SELECTED STORIES

By D. H. Lawrence

- PRINT/note "Man Who Loved Islands"
- 1 pg → notes/brief outline/ explanation of close Reading #2 due Monday.
- 4 copies, 2 pages → roughdraft Wednesday
- close Reading #2 due Friday

*extra credit for (good) showing annotations?

3

CONTENTS

THE PRUSSIAN OFFICER AND OTHER STORIES

ENGLAND, MY ENGLAND

OTHER STORIES

Love Among the Haystacks
✓ The Man Who Loved Islands
The Rocking Horse Winner
Things

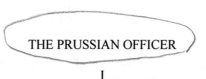

THE PRUSSIAN OFFICER

I

They had marched more than thirty kilometres since dawn, along the white, hot road where occasional thickets of trees threw a moment of shade, then out into the glare again. On either hand, the valley, wide and shallow, glittered with heat; dark green patches of rye, pale young corn, fallow and meadow and black pine woods spread in a dull, hot diagram under a glistening sky. But right in front the mountains ranged across, pale blue and very still, snow gleaming gently out of the deep atmosphere. And towards the mountains, on and on, the regiment marched between the rye fields and the meadows, between the scraggy fruit trees set regularly on either side the high road. The burnished, dark green rye threw off a suffocating heat, the mountains drew gradually nearer and more distinct. While the feet of the soldiers grew hotter, sweat ran through their hair under their helmets, and their knapsacks could burn no more in contact with their shoulders, but seemed instead to give off a cold, prickly sensation.

He walked on and on in silence, staring at the mountains ahead, that rose sheer out of the land, and stood fold behind fold, half earth, half heaven, the heaven, the barrier with slits of soft snow, in the pale, bluish peaks.

He could now walk almost without pain. At the start, he had determined not to limp. It had made him sick to take the first steps, and during the first mile or so, he had compressed his breath, and the cold drops of sweat had stood on his forehead. But he had walked it off. What were they after all but bruises! He had looked at them, as he was getting up: deep bruises on the backs of his thighs. And since he had made his first step in the morning, he had been conscious of them, till now he had a tight, hot place in his chest, with suppressing the pain, and holding himself in. There seemed no air when he breathed. But he walked almost lightly.

The Captain's hand had trembled at taking his coffee at dawn: his orderly saw it again. And he saw the fine figure of the Captain wheeling on horseback at the farm-house ahead, a handsome figure in pale blue uniform with facings of scarlet, and the metal gleaming on the black helmet and the sword-scabbard, and dark streaks of sweat coming on the silky bay horse. The orderly felt he was connected with that figure moving so suddenly on horseback: he followed it like a shadow, mute and inevitable and damned by it. And the officer was always aware of the tramp of the company behind, the march of his orderly among the men.

The Captain was a tall man of about forty, grey at the temples. He had a handsome, finely knit figure, and was one of the best horsemen in the West. His orderly, having to rub him down, admired the amazing riding-muscles of his loins.

For the rest, the orderly scarcely noticed the officer any more than he noticed himself. It was rarely he saw his master's face: he did not look at it. The Captain had reddish-brown, stiff hair, that he wore short upon his skull. His moustache was also cut short and bristly over a full, brutal mouth. His face was rather rugged, the cheeks thin. Perhaps the man was the more handsome for the deep lines in his face, the irritable tension of his brow, which gave him the look of a man who fights with life. His fair eyebrows stood bushy over light blue eyes that were always flashing with cold fire.

He was a Prussian aristocrat, haughty and overbearing. But his mother had been a Polish Countess. Having made too many gambling debts when he was young, he had ruined his prospects in the Army, and remained an infantry captain. He had never married: his position did not allow of it, and no woman had ever moved him to it. His time he spent riding—occasionally he rode one of his own horses at the races—and at the officers' club. Now and then he took himself a mistress. But after such an event, he returned to duty with his brow still more tense, his eyes still more hostile and irritable. With the men, however, he was merely impersonal, though a devil when roused; so that, on the whole, they feared him, but had no great aversion from him. They accepted him as the inevitable.

To his orderly he was at first cold and just and indifferent: he did not fuss over trifles. So that his servant knew practically nothing about him, except just what orders he would give, and how he wanted them obeyed. That was quite simple. Then the change gradually came.

The orderly was a youth of about twenty-two, of medium height, and well built. He had strong, heavy limbs, was swarthy, with a soft, black, young moustache. There was something altogether warm and young about him. He had firmly marked eyebrows over dark, expressionless eyes, that seemed never to have thought, only to have received life direct through his senses, and acted straight from instinct.

Gradually the officer had become aware of his servant's young, vigorous, unconscious presence about him. He could not get away from the sense of the youth's person, while he was in attendance. It was like a warm flame upon the older man's tense, rigid body, that had become almost unliving, fixed. There was something so free and self-contained about him, and something in the young fellow's movement, that made the officer aware of him. And this irritated the Prussian. He did not choose to be touched into life by his servant. He might easily have changed his man, but he did not. He now very rarely looked direct at his orderly, but kept his face averted, as if to avoid seeing him. And yet as the young soldier moved unthinking about the apartment, the elder watched him, and would notice the movement of his strong young shoulders under the blue cloth, the bend of his neck. And it irritated him. To see the soldier's young, brown, shapely peasant's hand grasp the loaf or the wine-bottle sent a flash of hate or of anger through the elder man's blood. It was not that the youth was clumsy: it was rather the blind, instinctive sureness of movement of an unhampered young animal that irritated the officer to such a degree.

Once, when a bottle of wine had gone over, and the red gushed out on to the tablecloth, the officer had started up with an oath, and his eyes, bluey like fire, had held those of the confused youth for a moment. It was a shock for the young soldier. He felt something sink deeper, deeper into his soul, where nothing had ever gone before. It left him rather blank and wondering. Some of his natural completeness in himself was gone, a little uneasiness took its place. And from that time an undiscovered feeling had held between the two men.

Henceforward the orderly was afraid of really meeting his master. His subconsciousness remembered those steely blue eyes and the harsh brows, and did not intend to meet them again. So he always stared past his master, and avoided him. Also, in a little anxiety, he waited for the three months to have gone, when his time would be up. He began to feel a constraint in the Captain's presence, and the soldier even more than the officer wanted to be left alone, in his neutrality as servant.

He had served the Captain for more than a year, and knew his duty. This he performed easily, as if it were natural to him. The officer and his commands he took for granted, as he took the sun and the rain, and he served as a matter of course. It did not implicate him personally.

But now if he were going to be forced into a personal interchange with his master he would be like a wild thing caught, he felt he must get away.

But the influence of the young soldier's being had penetrated through the officer's stiffened discipline, and perturbed the man in him. He, however, was a gentleman, with long, fine hands and cultivated movements, and was not going to allow such a thing as the stirring of his innate self. He was a man of passionate temper, who had always kept himself suppressed. Occasionally there had been a duel, an outburst before the soldiers. He knew himself to be always on the point of breaking out. But he kept himself hard to the idea of the Service. Whereas the young soldier seemed to live out his warm, full nature, to give it off in his very movements, which had a certain zest, such as wild animals have in free movement. And this irritated the officer more and more.

In spite of himself, the Captain could not regain his neutrality of feeling towards his orderly. Nor could he leave the man alone. In spite of himself, he watched him, gave him sharp orders, tried to take up as much of his time as possible. Sometimes he flew into a rage with the young soldier, and bullied him. Then the orderly shut himself off, as it were out of earshot, and waited, with sullen, flushed face, for the end of the noise. The words never pierced to his intelligence, he made himself, protectively, impervious to the feelings of his master.

He had a scar on his left thumb, a deep seam going across the knuckle. The officer had long suffered from it, and wanted to do something to it. Still it was there, ugly and brutal on the young, brown hand. At last the Captain's reserve gave way. One day, as the orderly was smoothing out the tablecloth, the officer pinned down his thumb with a pencil, asking:

"How did you come by that?"

The young man winced and drew back at attention.

"A wood axe, Herr Hauptmann," he answered.

The officer waited for further explanation. None came. The orderly went about his duties. The elder man was sullenly angry. His servant avoided him. And the next day he had to use all his will-power to avoid seeing the scarred thumb. He wanted to get hold of it and—A hot flame ran in his blood.

He knew his servant would soon be free, and would be glad. As yet, the soldier had held himself off from the elder man. The Captain grew madly irritable. He could not rest when the soldier was away, and when he was present, he glared at him with tormented eyes. He hated those fine, black brows over the unmeaning, dark eyes, he was infuriated by the free movement of the handsome limbs, which no military discipline could make stiff. And he became harsh and cruelly bullying, using contempt and satire. The young soldier only grew more mute and expressionless.

"What cattle were you bred by, that you can't keep straight eyes? Look me in the eyes when I speak to you."

And the soldier turned his dark eyes to the other's face, but there was no sight in them: he stared with the slightest possible cast, holding back his sight, perceiving the blue of his master's eyes, but receiving no look from them. And the elder man went pale, and his reddish eyebrows twitched. He gave his order, barrenly.

Once he flung a heavy military glove into the young soldier's face. Then he had the satisfaction of seeing the black eyes flare up into his own, like a blaze when straw is thrown on a fire. And he had laughed with a little tremor and a sneer.

But there were only two months more. The youth instinctively tried to keep himself intact: he tried to serve the officer as if the latter were an abstract authority and not a man. All his instinct was to avoid personal contact, even definite hate. But in spite of himself the hate grew, responsive to the officer's passion. However, he put it in the background. When he had left the Army he could dare acknowledge it. By nature he was active, and had many friends. He thought what amazing good fellows they were. But, without knowing it, he was alone. Now this solitariness was intensified. It would carry him through his term. But the officer seemed to be going irritably insane, and the youth was deeply frightened.

The soldier had a sweetheart, a girl from the mountains, independent and primitive. The two walked together, rather silently. He went with her, not to talk, but to have his arm round her, and for the physical contact. This eased him, made it easier for him to ignore the Captain; for he could rest with her held fast against his chest. And she, in some unspoken fashion, was there for him. They loved each other.

The Captain perceived it, and was mad with irritation. He kept the young man engaged all the evenings long, and took pleasure in the dark look that came on his face. Occasionally, the eyes of the two men met, those of the younger sullen and dark, doggedly unalterable, those of the elder sneering with restless contempt.

The officer tried hard not to admit the passion that had got hold of him. He would not know that his feeling for his orderly was anything but that of a man incensed by his stupid, perverse servant. So, keeping quite justified and conventional in his consciousness, he let the other thing run on. His nerves, however, were suffering. At last he slung the end of a belt in his servant's face. When he saw the youth start back, the pain-tears in his eyes and the blood on his mouth, he had felt at once a thrill of deep pleasure and of shame.

But this, he acknowledged to himself, was a thing he had never done before. The fellow was too exasperating. His own nerves must be going to pieces. He went away for some days with a woman.

It was a mockery of pleasure. He simply did not want the woman. But he stayed on for his time. At the end of it, he came back in an agony of irritation, torment, and misery. He rode all the evening, then came straight in to supper. His orderly was out. The officer sat with his long, fine hands lying on the table, perfectly still, and all his blood seemed to be corroding.

At last his servant entered. He watched the strong, easy young figure, the fine eyebrows, the thick black hair. In a week's time the youth had got back his old well-being. The hands of the officer twitched and seemed to be full of mad flame. The young man stood at attention, unmoving, shut off.

The meal went in silence. But the orderly seemed eager. He made a clatter with the dishes.

"Are you in a hurry?" asked the officer, watching the intent, warm face of his servant. The other did not reply.

"Will you answer my question?" said the Captain.

"Yes, sir," replied the orderly, standing with his pile of deep Army plates. The Captain waited, looked at him, then asked again:

"Are you in a hurry?"

"Yes, sir," came the answer, that sent a flash through the listener.

"For what?"

"I was going out, sir."

"I want you this evening."

There was a moment's hesitation. The officer had a curious stiffness of countenance.

"Yes, sir," replied the servant, in his throat.

"I want you to-morrow evening also—in fact, you may consider your evenings occupied, unless I give you leave."

The mouth with the young moustache set close.

"Yes, sir," answered the orderly, loosening his lips for a moment.

He again turned to the door.

"And why have you a piece of pencil in your ear?"

The orderly hesitated, then continued on his way without answering. He set the plates in a pile outside the door, took the stump of pencil from his ear, and put it in his pocket. He had been copying a verse for his sweetheart's birthday card. He returned to finish clearing the table. The officer's eyes were dancing, he had a little, eager smile.

"Why have you a piece of pencil in your ear?" he asked.

The orderly took his hands full of dishes. His master was standing near the great green stove, a little smile on his face, his chin thrust forward. When the young soldier saw him his heart suddenly ran hot. He felt blind. Instead of answering, he turned dazedly to the door. As he was crouching to set down the dishes, he was pitched forward by a kick from behind. The pots went in a stream down the stairs, he clung to the pillar of the banisters. And as he was rising he was kicked heavily again, and again, so that he clung sickly to the post for some moments. His master had gone swiftly into the room and closed the door. The maid-servant downstairs looked up the staircase and made a mocking face at the crockery disaster.

The officer's heart was plunging. He poured himself a glass of wine, part of which he spilled on the floor, and gulped the remainder, leaning against the cool, green stove. He heard his man collecting the dishes from the stairs. Pale, as if intoxicated, he waited. The servant entered again. The Captain's heart gave a pang, as of pleasure, seeing the young fellow bewildered and uncertain on his feet, with pain.

"Schöner!" he said.

The soldier was a little slower in coming to attention.

"Yes, sir!"

The youth stood before him, with pathetic young moustache, and fine eyebrows very distinct on his forehead of dark marble.

"I asked you a question."

"Yes, sir."

The officer's tone bit like acid.

"Why had you a pencil in your ear?"

Again the servant's heart ran hot, and he could not breathe. With dark, strained eyes, he looked at the officer, as if fascinated. And he stood there sturdily planted, unconscious. The withering smile came into the Captain's eyes, and he lifted his foot.

"I—I forgot it—sir," panted the soldier, his dark eyes fixed on the other man's dancing blue ones.

"What was it doing there?"

He saw the young man's breast heaving as he made an effort for words.

"I had been writing."

"Writing what?"

Again the soldier looked up and down. The officer could hear him panting. The smile came into the blue eyes. The soldier worked his dry throat, but could not speak. Suddenly the smile lit like a flame on the officer's face, and a kick came heavily against the orderly's thigh. The youth moved a pace sideways. His face went dead, with two black, staring eyes.

"Well?" said the officer.

The orderly's mouth had gone dry, and his tongue rubbed in it as on dry brown-paper. He worked his throat. The officer raised his foot. The servant went stiff.

"Some poetry, sir," came the crackling, unrecognizable sound of his voice.

"Poetry, what poetry?" asked the Captain, with a sickly smile.

Again there was the working in the throat. The Captain's heart had suddenly gone down heavily, and he stood sick and tired.

"For my girl, sir," he heard the dry, inhuman sound.

"Oh!" he said, turning away. "Clear the table."

"Click!" went the soldier's throat; then again, "click!" and then the half-articulate: "Yes, sir."

The young soldier was gone, looking old, and walking heavily.

The officer, left alone, held himself rigid, to prevent himself from thinking. His instinct warned him that he must not think. Deep inside him was the intense gratification of his passion, still working powerfully. Then there was a counter-action, a horrible breaking-down of something inside him, a whole agony of reaction. He stood there for an hour motionless, a chaos of sensations, but rigid with a will to keep blank his consciousness, to prevent his mind grasping. And he held himself so until the worst of the stress had passed, when he began to drink, drank himself to an intoxication, till he slept obliterated. When he woke in the morning he was shaken to the base of his nature. But he had fought off the realization of what he had done. He had prevented his mind from taking it in, had suppressed it along with his instincts, and the conscious man had nothing to do with it. He felt only as after a bout of intoxication, weak, but the affair itself all dim and not to be recovered. Of the drunkenness of his passion he successfully refused remembrance. And when his orderly appeared with coffee, the officer assumed the same self he had had the morning before. He refused the event of the past night—denied it had ever been—and was successful in his denial. He had not done any such thing—not he himself. Whatever there might be lay at the door of a stupid, insubordinate servant.

The orderly had gone about in a stupor all the evening. He drank some beer because he was parched, but not much, the alcohol made his feeling come back, and he could not bear it. He was dulled, as if nine-tenths of the ordinary man in him were inert. He crawled about disfigured. Still, when he thought of the kicks, he went sick, and when he thought of the threat of more kicking, in the room afterwards, his heart went hot and faint, and he panted, remembering the one that had come. He had been forced to say, "For my girl." He was much too done even to want to cry. His mouth hung slightly open, like an idiot's. He felt vacant, and wasted. So, he wandered at his work, painfully, and very slowly and clumsily, fumbling blindly with the brushes, and finding it difficult, when he sat down, to summon the energy to move again. His limbs, his jaw, were slack and nerveless. But he was very tired. He got to bed at last, and slept inert, relaxed, in a sleep that was rather stupor than slumber, a dead night of stupefaction shot through with gleams of anguish.

In the morning were the manoeuvres. But he woke even before the bugle sounded. The painful ache in his chest, the dryness of his throat, the awful steady feeling of misery made his eyes come awake and dreary at once. He knew, without thinking, what had happened. And he knew that the day had come again, when he must go on with his round. The last bit of darkness was being pushed out of the room. He would have to move his inert body and go on. He was so young, and had known so little trouble, that he was bewildered. He only wished it would stay night, so that he could lie still, covered up by the darkness. And yet nothing would prevent the day from coming, nothing would save him from having to get up and saddle the Captain's horse, and make the Captain's coffee. It was there, inevitable. And then, he thought, it was impossible. Yet they would not leave him free. He must go and take the coffee to the Captain. He was too stunned to understand it. He only knew it was inevitable—inevitable, however long he lay inert.

At last, after heaving at himself, for he seemed to be a mass of inertia, he got up. But he had to force every one of his movements from behind, with his will. He felt lost, and dazed, and helpless. Then he clutched hold of the bed, the pain was so keen. And looking at his thighs, he saw the darker bruises on his swarthy flesh and he knew that, if he pressed one of his fingers on one of the bruises, he should faint. But he did not want to faint—he did not want anybody to know. No one should ever know. It was between him and the Captain. There were only the two people in the world now—himself and the Captain.

Slowly, economically, he got dressed and forced himself to walk. Everything was obscure, except just what he had his hands on. But he managed to get through his work. The very pain revived his dull senses. The worst remained yet. He took the tray and went up to the Captain's room. The officer, pale and heavy, sat at the table. The orderly, as he saluted, felt himself put out of existence. He stood still for a moment submitting to his own nullification—then he gathered himself, seemed to regain himself, and then the Captain began to grow vague, unreal, and the younger soldier's heart beat up. He clung to this situation—that the Captain did not exist—so that he himself might live. But when he saw his officer's hand tremble as he took the coffee, he felt everything falling shattered. And he went away, feeling as if he himself were coming to pieces, disintegrated. And when the Captain was there on horseback, giving orders, while he himself stood, with rifle and knapsack, sick with pain, he felt as if he must shut his eyes—as if he must shut his eyes on everything. It was only the long agony of marching with a parched throat that filled him with one single, sleep-heavy intention: to save himself.

II

He was getting used even to his parched throat. That the snowy peaks were radiant among the sky, that the whity-green glacier-river twisted through its pale shoals, in the valley below, seemed almost supernatural. But he was going mad with fever and thirst. He plodded on uncomplaining. He did not want to speak, not to anybody. There were two gulls, like flakes of water and snow, over the river. The scent of green rye soaked in sunshine came like a sickness. And the march continued, monotonously, almost like a bad sleep.

At the next farm-house, which stood low and broad near the high road, tubs of water had been put out. The soldiers clustered round to drink. They took off their helmets, and the steam mounted from their wet hair. The Captain sat on horseback, watching. He needed to see his orderly. His helmet threw a dark shadow over his light, fierce eyes, but his moustache and mouth and chin were distinct in the sunshine. The orderly must move under the presence of the figure of the horseman. It was not that he was afraid, or cowed. It was as if he was disembowelled, made empty, like an empty shell. He felt himself as nothing, a shadow creeping under the sunshine. And, thirsty as he was, he could scarcely drink, feeling the Captain near him. He would not take off his helmet to wipe his wet hair. He wanted to stay in shadow, not to be forced into consciousness. Starting, he saw the light heel of the officer prick the belly of the horse; the Captain cantered away, and he himself could relapse into vacancy.

Nothing, however, could give him back his living place in the hot, bright morning. He felt like a gap among it all. Whereas the Captain was prouder, overriding. A hot flash went through the young servant's body. The Captain was firmer and prouder with life, he himself was empty as a shadow. Again the flash went through him, dazing him out. But his heart ran a little firmer.

The company turned up the hill, to make a loop for the return. Below, from among the trees, the farm-bell clanged. He saw the labourers, mowing barefoot at the thick grass, leave off their work and go downhill, their scythes hanging over their shoulders, like long, bright claws curving down behind them. They seemed like dream-people, as if they had no relation to himself. He felt as in a blackish dream: as if all the other things were there and had form, but he himself was only a consciousness, a gap that could think and perceive.

The soldiers were tramping silently up the glaring hillside. Gradually his head began to revolve, slowly, rhythmically. Sometimes it was dark before his eyes, as if he saw this world through a smoked glass, frail shadows and unreal. It gave him a pain in his head to walk.

The air was too scented, it gave no breath. All the lush greenstuff seemed to be issuing its sap, till the air was deathly, sickly with the smell of greenness. There was the perfume of clover, like pure honey and bees. Then there grew a faint acrid tang—they were near the beeches; and then a queer clattering noise, and a suffocating, hideous smell; they were passing a flock of sheep, a shepherd in a black smock, holding his crook. Why should the sheep huddle together under this fierce sun? He felt that the shepherd would not see him, though he could see the shepherd.

At last there was the halt. They stacked rifles in a conical stack, put down their kit in a scattered circle around it, and dispersed a little, sitting on a small knoll high on the hillside. The chatter began. The soldiers were steaming with heat, but were lively. He sat still, seeing the blue mountains rising upon the land, twenty kilometres away. There was a blue fold in the ranges, then out of that, at the foot, the broad, pale bed of the river, stretches of whity-green water between pinkish-grey shoals among the dark pine woods. There it was, spread out a long way off. And it seemed to come downhill, the river. There was a raft being steered, a mile away. It was a strange country. Nearer, a red-roofed, broad farm with white base and square dots of windows crouched beside the wall of beech foliage on the wood's edge. There were long strips of rye and clover and pale green corn. And just at his feet, below the knoll, was a darkish bog, where globe flowers stood breathless still on their slim stalks. And some of the pale gold bubbles were burst, and a broken fragment hung in the air. He thought he was going to sleep.

Suddenly something moved into this coloured mirage before his eyes. The Captain, a small, light-blue and scarlet figure, was trotting evenly between the strips of corn, along the level brow of the hill. And the man making flag-signals was coming on. Proud and sure moved the horseman's figure, the quick, bright thing, in which was concentrated all the light of this morning, which for the rest lay a fragile, shining shadow. Submissive, apathetic, the young soldier sat and stared. But as the horse slowed to a walk, coming up the last steep path, the great flash flared over the body and soul of the orderly. He sat waiting. The back of his head felt as if it were weighted with a heavy piece of fire. He did not want to eat. His hands trembled slightly as he moved them. Meanwhile the officer on horseback was approaching slowly and proudly. The tension grew in the orderly's soul.

Then again, seeing the Captain ease himself on the saddle, the flash blazed through him.

The Captain looked at the patch of light blue and scarlet, and dark heads, scattered closely on the hillside. It pleased him. The command pleased him. And he was feeling proud. His orderly was among them in common subjection. The officer rose a little on his stirrups to look. The young soldier sat with averted, dumb face. The Captain relaxed on his seat. His slim-legged, beautiful horse, brown as a beech nut, walked proudly uphill. The Captain passed into the zone of the company's atmosphere: a hot smell of men, of sweat, of leather. He knew it very well. After a word with the lieutenant, he went a few paces higher, and sat there, a dominant figure, his sweat-marked horse swishing its tail, while he looked down on his men, on his orderly, a nonentity among the crowd.

The young soldier's heart was like fire in his chest, and he breathed with difficulty. The officer, looking downhill, saw three of the young soldiers, two pails of water between them, staggering across a sunny green field. A table had been set up under a tree, and there the slim lieutenant stood, importantly busy. Then the Captain summoned himself to an act of courage. He called his orderly.

The flame leapt into the young soldier's throat as he heard the command, and he rose blindly, stifled. He saluted, standing below the officer. He did not look up. But there was the flicker in the Captain's voice.

"Go to the inn and fetch me . . ." the officer gave his commands. "Quick!" he added.

At the last word, the heart of the servant leapt with a flash, and he felt the strength come over his body. But he turned in mechanical obedience, and set off at a heavy run downhill, looking almost like a bear, his trousers bagging over his military boots. And the officer watched this blind, plunging run all the way.

But it was only the outside of the orderly's body that was obeying so humbly and mechanically. Inside had gradually accumulated a core into which all the energy of that young life was compact and concentrated. He executed his commission, and plodded quickly back uphill. There was a pain in his head, as he walked, that made him twist his features unknowingly. But hard there in the centre of his chest was himself, himself, firm, and not to be plucked to pieces.

The Captain had gone up into the wood. The orderly plodded through the hot, powerfully smelling zone of the company's atmosphere. He had a curious mass of energy inside him now. The Captain was less real than himself. He approached the green entrance to the wood. There, in the half-shade, he saw the horse standing, the sunshine and the flickering shadow of leaves dancing over his brown body. There was a clearing where timber had lately been felled. Here, in the gold-green shade beside the brilliant cup of sunshine, stood two figures, blue and pink, the bits of pink showing out plainly. The Captain was talking to his lieutenant.

The orderly stood on the edge of the bright clearing, where great trunks of trees, stripped and glistening, lay stretched like naked, brown-skinned bodies. Chips of wood littered the trampled floor, like splashed light, and the bases of the felled trees stood here and there, with their raw, level tops. Beyond was the brilliant, sunlit green of a beech.

"Then I will ride forward," the orderly heard his Captain say. The lieutenant saluted and strode away. He himself went forward. A hot flash passed through his belly, as he tramped towards his officer.

The Captain watched the rather heavy figure of the young soldier stumble forward, and his veins, too, ran hot. This was to be man to man between them. He yielded before the solid, stumbling figure with bent head. The orderly stooped and put the food on a level-sawn tree-base. The Captain watched the glistening, sun-inflamed, naked hands. He wanted to speak to the young soldier, but could not. The servant propped a bottle against his thigh, pressed open the cork, and poured out the beer into the mug. He kept his head bent. The Captain accepted the mug.

"Hot!" he said, as if amiably.

The flame sprang out of the orderly's heart, nearly suffocating him.

"Yes, sir," he replied, between shut teeth.

And he heard the sound of the Captain's drinking, and he clenched his fists, such a strong torment came into his wrists. Then came the faint clang of the closing pot-lid. He looked up. The Captain was watching him. He glanced swiftly away. Then he saw the officer stoop and take a piece of bread from the tree-base. Again the flash of flame went through the young soldier, seeing the stiff body stoop beneath him, and his hands jerked. He looked away. He could feel the officer was nervous. The bread fell as it was being broken. The officer ate the other piece. The two men stood tense and still, the master laboriously chewing his bread, the servant staring with averted face, his fist clenched.

Then the young soldier started. The officer had pressed open the lid of the mug again. The orderly watched the lid of the mug, and the white hand that clenched the handle, as if he were fascinated. It was raised. The youth followed it with his eyes. And then he saw the thin, strong throat of the elder man moving up and down as he drank, the strong jaw working. And the instinct which had been jerking at the young man's wrists suddenly jerked free. He jumped, feeling as if it were rent in two by a strong flame.

The spur of the officer caught in a tree-root, he went down backwards with a crash, the middle of his back thudding sickeningly against a sharp-edged tree-base, the pot flying away. And in a second the orderly, with serious, earnest young face, and underlip between his teeth, had got his knee in the officer's chest and was pressing the chin backward over the farther edge of the tree-stump, pressing, with all his heart behind in a passion of relief, the tension of his wrists exquisite with relief. And with the base of his palms he shoved at the chin, with all his might. And it was pleasant, too, to have that chin, that hard jaw already slightly rough with beard, in his hands. He did not relax one hair's breadth, but, all the force of all his blood exulting in his thrust, he shoved back the head of the other man, till there was a little "cluck" and a crunching sensation. Then he felt as if his head went to vapour. Heavy convulsions shook the body of the officer, frightening and horrifying the young soldier. Yet it pleased him, too, to repress them. It pleased him to keep his hands pressing back the chin, to feel the chest of the other man yield in expiration to the weight of his strong, young knees, to feel the hard twitchings of the prostrate body jerking his own whole frame, which was pressed down on it.

But it went still. He could look into the nostrils of the other man, the eyes he could scarcely see. How curiously the mouth was pushed out, exaggerating the full lips, and the moustache bristling up from them. Then, with a start, he noticed the nostrils gradually filled with blood. The red brimmed, hesitated, ran over, and went in a thin trickle down the face to the eyes.

It shocked and distressed him. Slowly, he got up. The body twitched and sprawled there, inert. He stood and looked at it in silence. It was a pity it was broken. It represented more than the thing which had kicked and bullied him. He was afraid to look at the eyes. They were hideous now, only the whites showing, and the blood running to them. The face of the orderly was drawn with horror at the sight. Well, it was so. In his heart he was satisfied. He had hated the face of the Captain. It was extinguished now. There was a heavy relief in the orderly's soul. That was as it should be. But he could not bear to see the long, military body lying broken over the tree-base, the fine fingers crisped. He wanted to hide it away.

Quickly, busily, he gathered it up and pushed it under the felled tree-trunks, which rested their beautiful, smooth length either end on logs. The face was horrible with blood. He covered it with the helmet. Then he pushed the limbs straight and decent, and brushed the dead leaves off the fine cloth of the uniform. So, it lay quite still in the shadow under there. A little strip of sunshine ran along the breast, from a chink between the logs. The orderly sat by it for a few moments. Here his own life also ended.

Then, through his daze, he heard the lieutenant, in a loud voice, explaining to the men outside the wood, that they were to suppose the bridge on the river below was held by the enemy. Now they were to march to the attack in such and such a manner. The lieutenant had no gift of expression. The orderly, listening from habit, got muddled. And when the lieutenant began it all again he ceased to hear.

He knew he must go. He stood up. It surprised him that the leaves were glittering in the sun, and the chips of wood reflecting white from the ground. For him a change had come over the world. But for the rest it had not—all seemed the same. Only he had left it. And he could not go back. It was his duty to return with the beer-pot and the bottle. He could not. He had left all that. The lieutenant was still hoarsely explaining. He must go, or they would overtake him. And he could not bear contact with anyone now.

He drew his fingers over his eyes, trying to find out where he was. Then he turned away. He saw the horse standing in the path. He went up to it and mounted. It hurt him to sit in the saddle. The pain of keeping his seat occupied him as they cantered through the wood. He would not have minded anything, but he could not get away from the sense of being divided from the others. The path led out of the trees. On the edge of the wood he pulled up and stood watching. There in the spacious sunshine of the valley soldiers were moving in a little swarm. Every now and then, a man harrowing on a strip of fallow shouted to his oxen, at the turn. The village and the white-towered church was small in the sunshine. And he no longer belonged to it—he sat there, beyond, like a man outside in the dark. He had gone out from everyday life into the unknown, and he could not, he even did not want to go back.

Turning from the sun-blazing valley, he rode deep into the wood. Tree-trunks, like people standing grey and still, took no notice as he went. A doe, herself a moving bit of sunshine and shadow, went running through the flecked shade. There were bright green rents in the foliage. Then it was all pine wood, dark and cool. And he was sick with pain, he had an intolerable great pulse in his head, and he was sick. He had never been ill in his life. He felt lost, quite dazed with all this.

Trying to get down from the horse, he fell, astonished at the pain and his lack of balance. The horse shifted uneasily. He jerked its bridle and sent it cantering jerkily away. It was his last connection with the rest of things.

But he only wanted to lie down and not be disturbed. Stumbling through the trees, he came on a quiet place where beeches and pine trees grew on a slope. Immediately he had lain down and closed his eyes, his consciousness went racing on without him. A big pulse of sickness beat in him as if it throbbed through the whole earth. He was burning with dry heat. But he was too busy, too tearingly active in the incoherent race of delirium to observe.

III

He came to with a start. His mouth was dry and hard, his heart beat heavily, but he had not the energy to get up. His heart beat heavily. Where was he?—the barracks—at home? There was something knocking. And, making an effort, he looked round—trees, and litter of greenery, and reddish, bright, still pieces of sunshine on the floor. He did not believe he was himself, he did not believe what he saw. Something was knocking. He made a struggle towards consciousness, but relapsed. Then he struggled again. And gradually his surroundings fell into relationship with himself. He knew, and a great pang of fear went through his heart. Somebody was knocking. He could see the heavy, black rags of a fir tree overhead. Then everything went black. Yet he did not believe he had closed his eyes. He had not. Out of the blackness sight slowly emerged again. And someone was knocking. Quickly, he saw the blood-disfigured face of his Captain, which he hated. And he held himself still with horror. Yet, deep inside him, he knew that it was so, the Captain should be dead. But the physical delirium got hold of him. Someone was knocking. He lay perfectly still, as if dead, with fear. And he went unconscious.

When he opened his eyes again, he started, seeing something creeping swiftly up a tree-trunk. It was a little bird. And the bird was whistling overhead. Tap-tap-tap—it was the small, quick bird rapping the tree-trunk with its beak, as if its head were a little round hammer. He watched it curiously. It shifted sharply, in its creeping fashion. Then, like a mouse, it slid down the bare trunk. Its swift creeping sent a flash of revulsion through him. He raised his head. It felt a great weight. Then, the little bird ran out of the shadow across a still patch of sunshine, its little head bobbing swiftly, its white legs twinkling brightly for a moment. How neat it was in its build, so compact, with pieces of white on its wings. There were several of them. They were so pretty—but they crept like swift, erratic mice, running here and there among the beech-mast.

He lay down again exhausted, and his consciousness lapsed. He had a horror of the little creeping birds. All his blood seemed to be darting and creeping in his head. And yet he could not move.

He came to with a further ache of exhaustion. There was the pain in his head, and the horrible sickness, and his inability to move. He had never been ill in his life. He did not know where he was or what he was. Probably he had got sunstroke. Or what else?—he had silenced the Captain for ever—some time ago—oh, a long time ago. There had been blood on his face, and his eyes had turned upwards. It was all right, somehow. It was peace. But now he had got beyond himself. He had never been here before. Was it life, or not life? He was by himself. They were in a big, bright place, those others, and he was outside. The town, all the country, a big bright place of light: and he was outside, here, in the darkened open beyond, where each thing existed alone. But they would all have to come out there sometime, those others. Little, and left behind him, they all were. There had been father and mother and sweetheart. What did they all matter? This was the open land.

He sat up. Something scuffled. It was a little, brown squirrel running in lovely, undulating bounds over the floor, its red tail completing the undulation of its body—and then, as it sat up, furling and unfurling. He watched it, pleased. It ran on again, friskily, enjoying itself. It flew wildly at another squirrel, and they were chasing each other, and making little scolding, chattering noises. The soldier wanted to speak to them. But only a hoarse sound came out of his throat. The squirrels burst away—they flew up the trees.

And then he saw the one peeping round at him, half-way up a tree-trunk. A start of fear went through him, though, in so far as he was conscious, he was amused. It still stayed, its little, keen face staring at him halfway up the tree-trunk, its little ears pricked up, its clawey little hands clinging to the bark, its white breast reared. He started from it in panic.

Struggling to his feet, he lurched away. He went on walking, walking, looking for something—for a drink. His brain felt hot and inflamed for want of water. He stumbled on. Then he did not know anything. He went unconscious as he walked. Yet he stumbled on, his mouth open.

When, to his dumb wonder, he opened his eyes on the world again, he no longer tried to remember what it was. There was thick, golden light behind golden-green glitterings, and tall, grey-purple shafts, and darknesses further off, surrounding him, growing deeper. He was conscious of a sense of arrival. He was amid the reality, on the real, dark bottom. But there was the thirst burning in his brain. He felt lighter, not so heavy. He supposed it was newness. The air was muttering with thunder. He thought he was walking wonderfully swiftly and was coming straight to relief—or was it to water?

Suddenly he stood still with fear. There was a tremendous flare of gold, immense— just a few dark trunks like bars between him and it. All the young level wheat was burnished gold glaring on its silky green. A woman, full-skirted, a black cloth on her head for head-dress, was passing like a block of shadow through the glistening, green corn, into the full glare. There was a farm, too, pale blue in shadow, and the timber black. And there was a church spire, nearly fused away in the gold. The woman moved on, away from him. He had no language with which to speak to her. She was the bright, solid unreality. She would make a noise of words that would confuse him, and her eyes would look at him without seeing him. She was crossing there to the other side. He stood against a tree.

When at last he turned, looking down the long, bare grove whose flat bed was already filling dark, he saw the mountains in a wonder-light, not far away, and radiant. Behind the soft, grey ridge of the nearest range the further mountains stood golden and pale grey, the snow all radiant like pure, soft gold. So still, gleaming in the sky, fashioned pure out of the ore of the sky, they shone in their silence. He stood and looked at them, his face illuminated. And like the golden, lustrous gleaming of the snow he felt his own thirst bright in him. He stood and gazed, leaning against a tree. And then everything slid away into space.

During the night the lightning fluttered perpetually, making the whole sky white. He must have walked again. The world hung livid round him for moments, fields a level sheen of grey-green light, trees in dark bulk, and the range of clouds black across a white sky. Then the darkness fell like a shutter, and the night was whole. A faint flutter of a half-revealed world, that could not quite leap out of the darkness!—Then there again stood a sweep of pallor for the land, dark shapes looming, a range of clouds hanging overhead. The world was a ghostly shadow, thrown for a moment upon the pure darkness, which returned ever whole and complete.

And the mere delirium of sickness and fever went on inside him—his brain opening and shutting like the night—then sometimes convulsions of terror from something with great eyes that stared round a tree—then the long agony of the march, and the sun decomposing his blood—then the pang of hate for the Captain, followed by a pang of tenderness and ease. But everything was distorted, born of an ache and resolving into an ache.

In the morning he came definitely awake. Then his brain flamed with the sole horror of thirstiness! The sun was on his face, the dew was steaming from his wet clothes. Like one possessed, he got up. There, straight in front of him, blue and cool and tender, the mountains ranged across the pale edge of the morning sky. He wanted them—he wanted them alone—he wanted to leave himself and be identified with them. They did not move, they were still soft, with white, gentle markings of snow. He stood still, mad with suffering, his hands crisping and clutching. Then he was twisting in a paroxysm on the grass.

He lay still, in a kind of dream of anguish. His thirst seemed to have separated itself from him, and to stand apart, a single demand. Then the pain he felt was another single self. Then there was the clog of his body, another separate thing. He was divided among all kinds of separate beings. There was some strange, agonized connection between them, but they were drawing further apart. Then they would all split. The sun, drilling down on him, was drilling through the bond. Then they would all fall, fall through the everlasting lapse of space. Then again, his consciousness reasserted itself. He roused on to his elbow and stared at the gleaming mountains. There they ranked, all still and wonderful between earth and heaven. He stared till his eyes went black, and the mountains, as they stood in their beauty, so clean and cool, seemed to have it, that which was lost in him.

IV

When the soldiers found him, three hours later, he was lying with his face over his arm, his black hair giving off heat under the sun. But he was still alive. Seeing the open, black mouth the young soldiers dropped him in horror.

He died in the hospital at night, without having seen again.

The doctors saw the bruises on his legs, behind, and were silent.

The bodies of the two men lay together, side by side, in the mortuary, the one white and slender, but laid rigidly at rest, the other looking as if every moment it must rouse into life again, so young and unused, from a slumber.

THE THORN IN THE FLESH

I

A wind was running, so that occasionally the poplars whitened as if a flame flew up them. The sky was broken and blue among moving clouds. Patches of sunshine lay on the level fields, and shadows on the rye and the vineyards. In the distance, very blue, the cathedral bristled against the sky, and the houses of the city of Metz clustered vaguely below, like a hill.

Among the fields by the lime trees stood the barracks, upon bare, dry ground, a collection of round-roofed huts of corrugated iron, where the soldiers' nasturtiums climbed brilliantly. There was a tract of vegetable garden at the side, with the soldiers' yellowish lettuces in rows, and at the back the big, hard drilling-yard surrounded by a wire fence.

At this time in the afternoon, the huts were deserted, all the beds pushed up, the soldiers were lounging about under the lime trees waiting for the call to drill. Bachmann sat on a bench in the shade that smelled sickly with blossom. Pale green, wrecked lime flowers were scattered on the ground. He was writing his weekly post card to his mother.

He was a fair, long, limber youth, good looking. He sat very still indeed, trying to write
his post card. His blue uniform, sagging on him as he sat bent over the card, disfigured
his youthful shape. His sunburnt hand waited motionless for the words to come. "Dear
mother"—was all he had written. Then he scribbled mechanically: "Many thanks for your
letter with what you sent. Everything is all right with me. We are just off to drill on the
fortifications—" Here he broke off and sat suspended, oblivious of everything, held in
some definite suspense. He looked again at the card. But he could write no more. Out of
the knot of his consciousness no word would come. He signed himself, and looked up, as
a man looks to see if anyone has noticed him in his privacy.

There was a self-conscious strain in his blue eyes, and a pallor about his mouth,
where the young, fair moustache glistened. He was almost girlish in his good looks and
his grace. But he had something of military consciousness, as if he believed in the
discipline for himself, and found satisfaction in delivering himself to his duty. There was
also a trace of youthful swagger and dare-devilry about his mouth and his limber body,
but this was in suppression now.

He put the post card in the pocket of his tunic, and went to join a group of his
comrades who were lounging in the shade, laughing and talking grossly. To-day he was
out of it. He only stood near to them for the warmth of the association. In his own
consciousness something held him down.

Presently they were summoned to ranks. The sergeant came out to take command.
He was a strongly built, rather heavy man of forty. His head was thrust forward, sunk a
little between his powerful shoulders, and the strong jaw was pushed out aggressively.
But the eyes were smouldering, the face hung slack and sodden with drink.

He gave his orders in brutal, barking shouts, and the little company moved forward,
out of the wire-fenced yard to the open road, marching rhythmically, raising the dust.
Bachmann, one of the inner file of four deep, marched in the airless ranks, half suffocated
with heat and dust and enclosure. Through the moving of his comrades' bodies, he could
see the small vines dusty by the roadside, the poppies among the tares fluttering and
blown to pieces, the distant spaces of sky and fields all free with air and sunshine. But he
was bound in a very dark enclosure of anxiety within himself.

He marched with his usual ease, being healthy and well adjusted. But his body went
on by itself. His spirit was clenched apart. And ever the few soldiers drew nearer and
nearer to the town, ever the consciousness of the youth became more gripped and
separate, his body worked by a kind of mechanical intelligence, a mere presence of mind.

They diverged from the high road and passed in single file down a path among trees.
All was silent and green and mysterious, with shadow of foliage and long, green,
undisturbed grass. Then they came out in the sunshine on a moat of water, which wound
silently between the long, flowery grass, at the foot of the earthworks, that rose in front in
terraces walled smooth on the face, but all soft with long grass at the top. Marguerite
daisies and lady's-slipper glimmered white and gold in the lush grass, preserved here in
the intense peace of the fortifications. Thickets of trees stood round about. Occasionally a
puff of mysterious wind made the flowers and the long grass that crested the earthworks
above bow and shake as with signals of oncoming alarm.

The group of soldiers stood at the end of the moat, in their light blue and scarlet
uniforms, very bright. The sergeant was giving them instructions, and his shout came
sharp and alarming in the intense, untouched stillness of the place. They listened, finding
it difficult to make the effort of understanding.

Then it was over, and the men were moving to make preparations. On the other side of the moat the ramparts rose smooth and clear in the sun, sloping slightly back. Along the summit grass grew and tall daisies stood ledged high, like magic, against the dark green of the tree-tops behind. The noise of the town, the running of tram-cars, was heard distinctly, but it seemed not to penetrate this still place.

The water of the moat was motionless. In silence the practice began. One of the soldiers took a scaling ladder, and passing along the narrow ledge at the foot of the earthworks, with the water of the moat just behind him, tried to get a fixture on the slightly sloping wall-face. There he stood, small and isolated, at the foot of the wall, trying to get his ladder settled. At last it held, and the clumsy, groping figure in the baggy blue uniform began to clamber up. The rest of the soldiers stood and watched. Occasionally the sergeant barked a command. Slowly the clumsy blue figure clambered higher up the wall-face. Bachmann stood with his bowels turned to water. The figure of the climbing soldier scrambled out on to the terrace up above, and moved, blue and distinct, among the bright green grass. The officer shouted from below. The soldier tramped along, fixed the ladder in another spot, and carefully lowered himself on to the rungs. Bachmann watched the blind foot groping in space for the ladder, and he felt the world fall away beneath him. The figure of the soldier clung cringing against the face of the wall, cleaving, groping downwards like some unsure insect working its way lower and lower, fearing every movement. At last, sweating and with a strained face, the figure had landed safely and turned to the group of soldiers. But still it had a stiffness and a blank, mechanical look, was something less than human.

Bachmann stood there heavy and condemned, waiting for his own turn and betrayal. Some of the men went up easily enough, and without fear. That only showed it could be done lightly, and made Bachmann's case more bitter. If only he could do it lightly, like that.

His turn came. He knew intuitively that nobody knew his condition. The officer just saw him as a mechanical thing. He tried to keep it up, to carry it through on the face of things. His inside gripped tight, as yet under control, he took the ladder and went along under the wall. He placed his ladder with quick success, and wild, quivering hope possessed him. Then blindly he began to climb. But the ladder was not very firm, and at every hitch a great, sick, melting feeling took hold of him. He clung on fast. If only he could keep that grip on himself, he would get through. He knew this, in agony. What he could not understand was the blind gush of white-hot fear, that came with great force whenever the ladder swerved, and which almost melted his belly and all his joints, and left him powerless. If once it melted all his joints and his belly, he was done. He clung desperately to himself. He knew the fear, he knew what it did when it came, he knew he had only to keep a firm hold. He knew all this. Yet, when the ladder swerved, and his foot missed, there was the great blast of fear blowing on his heart and bowels, and he was melting weaker and weaker, in a horror of fear and lack of control, melting to fall.

Yet he groped slowly higher and higher, always staring upwards with desperate face, and always conscious of the space below. But all of him, body and soul, was growing hot to fusion point. He would have to let go for very relief's sake. Suddenly his heart began to lurch. It gave a great, sickly swoop, rose, and again plunged in a swoop of horror. He lay against the wall inert as if dead, inert, at peace, save for one deep core of anxiety, which knew that it was not all over, that he was still high in space against the wall. But the chief effort of will was gone.

There came into his consciousness a small, foreign sensation. He woke up a little. What was it? Then slowly it penetrated him. His water had run down his leg. He lay there, clinging, still with shame, half conscious of the echo of the sergeant's voice thundering from below. He waited, in depths of shame beginning to recover himself. He had been shamed so deeply. Then he could go on, for his fear for himself was conquered. His shame was known and published. He must go on.

Slowly he began to grope for the rung above, when a great shock shook through him. His wrists were grasped from above, he was being hauled out of himself up, up to the safe ground. Like a sack he was dragged over the edge of the earthworks by the large hands, and landed there on his knees, grovelling in the grass to recover command of himself, to rise up on his feet.

Shame, blind, deep shame and ignominy overthrew his spirit and left it writhing. He stood there shrunk over himself, trying to obliterate himself.

Then the presence of the officer who had hauled him up made itself felt upon him. He heard the panting of the elder man, and then the voice came down on his veins like a fierce whip. He shrank in tension of shame.

"Put up your head—eyes front," shouted the enraged sergeant, and mechanically the soldier obeyed the command, forced to look into the eyes of the sergeant. The brutal, hanging face of the officer violated the youth. He hardened himself with all his might from seeing it. The tearing noise of the sergeant's voice continued to lacerate his body.

Suddenly he set back his head, rigid, and his heart leapt to burst. The face had suddenly thrust itself close, all distorted and showing the teeth, the eyes smouldering into him. The breath of the barking words was on his nose and mouth. He stepped aside in revulsion. With a scream the face was upon him again. He raised his arm, involuntarily, in self-defence. A shock of horror went through him, as he felt his forearm hit the face of the officer a brutal blow. The latter staggered, swerved back, and with a curious cry, reeled backwards over the ramparts, his hands clutching the air. There was a second of silence, then a crash to water.

Bachmann, rigid, looked out of his inner silence upon the scene. Soldiers were running.

"You'd better clear," said one young, excited voice to him. And with immediate instinctive decision he started to walk away from the spot. He went down the tree-hidden path to the high road where the trams ran to and from the town. In his heart was a sense of vindication, of escape. He was leaving it all, the military world, the shame. He was walking away from it.

Officers on horseback rode sauntering down the street, soldiers passed along the pavement. Coming to the bridge, Bachmann crossed over to the town that heaped before him, rising from the flat, picturesque French houses down below at the water's edge, up a jumble of roofs and chasms of streets, to the lovely dark cathedral with its myriad pinnacles making points at the sky.

He felt for the moment quite at peace, relieved from a great strain. So he turned along by the river to the public gardens. Beautiful were the heaped, purple lilac trees upon the green grass, and wonderful the walls of the horse-chestnut trees, lighted like an altar with white flowers on every ledge. Officers went by, elegant and all coloured, women and girls sauntered in the chequered shade. Beautiful it was, he walked in a vision, free.

II

But where was he going? He began to come out of his trance of delight and liberty. Deep within him he felt the steady burning of shame in the flesh. As yet he could not bear to think of it. But there it was, submerged beneath his attention, the raw, steady-burning shame.

It behoved him to be intelligent. As yet he dared not remember what he had done. He only knew the need to get away, away from everything he had been in contact with.

But how? A great pang of fear went through him. He could not bear his shamed flesh to be put again between the hands of authority. Already the hands had been laid upon him, brutally upon his nakedness, ripping open his shame and making him maimed, crippled in his own control.

Fear became an anguish. Almost blindly he was turning in the direction of the barracks. He could not take the responsibility of himself. He must give himself up to someone. Then his heart, obstinate in hope, became obsessed with the idea of his sweetheart. He would make himself her responsibility.

Blenching as he took courage, he mounted the small, quick-hurrying tram that ran out of the town in the direction of the barracks. He sat motionless and composed, static.

He got out at the terminus and went down the road. A wind was still running. He could hear the faint whisper of the rye, and the stronger swish as a sudden gust was upon it. No one was about. Feeling detached and impersonal, he went down a field-path between the low vines. Many little vine trees rose up in spires, holding out tender pink shoots, waving their tendrils. He saw them distinctly and wondered over them. In a field a little way off, men and women were taking up the hay. The bullock-waggon stood by on the path, the men in their blue shirts, the women with white cloths over their heads carried hay in their arms to the cart, all brilliant and distinct upon the shorn, glowing green acres. He felt himself looking out of darkness on to the glamorous, brilliant beauty of the world around him, outside him.

The Baron's house, where Emilie was maidservant, stood square and mellow among trees and garden and fields. It was an old French grange. The barracks was quite near. Bachmann walked, drawn by a single purpose, towards the courtyard. He entered the spacious, shadowy, sun-swept place. The dog, seeing a soldier, only jumped and whined for greeting. The pump stood peacefully in a corner, under a lime tree, in the shade.

The kitchen door was open. He hesitated, then walked in, speaking shyly and smiling involuntarily. The two women started, but with pleasure. Emilie was preparing the tray for afternoon coffee. She stood beyond the table, drawn up, startled, and challenging, and glad. She had the proud, timid eyes of some wild animal, some proud animal. Her black hair was closely banded, her grey eyes watched steadily. She wore a peasant dress of blue cotton sprigged with little red roses, that buttoned tight over her strong maiden breasts.

At the table sat another young woman, the nursery governess, who was picking cherries from a huge heap, and dropping them into a bowl. She was young, pretty, freckled.

"Good day!" she said pleasantly. "The unexpected."

Emilie did not speak. The flush came in her dark cheek. She still stood watching, between fear and a desire to escape, and on the other hand joy that kept her in his presence.

"Yes," he said, bashful and strained, while the eyes of the two women were upon him. "I've got myself in a mess this time."

"What?" asked the nursery governess, dropping her hands in her lap. Emilie stood rigid.

Bachmann could not raise his head. He looked sideways at the glistening, ruddy cherries. He could not recover the normal world.

"I knocked Sergeant Huber over the fortifications down into the moat," he said. "It was an accident—but—"

And he grasped at the cherries, and began to eat them, unknowing, hearing only Emilie's little exclamation.

"You knocked him over the fortifications!" echoed Fräulein Hesse in horror. "How?"

Spitting the cherry-stones into his hand, mechanically, absorbedly, he told them.

"Ach!" exclaimed Emilie sharply.

"And how did you get here?" asked Fräulein Hesse.

"I ran off," he said.

There was a dead silence. He stood, putting himself at the mercy of the women. There came a hissing from the stove, and a stronger smell of coffee. Emilie turned swiftly away. He saw her flat, straight back and her strong loins, as she bent over the stove.

"But what are you going to do?" said Fräulein Hesse, aghast.

"I don't know," he said, grasping at more cherries. He had come to an end.

"You'd better go to the barracks," she said. "We'll get the Herr Baron to come and see about it."

Emilie was swiftly and quietly preparing the tray. She picked it up, and stood with the glittering china and silver before her, impassive, waiting for his reply. Bachmann remained with his head dropped, pale and obstinate. He could not bear to go back.

"I'm going to try to get into France," he said.

"Yes, but they'll catch you," said Fräulein Hesse.

Emilie watched with steady, watchful grey eyes.

"I can have a try, if I could hide till to-night," he said.

Both women knew what he wanted. And they all knew it was no good. Emilie picked up the tray, and went out. Bachmann stood with his head dropped. Within himself he felt the dross of shame and incapacity.

"You'd never get away," said the governess.

"I can try," he said.

To-day he could not put himself between the hands of the military. Let them do as they liked with him to-morrow, if he escaped to-day.

They were silent. He ate cherries. The colour flushed bright into the cheek of the young governess.

Emilie returned to prepare another tray

"He could hide in your room," the governess said to her.

The girl drew herself away. She could not bear the intrusion.

"That is all I can think of that is safe from the children," said Fräulein Hesse.

Emilie gave no answer. Bachmann stood waiting for the two women. Emilie did not want the close contact with him.

"You could sleep with me," Fräulein Hesse said to her.

Emilie lifted her eyes and looked at the young man, direct, clear, reserving herself.

"Do you want that?" she asked, her strong virginity proof against him.

"Yes—yes—" he said uncertainly, destroyed by shame.

She put back her head.

"Yes," she murmured to herself.

Quickly she filled the tray, and went out.

"But you can't walk over the frontier in a night," said Fräulein Hesse.

"I can cycle," he said.

Emilie returned, a restraint, a neutrality, in her bearing.

"I'll see if it's all right," said the governess.

In a moment or two Bachmann was following Emilie through the square hall, where hung large maps on the walls. He noticed a child's blue coat with brass buttons on the peg, and it reminded him of Emilie walking holding the hand of the youngest child, whilst he watched, sitting under the lime tree. Already this was a long way off. That was a sort of freedom he had lost, changed for a new, immediate anxiety.

They went quickly, fearfully up the stairs and down a long corridor. Emilie opened her door, and he entered, ashamed, into her room.

"I must go down," she murmured, and she departed, closing the door softly.

It was a small, bare, neat room. There was a little dish for holy-water, a picture of the Sacred Heart, a crucifix, and a *prie-Dieu*. The small bed lay white and untouched, the wash-hand bowl of red earth stood on a bare table, there was a little mirror and a small chest of drawers. That was all.

Feeling safe, in sanctuary, he went to the window, looking over the courtyard at the shimmering, afternoon country. He was going to leave this land, this life. Already he was in the unknown.

He drew away into the room. The curious simplicity and severity of the little Roman Catholic bedroom was foreign but restoring to him. He looked at the crucifix. It was a long, lean, peasant Christ carved by a peasant in the Black Forest. For the first time in his life, Bachmann saw the figure as a human thing. It represented a man hanging there in helpless torture. He stared at it, closely, as if for new knowledge.

Within his own flesh burned and smouldered the restless shame. He could not gather himself together. There was a gap in his soul. The shame within him seemed to displace his strength and his manhood.

He sat down on his chair. The shame, the roused feeling of exposure acted on his brain, made him heavy, unutterably heavy.

Mechanically, his wits all gone, he took off his boots, his belt, his tunic, put them aside, and lay down, heavy, and fell into a kind of drugged sleep.

Emilie came in a little while, and looked at him. But he was sunk in sleep. She saw him lying there inert, and terribly still, and she was afraid. His shirt was unfastened at the throat. She saw his pure white flesh, very clean and beautiful. And he slept inert. His legs, in the blue uniform trousers, his feet in the coarse stockings, lay foreign on her bed. She went away.

III

She was uneasy, perturbed to her last fibre. She wanted to remain clear, with no touch on her. A wild instinct made her shrink away from any hands which might be laid on her.

She was a foundling, probably of some gipsy race, brought up in a Roman Catholic Rescue Home. A naïve, paganly religious being, she was attached to the Baroness, with whom she had served for seven years, since she was fourteen.

She came into contact with no one, unless it were with Ida Hesse, the governess. Ida was a calculating, good-natured, not very straight-forward flirt. She was the daughter of a poor country doctor. Having gradually come into connection with Emilie, more an alliance than an attachment, she put no distinction of grade between the two of them. They worked together, sang together, walked together, and went together to the rooms of Franz Brand, Ida's sweetheart. There the three talked and laughed together, or the women listened to Franz, who was a forester, playing on his violin.

In all this alliance there was no personal intimacy between the young women. Emilie was naturally secluded in herself, of a reserved, native race. Ida used her as a kind of weight to balance her own flighty movement. But the quick, shifty governess, occupied always in her dealings with admirers, did all she could to move the violent nature of Emilie towards some connection with men.

But the dark girl, primitive yet sensitive to a high degree, was fiercely virgin. Her blood flamed with rage when the common soldiers made the long, sucking, kissing noise behind her as she passed. She hated them for their almost jeering offers. She was well protected by the Baroness.

And her contempt of the common men in general was ineffable. But she loved the Baroness, and she revered the Baron, and she was at her ease when she was doing something for the service of a gentleman. Her whole nature was at peace in the service of real masters or mistresses. For her, a gentleman had some mystic quality that left her free and proud in service. The common soldiers were brutes, merely nothing. Her desire was to serve.

She held herself aloof. When, on Sunday afternoon, she had looked through the windows of the Reichshalle in passing, and had seen the soldiers dancing with the common girls, a cold revulsion and anger had possessed her. She could not bear to see the soldiers taking off their belts and pulling open their tunics, dancing with their shirts showing through the open, sagging tunic, their movements gross, their faces transfigured and sweaty, their coarse hands holding their coarse girls under the arm-pits, drawing the female up to their breasts. She hated to see them clutched breast to breast, the legs of the men moving grossly in the dance.

At evening, when she had been in the garden, and heard on the other side of the hedge the sexual inarticulate cries of the girls in the embraces of the soldiers, her anger had been too much for her, and she had cried, loud and cold:

"What are you doing there, in the hedge?"

She would have had them whipped.

But Bachmann was not quite a common soldier. Fräulein Hesse had found out about him, and had drawn him and Emilie together. For he was a handsome, blond youth, erect and walking with a kind of pride, unconscious yet clear. Moreover, he came of a rich farming stock, rich for many generations. His father was dead, his mother controlled the moneys for the time being. But if Bachmann wanted a hundred pounds at any moment, he could have them. By trade he, with one of his brothers, was a waggon-builder. The family had the farming, smithy, and waggon-building of their village. They worked because that was the form of life they knew. If they had chosen, they could have lived independent upon their means.

In this way, he was a gentleman in sensibility, though his intellect was not developed. He could afford to pay freely for things. He had, moreover, his native, fine breeding. Emilie wavered uncertainly before him. So he became her sweetheart, and she hungered after him. But she was virgin, and shy, and needed to be in subjection, because she was primitive and had no grasp on civilized forms of living, nor on civilized purposes.

IV

At six o'clock came the inquiry of the soldiers: Had anything been seen of Bachmann? Fräulein Hesse answered, pleased to be playing a rôle:

"No, I've not seen him since Sunday—have you, Emilie?"

"No, I haven't seen him," said Emilie, and her awkwardness was construed as bashfulness. Ida Hesse, stimulated, asked questions, and played her part.

"But it hasn't killed Sergeant Huber?" she cried in consternation.

"No. He fell into the water. But it gave him a bad shock, and smashed his foot on the side of the moat. He's in hospital. It's a bad look-out for Bachmann."

Emilie, implicated and captive, stood looking on. She was no longer free, working with all this regulated system which she could not understand and which was almost god-like to her. She was put out of her place. Bachmann was in her room, she was no longer the faithful in service serving with religious surety.

Her situation was intolerable to her. All evening long the burden was upon her, she could not live. The children must be fed and put to sleep. The Baron and Baroness were going out, she must give them light refreshment. The man-servant was coming in to supper after returning with the carriage. And all the while she had the insupportable feeling of being out of the order, self-responsible, bewildered. The control of her life should come from those above her, and she should move within that control. But now she was out of it, uncontrolled and troubled. More than that, the man, the lover, Bachmann, who was he, what was he? He alone of all men contained for her the unknown quantity which terrified her beyond her service. Oh, she had wanted him as a distant sweetheart, not close, like this, casting her out of her world.

When the Baron and Baroness had departed, and the young manservant had gone out to enjoy himself, she went upstairs to Bachmann. He had wakened up, and sat dimly in the room. Out in the open he heard the soldiers, his comrades, singing the sentimental songs of the nightfall, the drone of the concertina rising in accompaniment.

> "Wenn ich zu mei . . . nem Kinde geh' . . .
> In seinem Au . . . g die Mutter seh'. . . ."

But he himself was removed from it now. Only the sentimental cry of young, unsatisfied desire in the soldiers' singing penetrated his blood and stirred him subtly. He let his head hang; he had become gradually roused: and he waited in concentration, in another world.

The moment she entered the room where the man sat alone, waiting intensely, the thrill passed through her, she died in terror, and after the death, a great flame gushed up, obliterating her. He sat in trousers and shirt on the side of the bed. He looked up as she came in, and she shrank from his face. She could not bear it. Yet she entered near to him.

"Do you want anything to eat?" she said.

"Yes," he answered, and as she stood in the twilight of the room with him, he could only hear his heart beat heavily. He saw her apron just level with his face. She stood silent, a little distance off, as if she would be there for ever. He suffered.

As if in a spell she waited, standing motionless and looming there, he sat rather crouching on the side of the bed. A second will in him was powerful and dominating. She drew gradually nearer to him, coming up slowly, as if unconscious. His heart beat up swiftly. He was going to move.

As she came quite close, almost invisibly he lifted his arms and put them round her waist, drawing her with his will and desire. He buried his face into her apron, into the terrible softness of her belly. And he was a flame of passion intense about her. He had forgotten. Shame and memory were gone in a whole, furious flame of passion.

She was quite helpless. Her hands leapt, fluttered, and closed over his head, pressing it deeper into her belly, vibrating as she did so. And his arms tightened on her, his hands spread over her loins, warm as flame on her loveliness. It was intense anguish of bliss for her, and she lost consciousness.

When she recovered, she lay translated in the peace of satisfaction.

It was what she had had no inkling of, never known could be. She was strong with eternal gratitude. And he was there with her. Instinctively with an instinct of reverence and gratitude, her arms tightened in a little embrace upon him who held her thoroughly embraced.

And he was restored and completed, close to her. That little, twitching, momentary clasp of acknowledgment that she gave him in her satisfaction, roused his pride unconquerable. They loved each other, and all was whole. She loved him, he had taken her, she was given to him. It was right. He was given to her, and they were one, complete.

Warm, with a glow in their hearts and faces, they rose again, modest, but transfigured with happiness.

"I will get you something to eat," she said, and in joy and security of service again, she left him, making a curious little homage of departure. He sat on the side of the bed, escaped, liberated, wondering, and happy.

V

Soon she came again with the tray, followed by Fräulein Hesse. The two women watched him eat, watched the pride and wonder of his being, as he sat there blond and naïf again. Emilie felt rich and complete. Ida was a lesser thing than herself.

"And what are you going to do?" asked Fräulein Hesse, jealous.

"I must get away," he said.

But words had no meaning for him. What did it matter? He had the inner satisfaction and liberty.

"But you'll want a bicycle," said Ida Hesse.

"Yes," he said.

Emilie sat silent, removed and yet with him, connected with him in passion. She looked from this talk of bicycles and escape.

They discussed plans. But in two of them was the one will, that Bachmann should stay with Emilie. Ida Hesse was an outsider.

It was arranged, however, that Ida's lover should put out his bicycle, leave it at the hut where he sometimes watched. Bachmann should fetch it in the night, and ride into France. The hearts of all three beat hot in suspense, driven to thought. They sat in a fire of agitation.

Then Bachmann would get away to America, and Emilie would come and join him. They would be in a fine land then. The tale burned up again.

Emilie and Ida had to go round to Franz Brand's lodging. They departed with slight leave-taking. Bachmann sat in the dark, hearing the bugle for retreat sound out of the night. Then he remembered his post card to his mother. He slipped out after Emilie, gave it her to post. His manner was careless and victorious, hers shining and trustful. He slipped back to shelter.

There he sat on the side of the bed, thinking. Again he went over the events of the afternoon, remembering his own anguish of apprehension because he had known he could not climb the wall without fainting with fear. Still, a flush of shame came alight in him at the memory. But he said to himself: "What does it matter?—I can't help it, well then I can't. If I go up a height, I get absolutely weak, and can't help myself." Again memory came over him, and a gush of shame, like fire. But he sat and endured it. It had to be endured, admitted, and accepted. "I'm not a coward, for all that," he continued. "I'm not afraid of danger. If I'm made that way, that heights melt me and make me let go my water"—it was torture for him to pluck at this truth—"if I'm made like that, I shall have to abide by it, that's all. It isn't all of me." He thought of Emilie, and was satisfied. "What I am, I am; and let it be enough," he thought.

Having accepted his own defect, he sat thinking, waiting for Emilie, to tell her. She came at length, saying that Franz could not arrange about his bicycle this night. It was broken. Bachmann would have to stay over another day.

They were both happy. Emilie, confused before Ida, who was excited and prurient, came again to the young man. She was stiff and dignified with an agony of unusedness. But he took her between his hands, and uncovered her, and enjoyed almost like madness her helpless, virgin body that suffered so strongly, and that took its joy so deeply. While the moisture of torment and modesty was still in her eyes, she clasped him closer, and closer, to the victory and the deep satisfaction of both of them. And they slept together, he in repose still satisfied and peaceful, and she lying close in her static reality.

VI

In the morning, when the bugle sounded from the barracks they rose and looked out of the window. She loved his body that was proud and blond and able to take command. And he loved her body that was soft and eternal. They looked at the faint grey vapour of summer steaming off from the greenness and ripeness of the fields. There was no town anywhere, their look ended in the haze of the summer morning. Their bodies rested together, their minds tranquil. Then a little anxiety stirred in both of them from the sound of the bugle. She was called back to her old position, to realize the world of authority she did not understand but had wanted to serve. But this call died away again from her. She had all.

She went downstairs to her work, curiously changed. She was in a new world of her own, that she had never even imagined, and which was the land of promise for all that. In this she moved and had her being. And she extended it to her duties. She was curiously happy and absorbed. She had not to strive out of herself to do her work. The doing came from within her without call or command. It was a delicious outflow, like sunshine, the activity that flowed from her and put her tasks to rights.

Bachmann sat busily thinking. He would have to get all his plans ready. He must write to his mother, and she must send him money to Paris. He would go to Paris, and from thence, quickly, to America. It had to be done. He must make all preparations. The dangerous part was the getting into France. He thrilled in anticipation. During the day he would need a time-table of the trains going to Paris—he would need to think. It gave him delicious pleasure, using all his wits. It seemed such an adventure.

This one day, and he would escape then into freedom. What an agony of need he had for absolute, imperious freedom. He had won to his own being, in himself and Emilie, he had drawn the stigma from his shame, he was beginning to be himself. And now he wanted madly to be free to go on. A home, his work, and absolute freedom to move and to be, in her, with her, this was his passionate desire. He thought in a kind of ecstasy, living an hour of painful intensity.

Suddenly he heard voices, and a tramping of feet. His heart gave a great leap, then went still. He was taken. He had known all along. A complete silence filled his body and soul, a silence like death, a suspension of life and sound. He stood motionless in the bedroom, in perfect suspension.

Emilie was busy passing swiftly about the kitchen preparing the children's breakfasts when she heard the tramp of feet and the voice of the Baron. The latter had come in from the garden, and was wearing an old green linen suit. He was a man of middle stature, quick, finely made, and of whimsical charm. His right hand had been shot in the Franco-Prussian war, and now, as always when he was much agitated, he shook it down at his side, as if it hurt. He was talking rapidly to a young, stiff Ober-leutnant. Two private soldiers stood bearishly in the doorway.

Emilie, shocked out of herself, stood pale and erect, recoiling.

"Yes, if you think so, we can look," the Baron was hastily and irascibly saying.

"Emilie," he said, turning to the girl, "did you put a post card to the mother of this Bachmann in the box last evening?"

Emilie stood erect and did not answer.

"Yes?" said the Baron sharply.

"Yes, Herr Baron," replied Emilie, neutral.

The Baron's wounded hand shook rapidly in exasperation. The lieutenant drew himself up still more stiffly. He was right.

"And do you know anything of the fellow?" asked the Baron, looking at her with his blazing, greyish-golden eyes. The girl looked back at him steadily, dumb, but her whole soul naked before him. For two seconds he looked at her in silence. Then in silence, ashamed and furious, he turned away.

"Go up!" he said, with his fierce, peremptory command, to the young officer.

The lieutenant gave his order, in military cold confidence, to the soldiers. They all tramped across the hall. Emilie stood motionless, her life suspended.

The Baron marched swiftly upstairs and down the corridor, the lieutenant and the common soldiers followed. The Baron flung open the door of Emilie's room and looked at Bachmann, who stood watching, standing in shirt and trousers beside the bed, fronting the door. He was perfectly still. His eyes met the furious, blazing look of the Baron. The latter shook his wounded hand, and then went still. He looked into the eyes of the soldier, steadily. He saw the same naked soul exposed, as if he looked really into the man. And the man was helpless, the more helpless for his singular nakedness.

"Ha!" he exclaimed impatiently, turning to the approaching lieutenant.

The latter appeared in the doorway. Quickly his eyes travelled over the bare-footed youth. He recognized him as his object. He gave the brief command to dress.

Bachmann turned round for his clothes. He was very still, silent in himself. He was in an abstract, motionless world. That the two gentlemen and the two soldiers stood watching him, he scarcely realized. They could not see him.

Soon he was ready. He stood at attention. But only the shell of his body was at attention. A curious silence, a blankness, like something eternal, possessed him. He remained true to himself.

The lieutenant gave the order to march. The little procession went down the stairs with careful, respectful tread, and passed through the hall to the kitchen. There Emilie stood with her face uplifted, motionless and expressionless. Bachmann did not look at her. They knew each other. They were themselves. Then the little file of men passed out into the courtyard.

The Baron stood in the doorway watching the four figures in uniform pass through the chequered shadow under the lime trees. Bachmann was walking neutralized, as if he were not there. The lieutenant went brittle and long, the two soldiers lumbered beside. They passed out into the sunny morning, growing smaller, going towards the barracks.

The Baron turned into the kitchen. Emilie was cutting bread.

"So he stayed the night here?" he said.

The girl looked at him, scarcely seeing. She was too much herself. The Baron saw the dark, naked soul of her body in her unseeing eyes.

"What were you going to do?" he asked.

"He was going to America," she replied, in a still voice.

"Pah! You should have sent him straight back," fired the Baron.

Emilie stood at his bidding, untouched.

"He's done for now," he said.

But he could not bear the dark, deep nakedness of her eyes, that scarcely changed under this suffering.

"Nothing but a fool," he repeated, going away in agitation, and preparing himself for what he could do.

DAUGHTERS OF THE VICAR

I

Mr.. Lindley was first vicar of Aldecross. The cottages of this tiny hamlet had nestled in peace since their beginning, and the country folk had crossed the lanes and farm-lands, two or three miles, to the parish church at Greymeed, on the bright Sunday mornings.

But when the pits were sunk, blank rows of dwellings started up beside the high roads, and a new population, skimmed from the floating scum of workmen, was filled in, the cottages and the country people almost obliterated.

To suit the convenience of these new collier-inhabitants, a church must be built at Aldecross. There was not too much money. And so the little building crouched like a humped stone-and-mortar mouse, with two little turrets at the west corners for ears, in the fields near the cottages and the apple trees, as far as possible from the dwellings down the high road. It had an uncertain, timid look about it. And so they planted big-leaved ivy, to hide its shrinking newness. So that now the little church stands buried in its greenery, stranded and sleeping among the fields, while the brick houses elbow nearer and nearer, threatening to crush it down. It is already obsolete.

The Reverend Ernest Lindley, aged twenty-seven, and newly married, came from his curacy in Suffolk to take charge of his church. He was just an ordinary young man, who had been to Cambridge and taken orders. His wife was a self-assured young woman, daughter of a Cambridgeshire rector. Her father had spent the whole of his thousand a year, so that Mrs.. Lindley had nothing of her own. Thus the young married people came to Aldecross to live on a stipend of about a hundred and twenty pounds, and to keep up a superior position.

They were not very well received by the new, raw, disaffected population of colliers. Being accustomed to farm labourers, Mr.. Lindley had considered himself as belonging indisputably to the upper or ordering classes. He had to be humble to the county families, but still, he was of their kind, whilst the common people were something different. He had no doubts of himself.

He found, however, that the collier population refused to accept this arrangement. They had no use for him in their lives, and they told him so, callously. The women merely said, "they were throng," or else, "Oh, it's no good you coming here, we're Chapel." The men were quite good-humoured so long as he did not touch them too nigh, they were cheerfully contemptuous of him, with a preconceived contempt he was powerless against.

At last, passing from indignation to silent resentment, even, if he dared have acknowledged it, to conscious hatred of the majority of his flock, and unconscious hatred of himself, he confined his activities to a narrow round of cottages, and he had to submit. He had no particular character, having always depended on his position in society to give him position among men. Now he was so poor, he had no social standing even among the common vulgar tradespeople of the district, and he had not the nature nor the wish to make his society agreeable to them, nor the strength to impose himself where he would have liked to be recognized. He dragged on, pale and miserable and neutral.

At first his wife raged with mortification. She took on airs and used a high hand. But her income was too small, the wrestling with tradesmen's bills was too pitiful, she only met with general, callous ridicule when she tried to be impressive.

Wounded to the quick of her pride, she found herself isolated in an indifferent, callous population. She raged indoors and out. But soon she learned that she must pay too heavily for her outdoor rages, and then she only raged within the walls of the rectory. There her feeling was so strong, that she frightened herself. She saw herself hating her husband, and she knew that, unless she were careful, she would smash her form of life and bring catastrophe upon him and upon herself. So in very fear, she went quiet. She hid, bitter and beaten by fear, behind the only shelter she had in the world, her gloomy, poor parsonage.

Children were born one every year; almost mechanically, she continued to perform her maternal duty, which was forced upon her. Gradually, broken by the suppressing of her violent anger and misery and disgust, she became an invalid and took to her couch.

The children grew up healthy, but unwarmed and rather rigid. Their father and mother educated them at home, made them very proud and very genteel, put them definitely and cruelly in the upper classes, apart from the vulgar around them. So they lived quite isolated. They were good-looking, and had that curiously clean, semi-transparent look of the genteel, isolated poor.

Gradually Mr.. and Mrs.. Lindley lost all hold on life, and spent their hours, weeks and years merely haggling to make ends meet, and bitterly repressing and pruning their children into gentility, urging them to ambition, weighting them with duty. On Sunday morning the whole family, except the mother, went down the lane to church, the long-legged girls in skimpy frocks, the boys in black coats and long, grey, unfitting trousers. They passed by their father's parishioners with mute, clear faces, childish mouths closed in pride that was like a doom to them, and childish eyes already unseeing. Miss Mary, the eldest, was the leader. She was a long, slim thing with a fine profile and a proud, pure look of submission to a high fate. Miss Louisa, the second, was short and plump and obstinate-looking. She had more enemies than ideals. She looked after the lesser children, Miss Mary after the elder. The collier children watched this pale, distinguished procession of the vicar's family pass mutely by, and they were impressed by the air of gentility and distance, they made mock of the trousers of the small sons, they felt inferior in themselves, and hate stirred their hearts.

In her time, Miss Mary received as governess a few little daughters of tradesmen; Miss Louisa managed the house and went among her father's church-goers, giving lessons on the piano to the colliers' daughters at thirteen shillings for twenty-six lessons.

II

One winter morning, when his daughter Mary was about twenty years old, Mr. Lindley, a thin, unobtrusive figure in his black overcoat and his wideawake, went down into Aldecross with a packet of white papers under his arm. He was delivering the parish almanacs.

A rather pale, neutral man of middle age, he waited while the train thumped over the level-crossing, going up to the pit which rattled busily just along the line. A wooden-legged man hobbled to open the gate, Mr. Lindley passed on. Just at his left hand, below the road and the railway, was the red roof of a cottage, showing through the bare twigs of apple trees. Mr. Lindley passed round the low wall, and descended the worn steps that led from the highway down to the cottage which crouched darkly and quietly away below the rumble of passing trains and the clank of coal-carts in a quiet little under-world of its own. Snowdrops with tight-shut buds were hanging very still under the bare currant bushes.

The clergyman was just going to knock when he heard a clinking noise, and turning saw through the open door of a black shed just behind him an elderly woman in a black lace cap stooping among reddish big cans, pouring a very bright liquid into a tundish. There was a smell of paraffin. The woman put down her can, took the tundish and laid it on a shelf, then rose with a tin bottle. Her eyes met those of the clergyman.

"Oh, is it you, Mr. Lin'ley!" she said, in a complaining tone. "Go in."

The minister entered the house. In the hot kitchen sat a big, elderly man with a great grey beard, taking snuff. He grunted in a deep, muttering voice, telling the minister to sit down, and then took no more notice of him, but stared vacantly into the fire. Mr. Lindley waited.

The woman came in, the ribbons of her black lace cap, or bonnet, hanging on her shawl. She was of medium stature, everything about her was tidy. She went up a step out of the kitchen, carrying the paraffin tin. Feet were heard entering the room up the step. It was a little haberdashery shop, with parcels on the shelves of the walls, a big, old-fashioned sewing machine with tailor's work lying round it, in the open space. The woman went behind the counter, gave the child who had entered the paraffin bottle, and took from her a jug.

"My mother says shall yer put it down," said the child, and she was gone. The woman wrote in a book, then came into the kitchen with her jug. The husband, a very large man, rose and brought more coal to the already hot fire. He moved slowly and sluggishly. Already he was going dead; being a tailor, his large form had become an encumbrance to him. In his youth he had been a great dancer and boxer. Now he was taciturn, and inert. The minister had nothing to say, so he sought for his phrases. But John Durant took no notice, existing silent and dull.

Mrs. Durant spread the cloth. Her husband poured himself beer into a mug, and began to smoke and drink.

"Shall you have some?" he growled through his beard at the clergyman, looking slowly from the man to the jug, capable of this one idea.

"No, thank you," replied Mr. Lindley, though he would have liked some beer. He must set the example in a drinking parish.

"We need a drop to keep us going," said Mrs. Durant.

She had rather a complaining manner. The clergyman sat on uncomfortably while she laid the table for the half-past ten lunch. Her husband drew up to eat. She remained in her little round arm-chair by the fire.

She was a woman who would have liked to be easy in her life, but to whose lot had fallen a rough and turbulent family, and a slothful husband who did not care what became of himself or anybody. So, her rather good-looking square face was peevish, she had that air of having been compelled all her life to serve unwillingly, and to control where she did not want to control. There was about her, too, that masterful *aplomb* of a woman who has brought up and ruled her sons: but even them she had ruled unwillingly. She had enjoyed managing her little haberdashery-shop, riding in the carrier's cart to Nottingham, going through the big warehouses to buy her goods. But the fret of managing her sons she did not like. Only she loved her youngest boy, because he was her last, and she saw herself free.

This was one of the houses the clergyman visited occasionally. Mrs. Durant, as part of her regulation, had brought up all her sons in the Church. Not that she had any religion. Only, it was what she was used to. Mr. Durant was without religion. He read the fervently evangelical "Life of John Wesley" with a curious pleasure, getting from it a satisfaction as from the warmth of the fire, or a glass of brandy. But he cared no more about John Wesley, in fact, than about John Milton, of whom he had never heard.

Mrs. Durant took her chair to the table.

"I don't feel like eating," she sighed.

"Why—aren't you well?" asked the clergyman, patronizing.

"It isn't that," she sighed. She sat with shut, straight mouth. "I don't know what's going to become of us."

But the clergyman had ground himself down so long, that he could not easily sympathize.

"Have you any trouble?" he asked.

"Ay, have I any trouble!" cried the elderly woman. "I shall end my days in the workhouse."

The minister waited unmoved. What could she know of poverty, in her little house of plenty!

"I hope not," he said.

"And the one lad as I wanted to keep by me—" she lamented.

The minister listened without sympathy, quite neutral.

"And the lad as would have been a support to my old age! What is going to become of us?" she said.

The clergyman, justly, did not believe in the cry of poverty, but wondered what had become of the son.

"Has anything happened to Alfred?" he asked.

"We've got word he's gone for a Queen's sailor," she said sharply.

"He has joined the Navy!" exclaimed Mr. Lindley. "I think he could scarcely have done better—to serve his Queen and country on the sea . . ."

"He is wanted to serve *me*," she cried. "And I wanted my lad at home."

Alfred was her baby, her last, whom she had allowed herself the luxury of spoiling.

"You will miss him," said Mr. Lindley, "that is certain. But this is no regrettable step for him to have taken—on the contrary."

"That's easy for you to say, Mr. Lindley," she replied tartly. "Do you think I want my lad climbing ropes at another man's bidding, like a monkey—?"

"There is no *dishonour*, surely, in serving in the Navy?"

"Dishonour this dishonour that," cried the angry old woman. "He goes and makes a slave of himself, and he'll rue it."

Her angry, scornful impatience nettled the clergyman and silenced him for some moments.

"I do not see," he retorted at last, white at the gills and inadequate, "that the Queen's service is any more to be called slavery than working in a mine."

"At home he was at home, and his own master. *I* know he'll find a difference."

"It may be the making of him," said the clergyman. "It will take him away from bad companionship and drink."

Some of the Durants' sons were notorious drinkers, and Alfred was not quite steady.

"And why indeed shouldn't he have his glass?" cried the mother. "He picks no man's pocket to pay for it!"

The clergyman stiffened at what he thought was an allusion to his own profession, and his unpaid bills.

"With all due consideration, I am glad to hear he has joined the Navy," he said.

"Me with my old age coming on, and his father working very little! I'd thank you to be glad about something else besides that, Mr. Lindley."

The woman began to cry. Her husband, quite impassive, finished his lunch of meat-pie, and drank some beer. Then he turned to the fire, as if there were no one in the room but himself.

"I shall respect all men who serve God and their country on the sea, Mrs. Durant," said the clergyman stubbornly.

"That is very well, when they're not your sons who are doing the dirty work.—It makes a difference," she replied tartly.

"I should be proud if one of my sons were to enter the Navy."

"Ay—well—we're not all of us made alike—"

The minister rose. He put down a large folded paper.

"I've brought the almanac," he said.

Mrs. Durant unfolded it.

"I do like a bit of colour in things," she said, petulantly.

The clergyman did not reply.

"There's that envelope for the organist's fund—" said the old woman, and rising, she took the thing from the mantelpiece, went into the shop, and returned sealing it up.

"Which is all I can afford," she said.

Mr. Lindley took his departure, in his pocket the envelope containing Mrs. Durant's offering for Miss Louisa's services. He went from door to door delivering the almanacs, in dull routine. Jaded with the monotony of the business, and with the repeated effort of greeting half-known people, he felt barren and rather irritable. At last he returned home.

In the dining-room was a small fire. Mrs. Lindley, growing very stout, lay on her couch. The vicar carved the cold mutton; Miss Louisa, short and plump and rather flushed, came in from the kitchen; Miss Mary, dark, with a beautiful white brow and grey eyes, served the vegetables; the children chattered a little, but not exuberantly. The very air seemed starved.

"I went to the Durants," said the vicar, as he served out small portions of mutton; "it appears Alfred has run away to join the Navy."

"Do him good," came the rough voice of the invalid.

Miss Louisa, attending to the youngest child, looked up in protest.

"Why has he done that?" asked Mary's low, musical voice.

"He wanted some excitement, I suppose," said the vicar. "Shall we say grace?"

The children were arranged, all bent their heads, grace was pronounced, at the last word every face was being raised to go on with the interesting subject.

"He's just done the right thing, for once," came the rather deep voice of the mother; "save him from becoming a drunken sot, like the rest of them."

"They're not *all* drunken, mama," said Miss Louisa, stubbornly.

"It's no fault of their upbringing if they're not. Walter Durant is a standing disgrace."

"As I told Mrs. Durant," said the vicar, eating hungrily, "it is the best thing he could have done. It will take him away from temptation during the most dangerous years of his life—how old is he—nineteen?"

"Twenty," said Miss Louisa.

"Twenty!" repeated the vicar. "It will give him wholesome discipline and set before him some sort of standard of duty and honour—nothing could have been better for him. But—"

"We shall miss him from the choir," said Miss Louisa, as if taking opposite sides to her parents.

"That is as it may be," said the vicar. "I prefer to know he is safe in the Navy, than running the risk of getting into bad ways here."

"Was he getting into bad ways?" asked the stubborn Miss Louisa.

"You know, Louisa, he wasn't quite what he used to be," said Miss Mary gently and steadily. Miss Louisa shut her rather heavy jaw sulkily. She wanted to deny it, but she knew it was true.

For her he had been a laughing, warm lad, with something kindly and something rich about him. He had made her feel warm. It seemed the days would be colder since he had gone.

"Quite the best thing he could do," said the mother with emphasis.

"I think so," said the vicar. "But his mother was almost abusive because I suggested it."

He spoke in an injured tone.

"What does she care for her children's welfare?" said the invalid. "Their wages is all her concern."

"I suppose she wanted him at home with her," said Miss Louisa.

"Yes, she did—at the expense of his learning to be a drunkard like the rest of them," retorted her mother.

"George Durant doesn't drink," defended her daughter.

"Because he got burned so badly when he was nineteen—in the pit—and that frightened him. The Navy is a better remedy than that, at least."

"Certainly," said the vicar. "Certainly."

And to this Miss Louisa agreed. Yet she could not but feel angry that he had gone away for so many years. She herself was only nineteen.

III

It happened when Miss Mary was twenty-three years old, that Mr. Lindley was very ill. The family was exceedingly poor at the time, such a lot of money was needed, so little was forthcoming. Neither Miss Mary nor Miss Louisa had suitors. What chance had they? They met no eligible young men in Aldecross. And what they earned was a mere drop in a void. The girls' hearts were chilled and hardened with fear of this perpetual, cold penury, this narrow struggle, this horrible nothingness of their lives.

A clergyman had to be found for the church work. It so happened the son of an old friend of Mr. Lindley's was waiting three months before taking up his duties. He would come and officiate, for nothing. The young clergyman was keenly expected. He was not more than twenty-seven, a Master of Arts of Oxford, had written his thesis on Roman Law. He came of an old Cambridgeshire family, had some private means, was going to take a church in Northamptonshire with a good stipend, and was not married. Mrs. Lindley incurred new debts, and scarcely regretted her husband's illness.

But when Mr. Massy came, there was a shock of disappointment in the house. They had expected a young man with a pipe and a deep voice, but with better manners than Sidney, the eldest of the Lindleys. There arrived instead a small, chétif man, scarcely larger than a boy of twelve, spectacled, timid in the extreme, without a word to utter at first; yet with a certain inhuman self-sureness.

"What a little abortion!" was Mrs. Lindley's exclamation to herself on first seeing him, in his buttoned-up clerical coat. And for the first time for many days, she was profoundly thankful to God that all her children were decent specimens.

He had not normal powers of perception. They soon saw that he lacked the full range of human feelings, but had rather a strong, philosophical mind, from which he lived. His body was almost unthinkable, in intellect he was something definite. The conversation at once took a balanced, abstract tone when he participated. There was no spontaneous exclamation, no violent assertion or expression of personal conviction, but all cold, reasonable assertion. This was very hard on Mrs. Lindley. The little man would look at her, after one of her pronouncements, and then give, in his thin voice, his own calculated version, so that she felt as if she were tumbling into thin air through a hole in the flimsy floor on which their conversation stood. It was she who felt a fool. Soon she was reduced to a hardy silence.

Still, at the back of her mind, she remembered that he was an unattached gentleman, who would shortly have an income altogether of six or seven hundred a year. What did the man matter, if there were pecuniary ease! The man was a trifle thrown in. After twenty-two years her sentimentality was ground away, and only the millstone of poverty mattered to her. So she supported the little man as a representative of a decent income.

His most irritating habit was that of a sneering little giggle, all on his own, which came when he perceived or related some illogical absurdity on the part of another person. It was the only form of humour he had. Stupidity in thinking seemed to him exquisitely funny. But any novel was unintelligibly meaningless and dull, and to an Irish sort of humour he listened curiously, examining it like mathematics, or else simply not hearing. In normal human relationship he was not there. Quite unable to take part in simple everyday talk, he padded silently round the house, or sat in the dining-room looking nervously from side to side, always apart in a cold, rarefied little world of his own. Sometimes he made an ironic remark, that did not seem humanly relevant, or he gave his little laugh, like a sneer. He had to defend himself and his own insufficiency. And he answered questions grudgingly, with a yes or no, because he did not see their import and was nervous. It seemed to Miss Louisa he scarcely distinguished one person from another, but that he liked to be near her, or to Miss Mary, for some sort of contact which stimulated him unknown.

Apart from all this, he was the most admirable workman. He was unremittingly shy, but perfect in his sense of duty: as far as he could conceive Christianity, he was a perfect Christian. Nothing that he realized he could do for anyone did he leave undone, although he was so incapable of coming into contact with another being, that he could not proffer help. Now he attended assiduously to the sick man, investigated all the affairs of the parish or the church which Mr. Lindley had in control, straightened out accounts, made lists of the sick and needy, padded round with help and to see what he could do. He heard of Mrs. Lindley's anxiety about her sons, and began to investigate means of sending them to Cambridge. His kindness almost frightened Miss Mary. She honoured it so, and yet she shrank from it. For, in it all Mr. Massy seemed to have no sense of any person, any human being whom he was helping: he only realized a kind of mathematical working out, solving of given situations, a calculated well-doing. And it was as if he had accepted the Christian tenets as axioms. His religion consisted in what his scrupulous, abstract mind approved of.

Seeing his acts, Miss Mary must respect and honour him. In consequence she must serve him. To this she had to force herself, shuddering and yet desirous, but he did not perceive it. She accompanied him on his visiting in the parish, and whilst she was cold with admiration for him, often she was touched with pity for the little padding figure with bent shoulders, buttoned up to the chin in his overcoat. She was a handsome, calm girl, tall, with a beautiful repose. Her clothes were poor, and she wore a black silk scarf, having no furs. But she was a lady. As the people saw her walking down Aldecross beside Mr. Massy, they said:

"My word, Miss Mary's got a catch. Did ever you see such a sickly little shrimp!"

She knew they were talking so, and it made her heart grow hot against them, and she drew herself as it were protectively towards the little man beside her. At any rate, she could see and give honour to his genuine goodness.

He could not walk fast, or far.

"You have not been well?" she asked, in her dignified way.

"I have an internal trouble."

He was not aware of her slight shudder. There was silence, whilst she bowed to recover her composure, to resume her gentle manner towards him.

He was fond of Miss Mary. She had made it a rule of hospitality that he should always be escorted by herself or by her sister on his visits in the parish, which were not many. But some mornings she was engaged. Then Miss Louisa took her place. It was no good Miss Louisa's trying to adopt to Mr. Massy an attitude of queenly service. She was unable to regard him save with aversion. When she saw him from behind, thin and bent-shouldered, looking like a sickly lad of thirteen, she disliked him exceedingly, and felt a desire to put him out of existence. And yet a deeper justice in Mary made Louisa humble before her sister.

They were going to see Mr. Durant, who was paralysed and not expected to live. Miss Louisa was crudely ashamed at being admitted to the cottage in company with the little clergyman.

Mrs. Durant was, however, much quieter in the face of her real trouble.

38

"How is Mr. Durant?" asked Louisa.

"He is no different—and we don't expect him to be," was the reply. The little clergyman stood looking on.

They went upstairs. The three stood for some time looking at the bed, at the grey head of the old man on the pillow, the grey beard over the sheet. Miss Louisa was shocked and afraid.

"It is so dreadful," she said, with a shudder.

"It is how I always thought it would be," replied Mrs. Durant.

Then Miss Louisa was afraid of her. The two women were uneasy, waiting for Mr. Massy to say something. He stood, small and bent, too nervous to speak.

"Has he any understanding?" he asked at length.

"Maybe," said Mrs. Durant. "Can you hear, John?" she asked loudly. The dull blue eye of the inert man looked at her feebly.

"Yes, he understands," said Mrs. Durant to Mr. Massy. Except for the dull look in his eyes, the sick man lay as if dead. The three stood in silence. Miss Louisa was obstinate but heavy-hearted under the load of unlivingness. It was Mr. Massy who kept her there in discipline. His non-human will dominated them all.

Then they heard a sound below, a man's footsteps, and a man's voice called subduedly:

"Are you upstairs, mother?"

Mrs. Durant started and moved to the door. But already a quick, firm step was running up the stairs.

"I'm a bit early, mother," a troubled voice said, and on the landing they saw the form of the sailor. His mother came and clung to him. She was suddenly aware that she needed something to hold on to. He put his arms round her, and bent over her, kissing her.

"He's not gone, mother?" he asked anxiously, struggling to control his voice.

Miss Louisa looked away from the mother and son who stood together in the gloom on the landing. She could not bear it that she and Mr. Massy should be there. The latter stood nervously, as if ill at ease before the emotion that was running. He was a witness, nervous, unwilling, but dispassionate. To Miss Louisa's hot heart it seemed all, all wrong that they should be there.

Mrs. Durant entered the bedroom, her face wet.

"There's Miss Louisa and the vicar," she said, out of voice and quavering.

Her son, red-faced and slender, drew himself up to salute. But Miss Louisa held out her hand. Then she saw his hazel eyes recognize her for a moment, and his small white teeth showed in a glimpse of the greeting she used to love. She was covered with confusion. He went round to the bed; his boots clicked on the plaster floor, he bowed his head with dignity.

"How are you, dad?" he said, laying his hand on the sheet, faltering. But the old man stared fixedly and unseeing. The son stood perfectly still for a few minutes, then slowly recoiled. Miss Louisa saw the fine outline of his breast, under the sailor's blue blouse, as his chest began to heave.

"He doesn't know me," he said, turning to his mother. He gradually went white.

"No, my boy!" cried the mother, pitiful, lifting her face. And suddenly she put her face against his shoulder, he was stooping down to her, holding her against him, and she cried aloud for a moment or two. Miss Louisa saw his sides heaving, and heard the sharp hiss of his breath. She turned away, tears streaming down her face. The father lay inert upon the white bed, Mr. Massy looked queer and obliterated, so little now that the sailor with his sunburned skin was in the room. He stood waiting. Miss Louisa wanted to die, she wanted to have done. She dared not turn round again to look.

"Shall I offer a prayer?" came the frail voice of the clergyman, and all kneeled down.

Miss Louisa was frightened of the inert man upon the bed. Then she felt a flash of fear of Mr. Massy, hearing his thin, detached voice. And then, calmed, she looked up. On the far side of the bed were the heads of the mother and son, the one in the black lace cap, with the small white nape of the neck beneath, the other, with brown, sun-scorched hair too close and wiry to allow of a parting, and neck tanned firm, bowed as if unwillingly. The great grey beard of the old man did not move, the prayer continued. Mr. Massy prayed with a pure lucidity, that they all might conform to the higher Will. He was like something that dominated the bowed heads, something dispassionate that governed them inexorably. Miss Louisa was afraid of him. And she was bound, during the course of the prayer, to have a little reverence for him. It was like a foretaste of inexorable, cold death, a taste of pure justice.

That evening she talked to Mary of the visit. Her heart, her veins were possessed by the thought of Alfred Durant as he held his mother in his arms; then the break in his voice, as she remembered it again and again, was like a flame through her; and she wanted to see his face more distinctly in her mind, ruddy with the sun, and his golden-brown eyes, kind and careless, strained now with a natural fear, the fine nose tanned hard by the sun, the mouth that could not help smiling at her. And it went through her with pride, to think of his figure, a straight, fine jet of life.

"He is a handsome lad," said she to Miss Mary, as if he had not been a year older than herself. Underneath was the deeper dread, almost hatred, of the inhuman being of Mr. Massy. She felt she must protect herself and Alfred from him.

"When I felt Mr. Massy there," she said, "I almost hated him. What right had he to be there!"

"Surely he has all right," said Miss Mary after a pause. "He is really a Christian."

"He seems to me nearly an imbecile," said Miss Louisa.

Miss Mary, quiet and beautiful, was silent for a moment:

"Oh, no," she said. "Not *imbecile*—"

"Well then—he reminds me of a six months' child—or a five months' child—as if he didn't have time to get developed enough before he was born."

"Yes," said Miss Mary, slowly. "There is something lacking. But there is something wonderful in him: and he is really good—"

"Yes," said Miss Louisa, "it doesn't seem right that he should be. What right has *that* to be called goodness!"

"But it *is* goodness," persisted Mary. Then she added, with a laugh: "And come, you wouldn't deny that as well."

There was a doggedness in her voice. She went about very quietly. In her soul, she knew what was going to happen. She knew that Mr. Massy was stronger than she, and that she must submit to what he was. Her physical self was prouder, stronger than he, her physical self disliked and despised him. But she was in the grip of his moral, mental being. And she felt the days allotted out to her. And her family watched.

IV

A few days after, old Mr. Durant died. Miss Louisa saw Alfred once more, but he was stiff before her now, treating her not like a person, but as if she were some sort of will in command and he a separate, distinct will waiting in front of her. She had never felt such utter steel-plate separation from anyone. It puzzled her and frightened her. What had become of him? And she hated the military discipline—she was antagonistic to it. Now he was not himself. He was the will which obeys set over against the will which commands. She hesitated over accepting this. He had put himself out of her range. He had ranked himself inferior, subordinate to her. And that was how he would get away from her, that was how he would avoid all connection with her: by fronting her impersonally from the opposite camp, by taking up the abstract position of an inferior.

She went brooding steadily and sullenly over this, brooding and brooding. Her fierce, obstinate heart could not give way. It clung to its own rights. Sometimes she dismissed him. Why should he, inferior, trouble her?

Then she relapsed to him, and almost hated him. It was his way of getting out of it. She felt the cowardice of it, his calmly placing her in a superior class, and placing himself inaccessibly apart, in an inferior, as if she, the sentient woman who was fond of him, did not count. But she was not going to submit. Dogged in her heart she held on to him.

V

In six months' time Miss Mary had married Mr. Massy. There had been no love-making, nobody had made any remark. But everybody was tense and callous with expectation. When one day Mr. Massy asked for Mary's hand, Mr. Lindley started and trembled from the thin, abstract voice of the little man. Mr. Massy was very nervous, but so curiously absolute.

"I shall be very glad," said the vicar, "but of course the decision lies with Mary herself." And his still feeble hand shook as he moved a Bible on his desk.

The small man, keeping fixedly to his idea, padded out of the room to find Miss Mary. He sat a long time by her, while she made some conversation, before he had readiness to speak. She was afraid of what was coming, and sat stiff in apprehension. She felt as if her body would rise and fling him aside. But her spirit quivered and waited. Almost in expectation she waited, almost wanting him. And then she knew he would speak.

"I have already asked Mr. Lindley," said the clergyman, while suddenly she looked with aversion at his little knees, "if he would consent to my proposal." He was aware of his own disadvantage, but his will was set.

She went cold as she sat, and impervious, almost as if she had become stone. He waited a moment nervously. He would not persuade her. He himself never even heard persuasion, but pursued his own course. He looked at her, sure of himself, unsure of her, and said:

"Will you become my wife, Mary?"

Still her heart was hard and cold. She sat proudly.

"I should like to speak to mama first," she said.

"Very well," replied Mr. Massy. And in a moment he padded away.

Mary went to her mother. She was cold and reserved.

"Mr. Massy has asked me to marry him, mama," she said. Mrs. Lindley went on staring at her book. She was cramped in her feeling.

"Well, and what did you say?"

They were both keeping calm and cold.

"I said I would speak to you before answering him."

This was equivalent to a question. Mrs. Lindley did not want to reply to it. She shifted her heavy form irritably on the couch. Miss Mary sat calm and straight, with closed mouth.

"Your father thinks it would not be a bad match," said the mother, as if casually.

Nothing more was said. Everybody remained cold and shut-off. Miss Mary did not speak to Miss Louisa, the Reverend Ernest Lindley kept out of sight.

At evening Miss Mary accepted Mr. Massy.

"Yes, I will marry you," she said, with even a little movement of tenderness towards him. He was embarrassed, but satisfied. She could see him making some movement towards her, could feel the male in him, something cold and triumphant, asserting itself. She sat rigid, and waited.

When Miss Louisa knew, she was silent with bitter anger against everybody, even against Mary. She felt her faith wounded. Did the real things to her not matter after all? She wanted to get away. She thought of Mr. Massy. He had some curious power, some unanswerable right. He was a will that they could not controvert.—Suddenly a flush started in her. If he had come to her she would have flipped him out of the room. He was never going to touch her. And she was glad. She was glad that her blood would rise and exterminate the little man, if he came too near to her, no matter how her judgment was paralysed by him, no matter how he moved in abstract goodness. She thought she was perverse to be glad, but glad she was. "I would just flip him out of the room," she said, and she derived great satisfaction from the open statement. Nevertheless, perhaps she ought still to feel that Mary, on her plane, was a higher being than herself. But then Mary was Mary, and she was Louisa, and that also was inalterable.

Mary, in marrying him, tried to become a pure reason such as he was, without feeling or impulse. She shut herself up, she shut herself rigid against the agonies of shame and the terror of violation which came at first. She *would* not feel, and she *would* not feel. She was a pure will acquiescing to him. She elected a certain kind of fate. She would be good and purely just, she would live in a higher freedom than she had ever known, she would be free of mundane care, she was a pure will towards right. She had sold herself, but she had a new freedom. She had got rid of her body. She had sold a lower thing, her body, for a higher thing, her freedom from material things. She considered that she paid for all she got from her husband. So, in a kind of independence, she moved proud and free. She had paid with her body: that was henceforward out of consideration. She was glad to be rid of it. She had bought her position in the world—that henceforth was taken for granted. There remained only the direction of her activity towards charity and high-minded living.

She could scarcely bear other people to be present with her and her husband. Her private life was her shame. But then, she could keep it hidden. She lived almost isolated in the rectory of the tiny village miles from the railway. She suffered as if it were an insult to her own flesh, seeing the repulsion which some people felt for her husband, or the special manner they had of treating him, as if he were a "case". But most people were uneasy before him, which restored her pride.

If she had let herself, she would have hated him, hated his padding round the house, his thin voice devoid of human understanding, his bent little shoulders and rather incomplete face that reminded her of an abortion. But rigorously she kept to her position. She took care of him and was just to him. There was also a deep craven fear of him, something slave-like.

There was not much fault to be found with his behaviour. He was scrupulously just and kind according to his lights. But the male in him was cold and self-complete, and utterly domineering. Weak, insufficient little thing as he was, she had not expected this of him. It was something in the bargain she had not understood. It made her hold her head, to keep still. She knew, vaguely, that she was murdering herself. After all, her body was not quite so easy to get rid of. And this manner of disposing of it—ah, sometimes she felt she must rise and bring about death, lift her hand for utter denial of everything, by a general destruction.

He was almost unaware of the conditions about him. He did not fuss in the domestic way, she did as she liked in the house. Indeed, she was a great deal free of him. He would sit obliterated for hours. He was kind, and almost anxiously considerate. But when he considered he was right, his will was just blindly male, like a cold machine. And on most points he was logically right, or he had with him the right of the creed they both accepted. It was so. There was nothing for her to go against.

Then she found herself with child, and felt for the first time horror, afraid before God and man. This also she had to go through—it was the right. When the child arrived, it was a bonny, healthy lad. Her heart hurt in her body, as she took the baby between her hands. The flesh that was trampled and silent in her must speak again in the boy. After all, she had to live—it was not so simple after all. Nothing was finished completely. She looked and looked at the baby, and almost hated it, and suffered an anguish of love for it. She hated it because it made her live again in the flesh, when she *could* not live in the flesh, she could not. She wanted to trample her flesh down, down, extinct, to live in the mind. And now there was this child. It was too cruel, too racking. For she must love the child. Her purpose was broken in two again. She had to become amorphous, purposeless, without real being. As a mother, she was a fragmentary, ignoble thing.

Mr. Massy, blind to everything else in the way of human feeling, became obsessed by the idea of his child. When it arrived, suddenly it filled the whole world of feeling for him. It was his obsession, his terror was for its safety and well-being. It was something new, as if he himself had been born a naked infant, conscious of his own exposure, and full of apprehension. He who had never been aware of anyone else, all his life, now was aware of nothing but the child. Not that he ever played with it, or kissed it, or tended it. He did nothing for it. But it dominated him, it filled, and at the same time emptied his mind. The world was all baby for him.

This his wife must also bear, his question: "What is the reason that he cries?"—his reminder, at the first sound: "Mary, that is the child,"—his restlessness if the feeding-time were five minutes past. She had bargained for this—now she must stand by her bargain.

VI

Miss Louisa, at home in the dingy vicarage, had suffered a great deal over her sister's wedding. Having once begun to cry out against it, during the engagement, she had been silenced by Mary's quiet: "I don't agree with you about him, Louisa, I *want* to marry him." Then Miss Louisa had been angry deep in her heart, and therefore silent. This dangerous state started the change in her. Her own revulsion made her recoil from the hitherto undoubted Mary.

"I'd beg the streets barefoot first," said Miss Louisa, thinking of Mr. Massy.

But evidently Mary could perform a different heroism. So she, Louisa the practical, suddenly felt that Mary, her ideal, was questionable after all. How could she be pure—one cannot be dirty in act and spiritual in being. Louisa distrusted Mary's high spirituality. It was no longer genuine for her. And if Mary were spiritual and misguided, why did not her father protect her? Because of the money. He disliked the whole affair, but he backed away, because of the money. And the mother frankly did not care: her daughters could do as they liked. Her mother's pronouncement:

"Whatever happens to *him*, Mary is safe for life,"—so evidently and shallowly a calculation, incensed Louisa.

"I'd rather be safe in the workhouse," she cried.

"Your father will see to that," replied her mother brutally. This speech, in its indirectness, so injured Miss Louisa that she hated her mother deep, deep in her heart, and almost hated herself. It was a long time resolving itself out, this hate. But it worked and worked, and at last the young woman said:

"They are wrong—they are all wrong. They have ground out their souls for what isn't worth anything, and there isn't a grain of love in them anywhere. And I *will* have love. They want us to deny it. They've never found it, so they want to say it doesn't exist. But I *will* have it. I *will* love—it is my birthright. I will love the man I marry—that is all I care about."

So Miss Louisa stood isolated from everybody. She and Mary had parted over Mr. Massy. In Louisa's eyes, Mary was degraded, married to Mr. Massy. She could not bear to think of her lofty, spiritual sister degraded in the body like this. Mary was wrong, wrong, wrong: she was not superior, she was flawed, incomplete. The two sisters stood apart. They still loved each other, they would love each other as long as they lived. But they had parted ways. A new solitariness came over the obstinate Louisa, and her heavy jaw set stubbornly. She was going on her own way. But which way? She was quite alone, with a blank world before her. How could she be said to have any way? Yet she had her fixed will to love, to have the man she loved.

VII

When her boy was three years old, Mary had another baby, a girl. The three years had gone by monotonously. They might have been an eternity, they might have been brief as a sleep. She did not know. Only, there was always a weight on top of her, something that pressed down her life. The only thing that had happened was that Mr. Massy had had an operation. He was always exceedingly fragile. His wife had soon learned to attend to him mechanically, as part of her duty.

But this third year, after the baby girl had been born, Mary felt oppressed and depressed. Christmas drew near: the gloomy, unleavened Christmas of the rectory, where all the days were of the same dark fabric. And Mary was afraid. It was as if the darkness were coming upon her.

"Edward, I should like to go home for Christmas," she said, and a certain terror filled her as she spoke.

"But you can't leave baby," said her husband, blinking.

"We can all go."

He thought, and stared in his collective fashion.

"Why do you wish to go?" he asked.

"Because I need a change. A change would do me good, and it would be good for the milk."

He heard the will in his wife's voice, and was at a loss. Her language was unintelligible to him. And while she was breeding, either about to have a child, or nursing, he regarded her as a special sort of being.

"Wouldn't it hurt baby to take her by the train?" he said.

"No," replied the mother, "why should it?"

They went. When they were in the train, it began to snow. From the window of his first-class carriage the little clergyman watched the big flakes sweep by, like a blind drawn across the country. He was obsessed by thought of the baby, and afraid of the draughts of the carriage.

"Sit right in the corner," he said to his wife, "and hold baby close back."

She moved at his bidding, and stared out of the window. His eternal presence was like an iron weight on her brain. But she was going partially to escape for a few days.

"Sit on the other side, Jack," said the father. "It is less draughty. Come to this window."

He watched the boy in anxiety. But his children were the only beings in the world who took not the slightest notice of him.

"Look, mother, look!" cried the boy. "They fly right in my face"—he meant the snowflakes.

"Come into this corner," repeated his father, out of another world.

"He's jumped on this one's back, mother, an' they're riding to the bottom!" cried the boy, jumping with glee.

"Tell him to come on this side," the little man bade his wife.

"Jack, kneel on this cushion," said the mother, putting her white hand on the place.

The boy slid over in silence to the place she indicated, waited still for a moment, then almost deliberately, stridently cried:

"Look at all those in the corner, mother, making a heap," and he pointed to the cluster of snowflakes with finger pressed dramatically on the pane, and he turned to his mother a bit ostentatiously.

"All in a heap!" she said.

He had seen her face, and had her response, and he was somewhat assured. Vaguely uneasy, he was reassured if he could win her attention.

They arrived at the vicarage at half-past two, not having had lunch.

"How are you, Edward?" said Mr. Lindley, trying on his side to be fatherly. But he was always in a false position with his son-in-law, frustrated before him, therefore, as much as possible, he shut his eyes and ears to him. The vicar was looking thin and pale and ill-nourished. He had gone quite grey. He was, however, still haughty; but, since the growing-up of his children, it was a brittle haughtiness, that might break at any moment and leave the vicar only an impoverished, pitiable figure. Mrs. Lindley took all the notice of her daughter, and of the children. She ignored her son-in-law. Miss Louisa was clucking and laughing and rejoicing over the baby. Mr. Massy stood aside, a bent, persistent little figure.

"Oh a pretty!—a little pretty! oh a cold little pretty come in a railway-train!" Miss Louisa was cooing to the infant, crouching on the hearthrug opening the white woollen wraps and exposing the child to the fireglow.

"Mary," said the little clergyman, "I think it would be better to give baby a warm bath; she may take a cold."

"I think it is not necessary," said the mother, coming and closing her hand judiciously over the rosy feet and hands of the mite. "She is not chilly."

"Not a bit," cried Miss Louisa. "She's not caught cold."

"I'll go and bring her flannels," said Mr. Massy, with one idea.

"I can bath her in the kitchen then," said Mary, in an altered, cold tone.

"You can't, the girl is scrubbing there," said Miss Louisa. "Besides, she doesn't want a bath at this time of day."

"She'd better have one," said Mary, quietly, out of submission. Miss Louisa's gorge rose, and she was silent. When the little man padded down with the flannels on his arm, Mrs. Lindley asked:

"Hadn't *you* better take a hot bath, Edward?"

But the sarcasm was lost on the little clergyman. He was absorbed in the preparations round the baby.

The room was dull and threadbare, and the snow outside seemed fairy-like by comparison, so white on the lawn and tufted on the bushes. Indoors the heavy pictures hung obscurely on the walls, everything was dingy with gloom.

Except in the fireglow, where they had laid the bath on the hearth. Mrs. Massy, her black hair always smoothly coiled and queenly, kneeled by the bath, wearing a rubber apron, and holding the kicking child. Her husband stood holding the towels and the flannels to warm. Louisa, too cross to share in the joy of the baby's bath, was laying the table. The boy was hanging on the door-knob, wrestling with it to get out. His father looked round.

"Come away from the door, Jack," he said, ineffectually. Jack tugged harder at the knob as if he did not hear. Mr. Massy blinked at him.

"He must come away from the door, Mary," he said. "There will be a draught if it is opened."

"Jack, come away from the door, dear," said the mother, dexterously turning the shiny wet baby on to her towelled knee, then glancing round: "Go and tell Auntie Louisa about the train."

Louisa, also afraid to open the door, was watching the scene on the hearth. Mr. Massy stood holding the baby's flannel, as if assisting at some ceremonial. If everybody had not been subduedly angry, it would have been ridiculous.

"I want to see out of the window," Jack said. His father turned hastily.

"Do *you* mind lifting him on to a chair, Louisa," said Mary hastily. The father was too delicate.

When the baby was flannelled, Mr. Massy went upstairs and returned with four pillows, which he set in the fender to warm. Then he stood watching the mother feed her child, obsessed by the idea of his infant.

Louisa went on with her preparations for the meal. She could not have told why she was so sullenly angry. Mrs. Lindley, as usual, lay silently watching.

Mary carried her child upstairs, followed by her husband with the pillows. After a while he came down again.

"What is Mary doing? Why doesn't she come down to eat?" asked Mrs. Lindley.

"She is staying with baby. The room is rather cold. I will ask the girl to put in a fire." He was going absorbedly to the door.

"But Mary has had nothing to eat. It is *she* who will catch cold," said the mother, exasperated.

Mr. Massy seemed as if he did not hear. Yet he looked at his mother-in-law, and answered:

"I will take her something."

He went out. Mrs. Lindley shifted on her couch with anger. Miss Louisa glowered. But no one said anything, because of the money that came to the vicarage from Mr. Massy.

Louisa went upstairs. Her sister was sitting by the bed, reading a scrap of paper.

"Won't you come down and eat?" the younger asked.

"In a moment or two," Mary replied, in a quiet, reserved voice, that forbade anyone to approach her.

It was this that made Miss Louisa most furious. She went downstairs, and announced to her mother:

"I am going out. I may not be home to tea."

VIII

No one remarked on her exit. She put on her fur hat, that the village people knew so well, and the old Norfolk jacket. Louisa was short and plump and plain. She had her mother's heavy jaw, her father's proud brow, and her own grey, brooding eyes that were very beautiful when she smiled. It was true, as the people said, that she looked sulky. Her chief attraction was her glistening, heavy, deep-blond hair, which shone and gleamed with a richness that was not entirely foreign to her.

"Where am I going?" she said to herself, when she got outside in the snow. She did not hesitate, however, but by mechanical walking found herself descending the hill towards Old Aldecross. In the valley that was black with trees, the colliery breathed in stertorous pants, sending out high conical columns of steam that remained upright, whiter than the snow on the hills, yet shadowy, in the dead air. Louisa would not acknowledge to herself whither she was making her way, till she came to the railway crossing. Then the bunches of snow in the twigs of the apple tree that leaned towards the fence told her she must go and see Mrs. Durant. The tree was in Mrs. Durant's garden.

Alfred was now at home again, living with his mother in the cottage below the road. From the highway hedge, by the railway crossing, the snowy garden sheered down steeply, like the side of a hole, then dropped straight in a wall. In this depth the house was snug, its chimney just level with the road. Miss Louisa descended the stone stairs, and stood below in the little backyard, in the dimness and the semi-secrecy. A big tree leaned overhead, above the paraffin hut. Louisa felt secure from all the world down there. She knocked at the open door, then looked round. The tongue of garden narrowing in from the quarry bed was white with snow: she thought of the thick fringes of snowdrops it would show beneath the currant bushes in a month's time. The ragged fringe of pinks hanging over the garden brim behind her was whitened now with snow-flakes, that in summer held white blossom to Louisa's face. It was pleasant, she thought, to gather flowers that stooped to one's face from above.

She knocked again. Peeping in, she saw the scarlet glow of the kitchen, red firelight falling on the brick floor and on the bright chintz cushions. It was alive and bright as a peep-show. She crossed the scullery, where still an almanac hung. There was no one about. "Mrs. Durant," called Louisa softly, "Mrs. Durant."

She went up the brick step into the front room, that still had its little shop counter and its bundles of goods, and she called from the stair-foot. Then she knew Mrs. Durant was out.

She went into the yard to follow the old woman's footsteps up the garden path.

She emerged from the bushes and raspberry canes. There was the whole quarry bed, a wide garden white and dimmed, brindled with dark bushes, lying half submerged. On the left, overhead, the little colliery train rumbled by. Right away at the back was a mass of trees.

Louisa followed the open path, looking from right to left, and then she gave a cry of concern. The old woman was sitting rocking slightly among the ragged snowy cabbages. Louisa ran to her, found her whimpering with little, involuntary cries.

"Whatever have you done?" cried Louisa, kneeling in the snow.

"I've—I've—I was pulling a brussel-sprout stalk—and—oh-h!—something tore inside me. I've had a pain," the old woman wept from shock and suffering, gasping between her whimpers,—"I've had a pain there—a long time—and now—oh—oh!" She panted, pressed her hand on her side, leaned as if she would faint, looking yellow against the snow. Louisa supported her.

"Do you think you could walk now?" she asked.

"Yes," gasped the old woman.

Louisa helped her to her feet.

"Get the cabbage—I want it for Alfred's dinner," panted Mrs. Durant. Louisa picked up the stalk of brussel-sprouts, and with difficulty got the old woman indoors. She gave her brandy, laid her on the couch, saying:

"I'm going to send for a doctor—wait just a minute."

The young woman ran up the steps to the public-house a few yards away. The landlady was astonished to see Miss Louisa.

"Will you send for a doctor at once to Mrs. Durant," she said, with some of her father in her commanding tone.

"Is something the matter?" fluttered the landlady in concern.

Louisa, glancing out up the road, saw the grocer's cart driving to Eastwood. She ran and stopped the man, and told him.

Mrs. Durant lay on the sofa, her face turned away, when the young woman came back.

"Let me put you to bed," Louisa said. Mrs. Durant did not resist.

Louisa knew the ways of the working people. In the bottom drawer of the dresser she found dusters and flannels. With the old pit-flannel she snatched out the oven shelves, wrapped them up, and put them in the bed. From the son's bed she took a blanket, and, running down, set it before the fire. Having undressed the little old woman, Louisa carried her upstairs.

"You'll drop me, you'll drop me!" cried Mrs. Durant.

Louisa did not answer, but bore her burden quickly. She could not light a fire, because there was no fire-place in the bedroom. And the floor was plaster. So she fetched the lamp, and stood it lighted in one corner.

"It will air the room," she said.

"Yes," moaned the old woman.

Louisa ran with more hot flannels, replacing those from the oven shelves. Then she made a bran-bag and laid it on the woman's side. There was a big lump on the side of the abdomen.

"I've felt it coming a long time," moaned the old lady, when the pain was easier, "but I've not said anything; I didn't want to upset our Alfred."

Louisa did not see why "our Alfred" should be spared.

"What time is it?" came the plaintive voice.

"A quarter to four."

"Oh!" wailed the old lady, "he'll be here in half an hour, and no dinner ready for him."

"Let me do it?" said Louisa, gently.

"There's that cabbage—and you'll find the meat in the pantry—and there's an apple pie you can hot up. But *don't you* do it—!"

"Who will, then?" asked Louisa.

"I don't know," moaned the sick woman, unable to consider.

Louisa did it. The doctor came and gave serious examination. He looked very grave.

"What is it, doctor?" asked the old lady, looking up at him with old, pathetic eyes in which already hope was dead.

"I think you've torn the skin in which a tumour hangs," he replied.

"Ay!" she murmured, and she turned away.

"You see, she may die any minute—and it *may* be swaled away," said the old doctor to Louisa.

The young woman went upstairs again.

"He says the lump may be swaled away, and you may get quite well again," she said.

"Ay!" murmured the old lady. It did not deceive her. Presently she asked:

"Is there a good fire?"

"I think so," answered Louisa.

"He'll want a good fire," the mother said. Louisa attended to it.

Since the death of Durant, the widow had come to church occasionally, and Louisa had been friendly to her. In the girl's heart the purpose was fixed. No man had affected her as Alfred Durant had done, and to that she kept. In her heart, she adhered to him. A natural sympathy existed between her and his rather hard, materialistic mother.

Alfred was the most lovable of the old woman's sons. He had grown up like the rest, however, headstrong and blind to everything but his own will. Like the other boys, he had insisted on going into the pit as soon as he left school, because that was the only way speedily to become a man, level with all the other men. This was a great chagrin to his mother, who would have liked to have this last of her sons a gentleman.

But still he remained constant to her. His feeling for her was deep and unexpressed. He noticed when she was tired, or when she had a new cap. And he bought little things for her occasionally. She was not wise enough to see how much he lived by her.

At the bottom he did not satisfy her, he did not seem manly enough. He liked to read books occasionally, and better still he liked to play the piccolo. It amused her to see his head nod over the instrument as he made an effort to get the right note. It made her fond of him, with tenderness, almost pity, but not with respect. She wanted a man to be fixed, going his own way without knowledge of women. Whereas she knew Alfred depended on her. He sang in the choir because he liked singing. In the summer he worked in the garden, attended to the fowls and pigs. He kept pigeons. He played on Saturday in the cricket or football team. But to her he did not seem the man, the independent man her other boys had been. He was her baby—and whilst she loved him for it, she was a little bit contemptuous of him.

There grew up a little hostility between them. Then he began to drink, as the others had done; but not in their blind, oblivious way. He was a little self-conscious over it. She saw this, and she pitied it in him. She loved him most, but she was not satisfied with him because he was not free of her. He could not quite go his own way.

Then at twenty he ran away and served his time in the Navy. This made a man of him. He had hated it bitterly, the service, the subordination. For years he fought with himself under the military discipline, for his own self-respect, struggling through blind anger and shame and a cramping sense of inferiority. Out of humiliation and self-hatred, he rose into a sort of inner freedom. And his love for his mother, whom he idealised, remained the fact of hope and of belief.

He came home again, nearly thirty years old, but naïve and inexperienced as a boy, only with a silence about him that was new: a sort of dumb humility before life, a fear of living. He was almost quite chaste. A strong sensitiveness had kept him from women. Sexual talk was all very well among men, but somehow it had no application to living women. There were two things for him, the idea of women, with which he sometimes debauched himself, and real women, before whom he felt a deep uneasiness, and a need to draw away. He shrank and defended himself from the approach of any woman. And then he felt ashamed. In his innermost soul he felt he was not a man, he was less than the normal man. In Genoa he went with an under officer to a drinking house where the cheaper sort of girl came in to look for lovers. He sat there with his glass, the girls looked at him, but they never came to him. He knew that if they did come he could only pay for food and drink for them, because he felt a pity for them, and was anxious lest they lacked good necessities. He could not have gone with one of them: he knew it, and was ashamed, looking with curious envy at the swaggering, easy-passionate Italian whose body went to a woman by instinctive impersonal attraction. They were men, he was not a man. He sat feeling short, feeling like a leper. And he went away imagining sexual scenes between himself and a woman, walking wrapt in this indulgence. But when the ready woman presented herself, the very fact that she was a palpable woman made it impossible for him to touch her. And this incapacity was like a core of rottenness in him.

So several times he went, drunk, with his companions, to the licensed prostitute houses abroad. But the sordid insignificance of the experience appalled him. It had not been anything really: it meant nothing. He felt as if he were, not physically, but spiritually impotent: not actually impotent, but intrinsically so.

He came home with this secret, never changing burden of his unknown, unbestowed self torturing him. His navy training left him in perfect physical condition. He was sensible of, and proud of his body. He bathed and used dumb-bells, and kept himself fit. He played cricket and football. He read books and began to hold fixed ideas which he got from the Fabians. He played his piccolo, and was considered an expert. But at the bottom of his soul was always this canker of shame and incompleteness: he was miserable beneath all his healthy cheerfulness, he was uneasy and felt despicable among all his confidence and superiority of ideas. He would have changed with any mere brute, just to be free of himself, to be free of this shame of self-consciousness. He saw some collier lurching straight forward without misgiving, pursuing his own satisfactions, and he envied him. Anything, he would have given anything for this spontaneity and this blind stupidity which went to its own satisfaction direct.

IX

He was not unhappy in the pit. He was admired by the men, and well enough liked. It was only he himself who felt the difference between himself and the others. He seemed to hide his own stigma. But he was never sure that the others did not really despise him for a ninny, as being less a man than they were. Only he pretended to be more manly, and was surprised by the ease with which they were deceived. And, being naturally cheerful, he was happy at his work. He was sure of himself there. Naked to the waist, hot and grimy with labour, they squatted on their heels for a few minutes and talked, seeing each other dimly by the light of the safety lamps, while the black coal rose jutting round them, and the props of wood stood like little pillars in the low, black, very dark temple. Then the pony came and the gang-lad with a message from Number 7, or with a bottle of water from the horse-trough or some news of the world above. The day passed pleasantly enough. There was an ease, a go-as-you-please about the day underground, a delightful camaraderie of men shut off alone from the rest of the world, in a dangerous place, and a variety of labour, holing, loading, timbering, and a glamour of mystery and adventure in the atmosphere, that made the pit not unattractive to him when he had again got over his anguish of desire for the open air and the sea.

This day there was much to do and Durant was not in humour to talk. He went on working in silence through the afternoon.

"Loose-all" came, and they tramped to the bottom. The whitewashed underground office shone brightly. Men were putting out their lamps. They sat in dozens round the bottom of the shaft, down which black, heavy drops of water fell continuously into the sump. The electric lights shone away down the main underground road.

"Is it raining?" asked Durant.

"Snowing," said an old man, and the younger was pleased. He liked to go up when it was snowing.

"It'll just come right for Christmas," said the old man.

"Ay," replied Durant.

"A green Christmas, a fat churchyard," said the other sententiously.

Durant laughed, showing his small, rather pointed teeth.

The cage came down, a dozen men lined on. Durant noticed tufts of snow on the perforated, arched roof of the chain, and he was pleased.

He wondered how it liked its excursion underground. But already it was getting soppy with black water.

He liked things about him. There was a little smile on his face. But underlying it was the curious consciousness he felt in himself.

The upper world came almost with a flash, because of the glimmer of snow. Hurrying along the bank, giving up his lamp at the office, he smiled to feel the open about him again, all glimmering round him with snow. The hills on either side were pale blue in the dusk, and the hedges looked savage and dark. The snow was trampled between the railway lines. But far ahead, beyond the black figures of miners moving home, it became smooth again, spreading right up to the dark wall of the coppice.

To the west there was a pinkness, and a big star hovered half revealed. Below, the lights of the pit came out crisp and yellow among the darkness of the buildings, and the lights of Old Aldecross twinkled in rows down the bluish twilight.

Durant walked glad with life among the miners, who were all talking animatedly because of the snow. He liked their company, he liked the white dusky world. It gave him a little thrill to stop at the garden gate and see the light of home down below, shining on the silent blue snow.

X

By the big gate of the railway, in the fence, was a little gate, that he kept locked. As he unfastened it, he watched the kitchen light that shone on to the bushes and the snow outside. It was a candle burning till night set in, he thought to himself. He slid down the steep path to the level below. He liked making the first marks in the smooth snow. Then he came through the bushes to the house. The two women heard his heavy boots ring outside on the scraper, and his voice as he opened the door:

"How much worth of oil do you reckon to save by that candle, mother?" He liked a good light from the lamp.

He had just put down his bottle and snap-bag and was hanging his coat behind the scullery door, when Miss Louisa came upon him. He was startled, but he smiled.

His eyes began to laugh—then his face went suddenly straight, and he was afraid.

"Your mother's had an accident," she said.

"How?" he exclaimed.

"In the garden," she answered. He hesitated with his coat in his hands. Then he hung it up and turned to the kitchen.

"Is she in bed?" he asked.

"Yes," said Miss Louisa, who found it hard to deceive him. He was silent. He went into the kitchen, sat down heavily in his father's old chair, and began to pull off his boots. His head was small, rather finely shapen. His brown hair, close and crisp, would look jolly whatever happened. He wore heavy moleskin trousers that gave off the stale, exhausted scent of the pit. Having put on his slippers, he carried his boots into the scullery.

"What is it?" he asked, afraid.

"Something internal," she replied.

He went upstairs. His mother kept herself calm for his coming. Louisa felt his tread shake the plaster floor of the bedroom above.

"What have you done?" he asked.

"It's nothing, my lad," said the old woman, rather hard. "It's nothing. You needn't fret, my boy, it's nothing more the matter with me than I had yesterday, or last week. The doctor said I'd done nothing serious."

"What were you doing?" asked her son.

"I was pulling up a cabbage, and I suppose I pulled too hard; for, oh—there was such a pain—"

Her son looked at her quickly. She hardened herself.

"But who doesn't have a sudden pain sometimes, my boy. We all do."

"And what's it done?"

"I don't know," she said, "but I don't suppose it's anything."

The big lamp in the corner was screened with a dark green, so that he could scarcely see her face. He was strung tight with apprehension and many emotions. Then his brow knitted.

"What did you go pulling your inside out at cabbages for," he asked, "and the ground frozen? You'd go on dragging and dragging, if you killed yourself."

"Somebody's got to get them," she said.

"You needn't do yourself harm."

But they had reached futility.

Miss Louisa could hear plainly downstairs. Her heart sank. It seemed so hopeless between them.

"Are you sure it's nothing much, mother?" he asked, appealing, after a little silence.

"Ay, it's nothing," said the old woman, rather bitter.

"I don't want you to—to—to be badly—you know."

"Go an' get your dinner," she said. She knew she was going to die: moreover, the pain was torture just then. "They're only cosseting me up a bit because I'm an old woman. Miss Louisa's very good—and she'll have got your dinner ready, so you'd better go and eat it."

He felt stupid and ashamed. His mother put him off. He had to turn away. The pain burned in his bowels. He went downstairs. The mother was glad he was gone, so that she could moan with pain.

He had resumed the old habit of eating before he washed himself. Miss Louisa served his dinner. It was strange and exciting to her. She was strung up tense, trying to understand him and his mother. She watched him as he sat. He was turned away from his food, looking in the fire. Her soul watched him, trying to see what he was. His black face and arms were uncouth, he was foreign. His face was masked black with coal-dust. She could not see him, she could not even know him. The brown eyebrows, the steady eyes, the coarse, small moustache above the closed mouth—these were the only familiar indications. What was he, as he sat there in his pit-dirt? She could not see him, and it hurt her.

She ran upstairs, presently coming down with the flannels and the bran-bag, to heat them, because the pain was on again.

He was half-way through his dinner. He put down the fork, suddenly nauseated.

"They will soothe the wrench," she said. He watched, useless and left out.

"Is she bad?" he asked.

"I think she is," she answered.

It was useless for him to stir or comment. Louisa was busy. She went upstairs. The poor old woman was in a white, cold sweat of pain. Louisa's face was sullen with suffering as she went about to relieve her. Then she sat and waited. The pain passed gradually, the old woman sank into a state of coma. Louisa still sat silent by the bed. She heard the sound of water downstairs. Then came the voice of the old mother, faint but unrelaxing:

"Alfred's washing himself—he'll want his back washing—"

Louisa listened anxiously, wondering what the sick woman wanted.

"He can't bear if his back isn't washed—" the old woman persisted, in a cruel attention to his needs. Louisa rose and wiped the sweat from the yellowish brow.

"I will go down," she said soothingly.

"If you would," murmured the sick woman.

Louisa waited a moment. Mrs. Durant closed her eyes, having discharged her duty. The young woman went downstairs. Herself, or the man, what did they matter? Only the suffering woman must be considered.

Alfred was kneeling on the hearthrug, stripped to the waist, washing himself in a large panchion of earthenware. He did so every evening, when he had eaten his dinner; his brothers had done so before him. But Miss Louisa was strange in the house.

He was mechanically rubbing the white lather on his head, with a repeated, unconscious movement, his hand every now and then passing over his neck. Louisa watched. She had to brace herself to this also. He bent his head into the water, washed it free of soap, and pressed the water out of his eyes.

"Your mother said you would want your back washing," she said.

Curious how it hurt her to take part in their fixed routine of life! Louisa felt the almost repulsive intimacy being forced upon her. It was all so common, so like herding. She lost her own distinctness.

He ducked his face round, looking up at her in what was a very comical way. She had to harden herself.

"How funny he looks with his face upside down," she thought. After all, there was a difference between her and the common people. The water in which his arms were plunged was quite black, the soap-froth was darkish. She could scarcely conceive him as human. Mechanically, under the influence of habit, he groped in the black water, fished out soap and flannel, and handed them backward to Louisa. Then he remained rigid and submissive, his two arms thrust straight in the panchion, supporting the weight of his shoulders. His skin was beautifully white and unblemished, of an opaque, solid whiteness. Gradually Louisa saw it: this also was what he was. It fascinated her. Her feeling of separateness passed away: she ceased to draw back from contact with him and his mother. There was this living centre. Her heart ran hot. She had reached some goal in this beautiful, clear, male body. She loved him in a white, impersonal heat. But the sun-burnt, reddish neck and ears: they were more personal, more curious. A tenderness rose in her, she loved even his queer ears. A person—an intimate being he was to her. She put down the towel and went upstairs again, troubled in her heart. She had only seen one human being in her life—and that was Mary. All the rest were strangers. Now her soul was going to open, she was going to see another. She felt strange and pregnant.

"He'll be more comfortable," murmured the sick woman abstractedly, as Louisa entered the room. The latter did not answer. Her own heart was heavy with its own responsibility. Mrs. Durant lay silent awhile, then she murmured plaintively:

"You mustn't mind, Miss Louisa."

"Why should I?" replied Louisa, deeply moved.

"It's what we're used to," said the old woman.

And Louisa felt herself excluded again from their life. She sat in pain, with the tears of disappointment distilling her heart. Was that all?

Alfred came upstairs. He was clean, and in his shirt-sleeves. He looked a workman now. Louisa felt that she and he were foreigners, moving in different lives. It dulled her again. Oh, if she could only find some fixed relations, something sure and abiding.

"How do you feel?" he said to his mother.

"It's a bit better," she replied wearily, impersonally. This strange putting herself aside, this abstracting herself and answering him only what she thought good for him to hear, made the relations between mother and son poignant and cramping to Miss Louisa. It made the man so ineffectual, so nothing. Louisa groped as if she had lost him. The mother was real and positive—he was not very actual. It puzzled and chilled the young woman.

"I'd better fetch Mrs. Harrison?" he said, waiting for his mother to decide.

"I suppose we shall have to have somebody," she replied.

Miss Louisa stood by, afraid to interfere in their business. They did not include her in their lives, they felt she had nothing to do with them, except as a help from outside. She was quite external to them. She felt hurt and powerless against this unconscious difference. But something patient and unyielding in her made her say:

"I will stay and do the nursing: you can't be left."

The other two were shy, and at a loss for an answer.

"We s'll manage to get somebody," said the old woman wearily. She did not care very much what happened, now.

"I will stay until to-morrow, in any case," said Louisa. "Then we can see."

"I'm sure you've no right to trouble yourself," moaned the old woman. But she must leave herself in any hands.

Miss Louisa felt glad that she was admitted, even in an official capacity. She wanted to share their lives. At home they would need her, now Mary had come. But they must manage without her.

"I must write a note to the vicarage," she said.

Alfred Durant looked at her inquiringly, for her service. He had always that intelligent readiness to serve, since he had been in the Navy. But there was a simple independence in his willingness, which she loved. She felt nevertheless it was hard to get at him. He was so deferential, quick to take the slightest suggestion of an order from her, implicitly, that she could not get at the man in him.

He looked at her very keenly. She noticed his eyes were golden brown, with a very small pupil, the kind of eyes that can see a long way off. He stood alert, at military attention. His face was still rather weather-reddened.

"Do you want pen and paper?" he asked, with deferential suggestion to a superior, which was more difficult for her than reserve.

"Yes, please," she said.

He turned and went downstairs. He seemed to her so self-contained, so utterly sure in his movement. How was she to approach him? For he would take not one step towards her. He would only put himself entirely and impersonally at her service, glad to serve her, but keeping himself quite removed from her. She could see he felt real joy in doing anything for her, but any recognition would confuse him and hurt him. Strange it was to her, to have a man going about the house in his shirt-sleeves, his waistcoat unbuttoned, his throat bare, waiting on her. He moved well, as if he had plenty of life to spare. She was attracted by his completeness. And yet, when all was ready, and there was nothing more for him to do, she quivered, meeting his questioning look.

As she sat writing, he placed another candle near her. The rather dense light fell in two places on the overfoldings of her hair till it glistened heavy and bright, like a dense golden plumage folded up. Then the nape of her neck was very white, with fine down and pointed wisps of gold. He watched it as it were a vision, losing himself. She was all that was beyond him, of revelation and exquisiteness. All that was ideal and beyond him, she was that—and he was lost to himself in looking at her. She had no connection with him. He did not approach her. She was there like a wonderful distance. But it was a treat, having her in the house. Even with this anguish for his mother tightening about him, he was sensible of the wonder of living this evening. The candles glistened on her hair, and seemed to fascinate him. He felt a little awe of her, and a sense of uplifting, that he and she and his mother should be together for a time, in the strange, unknown atmosphere. And, when he got out of the house, he was afraid. He saw the stars above ringing with fine brightness, the snow beneath just visible, and a new night was gathering round him. He was afraid almost with obliteration. What was this new night ringing about him, and what was he? He could not recognize himself nor any of his surroundings. He was afraid to think of his mother. And yet his chest was conscious of her, and of what was happening to her. He could not escape from her, she carried him with her into an unformed, unknown chaos.

XI

He went up the road in an agony, not knowing what it was all about, but feeling as if a red-hot iron were gripped round his chest. Without thinking, he shook two or three tears on to the snow. Yet in his mind he did not believe his mother would die. He was in the grip of some greater consciousness. As he sat in the hall of the vicarage, waiting whilst Mary put things for Louisa into a bag, he wondered why he had been so upset. He felt abashed and humbled by the big house, he felt again as if he were one of the rank and file. When Miss Mary spoke to him, he almost saluted.

"An honest man," thought Mary. And the patronage was applied as salve to her own sickness. She had station, so she could patronize: it was almost all that was left to her. But she could not have lived without having a certain position. She could never have trusted herself outside a definite place, nor respected herself except as a woman of superior class.

As Alfred came to the latch-gate, he felt the grief at his heart again, and saw the new heavens. He stood a moment looking northward to the Plough climbing up the night, and at the far glimmer of snow in distant fields. Then his grief came on like physical pain. He held tight to the gate, biting his mouth, whispering "Mother!" It was a fierce, cutting, physical pain of grief, that came on in bouts, as his mother's pain came on in bouts, and was so acute he could scarcely keep erect. He did not know where it came from, the pain, nor why. It had nothing to do with his thoughts. Almost it had nothing to do with him. Only it gripped him and he must submit. The whole tide of his soul, gathering in its unknown towards this expansion into death, carried him with it helplessly, all the fritter of his thought and consciousness caught up as nothing, the heave passing on towards its breaking, taking him further than he had ever been. When the young man had regained himself, he went indoors, and there he was almost gay. It seemed to excite him. He felt in high spirits: he made whimsical fun of things. He sat on one side of his mother's bed, Louisa on the other, and a certain gaiety seized them all. But the night and the dread was coming on.

Alfred kissed his mother and went to bed. When he was half undressed the knowledge of his mother came upon him, and the suffering seized him in its grip like two hands, in agony. He lay on the bed screwed up tight. It lasted so long, and exhausted him so much, that he fell asleep, without having the energy to get up and finish undressing. He awoke after midnight to find himself stone cold. He undressed and got into bed, and was soon asleep again.

At a quarter to six he woke, and instantly remembered. Having pulled on his trousers and lighted a candle, he went into his mother's room. He put his hand before the candle flame so that no light fell on the bed.

"Mother!" he whispered.

"Yes," was the reply.

There was a hesitation.

"Should I go to work?"

He waited, his heart was beating heavily.

"I think I'd go, my lad."

His heart went down in a kind of despair.

"You want me to?"

He let his hand down from the candle flame. The light fell on the bed. There he saw Louisa lying looking up at him. Her eyes were upon him. She quickly shut her eyes and half buried her face in the pillow, her back turned to him. He saw the rough hair like bright vapour about her round head, and the two plaits flung coiled among the bedclothes. It gave him a shock. He stood almost himself, determined. Louisa cowered down. He looked, and met his mother's eyes. Then he gave way again, and ceased to be sure, ceased to be himself.

"Yes, go to work, my boy," said the mother.

"All right," replied he, kissing her. His heart was down at despair, and bitter. He went away.

"Alfred!" cried his mother faintly.

He came back with beating heart.

"What, mother?"

"You'll always do what's right, Alfred?" the mother asked, beside herself in terror now he was leaving her. He was too terrified and bewildered to know what she meant.

"Yes," he said.

She turned her cheek to him. He kissed her, then went away, in bitter despair. He went to work.

XII

By midday his mother was dead. The word met him at the pit-mouth. As he had known, inwardly, it was not a shock to him, and yet he trembled. He went home quite calmly, feeling only heavy in his breathing.

Miss Louisa was still at the house. She had seen to everything possible. Very succinctly, she informed him of what he needed to know. But there was one point of anxiety for her.

"You *did* half expect it—it's not come as a blow to you?" she asked, looking up at him. Her eyes were dark and calm and searching. She too felt lost. He was so dark and inchoate.

"I suppose—yes," he said stupidly. He looked aside, unable to endure her eyes on him.

"I could not bear to think you might not have guessed," she said.

He did not answer.

He felt it a great strain to have her near him at this time. He wanted to be alone. As soon as the relatives began to arrive, Louisa departed and came no more. While everything was arranging, and a crowd was in the house, whilst he had business to settle, he went well enough, with only those uncontrollable paroxysms of grief. For the rest, he was superficial. By himself, he endured the fierce, almost insane bursts of grief which passed again and left him calm, almost clear, just wondering. He had not known before that everything could break down, that he himself could break down, and all be a great chaos, very vast and wonderful. It seemed as if life in him had burst its bounds, and he was lost in a great, bewildering flood, immense and unpeopled. He himself was broken and spilled out amid it all. He could only breathe panting in silence. Then the anguish came on again.

When all the people had gone from the Quarry Cottage, leaving the young man alone with an elderly housekeeper, then the long trial began. The snow had thawed and frozen, a fresh fall had whitened the grey, this then began to thaw. The world was a place of loose grey slosh. Alfred had nothing to do in the evenings. He was a man whose life had been filled up with small activities. Without knowing it, he had been centralized, polarized in his mother. It was she who had kept him. Even now, when the old housekeeper had left him, he might still have gone on in his old way. But the force and balance of his life was lacking. He sat pretending to read, all the time holding his fists clenched, and holding himself in, enduring he did not know what. He walked the black and sodden miles of field-paths, till he was tired out: but all this was only running away from whence he must return. At work he was all right. If it had been summer he might have escaped by working in the garden till bedtime. But now, there was no escape, no relief, no help. He, perhaps, was made for action rather than for understanding; for doing than for being. He was shocked out of his activities, like a swimmer who forgets to swim.

For a week, he had the force to endure this suffocation and struggle, then he began to get exhausted, and knew it must come out. The instinct of self-preservation became strongest. But there was the question: Where was he to go? The public-house really meant nothing to him, it was no good going there. He began to think of emigration. In another country he would be all right. He wrote to the emigration offices.

On the Sunday after the funeral, when all the Durant people had attended church, Alfred had seen Miss Louisa, impassive and reserved, sitting with Miss Mary, who was proud and very distant, and with the other Lindleys, who were people removed. Alfred saw them as people remote. He did not think about it. They had nothing to do with his life. After service Louisa had come to him and shaken hands.

"My sister would like you to come to supper one evening, if you would be so good."

He looked at Miss Mary, who bowed. Out of kindness, Mary had proposed this to Louisa, disapproving of herself even as she did so. But she did not examine herself closely.

"Yes," said Durant awkwardly, "I'll come if you want me." But he vaguely felt that it was misplaced.

"You'll come to-morrow evening, then, about half-past six."

He went. Miss Louisa was very kind to him. There could be no music, because of the babies. He sat with his fists clenched on his thighs, very quiet and unmoved, lapsing, among all those people, into a kind of muse or daze. There was nothing between him and them. They knew it as well as he. But he remained very steady in himself, and the evening passed slowly. Mrs. Lindley called him "young man".

"Will you sit here, young man?"

He sat there. One name was as good as another. What had they to do with him?

Mr. Lindley kept a special tone for him, kind, indulgent, but patronizing. Durant took it all without criticism or offence, just submitting. But he did not want to eat—that troubled him, to have to eat in their presence. He knew he was out of place. But it was his duty to stay yet awhile. He answered precisely, in monosyllables.

When he left he winced with confusion. He was glad it was finished. He got away as quickly as possible. And he wanted still more intensely to go right away, to Canada.

Miss Louisa suffered in her soul, indignant with all of them, with him too, but quite unable to say why she was indignant.

XIII

Two evenings after, Louisa tapped at the door of the Quarry Cottage, at half-past six. He had finished dinner, the woman had washed up and gone away, but still he sat in his pit dirt. He was going later to the New Inn. He had begun to go there because he must go somewhere. The mere contact with other men was necessary to him, the noise, the warmth, the forgetful flight of the hours. But still he did not move. He sat alone in the empty house till it began to grow on him like something unnatural.

He was in his pit dirt when he opened the door.

"I have been wanting to call—I thought I would," she said, and she went to the sofa. He wondered why she wouldn't use his mother's round armchair. Yet something stirred in him, like anger, when the housekeeper placed herself in it.

"I ought to have been washed by now," he said, glancing at the clock, which was adorned with butterflies and cherries, and the name of "T. Brooks, Mansfield." He laid his black hands along his mottled dirty arms. Louisa looked at him. There was the reserve, and the simple neutrality towards her, which she dreaded in him. It made it impossible for her to approach him.

"I am afraid," she said, "that I wasn't kind in asking you to supper."

"I'm not used to it," he said, smiling with his mouth, showing the interspaced white teeth. His eyes, however, were steady and unseeing.

"It's not *that*," she said hastily. Her repose was exquisite and her dark grey eyes rich with understanding. He felt afraid of her as she sat there, as he began to grow conscious of her.

"How do you get on alone?" she asked.

He glanced away to the fire.

"Oh—" he answered, shifting uneasily, not finishing his answer.

Her face settled heavily.

"How close it is in this room. You have such immense fires. I will take off my coat," she said.

He watched her take off her hat and coat. She wore a cream cashmir blouse embroidered with gold silk. It seemed to him a very fine garment, fitting her throat and wrists close. It gave him a feeling of pleasure and cleanness and relief from himself.

"What were you thinking about, that you didn't get washed?" she asked, half intimately. He laughed, turning aside his head. The whites of his eyes showed very distinct in his black face.

"Oh," he said, "I couldn't tell you."

There was a pause.

"Are you going to keep this house on?" she asked.

He stirred in his chair, under the question.

"I hardly know," he said. "I'm very likely going to Canada."

Her spirit became very quiet and attentive.

"What for?" she asked.

Again he shifted restlessly on his seat.

"Well"—he said slowly—"to try the life."

"But which life?"

"There's various things—farming or lumbering or mining. I don't mind much what it is."

"And is that what you want?"

He did not think in these times, so he could not answer.

"I don't know," he said, "till I've tried."

She saw him drawing away from her for ever.

"Aren't you sorry to leave this house and garden?" she asked.

"I don't know," he answered reluctantly. "I suppose our Fred would come in—that's what he's wanting."

"You don't want to settle down?" she asked.

He was leaning forward on the arms of his chair. He turned to her. Her face was pale and set. It looked heavy and impassive, her hair shone richer as she grew white. She was to him something steady and immovable and eternal presented to him. His heart was hot in an anguish of suspense. Sharp twitches of fear and pain were in his limbs. He turned his whole body away from her. The silence was unendurable. He could not bear her to sit there any more. It made his heart go hot and stifled in his breast.

"Were you going out to-night?" she asked.

"Only to the New Inn," he said.

Again there was silence.

She reached for her hat. Nothing else was suggested to her. She *had* to go. He sat waiting for her to be gone, for relief. And she knew that if she went out of that house as she was, she went out a failure. Yet she continued to pin on her hat; in a moment she would have to go. Something was carrying her.

Then suddenly a sharp pang, like lightning, seared her from head to foot, and she was beyond herself.

"Do you want me to go?" she asked, controlled, yet speaking out of a fiery anguish, as if the words were spoken from her without her intervention.

He went white under his dirt.

"Why?" he asked, turning to her in fear, compelled.

"Do you want me to go?" she repeated.

"Why?" he asked again.

"Because I wanted to stay with you," she said, suffocated, with her lungs full of fire.

His face worked, he hung forward a little, suspended, staring straight into her eyes, in torment, in an agony of chaos, unable to collect himself. And as if turned to stone, she looked back into his eyes. Their souls were exposed bare for a few moments. It was agony. They could not bear it. He dropped his head, whilst his body jerked with little sharp twitchings.

She turned away for her coat. Her soul had gone dead in her. Her hands trembled, but she could not feel any more. She drew on her coat. There was a cruel suspense in the room. The moment had come for her to go. He lifted his head. His eyes were like agate, expressionless, save for the black points of torture. They held her, she had no will, no life any more. She felt broken.

"Don't you want me?" she said helplessly.

A spasm of torture crossed his eyes, which held her fixed.

"I—I—" he began, but he could not speak. Something drew him from his chair to her. She stood motionless, spellbound, like a creature given up as prey. He put his hand tentatively, uncertainly, on her arm. The expression of his face was strange and inhuman. She stood utterly motionless. Then clumsily he put his arms round her, and took her, cruelly, blindly, straining her till she nearly lost consciousness, till he himself had almost fallen.

Then, gradually, as he held her gripped, and his brain reeled round, and he felt himself falling, falling from himself, and whilst she, yielded up, swooned to a kind of death of herself, a moment of utter darkness came over him, and they began to wake up again as if from a long sleep. He was himself.

After a while his arms slackened, she loosened herself a little, and put her arms round him, as he held her. So they held each other close, and hid each against the other for assurance, helpless in speech. And it was ever her hands that trembled more closely upon him, drawing him nearer into her, with love.

And at last she drew back her face and looked up at him, her eyes wet, and shining with light. His heart, which saw, was silent with fear. He was with her. She saw his face all sombre and inscrutable, and he seemed eternal to her. And all the echo of pain came back into the rarity of bliss, and all her tears came up.

"I love you," she said, her lips drawn and sobbing. He put down his head against her, unable to hear her, unable to bear the sudden coming of the peace and passion that almost broke his heart. They stood together in silence whilst the thing moved away a little.

At last she wanted to see him. She looked up. His eyes were strange and glowing, with a tiny black pupil. Strange, they were, and powerful over her. And his mouth came to hers, and slowly her eyelids closed, as his mouth sought hers closer and closer, and took possession of her.

They were silent for a long time, too much mixed up with passion and grief and death to do anything but hold each other in pain and kiss with long, hurting kisses wherein fear was transfused into desire. At last she disengaged herself. He felt as if his heart were hurt, but glad, and he scarcely dared look at her.

"I'm glad," she said also.

He held her hands in passionate gratitude and desire. He had not yet the presence of mind to say anything. He was dazed with relief.

"I ought to go," she said.

He looked at her. He could not grasp the thought of her going, he knew he could never be separated from her any more. Yet he dared not assert himself. He held her hands tight.

"Your face is black," she said.

He laughed.

"Yours is a bit smudged," he said.

They were afraid of each other, afraid to talk. He could only keep her near to him. After a while she wanted to wash her face. He brought her some warm water, standing by and watching her. There was something he wanted to say, that he dared not. He watched her wiping her face, and making tidy her hair.

"They'll see your blouse is dirty," he said.

She looked at her sleeves and laughed for joy.

He was sharp with pride.

"What shall you do?" he asked.

"How?" she said.

He was awkward at a reply.

"About me," he said.

"What do you want me to do?" she laughed.

He put his hand out slowly to her. What did it matter!

"But make yourself clean," she said.

XIV

As they went up the hill, the night seemed dense with the unknown. They kept close together, feeling as if the darkness were alive and full of knowledge, all around them. In silence they walked up the hill. At first the street lamps went their way. Several people passed them. He was more shy than she, and would have let her go had she loosened in the least. But she held firm.

Then they came into the true darkness, between the fields. They did not want to speak, feeling closer together in silence. So they arrived at the Vicarage gate. They stood under the naked horse-chestnut tree.

"I wish you didn't have to go," he said.

She laughed a quick little laugh.

"Come to-morrow," she said, in a low tone, "and ask father."

She felt his hand close on hers.

She gave the same sorrowful little laugh of sympathy. Then she kissed him, sending him home.

At home, the old grief came on in another paroxysm, obliterating Louisa, obliterating even his mother for whom the stress was raging like a burst of fever in a wound. But something was sound in his heart.

XV

The next evening he dressed to go to the vicarage, feeling it was to be done, not imagining what it would be like. He would not take this seriously. He was sure of Louisa, and this marriage was like fate to him. It filled him also with a blessed feeling of fatality. He was not responsible, neither had her people anything really to do with it.

They ushered him into the little study, which was fireless. By and by the vicar came in. His voice was cold and hostile as he said:

"What can I do for you, young man?"

He knew already, without asking.

Durant looked up at him, again like a sailor before a superior. He had the subordinate manner. Yet his spirit was clear.

"I wanted, Mr. Lindley—" he began respectfully, then all the colour suddenly left his face. It seemed now a violation to say what he had to say. What was he doing there? But he stood on, because it had to be done. He held firmly to his own independence and self-respect. He must not be indecisive. He must put himself aside: the matter was bigger than just his personal self. He must not feel. This was his highest duty.

"You wanted—" said the vicar.

Durant's mouth was dry, but he answered with steadiness:

"Miss Louisa—Louisa—promised to marry me—"

"You asked Miss Louisa if she would marry you—yes—" corrected the vicar. Durant reflected he had not asked her this:

"If she would marry me, sir. I hope you—don't mind."

He smiled. He was a good-looking man, and the vicar could not help seeing it.

"And my daughter was willing to marry you?" said Mr. Lindley.

"Yes," said Durant seriously. It was pain to him, nevertheless. He felt the natural hostility between himself and the elder man.

"Will you come this way?" said the vicar. He led into the dining-room, where were Mary, Louisa, and Mrs. Lindley. Mr. Massy sat in a corner with a lamp.

"This young man has come on your account, Louisa?" said Mr. Lindley.

"Yes," said Louisa, her eyes on Durant, who stood erect, in discipline. He dared not look at her, but he was aware of her.

"You don't want to marry a collier, you little fool," cried Mrs. Lindley harshly. She lay obese and helpless upon the couch, swathed in a loose, dove-grey gown.

"Oh, hush, mother," cried Mary, with quiet intensity and pride.

"What means have you to support a wife?" demanded the vicar's wife roughly.

"I!" Durant replied, starting. "I think I can earn enough."

"Well, and how much?" came the rough voice.

"Seven and six a day," replied the young man.

"And will it get to be any more?"

"I hope so."

"And are you going to live in that poky little house?"

"I think so," said Durant, "if it's all right."

He took small offence, only was upset, because they would not think him good enough. He knew that, in their sense, he was not.

"Then she's a fool, I tell you, if she marries you," cried the mother roughly, casting her decision.

"After all, mama, it is Louisa's affair," said Mary distinctly, "and we must remember—"

"As she makes her bed, she must lie—but she'll repent it," interrupted Mrs. Lindley.

"And after all," said Mr. Lindley, "Louisa cannot quite hold herself free to act entirely without consideration for her family."

"What do you want, papa?" asked Louisa sharply.

"I mean that if you marry this man, it will make my position very difficult for me, particularly if you stay in this parish. If you were moving quite away, it would be simpler. But living here in a collier's cottage, under my nose, as it were—it would be almost unseemly. I have my position to maintain, and a position which may not be taken lightly."

"Come over here, young man," cried the mother, in her rough voice, "and let us look at you."

Durant, flushing, went over and stood—not quite at attention, so that he did not know what to do with his hands. Miss Louisa was angry to see him standing there, obedient and acquiescent. He ought to show himself a man.

"Can't you take her away and live out of sight?" said the mother. "You'd both of you be better off."

"Yes, we can go away," he said.

"Do you want to?" asked Miss Mary clearly.

He faced round. Mary looked very stately and impressive. He flushed.

"I do if it's going to be a trouble to anybody," he said.

"For yourself, you would rather stay?" said Mary.

"It's my home," he said, "and that's the house I was born in."

"Then"—Mary turned clearly to her parents, "I really don't see how you can make the conditions, papa. He has his own rights, and if Louisa wants to marry him—"

"Louisa, Louisa!" cried the father impatiently. "I cannot understand why Louisa should not behave in the normal way. I cannot see why she should only think of herself, and leave her family out of count. The thing is enough in itself, and she ought to try to ameliorate it as much as possible. And if—"

"But I love the man, papa," said Louisa.

"And I hope you love your parents, and I hope you want to spare them as much of the—the loss of prestige, as possible."

"We *can* go away to live," said Louisa, her face breaking to tears. At last she was really hurt.

"Oh, yes, easily," Durant replied hastily, pale, distressed.

There was dead silence in the room.

"I think it would really be better," murmured the vicar, mollified.

"Very likely it would," said the rough-voiced invalid.

"Though I think we ought to apologize for asking such a thing," said Mary haughtily.

"No," said Durant. "It will be best all round." He was glad there was no more bother.

"And shall we put up the banns here or go to the registrar?" he asked clearly, like a challenge.

"We will go to the registrar," replied Louisa decidedly.

Again there was a dead silence in the room.

"Well, if you will have your own way, you must go your own way," said the mother emphatically.

All the time Mr. Massy had sat obscure and unnoticed in a corner of the room. At this juncture he got up, saying:

"There is baby, Mary."

Mary rose and went out of the room, stately; her little husband padded after her. Durant watched the fragile, small man go, wondering.

"And where," asked the vicar, almost genial, "do you think you will go when you are married?"

Durant started.

"I was thinking of emigrating," he said.

"To Canada? or where?"

"I think to Canada."

"Yes, that would be very good."

Again there was a pause.

"We shan't see much of you then, as a son-in-law," said the mother, roughly but amicably.

"Not much," he said.

Then he took his leave. Louisa went with him to the gate. She stood before him in distress.

"You won't mind them, will you?" she said humbly.

"I don't mind them, if they don't mind me!" he said. Then he stooped and kissed her.

"Let us be married soon," she murmured, in tears.

"All right," he said. "I'll go to-morrow to Barford."

A FRAGMENT OF STAINED GLASS

Beauvale is, or was, the largest parish in England. It is thinly populated, only just netting the stragglers from shoals of houses in three large mining villages. For the rest, it holds a great tract of woodland, fragment of old Sherwood, a few hills of pasture and arable land, three collieries, and, finally, the ruins of a Cistercian abbey. These ruins lie in a still rich meadow at the foot of the last fall of woodland, through whose oaks shines a blue of hyacinths, like water, in May-time. Of the abbey, there remains only the east wall of the chancel standing, a wild thick mass of ivy weighting one shoulder, while pigeons perch in the tracery of the lofty window. This is the window in question.

The vicar of Beauvale is a bachelor of forty-two years. Quite early in life some illness caused a slight paralysis of his right side, so that he drags a little, and so that the right corner of his mouth is twisted up into his cheek with a constant grimace, unhidden by a heavy moustache. There is something pathetic about this twist on the vicar's countenance: his eyes are so shrewd and sad. It would be hard to get near to Mr. Colbran. Indeed, now, his soul had some of the twist of his face, so that, when he is not ironical, he is satiric. Yet a man of more complete tolerance and generosity scarcely exists. Let the boors mock him, he merely smiles on the other side, and there is no malice in his eyes, only a quiet expression of waiting till they have finished. His people do not like him, yet none could bring forth an accusation against him, save, that "You never can tell when he's having you."

I dined the other evening with the vicar in his study. The room scandalizes the neighbourhood because of the statuary which adorns it: a Laocoon and other classic copies, with bronze and silver Italian Renaissance work. For the rest, it is all dark and tawny.

Mr. Colbran is an archaeologist. He does not take himself seriously, however, in his hobby, so that nobody knows the worth of his opinions on the subject.

"Here you are," he said to me after dinner, "I've found another paragraph for my great work."

"What's that?" I asked.

"Haven't I told you I was compiling a Bible of the English people—the Bible of their hearts—their exclamations in presence of the unknown? I've found a fragment at home, a jump at God from Beauvale."

"Where?" I asked, startled.

The vicar closed his eyes whilst looking at me.

"Only on parchment," he said.

Then, slowly, he reached for a yellow book, and read, translating as he went:

"Then, while we chanted, came a crackling at the window, at the great east window, where hung our Lord on the Cross. It was a malicious covetous Devil wrathed by us, rended the lovely image of the glass. We saw the iron clutches of the fiend pick the window, and a face flaming red like fire in a basket did glower down on us. Our hearts melted away, our legs broke, we thought to die. The breath of the wretch filled the chapel.

"But our dear Saint, etc., etc., came hastening down heaven to defend us. The fiend began to groan and bray—he was daunted and beat off.

"When the sun uprose, and it was morning, some went out in dread upon the thin snow. There the figure of our Saint was broken and thrown down, whilst in the window was a wicked hole as from the Holy Wounds the Blessed Blood was run out at the touch of the Fiend, and on the snow was the Blood, sparkling like gold. Some gathered it up for the joy of this House. . . ."

"Interesting," I said. "Where's it from?"

"Beauvale records—fifteenth century."

"Beauvale Abbey," I said; "they were only very few, the monks. What frightened them, I wonder."

"I wonder," he repeated.

"Somebody climbed up," I supposed, "and attempted to get in."

"What?" he exclaimed, smiling.

"Well, what do you think?"

"Pretty much the same," he replied. "I glossed it out for my book."

"Your great work? Tell me."

He put a shade over the lamp so that the room was almost in darkness.

"Am I more than a voice?" he asked.

"I can see your hand," I replied. He moved entirely from the circle of light. Then his voice began, sing-song, sardonic:

"I was a serf in Rollestoun's Newthorpe Manor, master of the stables I was. One day a horse bit me as I was grooming him. He was an old enemy of mine. I fetched him a blow across the nose. Then, when he got a chance, he lashed out at me and caught me a gash over the mouth. I snatched at a hatchet and cut his head. He yelled, fiend as he was, and strained for me with all his teeth bare. I brought him down.

"For killing him they flogged me till they thought I was dead. I was sturdy, because we horse-serfs got plenty to eat. I was sturdy, but they flogged me till I did not move. The next night I set fire to the stables, and the stables set fire to the house. I watched and saw the red flame rise and look out of the window, I saw the folk running, each for himself, master no more than one of a frightened party. It was freezing, but the heat made me sweat. I saw them all turn again to watch, all rimmed with red. They cried, all of them when the roof went in, when the sparks splashed up at rebound. They cried then like dogs at the bagpipes howling. Master cursed me, till I laughed as I lay under a bush quite near.

"As the fire went down I got frightened. I ran for the woods, with fire blazing in my eyes and crackling in my ears. For hours I was all fire. Then I went to sleep under the bracken. When I woke it was evening. I had no mantle, was frozen stiff. I was afraid to move, lest all the sores of my back should be broken like thin ice. I lay still until I could bear my hunger no longer. I moved then to get used to the pain of movement, when I began to hunt for food. There was nothing to be found but hips.

"After wandering about till I was faint I dropped again in the bracken. The boughs above me creaked with frost. I started and looked round. The branches were like hair among the starlight. My heart stood still. Again there was a creak, creak, and suddenly a whoop, that whistled in fading. I fell down in the bracken like dead wood. Yet, by the peculiar whistling sound at the end, I knew it was only the ice bending or tightening in the frost. I was in the woods above the lake, only two miles from the Manor. And yet, when the lake whooped hollowly again, I clutched the frozen soil, every one of my muscles as stiff as the stiff earth. So all the night long I dare not move my face, but pressed it flat down, and taut I lay as if pegged down and braced.

"When morning came still I did not move, I lay still in a dream. By afternoon my ache was such it enlivened me. I cried, rocking my breath in the ache of moving. Then again I became fierce. I beat my hands on the rough bark to hurt them, so that I should not ache so much. In such a rage I was I swung my limbs to torture till I fell sick with pain. Yet I fought the hurt, fought it and fought by twisting and flinging myself, until it was overcome. Then the evening began to draw on. All day the sun had not loosened the frost. I felt the sky chill again towards afternoon. Then I knew the night was coming, and, remembering the great space I had just come through, horrible so that it seemed to have made me another man, I fled across the wood.

"But in my running I came upon the oak where hanged five bodies. There they must hang, bar-stiff, night after night. It was a terror worse than any. Turning, blundering through the forest, I came out where the trees thinned, where only hawthorns, ragged and shaggy, went down to the lake's edge.

"The sky across was red, the ice on the water glistened as if it were warm. A few wild geese sat out like stones on the sheet of ice. I thought of Martha. She was the daughter of the miller at the upper end of the lake. Her hair was red like beech leaves in a wind. When I had gone often to the mill with the horses she had brought me food.

"'I thought,' said I to her, "twas a squirrel sat on your shoulder. 'Tis your hair fallen loose.'

"'They call me the fox,' she said.

"'Would I were your dog,' said I. She would bring me bacon and good bread, when I called at the mill with the horses. The thought of cakes of bread and of bacon made me reel as if drunk. I had torn at the rabbit holes, I had chewed wood all day. In such a dimness was my head that I felt neither the soreness of my wounds nor the cuts of thorns on my knees, but stumbled towards the mill, almost past fear of man and death, panting with fear of the darkness that crept behind me from trunk to trunk.

"Coming to the gap in the wood, below which lay the pond, I heard no sound. Always I knew the place filled with the buzz of water, but now it was silent. In fear of this stillness I ran forward, forgetting myself, forgetting the frost. The wood seemed to pursue me. I fell, just in time, down by a shed wherein were housed the few wintry pigs. The miller came riding in on his horse, and the barking of dogs was for him. I heard him curse the day, curse his servant, curse me, whom he had been out to hunt, in his rage of wasted labour, curse all. As I lay I heard inside the shed a sucking. Then I knew that the sow was there, and that the most of her sucking pigs would be already killed for tomorrow's Christmas. The miller, from forethought to have young at that time, made profit by his sucking pigs that were sold for the mid-winter feast.

"When in a moment all was silent in the dusk, I broke the bar and came into the shed. The sow grunted, but did not come forth to discover me. By and by I crept in towards her warmth. She had but three young left, which now angered her, she being too full of milk. Every now and again she slashed at them and they squealed. Busy as she was with them, I in the darkness advanced towards her. I trembled so that scarce dared I trust myself near her, for long dared not put my naked face towards her. Shuddering with hunger and fear, I at last fed of her, guarding my face with my arm. Her own full young tumbled squealing against me, but she, feeling her ease, lay grunting. At last I, too, lay drunk, swooning.

"I was roused by the shouting of the miller. He, angered by his daughter who wept, abused her, driving her from the house to feed the swine. She came, bowing under a yoke, to the door of the shed. Finding the pin broken she stood afraid, then, as the sow grunted, she came cautiously in. I took her with my arm, my hand over her mouth. As she struggled against my breast my heart began to beat loudly. At last she knew it was I. I clasped her. She hung in my arms, turning away her face, so that I kissed her throat. The tears blinded my eyes, I know not why, unless it were the hurt of my mouth, wounded by the horse, was keen.

"'They will kill you,' she whispered.

"'No,' I answered.

"And she wept softly. She took my head in her arms and kissed me, wetting me with her tears, brushing me with her keen hair, warming me through.

"'I will not go away from here,' I said. 'Bring me a knife, and I will defend myself.'

"'No,' she wept. 'Ah, no!'

"When she went I lay down, pressing my chest where she had rested on the earth, lest being alone were worse emptiness than hunger.

"Later she came again. I saw her bend in the doorway, a lanthorn hanging in front. As she peered under the redness of her falling hair, I was afraid of her. But she came with food. We sat together in the dull light. Sometimes still I shivered and my throat would not swallow.

"'If,' said I, 'I eat all this you have brought me, I shall sleep till somebody finds me.'

"Then she took away the rest of the meat.

"'Why,' said I, 'should I not eat?' She looked at me in tears of fear.

"'What?' I said, but still she had no answer. I kissed her, and the hurt of my wounded mouth angered me.

"'Now there is my blood,' said I, 'on your mouth.' Wiping her smooth hand over her lips, she looked thereat, then at me.

"'Leave me,' I said, 'I am tired.' She rose to leave me.

"'But bring a knife,' I said. Then she held the lanthorn near my face, looking as at a picture.

"'You look to me,' she said, 'like a stirk that is roped for the axe. Your eyes are dark, but they are wide open.'

"'Then I will sleep,' said I, 'but will not wake too late.'

"'Do not stay here,' she said.

"'I will not sleep in the wood,' I answered, and it was my heart that spoke, 'for I am afraid. I had better be afraid of the voice of man and dogs, than the sounds in the woods. Bring me a knife, and in the morning I will go. Alone will I not go now.'

"'The searchers will take you,' she said.

"'Bring me a knife,' I answered.

"'Ah, go,' she wept.

"'Not now—I will not—'

"With that she lifted the lanthorn, lit up her own face and mine. Her blue eyes dried of tears. Then I took her to myself, knowing she was mine.

"'I will come again,' she said.

"She went, and I folded my arms, lay down and slept.

"When I woke, she was rocking me wildly to rouse me.

"'I dreamed,' said I, 'that a great heap, as if it were a hill, lay on me and above me.'

"She put a cloak over me, gave me a hunting-knife and a wallet of food, and other things I did not note. Then under her own cloak she hid the lanthorn.

"'Let us go,' she said, and blindly I followed her.

"When I came out into the cold someone touched my face and my hair.

"'Ha!' I cried, 'who now—?' Then she swiftly clung to me, hushed me.

"'Someone has touched me,' I said aloud, still dazed with sleep.

"'Oh hush!' she wept. ''Tis snowing.' The dogs within the house began to bark. She fled forward, I after her. Coming to the ford of the stream she ran swiftly over, but I broke through the ice. Then I knew where I was. Snowflakes, fine and rapid, were biting at my face. In the wood there was no wind nor snow.

"'Listen,' said I to her, 'listen, for I am locked up with sleep.'

"'I hear roaring overhead,' she answered. 'I hear in the trees like great bats squeaking.'

"'Give me your hand,' said I.

"We heard many noises as we passed. Once as there uprose a whiteness before us, she cried aloud.

"'Nay,' said I, 'do not untie thy hand from mine,' and soon we were crossing fallen snow. But ever and again she started back from fear.

"'When you draw back my arm,' I said, angry, 'you loosed a weal on my shoulder.'

"Thereafter she ran by my side, like a fawn beside its mother.

"'We will cross the valley and gain the stream,' I said. 'That will lead us on its ice as on a path deep into the forest. There we can join the outlaws. The wolves are driven from this part. They have followed the driven deer.'

"We came directly on a large gleam that shaped itself up among flying grains of snow.

"'Ah!' she cried, and she stood amazed.

"Then I thought we had gone through the bounds into faery realm, and I was no more a man. How did I know what eyes were gleaming at me between the snow, what cunning spirits in the draughts of air? So I waited for what would happen, and I forgot her, that she was there. Only I could feel the spirits whirling and blowing about me.

"Whereupon she clung upon me, kissing me lavishly, and, were dogs or men or demons come upon us at that moment, she had let us be stricken down, nor heeded not. So we moved forward to the shadow that shone in colours upon the passing snow. We found ourselves under a door of light which shed its colours mixed with snow. This Martha had never seen, nor I, this door open for a red and brave issuing like fires. We wondered.

"'It is faery,' she said, and after a while, 'Could one catch such—Ah, no!'

"Through the snow shone bunches of red and blue.

"'Could one have such a little light like a red flower—only a little, like a rose-berry scarlet on one's breast!—then one were singled out as Our Lady.'

"I flung off my cloak and my burden to climb up the face of the shadow. Standing on rims of stone, then in pockets of snow, I reached upward. My hand was red and blue, but I could not take the stuff. Like colour of a moth's wing it was on my hand, it flew on the increasing snow. I stood higher on the head of a frozen man, reached higher my hand. Then I felt the bright stuff cold. I could not pluck it off. Down below she cried to me to come again to her. I felt a rib that yielded, I struck at it with my knife. There came a gap in the redness. Looking through I saw below as it were white stunted angels, with sad faces lifted in fear. Two faces they had each, and round rings of hair. I was afraid. I grasped the shining red, I pulled. Then the cold man under me sank, so I fell as if broken on to the snow.

"Soon I was risen again, and we were running downwards towards the stream. We felt ourselves eased when the smooth road of ice was beneath us. For a while it was resting, to travel thus evenly. But the wind blew round us, the snow hung upon us, we leaned us this way and that, towards the storm. I drew her along, for she came as a bird that stems lifting and swaying against the wind. By and by the snow came smaller, there was not wind in the wood. Then I felt nor labour, nor cold. Only I knew the darkness drifted by on either side, that overhead was a lane of paleness where a moon fled us before. Still, I can feel the moon fleeing from me, can feel the trees passing round me in slow dizzy reel, can feel the hurt of my shoulder and my straight arm torn with holding her. I was following the moon and the stream, for I knew where the water peeped from its burrow in the ground there were shelters of the outlaw. But she fell, without sound or sign.

"I gathered her up and climbed the bank. There all round me hissed the larchwood, dry beneath, and laced with its dry-fretted cords. For a little way I carried her into the trees. Then I laid her down till I cut flat hairy boughs. I put her in my bosom on this dry bed, so we swooned together through the night. I laced her round and covered her with myself, so she lay like a nut within its shell.

"Again, when morning came, it was pain of cold that woke me. I groaned, but my heart was warm as I saw the heap of red hair in my arms. As I looked at her, her eyes opened into mine. She smiled—from out of her smile came fear. As if in a trap she pressed back her head.

"'We have no flint,' said I.

"'Yes—in the wallet, flint and steel and tinder box,' she answered.

"'God yield you blessing,' I said.

"In a place a little open I kindled a fire of larch boughs. She was afraid of me, hovering near, yet never crossing a space.

"'Come,' said I, 'let us eat this food.'

"'Your face,' she said, 'is smeared with blood.'

"I opened out my cloak.

"'But come,' said I, 'you are frosted with cold.'

"I took a handful of snow in my hand, wiping my face with it, which then I dried on my cloak.

"'My face is no longer painted with blood, you are no longer afraid of me. Come here then, sit by me while we eat.'

"But as I cut the cold bread for her, she clasped me suddenly, kissing me. She fell before me, clasped my knees to her breast, weeping. She laid her face down to my feet, so that her hair spread like a fire before me. I wondered at the woman. 'Nay,' I cried. At that she lifted her face to me from below. 'Nay,' I cried, feeling my tears fall. With her head on my breast, my own tears rose from their source, wetting my cheek and her hair, which was wet with the rain of my eyes.

"Then I remembered and took from my bosom the coloured light of that night before. I saw it was black and rough.

"'Ah,' said I, 'this is magic.'

"'The black stone!' she wondered.

"'It is the red light of the night before,' I said.

"'It is magic,' she answered.

"'Shall I throw it?' said I, lifting the stone, 'shall I throw it away, for fear?'

"'It shines!' she cried, looking up. 'It shines like the eye of a creature at night, the eye of a wolf in the doorway.'

"''Tis magic,' I said, 'let me throw it from us.' But nay, she held my arm.

"'It is red and shining,' she cried.

"'It is a bloodstone,' I answered. 'It will hurt us, we shall die in blood.'

"'But give it to me,' she answered.

"'It is red of blood,' I said.

"'Ah, give it to me,' she called.

"'It is my blood,' I said.

"'Give it,' she commanded, low.

"'It is my life-stone,' I said.

"'Give it me,' she pleaded.

"'I gave it her. She held it up, she smiled, she smiled in my face, lifting her arms to me. I took her with my mouth, her mouth, her white throat. Nor she ever shrank, but trembled with happiness.

"What woke us, when the woods were filling again with shadow, when the fire was out, when we opened our eyes and looked up as if drowned, into the light which stood bright and thick on the tree-tops, what woke us was the sound of wolves. . . ."

"Nay," said the vicar, suddenly rising, "they lived happily ever after."

"No," I said.

THE SHADES OF SPRING

I

It was a mile nearer through the wood. Mechanically, Syson turned up by the forge and lifted the field-gate. The blacksmith and his mate stood still, watching the trespasser. But Syson looked too much a gentleman to be accosted. They let him go in silence across the small field to the wood.

There was not the least difference between this morning and those of the bright springs, six or eight years back. White and sandy-gold fowls still scratched round the gate, littering the earth and the field with feathers and scratched-up rubbish. Between the two thick holly bushes in the wood-hedge was the hidden gap, whose fence one climbed to get into the wood; the bars were scored just the same by the keeper's boots. He was back in the eternal.

Syson was extraordinarily glad. Like an uneasy spirit he had returned to the country of his past, and he found it waiting for him, unaltered. The hazel still spread glad little hands downwards, the bluebells here were still wan and few, among the lush grass and in shade of the bushes.

The path through the wood, on the very brow of a slope, ran winding easily for a time. All around were twiggy oaks, just issuing their gold, and floor spaces diapered with woodruff, with patches of dog-mercury and tufts of hyacinth. Two fallen trees still lay across the track. Syson jolted down a steep, rough slope, and came again upon the open land, this time looking north as through a great window in the wood. He stayed to gaze over the level fields of the hill-top, at the village which strewed the bare upland as if it had tumbled off the passing waggons of industry, and been forsaken. There was a stiff, modern, grey little church, and blocks and rows of red dwellings lying at random; at the back, the twinkling headstocks of the pit, and the looming pit-hill. All was naked and out-of-doors, not a tree! It was quite unaltered.

Syson turned, satisfied, to follow the path that sheered downhill into the wood. He was curiously elated, feeling himself back in an enduring vision. He started. A keeper was standing a few yards in front, barring the way.

"Where might you be going this road, sir?" asked the man. The tone of his question had a challenging twang. Syson looked at the fellow with an impersonal, observant gaze. It was a young man of four or five and twenty, ruddy and well favoured. His dark blue eyes now stared aggressively at the intruder. His black moustache, very thick, was cropped short over a small, rather soft mouth. In every other respect the fellow was manly and good-looking. He stood just above middle height; the strong forward thrust of his chest, and the perfect ease of his erect, self-sufficient body, gave one the feeling that he was taut with animal life, like the thick jet of a fountain balanced in itself. He stood with the butt of his gun on the ground, looking uncertainly and questioningly at Syson. The dark, restless eyes of the trespasser, examining the man and penetrating into him without heeding his office, troubled the keeper and made him flush.

"Where is Naylor? Have you got his job?" Syson asked.

"You're not from the House, are you?" inquired the keeper. It could not be, since everyone was away.

"No, I'm not from the House," the other replied. It seemed to amuse him.

"Then might I ask where you were making for?" said the keeper, nettled.

"Where I am making for?" Syson repeated. "I am going to Willey-Water Farm."

"This isn't the road."

"I think so. Down this path, past the well, and out by the white gate."

"But that's not the public road."

"I suppose not. I used to come so often, in Naylor's time, I had forgotten. Where is he, by the way?"

"Crippled with rheumatism," the keeper answered reluctantly.

"Is he?" Syson exclaimed in pain.

"And who might you be?" asked the keeper, with a new intonation.

"John Adderley Syson; I used to live in Cordy Lane."

"Used to court Hilda Millership?"

Syson's eyes opened with a pained smile. He nodded. There was an awkward silence.

"And you—who are you?" asked Syson.

"Arthur Pilbeam—Naylor's my uncle," said the other.

"You live here in Nuttall?"

"I'm lodgin' at my uncle's—at Naylor's."

"I see!"

"Did you say you was goin' down to Willey-Water?" asked the keeper.

"Yes."

There was a pause of some moments, before the keeper blurted: "*I'm* courtin' Hilda Millership."

The young fellow looked at the intruder with a stubborn defiance, almost pathetic. Syson opened new eyes.

"Are you?" he said, astonished. The keeper flushed dark.

"She and me are keeping company," he said.

"I didn't know!" said Syson. The other man waited uncomfortably.

"What, is the thing settled?" asked the intruder.

"How, settled?" retorted the other sulkily.

"Are you going to get married soon, and all that?"

The keeper stared in silence for some moments, impotent.

"I suppose so," he said, full of resentment.

"Ah!" Syson watched closely.

"I'm married myself," he added, after a time.

"You are?" said the other incredulously.

Syson laughed in his brilliant, unhappy way.

"This last fifteen months," he said.

The keeper gazed at him with wide, wondering eyes, apparently thinking back, and trying to make things out.

"Why, didn't you know?" asked Syson.

"No, I didn't," said the other sulkily.

There was silence for a moment.

"Ah well!" said Syson, "I will go on. I suppose I may."

The keeper stood in silent opposition. The two men hesitated in the open, grassy space, set around with small sheaves of sturdy bluebells; a little open platform on the brow of the hill. Syson took a few indecisive steps forward, then stopped.

"I say, how beautiful!" he cried.

He had come in full view of the downslope. The wide path ran from his feet like a river, and it was full of bluebells, save for a green winding thread down the centre, where the keeper walked. Like a stream the path opened into azure shallows at the levels, and there were pools of bluebells, with still the green thread winding through, like a thin current of ice-water through blue lakes. And from under the twig-purple of the bushes swam the shadowed blue, as if the flowers lay in flood water over the woodland.

"Ah, isn't it lovely!" Syson exclaimed; this was his past, the country he had abandoned, and it hurt him to see it so beautiful. Woodpigeons cooed overhead, and the air was full of the brightness of birds singing.

"If you're married, what do you keep writing to her for, and sending her poetry books and things?" asked the keeper. Syson stared at him, taken aback and humiliated. Then he began to smile.

"Well," he said, "I did not know about you . . ."

Again the keeper flushed darkly.

"But if you are married—" he charged.

"I am," answered the other cynically.

Then, looking down the blue, beautiful path, Syson felt his own humiliation. "What right *have* I to hang on to her?" he thought, bitterly self-contemptuous.

"She knows I'm married and all that," he said.

"But you keep sending her books," challenged the keeper.

Syson, silenced, looked at the other man quizzically, half pitying. Then he turned.

"Good day," he said, and was gone. Now, everything irritated him: the two sallows, one all gold and perfume and murmur, one silver-green and bristly, reminded him, that here he had taught her about pollination. What a fool he was! What god-forsaken folly it all was!

"Ah well," he said to himself; "the poor devil seems to have a grudge against me. I'll do my best for him." He grinned to himself, in a very bad temper.

II

The farm was less than a hundred yards from the wood's edge. The wall of trees formed the fourth side to the open quadrangle. The house faced the wood. With tangled emotions, Syson noted the plum blossom falling on the profuse, coloured primroses, which he himself had brought here and set. How they had increased! There were thick tufts of scarlet, and pink, and pale purple primroses under the plum trees. He saw somebody glance at him through the kitchen window, heard men's voices.

The door opened suddenly: very womanly she had grown! He felt himself going pale.

"You?—Addy!" she exclaimed, and stood motionless.

"Who?" called the farmer's voice. Men's low voices answered. Those low voices, curious and almost jeering, roused the tormented spirit in the visitor. Smiling brilliantly at her, he waited.

"Myself—why not?" he said.

The flush burned very deep on her cheek and throat.

"We are just finishing dinner," she said.

"Then I will stay outside." He made a motion to show that he would sit on the red earthenware pipkin that stood near the door among the daffodils, and contained the drinking water.

"Oh no, come in," she said hurriedly. He followed her. In the doorway, he glanced swiftly over the family, and bowed. Everyone was confused. The farmer, his wife, and the four sons sat at the coarsely laid dinner-table, the men with arms bare to the elbows.

"I am sorry I come at lunch-time," said Syson.

"Hello, Addy!" said the farmer, assuming the old form of address, but his tone cold. "How are you?"

And he shook hands.

"Shall you have a bit?" he invited the young visitor, but taking for granted the offer would be refused. He assumed that Syson was become too refined to eat so roughly. The young man winced at the imputation.

"Have you had any dinner?" asked the daughter.

"No," replied Syson. "It is too early. I shall be back at half-past one."

"You call it lunch, don't you?" asked the eldest son, almost ironical. He had once been an intimate friend of this young man.

"We'll give Addy something when we've finished," said the mother, an invalid, deprecating.

"No—don't trouble. I don't want to give you any trouble," said Syson.

"You could allus live on fresh air an' scenery," laughed the youngest son, a lad of nineteen.

Syson went round the buildings, and into the orchard at the back of the house, where daffodils all along the hedgerow swung like yellow, ruffled birds on their perches. He loved the place extraordinarily, the hills ranging round, with bear-skin woods covering their giant shoulders, and small red farms like brooches clasping their garments; the blue streak of water in the valley, the bareness of the home pasture, the sound of myriad-threaded bird-singing, which went mostly unheard. To his last day, he would dream of this place, when he felt the sun on his face, or saw the small handfuls of snow between the winter twigs, or smelt the coming of spring.

Hilda was very womanly. In her presence he felt constrained. She was twenty-nine, as he was, but she seemed to him much older. He felt foolish, almost unreal, beside her. She was so static. As he was fingering some shed plum blossom on a low bough, she came to the back door to shake the table-cloth. Fowls raced from the stack-yard, birds rustled from the trees. Her dark hair was gathered up in a coil like a crown on her head. She was very straight, distant in her bearing. As she folded the cloth, she looked away over the hills.

Presently Syson returned indoors. She had prepared eggs and curd cheese, stewed gooseberries and cream.

"Since you will dine to-night," she said, "I have only given you a light lunch."

"It is awfully nice," he said. "You keep a real idyllic atmosphere—your belt of straw and ivy buds."

Still they hurt each other.

He was uneasy before her. Her brief, sure speech, her distant bearing, were unfamiliar to him. He admired again her grey-black eyebrows, and her lashes. Their eyes met. He saw, in the beautiful grey and black of her glance, tears and a strange light, and at the back of all, calm acceptance of herself, and triumph over him.

He felt himself shrinking. With an effort he kept up the ironic manner.

She sent him into the parlour while she washed the dishes. The long low room was refurnished from the Abbey sale, with chairs upholstered in claret-coloured rep, many years old, and an oval table of polished walnut, and another piano, handsome, though still antique. In spite of the strangeness, he was pleased. Opening a high cupboard let into the thickness of the wall, he found it full of his books, his old lesson-books, and volumes of verse he had sent her, English and German. The daffodils in the white window-bottoms shone across the room, he could almost feel their rays. The old glamour caught him again. His youthful water-colours on the wall no longer made him grin; he remembered how fervently he had tried to paint for her, twelve years before.

She entered, wiping a dish, and he saw again the bright, kernel-white beauty of her arms.

"You are quite splendid here," he said, and their eyes met.

"Do you like it?" she asked. It was the old, low, husky tone of intimacy. He felt a quick change beginning in his blood. It was the old, delicious sublimation, the thinning, almost the vaporizing of himself, as if his spirit were to be liberated.

"Aye," he nodded, smiling at her like a boy again. She bowed her head.

"This was the countess's chair," she said in low tones. "I found her scissors down here between the padding."

"Did you? Where are they?"

Quickly, with a lilt in her movement, she fetched her work-basket, and together they examined the long-shanked old scissors.

"What a ballad of dead ladies!" he said, laughing, as he fitted his fingers into the round loops of the countess's scissors.

"I knew you could use them," she said, with certainty. He looked at his fingers, and at the scissors. She meant his fingers were fine enough for the small-looped scissors.

"That is something to be said for me," he laughed, putting the scissors aside. She turned to the window. He noticed the fine, fair down on her cheek and her upper lip, and her soft, white neck, like the throat of a nettle flower, and her fore-arms, bright as newly blanched kernels. He was looking at her with new eyes, and she was a different person to him. He did not know her. But he could regard her objectively now.

"Shall we go out awhile?" she asked.

"Yes!" he answered. But the predominant emotion, that troubled the excitement and perplexity of his heart, was fear, fear of that which he saw. There was about her the same manner, the same intonation in her voice, now as then, but she was not what he had known her to be. He knew quite well what she had been for him. And gradually he was realizing that she was something quite other, and always had been.

She put no covering on her head, merely took off her apron, saying, "We will go by the larches." As they passed the old orchard, she called him in to show him a blue-tit's nest in one of the apple trees, and a sycock's in the hedge. He rather wondered at her surety, at a certain hardness like arrogance hidden under her humility.

"Look at the apple buds," she said, and he then perceived myriads of little scarlet balls among the drooping boughs. Watching his face, her eyes went hard. She saw the scales were fallen from him, and at last he was going to see her as she was. It was the thing she had most dreaded in the past, and most needed, for her soul's sake. Now he was going to see her as she was. He would not love her, and he would know he never could have loved her. The old illusion gone, they were strangers, crude and entire. But he would give her her due—she would have her due from him.

She was brilliant as he had not known her. She showed him nests: a jenny wren's in a low bush.

"See this jinty's!" she exclaimed.

He was surprised to hear her use the local name. She reached carefully through the thorns, and put her fingers in the nest's round door.

"Five!" she said. "Tiny little things."

She showed him nests of robins, and chaffinches, and linnets, and buntings; of a wagtail beside the water.

"And if we go down, nearer the lake, I will show you a kingfisher's . . ."

"Among the young fir trees," she said, "there's a throstle's or a blackie's on nearly every bough, every ledge. The first day, when I had seen them all, I felt as if I mustn't go in the wood. It seemed a city of birds: and in the morning, hearing them all, I thought of the noisy early markets. I was afraid to go in my own wood."

She was using the language they had both of them invented. Now it was all her own. He had done with it. She did not mind his silence, but was always dominant, letting him see her wood. As they came along a marshy path where forget-me-nots were opening in a rich blue drift: "We know all the birds, but there are many flowers we can't find out," she said. It was half an appeal to him, who had known the names of things.

She looked dreamily across to the open fields that slept in the sun.

"I have a lover as well, you know," she said, with assurance, yet dropping again almost into the intimate tone.

This woke in him the spirit to fight her.

"I think I met him. He is good-looking—also in Arcady."

Without answering, she turned into a dark path that led up-hill, where the trees and undergrowth were very thick.

"They did well," she said at length, "to have various altars to various gods, in old days."

"Ah yes!" he agreed. "To whom is the new one?"

"There are no old ones," she said. "I was always looking for this."

"And whose is it?" he asked.

"I don't know," she said, looking full at him.

"I'm very glad, for your sake," he said, "that you are satisfied."

"Aye—but the man doesn't matter so much," she said. There was a pause.

"No!" he exclaimed, astonished, yet recognizing her as her real self.

"It is one's self that matters," she said. "Whether one is being one's own self and serving one's own God."

There was silence, during which he pondered. The path was almost flowerless, gloomy. At the side, his heels sank into soft clay.

III

"I," she said, very slowly, "I was married the same night as you."

He looked at her.

"Not legally, of course," she replied. "But—actually."

"To the keeper?" he said, not knowing what else to say.

She turned to him.

"You thought I could not?" she said. But the flush was deep in her cheek and throat, for all her assurance.

Still he would not say anything.

"You see"—she was making an effort to explain—"I had to understand also."

"And what does it amount to, this *understanding*?" he asked.

"A very great deal—does it not to you?" she replied. "One is free."

"And you are not disappointed?"

"Far from it!" Her tone was deep and sincere.

"You love him?"

"Yes, I love him."

"Good!" he said.

This silenced her for a while.

"Here, among his things, I love him," she said.

His conceit would not let him be silent.

"It needs this setting?" he asked.

"It does," she cried. "You were always making me to be not myself."

He laughed shortly.

"But is it a matter of surroundings?" he said. He had considered her all spirit.

"I am like a plant," she replied. "I can only grow in my own soil."

They came to a place where the undergrowth shrank away, leaving a bare, brown space, pillared with the brick-red and purplish trunks of pine trees. On the fringe, hung the sombre green of elder trees, with flat flowers in bud, and below were bright, unfurling pennons of fern. In the midst of the bare space stood a keeper's log hut. Pheasant-coops were lying about, some occupied by a clucking hen, some empty.

Hilda walked over the brown pine-needles to the hut, took a key from among the eaves, and opened the door. It was a bare wooden place with a carpenter's bench and form, carpenter's tools, an axe, snares, straps, some skins pegged down, everything in order. Hilda closed the door. Syson examined the weird flat coats of wild animals, that were pegged down to be cured. She turned some knotch in the side wall, and disclosed a second, small apartment.

"How romantic!" said Syson.

"Yes. He is very curious—he has some of a wild animal's cunning—in a nice sense—and he is inventive, and thoughtful—but not beyond a certain point."

She pulled back a dark green curtain. The apartment was occupied almost entirely by a large couch of heather and bracken, on which was spread an ample rabbit-skin rug. On the floor were patchwork rugs of cat-skin, and a red calf-skin, while hanging from the wall were other furs. Hilda took down one, which she put on. It was a cloak of rabbit-skin and of white fur, with a hood, apparently of the skins of stoats. She laughed at Syson from out of this barbaric mantle, saying:

"What do you think of it?"

"Ah—! I congratulate you on your man," he replied.

"And look!" she said.

In a little jar on a shelf were some sprays, frail and white, of the first honeysuckle.

"They will scent the place at night," she said.

He looked round curiously.

"Where does he come short, then?" he asked. She gazed at him for a few moments. Then, turning aside:

"The stars aren't the same with him," she said. "You could make them flash and quiver, and the forget-me-nots come up at me like phosphorescence. You could make things *wonderful*. I have found it out—it is true. But I have them all for myself, now."

He laughed, saying:

"After all, stars and forget-me-nots are only luxuries. You ought to make poetry."

"Aye," she assented. "But I have them all now."

Again he laughed bitterly at her.

She turned swiftly. He was leaning against the small window of the tiny, obscure room, and was watching her, who stood in the doorway, still cloaked in her mantle. His cap was removed, so she saw his face and head distinctly in the dim room. His black, straight, glossy hair was brushed clean back from his brow. His black eyes were watching her, and his face, that was clear and cream, and perfectly smooth, was flickering.

"We are very different," she said bitterly.

Again he laughed.

"I see you disapprove of me," he said.

"I disapprove of what you have become," she said.

"You think we might"—he glanced at the hut—"have been like this—you and I?"

She shook her head.

"You! no; never! You plucked a thing and looked at it till you had found out all you wanted to know about it, then you threw it away," she said.

"Did I?" he asked. "And could your way never have been my way? I suppose not."

"Why should it?" she said. "I am a separate being."

"But surely two people sometimes go the same way," he said.

"You took me away from myself," she said.

He knew he had mistaken her, had taken her for something she was not. That was his fault, not hers.

"And did you always know?" he asked.

"No—you never let me know. You bullied me. I couldn't help myself. I was glad when you left me, really."

"I know you were," he said. But his face went paler, almost deathly luminous.

"Yet," he said, "it was you who sent me the way I have gone."

"I!" she exclaimed, in pride.

"You *would* have me take the Grammar School scholarship—and you would have me foster poor little Botell's fervent attachment to me, till he couldn't live without me—and because Botell was rich and influential. You triumphed in the wine-merchant's offer to send me to Cambridge, to befriend his only child. You wanted me to rise in the world. And all the time you were sending me away from you—every new success of mine put a separation between us, and more for you than for me. You never wanted to come with me: you wanted just to send me to see what it was like. I believe you even wanted me to marry a lady. You wanted to triumph over society in me."

"And I am responsible," she said, with sarcasm.

"I distinguished myself to satisfy you," he replied.

"Ah!" she cried, "you always wanted change, change, like a child."

"Very well! And I am a success, and I know it, and I do some good work. But—I thought you were different. What right have you to a man?"

"What do you want?" she said, looking at him with wide, fearful eyes.

He looked back at her, his eyes pointed, like weapons.

"Why, nothing," he laughed shortly.

There was a rattling at the outer latch, and the keeper entered. The woman glanced round, but remained standing, fur-cloaked, in the inner doorway. Syson did not move.

The other man entered, saw, and turned away without speaking. The two also were silent.

Pilbeam attended to his skins.

"I must go," said Syson.

"Yes," she replied.

"Then I give you 'To our vast and varying fortunes.'" He lifted his hand in pledge.

"'To our vast and varying fortunes,'" she answered gravely, and speaking in cold tones.

"Arthur!" she said.

The keeper pretended not to hear. Syson, watching keenly, began to smile. The woman drew herself up.

"Arthur!" she said again, with a curious upward inflection, which warned the two men that her soul was trembling on a dangerous crisis.

The keeper slowly put down his tool and came to her.

"Yes," he said.

"I wanted to introduce you," she said, trembling.

"I've met him a'ready," said the keeper.

"Have you? It is Addy, Mr. Syson, whom you know about.—This is Arthur, Mr. Pilbeam," she added, turning to Syson. The latter held out his hand to the keeper, and they shook hands in silence.

"I'm glad to have met you," said Syson. "We drop our correspondence, Hilda?"

"Why need we?" she asked.

The two men stood at a loss.

"*Is* there no need?" said Syson.

Still she was silent.

"It is as you will," she said.

They went all three together down the gloomy path.

"'*Qu'il était bleu, le ciel, et grand l'espoir,*'" quoted Syson, not knowing what to say.

"What do you mean?" she said. "Besides, *we* can't walk in *our* wild oats—we never sowed any."

Syson looked at her. He was startled to see his young love, his nun, his Botticelli angel, so revealed. It was he who had been the fool. He and she were more separate than any two strangers could be. She only wanted to keep up a correspondence with him—and he, of course, wanted it kept up, so that he could write to her, like Dante to some Beatrice who had never existed save in the man's own brain.

At the bottom of the path she left him. He went along with the keeper, towards the open, towards the gate that closed on the wood. The two men walked almost like friends. They did not broach the subject of their thoughts.

Instead of going straight to the high-road gate, Syson went along the wood's edge, where the brook spread out in a little bog, and under the alder trees, among the reeds, great yellow stools and bosses of marigolds shone. Threads of brown water trickled by, touched with gold from the flowers. Suddenly there was a blue flash in the air, as a kingfisher passed.

Syson was extraordinarily moved. He climbed the bank to the gorse bushes, whose sparks of blossom had not yet gathered into a flame. Lying on the dry brown turf, he discovered sprigs of tiny purple milkwort and pink spots of lousewort. What a wonderful world it was—marvellous, for ever new. He felt as if it were underground, like the fields of monotone hell, notwithstanding. Inside his breast was a pain like a wound. He remembered the poem of William Morris, where in the Chapel of Lyonesse a knight lay wounded, with the truncheon of a spear deep in his breast, lying always as dead, yet did not die, while day after day the coloured sunlight dipped from the painted window across the chancel, and passed away. He knew now it never had been true, that which was between him and her, not for a moment. The truth had stood apart all the time.

Syson turned over. The air was full of the sound of larks, as if the sunshine above were condensing and falling in a shower. Amid this bright sound, voices sounded small and distinct.

"But if he's married, an' quite willing to drop it off, what has ter against it?" said the man's voice.

"I don't want to talk about it now. I want to be alone."

Syson looked through the bushes. Hilda was standing in the wood, near the gate. The man was in the field, loitering by the hedge, and playing with the bees as they settled on the white bramble flowers.

There was silence for a while, in which Syson imagined her will among the brightness of the larks. Suddenly the keeper exclaimed "Ah!" and swore. He was gripping at the sleeve of his coat, near the shoulder. Then he pulled off his jacket, threw it on the ground, and absorbedly rolled up his shirt sleeve right to the shoulder.

"Ah!" he said vindictively, as he picked out the bee and flung it away. He twisted his fine, bright arm, peering awkwardly over his shoulder.

"What is it?" asked Hilda.

"A bee—crawled up my sleeve," he answered.

"Come here to me," she said.

The keeper went to her, like a sulky boy. She took his arm in her hands.

"Here it is—and the sting left in—poor bee!"

She picked out the sting, put her mouth to his arm, and sucked away the drop of poison. As she looked at the red mark her mouth had made, and at his arm, she said, laughing:

"That is the reddest kiss you will ever have."

When Syson next looked up, at the sound of voices, he saw in the shadow the keeper with his mouth on the throat of his beloved, whose head was thrown back, and whose hair had fallen, so that one rough rope of dark brown hair hung across his bare arm.

"No," the woman answered. "I am not upset because he's gone. You won't understand . . ."

Syson could not distinguish what the man said. Hilda replied, clear and distinct:

"You know I love you. He has gone quite out of my life—don't trouble about him . . ." He kissed her, murmuring. She laughed hollowly.

"Yes," she said, indulgent. "We will be married, we will be married. But not just yet." He spoke to her again. Syson heard nothing for a time. Then she said:

"You must go home, now, dear—you will get no sleep."

Again was heard the murmur of the keeper's voice, troubled by fear and passion.

"But why should we be married at once?" she said. "What more would you have, by being married? It is most beautiful as it is."

At last he pulled on his coat and departed. She stood at the gate, not watching him, but looking over the sunny country.

When at last she had gone, Syson also departed, going back to town.

SECOND BEST

"Oh, I'm tired!" Frances exclaimed petulantly, and in the same instant she dropped down on the turf, near the hedge-bottom. Anne stood a moment surprised, then, accustomed to the vagaries of her beloved Frances, said:

"Well, and aren't you always likely to be tired, after travelling that blessed long way from Liverpool yesterday?" and she plumped down beside her sister. Anne was a wise young body of fourteen, very buxom, brimming with common sense. Frances was much older, about twenty-three, and whimsical, spasmodic. She was the beauty and the clever child of the family. She plucked the goose-grass buttons from her dress in a nervous, desperate fashion. Her beautiful profile, looped above with black hair, warm with the dusky-and-scarlet complexion of a pear, was calm as a mask, her thin brown hand plucked nervously.

"It's not the journey," she said, objecting to Anne's obtuseness. Anne looked inquiringly at her darling. The young girl, in her self-confident, practical way, proceeded to reckon up this whimsical creature. But suddenly she found herself full in the eyes of Frances; felt two dark, hectic eyes flaring challenge at her, and she shrank away. Frances was peculiar for these great, exposed looks, which disconcerted people by their violence and their suddenness.

"What's a matter, poor old duck?" asked Anne, as she folded the slight, wilful form of her sister in her arms. Frances laughed shakily, and nestled down for comfort on the budding breasts of the strong girl.

"Oh, I'm only a bit tired," she murmured, on the point of tears.

"Well, of course you are, what do you expect?" soothed Anne. It was a joke to Frances that Anne should play elder, almost mother to her. But then, Anne was in her unvexed teens; men were like big dogs to her: while Frances, at twenty-three, suffered a good deal.

The country was intensely morning-still. On the common everything shone beside its shadow, and the hillside gave off heat in silence. The brown turf seemed in a low state of combustion, the leaves of the oaks were scorched brown. Among the blackish foliage in the distance shone the small red and orange of the village.

The willows in the brook-course at the foot of the common suddenly shook with a dazzling effect like diamonds. It was a puff of wind. Anne resumed her normal position. She spread her knees, and put in her lap a handful of hazel nuts, whity-green leafy things, whose one cheek was tanned between brown and pink. These she began to crack and eat. Frances, with bowed head, mused bitterly.

"Eh, you know Tom Smedley?" began the young girl, as she pulled a tight kernel out of its shell.

"I suppose so," replied Frances sarcastically.

"Well, he gave me a wild rabbit what he'd caught, to keep with my tame one—and it's living."

"That's a good thing," said Frances, very detached and ironic.

"Well, it *is*! He reckoned he'd take me to Ollerton Feast, but he never did. Look here, he took a servant from the rectory; I saw him."

"So he ought," said Frances.

"No, he oughtn't! and I told him so. And I told him I should tell you—an' I have done."

Click and snap went a nut between her teeth. She sorted out the kernel, and chewed complacently.

"It doesn't make much difference," said Frances.

"Well, 'appen it doesn't; but I was mad with him all the same."

"Why?"

"Because I was; he's no right to go with a servant."

"He's a perfect right," persisted Frances, very just and cold.

"No, he hasn't, when he'd said he'd take me."

Frances burst into a laugh of amusement and relief.

"Oh, no; I'd forgot that," she said, adding, "And what did he say when you promised to tell me?"

"He laughed and said, 'he won't fret her fat over that.'"

"And she won't," sniffed Frances.

There was silence. The common, with its sere, blonde-headed thistles, its heaps of silent bramble, its brown-husked gorse in the glare of sunshine, seemed visionary. Across the brook began the immense pattern of agriculture, white chequering of barley stubble, brown squares of wheat, khaki patches of pasture, red stripes of fallow, with the woodland and the tiny village dark like ornaments, leading away to the distance, right to the hills, where the check-pattern grew smaller and smaller, till, in the blackish haze of heat, far off, only the tiny white squares of barley stubble showed distinct.

"Eh, I say, here's a rabbit hole!" cried Anne suddenly. "Should we watch if one comes out? You won't have to fidget, you know."

The two girls sat perfectly still. Frances watched certain objects in her surroundings: they had a peculiar, unfriendly look about them: the weight of greenish elderberries on their purpling stalks; the twinkling of the yellowing crab-apples that clustered high up in the hedge, against the sky: the exhausted, limp leaves of the primroses lying flat in the hedge-bottom: all looked strange to her. Then her eyes caught a movement. A mole was moving silently over the warm, red soil, nosing, shuffling hither and thither, flat, and dark as a shadow, shifting about, and as suddenly brisk, and as silent, like a very ghost of *joie de vivre*. Frances started, from habit was about to call on Anne to kill the little pest. But, to-day, her lethargy of unhappiness was too much for her. She watched the little brute paddling, snuffing, touching things to discover them, running in blindness, delighted to ecstasy by the sunlight and the hot, strange things that caressed its belly and its nose. She felt a keen pity for the little creature.

"Eh, our Fran, look there! It's a mole."

Anne was on her feet, standing watching the dark, unconscious beast. Frances frowned with anxiety.

"It doesn't run off, does it?" said the young girl softly. Then she stealthily approached the creature. The mole paddled fumblingly away. In an instant Anne put her foot upon it, not too heavily. Frances could see the struggling, swimming movement of the little pink hands of the brute, the twisting and twitching of its pointed nose, as it wrestled under the sole of the boot.

"It *does* wriggle!" said the bonny girl, knitting her brows in a frown at the eerie sensation. Then she bent down to look at her trap. Frances could now see, beyond the edge of the boot-sole, the heaving of the velvet shoulders, the pitiful turning of the sightless face, the frantic rowing of the flat, pink hands.

"Kill the thing," she said, turning away her face.

"Oh—I'm not," laughed Anne, shrinking. "You can, if you like."

"I *don't* like," said Frances, with quiet intensity.

After several dabbling attempts, Anne succeeded in picking up the little animal by the scruff of its neck. It threw back its head, flung its long blind snout from side to side, the mouth open in a peculiar oblong, with tiny pinkish teeth at the edge. The blind, frantic mouth gaped and writhed. The body, heavy and clumsy, hung scarcely moving.

"Isn't it a snappy little thing," observed Anne twisting to avoid the teeth.

"What are you going to do with it?" asked Frances sharply.

"It's got to be killed—look at the damage they do. I s'll take it home and let dadda or somebody kill it. I'm not going to let it go."

She swaddled the creature clumsily in her pocket-handkerchief and sat down beside her sister. There was an interval of silence, during which Anne combated the efforts of the mole.

"You've not had much to say about Jimmy this time. Did you see him often in Liverpool?" Anne asked suddenly.

"Once or twice," replied Frances, giving no sign of how the question troubled her.

"And aren't you sweet on him any more, then?"

"I should think I'm not, seeing that he's engaged."

"Engaged? Jimmy Barrass! Well, of all things! I never thought *he'd* get engaged."

"Why not, he's as much right as anybody else?" snapped Frances.

Anne was fumbling with the mole.

"'Appen so," she said at length; "but I never thought Jimmy would, though."

"Why not?" snapped Frances.

"*I* don't know—this blessed mole, it'll not keep still!—who's he got engaged to?"

"How should I know?"

"I thought you'd ask him; you've known him long enough. I s'd think he thought he'd get engaged now he's a Doctor of Chemistry."

Frances laughed in spite of herself.

"What's that got to do with it?" she asked.

"I'm sure it's got a lot. He'll want to feel *somebody* now, so he's got engaged. Hey, stop it; go in!"

But at this juncture the mole almost succeeded in wriggling clear. It wrestled and twisted frantically, waved its pointed blind head, its mouth standing open like a little shaft, its big, wrinkled hands spread out.

"Go in with you!" urged Anne, poking the little creature with her forefinger, trying to get it back into the handkerchief. Suddenly the mouth turned like a spark on her finger.

"Oh!" she cried, "he's bit me."

She dropped him to the floor. Dazed, the blind creature fumbled round. Frances felt like shrieking. She expected him to dart away in a flash, like a mouse, and there he remained groping; she wanted to cry to him to be gone. Anne, in a sudden decision of wrath, caught up her sister's walking-cane. With one blow the mole was dead. Frances was startled and shocked. One moment the little wretch was fussing in the heat, and the next it lay like a little bag, inert and black—not a struggle, scarce a quiver.

"It is dead!" Frances said breathlessly. Anne took her finger from her mouth, looked at the tiny pinpricks, and said:

"Yes, he is, and I'm glad. They're vicious little nuisances, moles are."

With which her wrath vanished. She picked up the dead animal.

"Hasn't it got a beautiful skin," she mused, stroking the fur with her forefinger, then with her cheek.

"Mind," said Frances sharply. "You'll have the blood on your skirt!"

One ruby drop of blood hung on the small snout, ready to fall. Anne shook it off on to some harebells. Frances suddenly became calm; in that moment, grown-up.

"I suppose they have to be killed," she said, and a certain rather dreary indifference succeeded to her grief. The twinkling crab-apples, the glitter of brilliant willows now seemed to her trifling, scarcely worth the notice. Something had died in her, so that things lost their poignancy. She was calm, indifference overlying her quiet sadness. Rising, she walked down to the brook course.

"Here, wait for me," cried Anne, coming tumbling after.

Frances stood on the bridge, looking at the red mud trodden into pockets by the feet of cattle. There was not a drain of water left, but everything smelled green, succulent. Why did she care so little for Anne, who was so fond of her? she asked herself. Why did she care so little for anyone? She did not know, but she felt a rather stubborn pride in her isolation and indifference.

They entered a field where stooks of barley stood in rows, the straight, blonde tresses of the corn streaming on to the ground. The stubble was bleached by the intense summer, so that the expanse glared white. The next field was sweet and soft with a second crop of seeds; thin, straggling clover whose little pink knobs rested prettily in the dark green. The scent was faint and sickly. The girls came up in single file, Frances leading.

Near the gate a young man was mowing with the scythe some fodder for the afternoon feed of the cattle. As he saw the girls he left off working and waited in an aimless kind of way. Frances was dressed in white muslin, and she walked with dignity, detached and forgetful. Her lack of agitation, her simple, unheeding advance made him nervous. She had loved the far-off Jimmy for five years, having had in return his half-measures. This man only affected her slightly.

Tom was of medium stature, energetic in build. His smooth, fair-skinned face was burned red, not brown, by the sun, and this ruddiness enhanced his appearance of good humour and easiness. Being a year older than Frances, he would have courted her long ago had she been so inclined. As it was, he had gone his uneventful way amiably, chatting with many a girl, but remaining unattached, free of trouble for the most part. Only he knew he wanted a woman. He hitched his trousers just a trifle self-consciously as the girls approached. Frances was a rare, delicate kind of being, whom he realized with a queer and delicious stimulation in his veins. She gave him a slight sense of suffocation. Somehow, this morning, she affected him more than usual. She was dressed in white. He, however, being matter-of-fact in his mind, did not realize. His feeling had never become conscious, purposive.

Frances knew what she was about. Tom was ready to love her as soon as she would show him. Now that she could not have Jimmy, she did not poignantly care. Still, she would have something. If she could not have the best—Jimmy, whom she knew to be something of a snob—she would have the second best, Tom. She advanced rather indifferently.

"You are back, then!" said Tom. She marked the touch of uncertainty in his voice.

"No," she laughed, "I'm still in Liverpool," and the undertone of intimacy made him burn.

"This isn't you, then?" he asked.

Her heart leapt up in approval. She looked in his eyes, and for a second was with him.

"Why, what do you think?" she laughed.

He lifted his hat from his head with a distracted little gesture. She liked him, his quaint ways, his humour, his ignorance, and his slow masculinity.

"Here, look here, Tom Smedley," broke in Anne.

"A moudiwarp! Did you find it dead?" he asked.

"No, it bit me," said Anne.

"Oh, aye! An' that got your rag out, did it?"

"No, it didn't!" Anne scolded sharply. "Such language!"

"Oh, what's up wi' it?"

"I can't bear you to talk broad."

"Can't you?"

He glanced at Frances.

"It isn't nice," Frances said. She did not care, really. The vulgar speech jarred on her as a rule; Jimmy was a gentleman. But Tom's manner of speech did not matter to her.

"I like you to talk *nicely*," she added.

"Do you," he replied, tilting his hat, stirred.

"And generally you *do*, you know," she smiled.

"I s'll have to have a try," he said, rather tensely gallant.

"What?" she asked brightly.

"To talk nice to you," he said. Frances coloured furiously, bent her head for a moment, then laughed gaily, as if she liked this clumsy hint.

"Eh now, you mind what you're saying," cried Anne, giving the young man an admonitory pat.

"You wouldn't have to give yon mole many knocks like that," he teased, relieved to get on safe ground, rubbing his arm.

"No indeed, it died in one blow," said Frances, with a flippancy that was hateful to her.

"You're not so good at knockin' 'em?" he said, turning to her.

"I don't know, if I'm cross," she said decisively.

"No?" he replied, with alert attentiveness.

"I could," she added, harder, "if it was necessary."

He was slow to feel her difference.

"And don't you consider it is necessary?" he asked, with misgiving.

"W—ell—is it?" she said, looking at him steadily, coldly.

"I reckon it is," he replied, looking away, but standing stubborn.

She laughed quickly.

"But it isn't necessary for *me*," she said, with slight contempt.

"Yes, that's quite true," he answered.

She laughed in a shaky fashion.

"*I know it is*," she said; and there was an awkward pause.

"Why, would you *like* me to kill moles then?" she asked tentatively, after a while.

"They do us a lot of damage," he said, standing firm on his own ground, angered.

"Well, I'll see the next time I come across one," she promised, defiantly. Their eyes met, and she sank before him, her pride troubled. He felt uneasy and triumphant and baffled, as if fate had gripped him. She smiled as she departed.

"Well," said Anne, as the sisters went through the wheat stubble; "I don't know what you two's been jawing about, I'm sure."

"Don't you?" laughed Frances significantly.

"No, I don't. But, at any rate, Tom Smedley's a good deal better to my thinking than Jimmy, so there—and nicer."

"Perhaps he is," said Frances coldly.

And the next day, after a secret, persistent hunt, she found another mole playing in the heat. She killed it, and in the evening, when Tom came to the gate to smoke his pipe after supper, she took him the dead creature.

"Here you are then!" she said.

"Did you catch it?" he replied, taking the velvet corpse into his fingers and examining it minutely. This was to hide his trepidation.

"Did you think I couldn't?" she asked, her face very near his.

"Nay, I didn't know."

She laughed in his face, a strange little laugh that caught her breath, all agitation, and tears, and recklessness of desire. He looked frightened and upset. She put her hand to his arm.

"Shall you go out wi' me?" he asked, in a difficult, troubled tone.

She turned her face away, with a shaky laugh. The blood came up in him, strong, overmastering. He resisted it. But it drove him down, and he was carried away. Seeing the winsome, frail nape of her neck, fierce love came upon him for her, and tenderness.

"We s'll 'ave to tell your mother," he said. And he stood, suffering, resisting his passion for her.

"Yes," she replied, in a dead voice. But there was a thrill of pleasure in this death.

THE SHADOW IN THE ROSE GARDEN

A rather small young man sat by the window of a pretty seaside cottage trying to persuade himself that he was reading the newspaper. It was about half-past eight in the morning. Outside, the glory roses hung in the morning sunshine like little bowls of fire tipped up. The young man looked at the table, then at the clock, then at his own big silver watch. An expression of stiff endurance came on to his face. Then he rose and reflected on the oil-paintings that hung on the walls of the room, giving careful but hostile attention to "The Stag at Bay". He tried the lid of the piano, and found it locked. He caught sight of his own face in a little mirror, pulled his brown moustache, and an alert interest sprang into his eyes. He was not ill-favoured. He twisted his moustache. His figure was rather small, but alert and vigorous. As he turned from the mirror a look of self-commiseration mingled with his appreciation of his own physiognomy.

In a state of self-suppression, he went through into the garden. His jacket, however, did not look dejected. It was new, and had a smart and self-confident air, sitting upon a confident body. He contemplated the Tree of Heaven that flourished by the lawn, then sauntered on to the next plant. There was more promise in a crooked apple tree covered with brown-red fruit. Glancing round, he broke off an apple and, with his back to the house, took a clean, sharp bite. To his surprise the fruit was sweet. He took another. Then again he turned to survey the bedroom windows overlooking the garden. He started, seeing a woman's figure; but it was only his wife. She was gazing across to the sea, apparently ignorant of him.

For a moment or two he looked at her, watching her. She was a good-looking woman, who seemed older than he, rather pale, but healthy, her face yearning. Her rich auburn hair was heaped in folds on her forehead. She looked apart from him and his world, gazing away to the sea. It irked her husband that she should continue abstracted and in ignorance of him; he pulled poppy fruits and threw them at the window. She started, glanced at him with a wild smile, and looked away again. Then almost immediately she left the window. He went indoors to meet her. She had a fine carriage, very proud, and wore a dress of soft white muslin.

"I've been waiting long enough," he said.

"For me or for breakfast?" she said lightly. "You know we said nine o'clock. I should have thought you could have slept after the journey."

"You know I'm always up at five, and I couldn't stop in bed after six. You might as well be in pit as in bed, on a morning like this."

"I shouldn't have thought the pit would occur to you, here."

She moved about examining the room, looking at the ornaments under glass covers. He, planted on the hearthrug, watched her rather uneasily, and grudgingly indulgent. She shrugged her shoulders at the apartment.

"Come," she said, taking his arm, "let us go into the garden till Mrs. Coates brings the tray."

"I hope she'll be quick," he said, pulling his moustache. She gave a short laugh, and leaned on his arm as they went. He had lighted a pipe.

Mrs. Coates entered the room as they went down the steps. The delightful, erect old lady hastened to the window for a good view of her visitors. Her china-blue eyes were bright as she watched the young couple go down the path, he walking in an easy, confident fashion, with his wife, on his arm. The landlady began talking to herself in a soft, Yorkshire accent.

"Just of a height they are. She wouldn't ha' married a man less than herself in stature, I think, though he's not her equal otherwise." Here her granddaughter came in, setting a tray on the table. The girl went to the old woman's side.

"He's been eating the apples, gran'," she said.

"Has he, my pet? Well, if he's happy, why not?"

Outside, the young, well-favoured man listened with impatience to the chink of the teacups. At last, with a sigh of relief, the couple came in to breakfast. After he had eaten for some time, he rested a moment and said:

"Do you think it's any better place than Bridlington?"

"I do," she said, "infinitely! Besides, I am at home here—it's not like a strange sea-side place to me."

"How long were you here?"

"Two years."

He ate reflectively.

"I should ha' thought you'd rather go to a fresh place," he said at length.

She sat very silent, and then, delicately, put out a feeler.

"Why?" she said. "Do you think I shan't enjoy myself?"

He laughed comfortably, putting the marmalade thick on his bread.

"I hope so," he said.

She again took no notice of him.

"But don't say anything about it in the village, Frank," she said casually. "Don't say who I am, or that I used to live here. There's nobody I want to meet, particularly, and we should never feel free if they knew me again."

"Why did you come, then?"

"'Why?' Can't you understand why?"

"Not if you don't want to know anybody."

"I came to see the place, not the people."

He did not say any more.

"Women," she said, "are different from men. I don't know why I wanted to come—but I did."

She helped him to another cup of coffee, solicitously.

"Only," she resumed, "don't talk about me in the village." She laughed shakily. "I don't want my past brought up against me, you know." And she moved the crumbs on the cloth with her finger-tip.

He looked at her as he drank his coffee; he sucked his moustache, and putting down his cup, said phlegmatically:

"I'll bet you've had a lot of past."

She looked with a little guiltiness, that flattered him, down at the tablecloth.

"Well," she said, caressive, "you won't give me away, who I am, will you?"

"No," he said, comforting, laughing, "I won't give you away."

He was pleased.

She remained silent. After a moment or two she lifted her head, saying:

"I've got to arrange with Mrs. Coates, and do various things. So you'd better go out by yourself this morning—and we'll be in to dinner at one."

"But you can't be arranging with Mrs. Coates all morning," he said.

"Oh, well—then I've some letters to write, and I must get that mark out of my skirt. I've got plenty of little things to do this morning. You'd better go out by yourself."

He perceived that she wanted to be rid of him, so that when she went upstairs, he took his hat and lounged out on to the cliffs, suppressedly angry.

Presently she too came out. She wore a hat with roses, and a long lace scarf hung over her white dress. Rather nervously, she put up her sunshade, and her face was half-hidden in its coloured shadow. She went along the narrow track of flag-stones that were worn hollow by the feet of the fishermen. She seemed to be avoiding her surroundings, as if she remained safe in the little obscurity of her parasol.

She passed the church, and went down the lane till she came to a high wall by the wayside. Under this she went slowly, stopping at length by an open doorway, which shone like a picture of light in the dark wall. There in the magic beyond the doorway, patterns of shadow lay on the sunny court, on the blue and white sea-pebbles of its paving, while a green lawn glowed beyond, where a bay tree glittered at the edges. She tiptoed nervously into the courtyard, glancing at the house that stood in shadow. The uncurtained windows looked black and soulless, the kitchen door stood open. Irresolutely she took a step forward, and again forward, leaning, yearning, towards the garden beyond.

She had almost gained the corner of the house when a heavy step came crunching through the trees. A gardener appeared before her. He held a wicker tray on which were rolling great, dark red gooseberries, overripe. He moved slowly.

"The garden isn't open today," he said quietly to the attractive woman, who was poised for retreat.

For a moment she was silent with surprise. How should it be public at all?

"When is it open?" she asked, quick-witted.

"The rector lets visitors in on Fridays and Tuesdays."

She stood still, reflecting. How strange to think of the rector opening his garden to the public!

"But everybody will be at church," she said coaxingly to the man. "There'll be nobody here, will there?"

He moved, and the big gooseberries rolled.

"The rector lives at the new rectory," he said.

The two stood still. He did not like to ask her to go. At last she turned to him with a winning smile.

"Might I have *one* peep at the roses?" she coaxed, with pretty wilfulness.

"I don't suppose it would matter," he said, moving aside: "you won't stop long—"

She went forward, forgetting the gardener in a moment. Her face became strained, her movements eager. Glancing round, she saw all the windows giving on to the lawn were curtainless and dark. The house had a sterile appearance, as if it were still used, but not inhabited. A shadow seemed to go over her. She went across the lawn towards the garden, through an arch of crimson ramblers, a gate of colour. There beyond lay the soft blue sea with the bay, misty with morning, and the farthest headland of black rock jutting dimly out between blue and blue of the sky and water. Her face began to shine, transfigured with pain and joy. At her feet the garden fell steeply, all a confusion of flowers, and away below was the darkness of tree-tops covering the beck.

She turned to the garden that shone with sunny flowers around her. She knew the little corner where was the seat beneath the yew tree. Then there was the terrace where a great host of flowers shone, and from this, two paths went down, one at each side of the garden. She closed her sunshade and walked slowly among the many flowers. All round were rose bushes, big banks of roses, then roses hanging and tumbling from pillars, or roses balanced on the standard bushes. By the open earth were many other flowers. If she lifted her head, the sea was upraised beyond, and the Cape.

Slowly she went down one path, lingering, like one who has gone back into the past. Suddenly she was touching some heavy crimson roses that were soft as velvet, touching them thoughtfully, without knowing, as a mother sometimes fondles the hand of her child. She leaned slightly forward to catch the scent. Then she wandered on in abstraction. Sometimes a flame-coloured, scentless rose would hold her arrested. She stood gazing at it as if she could not understand it. Again the same softness of intimacy came over her, as she stood before a tumbling heap of pink petals. Then she wondered over the white rose, that was greenish, like ice, in the centre. So, slowly, like a white, pathetic butterfly, she drifted down the path, coming at last to a tiny terrace all full of roses. They seemed to fill the place, a sunny, gay throng. She was shy of them, they were so many and so bright. They seemed to be conversing and laughing. She felt herself in a strange crowd. It exhilarated her, carried her out of herself. She flushed with excitement. The air was pure scent.

Hastily, she went to a little seat among the white roses, and sat down. Her scarlet sunshade made a hard blot of colour. She sat quite still, feeling her own existence lapse. She was no more than a rose, a rose that could not quite come into blossom, but remained tense. A little fly dropped on her knee, on her white dress. She watched it, as if it had fallen on a rose. She was not herself.

Then she started cruelly as a shadow crossed her and a figure moved into her sight. It was a man who had come in slippers, unheard. He wore a linen coat. The morning was shattered, the spell vanished away. She was only afraid of being questioned. He came forward. She rose. Then, seeing him, the strength went from her and she sank on the seat again.

He was a young man, military in appearance, growing slightly stout. His black hair was brushed smooth and bright, his moustache was waxed. But there was something rambling in his gait. She looked up, blanched to the lips, and saw his eyes. They were black, and stared without seeing. They were not a man's eyes. He was coming towards her.

He stared at her fixedly, made unconscious salute, and sat down beside her on the seat. He moved on the bench, shifted his feet, saying, in a gentlemanly, military voice:

"I don't disturb you—do I?"

She was mute and helpless. He was scrupulously dressed in dark clothes and a linen coat. She could not move. Seeing his hands, with the ring she knew so well upon the little finger, she felt as if she were going dazed. The whole world was deranged. She sat unavailing. For his hands, her symbols of passionate love, filled her with horror as they rested now on his strong thighs.

"May I smoke?" he asked intimately, almost secretly, his hand going to his pocket.

She could not answer, but it did not matter, he was in another world. She wondered, craving, if he recognized her—if he could recognize her. She sat pale with anguish. But she had to go through it.

"I haven't got any tobacco," he said thoughtfully.

But she paid no heed to his words, only she attended to him. Could he recognize her, or was it all gone? She sat still in a frozen kind of suspense.

"I smoke John Cotton," he said, "and I must economize with it, it is expensive. You know, I'm not very well off while these lawsuits are going on."

"No," she said, and her heart was cold, her soul kept rigid.

He moved, made a loose salute, rose, and went away. She sat motionless. She could see his shape, the shape she had loved, with all her passion: his compact, soldier's head, his fine figure now slackened. And it was not he. It only filled her with horror too difficult to know.

Suddenly he came again, his hand in his jacket pocket.

"Do you mind if I smoke?" he said. "Perhaps I shall be able to see things more clearly."

He sat down beside her again, filling a pipe. She watched his hands with the fine strong fingers. They had always inclined to tremble slightly. It had surprised her, long ago, in such a healthy man. Now they moved inaccurately, and the tobacco hung raggedly out of the pipe.

"I have legal business to attend to. Legal affairs are always so uncertain. I tell my solicitor exactly, precisely what I want, but I can never get it done."

She sat and heard him talking. But it was not he. Yet those were the hands she had kissed, there were the glistening, strange black eyes that she had loved. Yet it was not he. She sat motionless with horror and silence. He dropped his tobacco pouch, and groped for it on the ground. Yet she must wait if he would recognize her. Why could she not go! In a moment he rose.

"I must go at once," he said. "The owl is coming." Then he added confidentially: "His name isn't really the owl, but I call him that. I must go and see if he has come."

She rose too. He stood before her, uncertain. He was a handsome, soldierly fellow, and a lunatic. Her eyes searched him, and searched him, to see if he would recognize her, if she could discover him.

"You don't know me?" she asked, from the terror of her soul, standing alone.

He looked back at her quizzically. She had to bear his eyes. They gleamed on her, but with no intelligence. He was drawing nearer to her.

"Yes, I do know you," he said, fixed, intent, but mad, drawing his face nearer hers. Her horror was too great. The powerful lunatic was coming too near to her.

A man approached, hastening.

"The garden isn't open this morning," he said.

The deranged man stopped and looked at him. The keeper went to the seat and picked up the tobacco pouch left lying there.

"Don't leave your tobacco, sir," he said, taking it to the gentleman in the linen coat.

"I was just asking this lady to stay to lunch," the latter said politely. "She is a friend of mine."

The woman turned and walked swiftly, blindly, between the sunny roses, out of the garden, past the house with the blank, dark windows, through the sea-pebbled courtyard to the street. Hastening and blind, she went forward without hesitating, not knowing whither. Directly she came to the house she went upstairs, took off her hat, and sat down on the bed. It was as if some membrane had been torn in two in her, so that she was not an entity that could think and feel. She sat staring across at the window, where an ivy spray waved slowly up and down in the sea wind. There was some of the uncanny luminousness of the sunlit sea in the air. She sat perfectly still, without any being. She only felt she might be sick, and it might be blood that was loose in her torn entrails. She sat perfectly still and passive.

After a time she heard the hard tread of her husband on the floor below, and, without herself changing, she registered his movement. She heard his rather disconsolate footsteps go out again, then his voice speaking, answering, growing cheery, and his solid tread drawing near.

He entered, ruddy, rather pleased, an air of complacency about his alert figure. She moved stiffly. He faltered in his approach.

"What's the matter?" he asked a tinge of impatience in his voice. "Aren't you feeling well?"

This was torture to her.

"Quite," she replied.

His brown eyes became puzzled and angry.

"What is the matter?" he said.

"Nothing."

He took a few strides, and stood obstinately, looking out of the window.

"Have you run up against anybody?" he asked.

"Nobody who knows me," she said.

His hands began to twitch. It exasperated him, that she was no more sensible of him than if he did not exist. Turning on her at length, driven, he asked:

"Something has upset you hasn't it?"

"No, why?" she said neutral. He did not exist for her, except as an irritant.

His anger rose, filling the veins in his throat.

"It seems like it," he said, making an effort not to show his anger, because there seemed no reason for it. He went away downstairs. She sat still on the bed, and with the residue of feeling left to her, she disliked him because he tormented her. The time went by. She could smell the dinner being served, the smoke of her husband's pipe from the garden. But she could not move. She had no being. There was a tinkle of the bell. She heard him come indoors. And then he mounted the stairs again. At every step her heart grew tight in her. He opened the door.

"Dinner is on the table," he said.

It was difficult for her to endure his presence, for he would interfere with her. She could not recover her life. She rose stiffly and went down. She could neither eat nor talk during the meal. She sat absent, torn, without any being of her own. He tried to go on as if nothing were the matter. But at last he became silent with fury. As soon as it was possible, she went upstairs again, and locked the bedroom door. She must be alone. He went with his pipe into the garden. All his suppressed anger against her who held herself superior to him filled and blackened his heart. Though he had not know it, yet he had never really won her, she had never loved him. She had taken him on sufference. This had foiled him. He was only a labouring electrician in the mine, she was superior to him. He had always given way to her. But all the while, the injury and ignominy had been working in his soul because she did not hold him seriously. And now all his rage came up against her.

He turned and went indoors. The third time, she heard him mounting the stairs. Her heart stood still. He turned the catch and pushed the door—it was locked. He tried it again, harder. Her heart was standing still.

"Have you fastened the door?" he asked quietly, because of the landlady.

"Yes. Wait a minute."

She rose and turned the lock, afraid he would burst it. She felt hatred towards him, because he did not leave her free. He entered, his pipe between his teeth, and she returned to her old position on the bed. He closed the door and stood with his back to it.

"What's the matter?" he asked determinedly.

She was sick with him. She could not look at him.

"Can't you leave me alone?" she replied, averting her face from him.

He looked at her quickly, fully, wincing with ignominy. Then he seemed to consider for a moment.

"There's something up with you, isn't there?" he asked definitely.

"Yes," she said, "but that's no reason why you should torment me."

"I don't torment you. What's the matter?"

"Why should you know?" she cried, in hate and desperation.

Something snapped. He started and caught his pipe as it fell from his mouth. Then he pushed forward the bitten-off mouth-piece with his tongue, took it from off his lips, and looked at it. Then he put out his pipe, and brushed the ash from his waistcoat. After which he raised his head.

"I want to know," he said. His face was greyish pale, and set uglily.

Neither looked at the other. She knew he was fired now. His heart was pounding heavily. She hated him, but she could not withstand him. Suddenly she lifted her head and turned on him.

"What right have you to know?" she asked.

He looked at her. She felt a pang of surprise for his tortured eyes and his fixed face. But her heart hardened swiftly. She had never loved him. She did not love him now.

But suddenly she lifted her head again swiftly, like a thing that tries to get free. She wanted to be free of it. It was not him so much, but it, something she had put on herself, that bound her so horribly. And having put the bond on herself, it was hardest to take it off. But now she hated everything and felt destructive. He stood with his back to the door, fixed, as if he would oppose her eternally, till she was extinguished. She looked at him. Her eyes were cold and hostile. His workman's hands spread on the panels of the door behind him.

"You know I used to live here?" she began, in a hard voice, as if wilfully to wound him. He braced himself against her, and nodded.

"Well, I was companion to Miss Birch of Torril Hall—she and the rector were friends, and Archie was the rector's son." There was a pause. He listened without knowing what was happening. He stared at his wife. She was squatted in her white dress on the bed, carefully folding and re-folding the hem of her skirt. Her voice was full of hostility.

"He was an officer—a sub-lieutenant—then he quarrelled with his colonel and came out of the army. At any rate"—she plucked at her skirt hem, her husband stood motionless, watching her movements which filled his veins with madness—"he was awfully fond of me, and I was of him—awfully."

"How old was he?" asked the husband.

"When—when I first knew him? Or when he went away?—"

"When you first knew him."

"When I first knew him, he was twenty-six—now—he's thirty-one—nearly thirty-two—because I'm twenty-nine, and he is nearly three years older—"

She lifted her head and looked at the opposite wall.

"And what then?" said her husband.

She hardened herself, and said callously:

"We were as good as engaged for nearly a year, though nobody knew—at least—they talked—but—it wasn't open. Then he went away—"

"He chucked you?" said the husband brutally, wanting to hurt her into contact with himself. Her heart rose wildly with rage. Then "Yes", she said, to anger him. He shifted from one foot to the other, giving a "Ph!" of rage. There was silence for a time.

"Then," she resumed, her pain giving a mocking note to her words, "he suddenly went out to fight in Africa, and almost the very day I first met you, I heard from Miss Birch he'd got sunstroke—and two months after, that he was dead—"

"That was before you took on with me?" said the husband.

There was no answer. Neither spoke for a time. He had not understood. His eyes were contracted uglily.

"So you've been looking at your old courting places!" he said. "That was what you wanted to go out by yourself for this morning."

Still she did not answer him anything. He went away from the door to the window. He stood with his hands behind him, his back to her. She looked at him. His hands seemed gross to her, the back of his head paltry.

At length, almost against his will, he turned round, asking:

"How long were you carrying on with him?"

"What do you mean?" she replied coldly.

"I mean how long were you carrying on with him?"

She lifted her head, averting her face from him. She refused to answer. Then she said:

"I don't know what you mean, by carrying on. I loved him from the first days I met him—two months after I went to stay with Miss Birch."

"And do you reckon he loved you?" he jeered.

"I know he did."

"How do you know, if he'd have no more to do with you?"

There was a long silence of hate and suffering.

"And how far did it go between you?" he asked at length, in a frightened, stiff voice.

"I hate your not-straightforward questions," she cried, beside herself with his baiting. "We loved each other, and we *were* lovers—we were. I don't care what *you* think: what have you got to do with it? We were lovers before ever I knew you—"

"Lovers—lovers," he said, white with fury. "You mean you had your fling with an army man, and then came to me to marry you when you'd done—"

She sat swallowing her bitterness. There was a long pause.

"Do you mean to say you used to go—the whole hogger?" he asked, still incredulous.

"Why, what else do you think I mean?" she cried brutally.

He shrank, and became white, impersonal. There was a long, paralysed silence. He seemed to have gone small.

"You never thought to tell me all this before I married you," he said, with bitter irony, at last.

"You never asked me," she replied.

"I never thought there was any need."

"Well, then, you *should* think."

He stood with expressionless, almost childlike set face, revolving many thoughts, whilst his heart was mad with anguish.

Suddenly she added:

"And I saw him today," she said. "He is not dead, he's mad."

Her husband looked at her, startled.

"Mad!' he said involuntarily.

"A lunatic," she said. It almost cost her her reason to utter the word. There was a pause.

"Did he know you?" asked the husband in a small voice.

"No," she said.

He stood and looked at her. At last he had learned the width of the breach between them. She still squatted on the bed. He could not go near her. It would be violation to each of them to be brought into contact with the other. The thing must work itself out. They were both shocked so much, they were impersonal, and no longer hated each other. After some minutes he left her and went out.

GOOSE FAIR

I

Through the gloom of evening, and the flare of torches of the night before the fair, through the still fogs of the succeeding dawn came paddling the weary geese, lifting their poor feet that had been dipped in tar for shoes, and trailing them along the cobble-stones into the town. Last of all, in the afternoon, a country girl drove in her dozen birds, disconsolate because she was so late. She was a heavily built girl, fair, with regular features, and yet unprepossessing. She needed chiselling down, her contours were brutal. Perhaps it was weariness that hung her eyelids a little lower than was pleasant. When she spoke to her clumsily lagging birds it was in a snarling nasal tone. One of the silly things sat down in the gutter and refused to move. It looked very ridiculous, but also rather pitiful, squat there with its head up, refusing to be urged on by the ungentle toe of the girl. The latter swore heavily, then picked up the great complaining bird, and fronting her road stubbornly, drove on the lamentable eleven.

No one had noticed her. This afternoon the women were not sitting chatting on their doorsteps, seaming up the cotton hose, or swiftly passing through their fingers the piled white lace; and in the high dark houses the song of the hosiery frames was hushed: "Shackety-boom, Shackety-shackety-boom, Z—zzz!" As she dragged up Hollow Stone, people returned from the fair chaffed her and asked her what o'clock it was. She did not reply, her look was sullen. The Lace Market was quiet as the Sabbath: even the great brass plates on the doors were dull with neglect. There seemed an afternoon atmosphere of raw discontent. The girl stopped a moment before the dismal prospect of one of the great warehouses that had been gutted with fire. She looked at the lean, threatening walls, and watched her white flock waddling in reckless misery below, and she would have laughed out loud had the wall fallen flat upon them and relieved her of them. But the wall did not fall, so she crossed the road, and walking on the safe side, hurried after her charge. Her look was even more sullen. She remembered the state of trade—Trade, the invidious enemy; Trade, which thrust out its hand and shut the factory doors, and pulled the stockingers off their seats, and left the web half-finished on the frame; Trade, which mysteriously choked up the sources of the rivulets of wealth, and blacker and more secret than a pestilence, starved the town. Through this morose atmosphere of bad trade, in the afternoon of the first day of the fair, the girl strode down to the Poultry with eleven sound geese and one lame one to sell.

The Frenchmen were at the bottom of it! So everybody said, though nobody quite knew how. At any rate, they had gone to war with the Prussians and got beaten, and trade was ruined in Nottingham!

A little fog rose up, and the twilight gathered around. Then they flared abroad their torches in the fair, insulting the night. The girl still sat in the Poultry, and her weary geese unsold on the stones, illuminated by the hissing lamp of a man who sold rabbits and pigeons and such-like assorted live-stock.

II

In another part of the town, near Sneinton Church, another girl came to the door to look at the night. She was tall and slender, dressed with the severe accuracy which marks the girl of superior culture. Her hair was arranged with simplicity about the long, pale, cleanly cut face. She leaned forward very slightly to glance down the street, listening. She very carefully preserved the appearance of having come quite casually to the door, yet she lingered and lingered and stood very still to listen when she heard a footstep, but when it proved to be only a common man, she drew herself up proudly and looked with a small smile over his head. He hesitated to glance into the open hall, lighted so spaciously with a scarlet-shaded lamp, and at the slim girl in brown silk lifted up before the light. But she, she looked over his head. He passed on.

Presently she started and hung in suspense. Somebody was crossing the road. She ran down the steps in a pretty welcome, not effuse, saying in quick, but accurately articulated words: "Will! I began to think you'd gone to the fair. I came out to listen to it. I felt almost sure you'd gone. You're coming in, aren't you?" She waited a moment anxiously. "We expect you to dinner, you know," she added wistfully.

The man, who had a short face and spoke with his lip curling up on one side, in a drawling speech with ironically exaggerated intonation, replied after a short hesitation:

"I'm awfully sorry, I am, straight, Lois. It's a shame. I've got to go round to the biz. Man proposes—the devil disposes." He turned aside with irony in the darkness.

"But surely, Will!" remonstrated the girl, keenly disappointed.

"Fact, Lois.—I feel wild about it myself. But I've got to go down to the works. They may be getting a bit warm down there, you know"—he jerked his head in the direction of the fair. "If the Lambs get frisky!—they're a bit off about the work, and they'd just be in their element if they could set a lighted match to something—"

"Will, you don't think—!" exclaimed the girl, laying her hand on his arm in the true fashion of romance, and looking up at him earnestly.

"Dad's not sure," he replied, looking down at her with gravity. They remained in this attitude for a moment, then he said:

"I might stop a bit. It's all right for an hour, I should think."

She looked at him earnestly, then said in tones of deep disappointment and of fortitude: "No, Will, you must go. You'd better go—"

"It's a shame!" he murmured, standing a moment at a loose end. Then, glancing down the street to see he was alone, he put his arm round her waist and said in a difficult voice: "How goes it?"

She let him keep her for a moment, then he kissed her as if afraid of what he was doing. They were both uncomfortable.

"Well—!" he said at length.

"Good night!" she said, setting him free to go.

He hung a moment near her, as if ashamed. Then "Good night," he answered, and he broke away. She listened to his footsteps in the night, before composing herself to turn indoors.

"Helloa!" said her father, glancing over his paper as she entered the dining-room. "What's up, then?"

"Oh, nothing," she replied, in her calm tones. "Will won't be here to dinner tonight."

"What, gone to the fair?"

"No."

"Oh! What's got him then?"

Lois looked at her father, and answered:

"He's gone down to the factory. They are afraid of the hands."

Her father looked at her closely.

"Oh, aye!" he answered, undecided, and they sat down to dinner.

III

Lois returned very early. She had a fire in her bedroom. She drew the curtains and stood holding aside a heavy fold, looking out at the night. She could see only the nothingness of the fog; not even the glare of the fair was evident, though the noise clamoured small in the distance. In front of everything she could see her own faint image. She crossed to the dressing-table, and there leaned her face to the mirror, and looked at herself. She looked a long time, then she rose, changed her dress for a dressing-jacket, and took up *Sesame and Lilies*.

Late in the night she was roused from sleep by a bustle in the house. She sat up and heard a hurrying to and fro and the sound of anxious voices. She put on her dressing-gown and went out to her mother's room. Seeing her mother at the head of the stairs, she said in her quick, clean voice:

"Mother, what it it?"

"Oh, child, don't ask me! Go to bed, dear, do! I shall surely be worried out of my life."

"Mother, what is it?" Lois was sharp and emphatic.

"I hope your father won't go. Now I do hope your father won't go. He's got a cold as it is."

"Mother, tell me what is it?" Lois took her mother's arm.

"It's Selby's. I should have thought you would have heard the fire-engine, and Jack isn't in yet. I hope we're safe!" Lois returned to her bedroom and dressed. She coiled her plaited hair, and having put on a cloak, left the house.

She hurried along under the fog-dripping trees towards the meaner part of the town. When she got near, she saw a glare in the fog, and closed her lips tight. She hastened on till she was in the crowd. With peaked, noble face she watched the fire. Then she looked a little wildly over the fire-reddened faces in the crowd, and catching sight of her father, hurried to him.

"Oh, Dadda—is he safe? Is Will safe—?"

"Safe, aye, why not? You've no business here. Here, here's Sampson, he'll take you home. I've enough to bother me; there's my own place to watch. Go home now, I can't do with you here."

"Have you seen Will?" she asked.

"Go home—Sampson, just take Miss Lois home—now!"

"You don't really know where he is—father?"

"Go home now—I don't want you here—" her father ordered peremptorily.

The tears sprang to Lois' eyes. She looked at the fire and the tears were quickly dried by fear. The flames roared and struggled upward. The great wonder of the fire made her forget even her indignation at her father's light treatment of herself and of her lover. There was a crashing and bursting of timber, as the first floor fell in a mass into the blazing gulf, splashing the fire in all directions, to the terror of the crowd. She saw the steel of the machines growing white-hot and twisting like flaming letters. Piece after piece of the flooring gave way, and the machines dropped in red ruin as the wooden framework burned out. The air became unbreathable; the fog was swallowed up: sparks went rushing up as if they would burn the dark heavens; sometimes cards of lace went whirling into the gulf of the sky, waving with wings of fire. It was dangerous to stand near this great cup of roaring destruction.

Sampson, the grey old manager of Buxton and Co's, led her away as soon as she would turn her face to listen to him. He was a stout, irritable man. He elbowed his way roughly through the crowd, and Lois followed him, her head high, her lips closed. He led her for some distance without speaking, then at last, unable to contain his garrulous irritability, he broke out:

"What do they expect? What can they expect? They can't expect to stand a bad time. They spring up like mushrooms as big as a house-side, but there's no stability in 'em. I remember William Selby when he'd run on my errands. Yes, there's some as can make much out of little, and there's some as can make much out of nothing, but they find it won't last. William Selby's sprung up in a day, and he'll vanish in a night. You can't trust to luck alone. Maybe he thinks it's a lucky thing this fire has come when things are looking black. But you can't get out of it as easy as that. There's been a few too many of 'em. No, indeed, a fire's the last thing I should hope to come to—the very last!"

Lois hurried and hurried, so that she brought the old manager panting in distress up the steps of her home. She could not bear to hear him talking so. They could get no one to open the door for some time. When at last Lois ran upstairs, she found her mother dressed, but all unbuttoned again, lying back in the chair in her daughter's room, suffering from palpitation of the heart, with *Sesame and Lilies* crushed beneath her. Lois administered brandy, and her decisive words and movements helped largely to bring the good lady to a state of recovery sufficient to allow of her returning to her own bedroom.

Then Lois locked the door. She glanced at her fire-darkened face, and taking the flattened Ruskin out of the chair, sat down and wept. After a while she calmed herself, rose, and sponged her face. Then once more on that fatal night she prepared for rest. Instead, however, or retiring, she pulled a silk quilt from her disordered bed and wrapping it round her, sat miserably to think. It was two o'clock in the morning.

IV

The fire was sunk to cold ashes in the grate, and the grey morning was creeping through the half-opened curtains like a thing ashamed, when Lois awoke. It was painful to move her head: her neck was cramped. The girl awoke in full recollection. She sighed, roused herself and pulled the quilt closer about her. For a little while she sat and mused. A pale, tragic resignation fixed her face like a mask. She remembered her father's irritable answer to her question concerning her lover's safety—"Safe, aye—why not?" She knew that he suspected the factory of having been purposely set on fire. But then, he had never liked Will. And yet—and yet—Lois' heart was heavy as lead. She felt her lover was guilty. And she felt she must hide her secret of his last communication to her. She saw herself being cross-examined—"When did you last see this man?" But she would hide what he had said about watching at the works. How dreary it was—and how dreadful. Her life was ruined now, and nothing mattered any more. She must only behave with dignity, and submit to her own obliteration. For even if Will were never accused, she knew in her heart he was guilty. She knew it was over between them.

It was dawn among the yellow fog outside, and Lois, as she moved mechanically about her toilet, vaguely felt that all her days would arrive slowly struggling through a bleak fog. She felt an intense longing at this uncanny hour to slough the body's trammelled weariness and to issue at once into the new bright warmth of the far Dawn where a lover waited transfigured; it is so easy and pleasant in imagination to step out of the chill grey dampness of another terrestrial daybreak, straight into the sunshine of the eternal morning! And who can escape his hour? So Lois performed the meaningless routine of her toilet, which at last she made meaningful when she took her black dress, and fastened a black jet brooch at her throat.

Then she went downstairs and found her father eating a mutton chop. She quickly approached and kissed him on the forehead. Then she retreated to the other end of the table. Her father looked tired, even haggard.

"You are early," he said, after a while. Lois did not reply. Her father continued to eat for a few moments, then he said:

"Have a chop—here's one! Ring for a hot plate. Eh, what? Why not?"

Lois was insulted, but she gave no sign. She sat down and took a cup of coffee, making no pretence to eat. Her father was absorbed, and had forgotten her.

"Our Jack's not come home yet," he said at last.

Lois stirred faintly. "Hasn't he?" she said.

"No." There was silence for a time. Lois was frightened. Had something happened also to her brother? This fear was closer and more irksome.

"Selby's was cleaned out, gutted. We had a near shave of it—"

"You have no loss, Dadda?"

"Nothing to mention." After another silence, her father said:

"I'd rather be myself than William Selby. Of course it may merely be bad luck—you don't know. But whatever it was, I wouldn't like to add one to the list of fires just now. Selby was at the 'George' when it broke out—I don't know where the lad was—!"

"Father," broke in Lois, "why do you talk like that? Why do you talk as if Will had done it?" She ended suddenly. Her father looked at her pale, mute face.

"I don't talk as if Will had done it," he said. "I don't even think it."

Feeling she was going to cry, Lois rose and left the room. Her father sighed, and leaning his elbows on his knees, whistled faintly into the fire. He was not thinking about her.

Lois went down to the kitchen and asked Lucy, the parlour-maid, to go out with her. She somehow shrank from going alone, lest people should stare at her overmuch: and she felt an overpowering impulse to go to the scene of the tragedy, to judge for herself.

The churches were chiming half-past eight when the young lady and the maid set off down the street. Nearer the fair, swarthy, thin-legged men were pushing barrels of water towards the market-place, and the gipsy women, with hard brows, and dressed in tight velvet bodices, hurried along the pavement with jugs of milk, and great brass water ewers and loaves and breakfast parcels. People were just getting up, and in the poorer streets was a continual splash of tea-leaves, flung out on to the cobble-stones. A teapot came crashing down from an upper story just behind Lois, and she, starting round and looking up, thought that the trembling, drink-bleared man at the upper window, who was stupidly staring after his pot, had had designs on her life; and she went on her way shuddering at the grim tragedy of life.

In the dull October morning the ruined factory was black and ghastly. The window-frames were all jagged, and the walls stood gaunt. Inside was a tangle of twisted *débris*, the iron, in parts red with bright rust, looking still hot; the charred wood was black and satiny; from dishevelled heaps, sodden with water, a faint smoke rose dimly. Lois stood and looked. If he had done that! He might even be dead there, burned to ash and lost for ever. It was almost soothing to feel so. He would be safe in the eternity which now she must hope in.

At her side the pretty, sympathetic maid chatted plaintively. Suddenly, from one of her lapses into silence, she exclaimed:

"Why if there isn't Mr. Jack!"

Lois turned suddenly and saw her brother and her lover approaching her. Both looked soiled, untidy and wan. Will had a black eye, some ten hours old, well coloured. Lois turned very pale as they approached. They were looking gloomily at the factory, and for a moment did not notice the girls.

"I'll be jiggered if there ain't our Lois!" exclaimed Jack, the reprobate, swearing under his breath.

"Oh, God!" exclaimed the other in disgust.

"Jack, where have you been?" said Lois sharply, in keen pain, not looking at her lover. Her sharp tone of suffering drove her lover to defend himself with an affectation of comic recklessness.

"In quod," replied her brother, smiling sickly.

"Jack!" cried his sister very sharply.

"Fact."

Will Selby shuffled on his feet and smiled, trying to turn away his face so that she should not see his black eye. She glanced at him. He felt her boundless anger and contempt, and with great courage he looked straight at her, smiling ironically. Unfortunately his smile would not go over his swollen eye, which remained grave and lurid.

"Do I look pretty?" he inquired with a hateful twist of his lip.

"Very!" she replied.

"I thought I did," he replied. And he turned to look at his father's ruined works, and he felt miserable and stubborn. The girl standing there so clean and out of it all! Oh, God, he felt sick. He turned to go home.

The three went together, Lois silent in anger and resentment. Her brother was tired and overstrung, but not suppressed. He chattered on blindly.

"It was a lark we had! We met Bob Osborne and Freddy Mansell coming down Poultry. There was girl with some geese. She looked a tanger sitting there, all like statues, her and the geese. It was Will who began it. He offered her three-pence and asked her to begin the show. She called him a—she called him something, and then somebody poked an old gander to stir him up, and somebody squirted him in the eye. He upped and squawked and started off with his neck out. Laugh! We nearly killed ourselves, keeping back those old birds with squirts and teasers. Oh, Lum! Those old geese, oh, scrimmy, they didn't know where to turn, they fairly went off their dots, coming at us right an' left, and such a row—it was fun, you never knew! Then the girl she got up and knocked somebody over the jaw, and we were right in for it. Well, in the end, Billy here got hold of her round the waist—"

"Oh, dry it up!" exclaimed Will bitterly.

Jack looked at him, laughed mirthlessly, and continued: "An' we said we'd buy her birds. So we got hold of one goose apiece—an' they took some holding, I can tell you—and off we set round the fair, Billy leading with the girl. The bloomin' geese squawked an' pecked. Laugh—I thought I should a' died. Well, then we wanted the girl to have her birds back—and then she fired up. She got some other chaps on her side, and there was a proper old row. The girl went tooth and nail for Will there—she was dead set against him. She gave him a black eye, by gum, and we went at it, I can tell you. It was a free fight, a beauty, an' we got run in. I don't know what became of the girl."

Lois surveyed the two men. There was no glimmer of a smile on her face, though the maid behind her was sniggering. Will was very bitter. He glanced at his sweetheart and at the ruined factory.

"How's dad taken it?" he asked, in a biting, almost humble tone.

"I don't know," she replied coldly. "Father's in an awful way. I believe everybody thinks you set the place on fire."

Lois drew herself up. She had delivered her blow. She drew herself up in cold condemnation and for a moment enjoyed her complete revenge. He was despicable, abject in his dishevelled, disfigured, unwashed condition.

"Aye, well, they made a mistake for once," he replied, with a curl of the lip.

Curiously enough, they walked side by side as if they belonged to each other. She was his conscience-keeper. She was far from forgiving him, but she was still farther from letting him go. And he walked at her side like a boy who had to be punished before he can be exonerated. He submitted. But there was a genuine bitter contempt in the curl of his lip.

THE WHITE STOCKING

I

"I'm getting up, Teddilinks," said Mrs. Whiston, and she sprang out of bed briskly.

"What the Hanover's got you?" asked Whiston.

"Nothing. Can't I get up?" she replied animatedly.

It was about seven o'clock, scarcely light yet in the cold bedroom. Whiston lay still and looked at his wife. She was a pretty little thing, with her fleecy, short black hair all tousled . . . He watched her as she dressed quickly, flicking her small, delightful limbs, throwing her clothes about her. Her slovenliness and untidiness did not trouble him. When she picked up the edge of her petticoat, ripped off a torn string of white lace, and flung it on the dressing-table, her careless abandon made his spirit glow. She stood before the mirror and roughly scrambled together her profuse little mane of hair. He watched the quickness and softness of her young shoulders, calmly, like a husband, and appreciatively.

"Rise up," she cried, turning to him with a quick wave of her arm—"and shine forth."

They had been married two years. But still, when she had gone out of the room, he felt as if all his light and warmth were taken away, he became aware of the raw, cold morning. So he rose himself, wondering casually what had roused her so early. Usually she lay in bed as late as she could.

Whiston fastened a belt round his loins and went downstairs in shirt and trousers. He heard her singing in her snatchy fashion. The stairs creaked under his weight. He passed down the narrow little passage, which she called a hall, of the seven and sixpenny house which was his first home.

He was a shapely young fellow of about twenty-eight, sleepy now and easy with well-being. He heard the water drumming into the kettle, and she began to whistle. He loved the quick way she dodged the supper cups under the tap to wash them for breakfast. She looked an untidy minx, but she was quick and handy enough.

"Teddilinks," she cried.

"What?"

"Light a fire, quick."

She wore an old, sack-like dressing-jacket of black silk pinned across her breast. But one of the sleeves, coming unfastened, showed some delightful pink upper-arm.

"Why don't you sew your sleeve up?" he said, suffering from the sight of the exposed soft flesh.

"Where?" she cried, peering round. "Nuisance," she said, seeing the gap, then with light fingers went on drying the cups.

The kitchen was of fair size, but gloomy. Whiston poked out the dead ashes.

Suddenly a thud was heard at the door down the passage.

"I'll go," cried Mrs. Whiston, and she was gone down the hall.

The postman was a ruddy-faced man who had been a soldier. He smiled broadly, handing her some packages.

"They've not forgot you," he said impudently.

"No—lucky for them," she said, with a toss of the head. But she was interested only in her envelopes this morning. The postman waited inquisitively, smiling in an ingratiating fashion. She slowly, abstractedly, as if she did not know anyone was there, closed the door in his face, continuing to look at the addresses on her letters.

She tore open the thin envelope. There was a long, hideous, cartoon valentine. She smiled briefly and dropped it on the floor. Struggling with the string of a packet, she opened a white cardboard box, and there lay a white silk handkerchief packed neatly under the paper lace of the box, and her initial, worked in heliotrope, fully displayed. She smiled pleasantly, and gently put the box aside. The third envelope contained another white packet—apparently a cotton handkerchief neatly folded. She shook it out. It was a long white stocking, but there was a little weight in the toe. Quickly, she thrust down her arm, wriggling her fingers into the toe of the stocking, and brought out a small box. She peeped inside the box, then hastily opened a door on her left hand, and went into the little, cold sitting-room. She had her lower lip caught earnestly between her teeth.

With a little flash of triumph, she lifted a pair of pearl ear-rings from the small box, and she went to the mirror. There, earnestly, she began to hook them through her ears, looking at herself sideways in the glass. Curiously concentrated and intent she seemed as she fingered the lobes of her ears, her head bent on one side.

Then the pearl ear-rings dangled under her rosy, small ears. She shook her head sharply, to see the swing of the drops. They went chill against her neck, in little, sharp touches. Then she stood still to look at herself, bridling her head in the dignified fashion. Then she simpered at herself. Catching her own eye, she could not help winking at herself and laughing.

She turned to look at the box. There was a scrap of paper with this posy:

"Pearls may be fair, but thou art fairer.
Wear these for me, and I'll love the wearer."

She made a grimace and a grin. But she was drawn to the mirror again, to look at her ear-rings.

Whiston had made the fire burn, so he came to look for her. When she heard him, she started round quickly, guiltily. She was watching him with intent blue eyes when he appeared.

He did not see much, in his morning-drowsy warmth. He gave her, as ever, a feeling of warmth and slowness. His eyes were very blue, very kind, his manner simple.

"What ha' you got?" he asked.

"Valentines," she said briskly, ostentatiously turning to show him the silk handkerchief. She thrust it under his nose. "Smell how good," she said.

"Who's that from?" he replied, without smelling.

"It's a valentine," she cried. "How da I know who it's from?"

"I'll bet you know," he said.

"Ted!—I don't!" she cried, beginning to shake her head, then stopping because of the ear-rings.

He stood still a moment, displeased.

"They've no right to send you valentines, now," he said.

"Ted!—Why not? You're not jealous, are you? I haven't the least idea who it's from. Look—there's my initial"—she pointed with an emphatic finger at the heliotrope embroidery—

> "E for Elsie,
> Nice little gelsie,"

she sang.

"Get out," he said. "You know who it's from."

"Truth, I don't," she cried.

He looked round, and saw the white stocking lying on a chair.

"Is this another?" he said.

"No, that's a sample," she said. "There's only a comic." And she fetched in the long cartoon.

He stretched it out and looked at it solemnly.

"Fools!" he said, and went out of the room.

She flew upstairs and took off the ear-rings. When she returned, he was crouched before the fire blowing the coals. The skin of his face was flushed, and slightly pitted, as if he had had small-pox. But his neck was white and smooth and goodly. She hung her arms round his neck as he crouched there, and clung to him. He balanced on his toes.

"This fire's a slow-coach," he said.

"And who else is a slow-coach?" she said.

"One of us two, I know," he said, and he rose carefully. She remained clinging round his neck, so that she was lifted off her feet.

"Ha!—swing me," she cried.

He lowered his head, and she hung in the air, swinging from his neck, laughing. Then she slipped off.

"The kettle is singing," she sang, flying for the teapot. He bent down again to blow the fire. The veins in his neck stood out, his shirt collar seemed too tight.

> "Doctor Wyer,
> Blow the fire,
> Puff! puff! puff!"

she sang, laughing.

He smiled at her.

She was so glad because of her pearl ear-rings.

Over the breakfast she grew serious. He did not notice. She became portentous in her gravity. Almost it penetrated through his steady good-humour to irritate him.

"Teddy!" she said at last.

"What?" he asked.

"I told you a lie," she said, humbly tragic.

His soul stirred uneasily.

"Oh aye?" he said casually.

She was not satisfied. He ought to be more moved.

"Yes," she said.

He cut a piece of bread.

"Was it a good one?" he asked.

She was piqued. Then she considered—was it a good one? Then she laughed.

"No," she said, "it wasn't up to much."

"Ah!" he said easily, but with a steady strength of fondness for her in his tone. "Get it out then."

It became a little more difficult.

"You know that white stocking," she said earnestly. "I told you a lie. It wasn't a sample. It was a valentine."

A little frown came on his brow.

"Then what did you invent it as a sample for?" he said. But he knew this weakness of hers. The touch of anger in his voice frightened her.

"I was afraid you'd be cross," she said pathetically.

"I'll bet you were vastly afraid," he said.

"I *was*, Teddy."

There was a pause. He was resolving one or two things in his mind.

"And who sent it?" he asked.

"I can guess," she said, "though there wasn't a word with it—except—"

She ran to the sitting-room and returned with a slip of paper.

> "Pearls may be fair, but thou art fairer.
> Wear these for me, and I'll love the wearer."

He read it twice, then a dull red flush came on his face.

"And *who* do you guess it is?" he asked, with a ringing of anger in his voice.

"I suspect it's Sam Adams," she said, with a little virtuous indignation.

Whiston was silent for a moment.

"Fool!" he said. "An' what's it got to do with pearls?—and how can he say 'wear these for me' when there's only one? He hasn't got the brain to invent a proper verse."

He screwed the sup of paper into a ball and flung it into the fire.

"I suppose he thinks it'll make a pair with the one last year," she said.

"Why, did he send one then?"

"Yes. I thought you'd be wild if you knew."

His jaw set rather sullenly.

Presently he rose, and went to wash himself, rolling back his sleeves and pulling open his shirt at the breast. It was as if his fine, clear-cut temples and steady eyes were degraded by the lower, rather brutal part of his face. But she loved it. As she whisked about, clearing the table, she loved the way in which he stood washing himself. He was such a man. She liked to see his neck glistening with water as he swilled it. It amused her and pleased her and thrilled her. He was so sure, so permanent, he had her so utterly in his power. It gave her a delightful, mischievous sense of liberty. Within his grasp, she could dart about excitingly.

He turned round to her, his face red from the cold water, his eyes fresh and very blue.

"You haven't been seeing anything of him, have you?" he asked roughly.

"Yes," she answered, after a moment, as if caught guilty. "He got into the tram with me, and he asked me to drink a coffee and a Benedictine in the Royal."

"You've got it off fine and glib," he said sullenly. "And did you?"

"Yes," she replied, with the air of a traitor before the rack.

The blood came up into his neck and face, he stood motionless, dangerous.

"It was cold, and it was such fun to go into the Royal," she said.

"You'd go off with a nigger for a packet of chocolate," he said, in anger and contempt, and some bitterness. Queer how he drew away from her, cut her off from him.

"Ted—how beastly!" she cried. "You know quite well—" She caught her lip, flushed, and the tears came to her eyes.

He turned away, to put on his necktie. She went about her work, making a queer pathetic little mouth, down which occasionally dripped a tear.

He was ready to go. With his hat jammed down on his head, and his overcoat buttoned up to his chin, he came to kiss her. He would be miserable all the day if he went without. She allowed herself to be kissed. Her cheek was wet under his lips, and his heart burned. She hurt him so deeply. And she felt aggrieved, and did not quite forgive him.

In a moment she went upstairs to her ear-rings. Sweet they looked nestling in the little drawer—sweet! She examined them with voluptuous pleasure, she threaded them in her ears, she looked at herself, she posed and postured and smiled, and looked sad and tragic and winning and appealing, all in turn before the mirror. And she was happy, and very pretty.

She wore her ear-rings all morning, in the house. She was self-conscious, and quite brilliantly winsome, when the baker came, wondering if he would notice. All the tradesmen left her door with a glow in them, feeling elated, and unconsciously favouring the delightful little creature, though there had been nothing to notice in her behaviour.

She was stimulated all the day. She did not think about her husband. He was the permanent basis from which she took these giddy little flights into nowhere. At night, like chickens and curses, she would come home to him, to roost.

Meanwhile Whiston, a traveller and confidential support of a small firm, hastened about his work, his heart all the while anxious for her, yearning for surety, and kept tense by not getting it.

II

She had been a warehouse girl in Adams's lace factory before she was married. Sam Adams was her employer. He was a bachelor of forty, growing stout, a man well dressed and florid, with a large brown moustache and thin hair. From the rest of his well-groomed, showy appearance, it was evident his baldness was a chagrin to him. He had a good presence, and some Irish blood in his veins.

His fondness for the girls, or the fondness of the girls for him, was notorious. And Elsie, quick, pretty, almost witty little thing—she *seemed* witty, although, when her sayings were repeated, they were entirely trivial—she had a great attraction for him. He would come into the warehouse dressed in a rather sporting reefer coat, of fawn colour, and trousers of fine black-and-white check, a cap with a big peak and a scarlet carnation in his button-hole, to impress her. She was only half impressed. He was too loud for her good taste. Instinctively perceiving this, he sobered down to navy blue. Then a well-built man, florid, with large brown whiskers, smart navy blue suit, fashionable boots, and manly hat, he was the irreproachable. Elsie was impressed.

But meanwhile Whiston was courting her, and she made splendid little gestures, before her bedroom mirror, of the constant-and-true sort.

"True, true till death—"

That was her song. Whiston was made that way, so there was no need to take thought for him.

Every Christmas Sam Adams gave a party at his house, to which he invited his superior work-people—not factory hands and labourers, but those above. He was a generous man in his way, with a real warm feeling for giving pleasure.

Two years ago Elsie had attended this Christmas-party for the last time. Whiston had accompanied her. At that time he worked for Sam Adams.

She had been very proud of herself, in her close-fitting, full-skirted dress of blue silk. Whiston called for her. Then she tripped beside him, holding her large cashmere shawl across her breast. He strode with long strides, his trousers handsomely strapped under his boots, and her silk shoes bulging the pockets of his full-skirted overcoat.

They passed through the park gates, and her spirits rose. Above them the Castle Rock looked grandly in the night, the naked trees stood still and dark in the frost, along the boulevard.

They were rather late. Agitated with anticipation, in the cloak-room she gave up her shawl, donned her silk shoes, and looked at herself in the mirror. The loose bunches of curls on either side her face danced prettily, her mouth smiled.

She hung a moment in the door of the brilliantly lighted room. Many people were moving within the blaze of lamps, under the crystal chandeliers, the full skirts of the women balancing and floating, the side-whiskers and white cravats of the men bowing above. Then she entered the light.

In an instant Sam Adams was coming forward, lifting both his arms in boisterous welcome. There was a constant red laugh on his face.

"Come late, would you," he shouted, "like royalty."

He seized her hands and led her forward. He opened his mouth wide when he spoke, and the effect of the warm, dark opening behind the brown whiskers was disturbing. But she was floating into the throng on his arm. He was very gallant.

"Now then," he said, taking her card to write down the dances, "I've got carte blanche, haven't I?"

"Mr. Whiston doesn't dance," she said.

"I am a lucky man!" he said, scribbling his initials. "I was born with an *amourette* in my mouth."

He wrote on, quietly. She blushed and laughed, not knowing what it meant.

"Why, what is that?" she said.

"It's you, even littler than you are, dressed in little wings," he said.

"I should have to be pretty small to get in your mouth," she said.

"You think you're too big, do you!" he said easily.

He handed her her card, with a bow.

"Now I'm set up, my darling, for this evening," he said.

Then, quick, always at his ease, he looked over the room. She waited in front of him. He was ready. Catching the eye of the band, he nodded. In a moment, the music began. He seemed to relax, giving himself up.

"Now then, Elsie," he said, with a curious caress in his voice that seemed to lap the outside of her body in a warm glow, delicious. She gave herself to it. She liked it.

He was an excellent dancer. He seemed to draw her close in to him by some male warmth of attraction, so that she became all soft and pliant to him, flowing to his form, whilst he united her with him and they lapsed along in one movement. She was just carried in a kind of strong, warm flood, her feet moved of themselves, and only the music threw her away from him, threw her back to him, to his clasp, in his strong form moving against her, rhythmically, deliriously.

When it was over, he was pleased and his eyes had a curious gleam which thrilled her and yet had nothing to do with her. Yet it held her. He did not speak to her. He only looked straight into her eyes with a curious, gleaming look that disturbed her fearfully and deliriously. But also there was in his look some of the automatic irony of the *roué*. It left her partly cold. She was not carried away.

She went, driven by an opposite, heavier impulse, to Whiston. He stood looking gloomy, trying to admit that she had a perfect right to enjoy herself apart from him. He received her with rather grudging kindliness.

"Aren't you going to play whist?" she asked.

"Aye," he said. "Directly."

"I do wish you could dance."

"Well, I can't," he said. "So you enjoy yourself."

"But I should enjoy it better if I could dance with you."

"Nay, you're all right," he said. "I'm not made that way."

"Then you ought to be!" she cried.

"Well, it's my fault, not yours. You enjoy yourself," he bade her. Which she proceeded to do, a little bit irked.

She went with anticipation to the arms of Sam Adams, when the time came to dance with him. It was so gratifying, irrespective of the man. And she felt a little grudge against Whiston, soon forgotten when her host was holding her near to him, in a delicious embrace. And she watched his eyes, to meet the gleam in them, which gratified her.

She was getting warmed right through, the glow was penetrating into her, driving away everything else. Only in her heart was a little tightness, like conscience.

When she got a chance, she escaped from the dancing-room to the card-room. There, in a cloud of smoke, she found Whiston playing cribbage. Radiant, roused, animated, she came up to him and greeted him. She was too strong, too vibrant a note in the quiet room. He lifted his head, and a frown knitted his gloomy forehead.

"Are you playing cribbage? Is it exciting? How are you getting on?" she chattered.

He looked at her. None of these questions needed answering, and he did not feel in touch with her. She turned to the cribbage-board.

"Are you white or red?" she asked.

"He's red," replied the partner.

"Then you're losing," she said, still to Whiston. And she lifted the red peg from the board. "One—two—three—four—five—six—seven—eight—Right up there you ought to jump—"

"Now put it back in its right place," said Whiston.

"Where was it?" she asked gaily, knowing her transgression. He took the little red peg away from her and stuck it in its hole.

The cards were shuffled.

"What a shame you're losing!" said Elsie.

"You'd better cut for him," said the partner.

She did so, hastily. The cards were dealt. She put her hand on his shoulder, looking at his cards.

"It's good," she cried, "isn't it?"

He did not answer, but threw down two cards. It moved him more strongly than was comfortable, to have her hand on his shoulder, her curls dangling and touching his ears, whilst she was roused to another man. It made the blood flame over him.

At that moment Sam Adams appeared, florid and boisterous, intoxicated more with himself, with the dancing, than with wine. In his eyes the curious, impersonal light gleamed.

"I thought I should find you here, Elsie," he cried boisterously, a disturbing, high note in his voice.

"What made you think so?" she replied, the mischief rousing in her.

The florid, well-built man narrowed his eyes to a smile.

"I should never look for you among the ladies," he said, with a kind of intimate, animal call to her. He laughed, bowed, and offered her his arm.

"Madam, the music waits."

She went almost helplessly, carried along with him, unwilling, yet delighted.

That dance was an intoxication to her. After the first few steps, she felt herself slipping away from herself. She almost knew she was going, she did not even want to go. Yet she must have chosen to go. She lay in the arm of the steady, close man with whom she was dancing, and she seemed to swim away out of contact with the room, into him. She had passed into another, denser element of him, an essential privacy. The room was all vague around her, like an atmosphere, like under sea, with a flow of ghostly, dumb movements. But she herself was held real against her partner, and it seemed she was connected with him, as if the movements of his body and limbs were her own movements, yet not her own movements—and oh, delicious! He also was given up, oblivious, concentrated, into the dance. His eye was unseeing. Only his large, voluptuous body gave off a subtle activity. His fingers seemed to search into her flesh. Every moment, and every moment, she felt she would give way utterly, and sink molten: the fusion point was coming when she would fuse down into perfect unconsciousness at his feet and knees. But he bore her round the room in the dance, and he seemed to sustain all her body with his limbs, his body, and his warmth seemed to come closer into her, nearer, till it would fuse right through her, and she would be as liquid to him, as an intoxication only.

It was exquisite. When it was over, she was dazed, and was scarcely breathing. She stood with him in the middle of the room as if she were alone in a remote place. He bent over her. She expected his lips on her bare shoulder, and waited. Yet they were not alone, they were not alone. It was cruel.

"'Twas good, wasn't it, my darling?" he said to her, low and delighted. There was a strange impersonality about his low, exultant call that appealed to her irresistibly. Yet why was she aware of some part shut off in her? She pressed his arm, and he led her towards the door.

She was not aware of what she was doing, only a little grain of resistant trouble was in her. The man, possessed, yet with a superficial presence of mind, made way to the dining-room, as if to give her refreshment, cunningly working to his own escape with her. He was molten hot, filmed over with presence of mind, and bottomed with cold disbelief.

In the dining-room was Whiston, carrying coffee to the plain, neglected ladies. Elsie saw him, but felt as if he could not see her. She was beyond his reach and ken. A sort of fusion existed between her and the large man at her side. She ate her custard, but an incomplete fusion all the while sustained and contained her within the being of her employer.

But she was growing cooler. Whiston came up. She looked at him, and saw him with different eyes. She saw his slim, young man's figure real and enduring before her. That was he. But she was in the spell with the other man, fused with him, and she could not be taken away.

"Have you finished your cribbage?" she asked, with hasty evasion of him.

"Yes," he replied. "Aren't you getting tired of dancing?"

"Not a bit," she said.

"Not she," said Adams heartily. "No girl with any spirit gets tired of dancing.—Have something else, Elsie. Come—sherry. Have a glass of sherry with us, Whiston."

Whilst they sipped the wine, Adams watched Whiston almost cunningly, to find his advantage.

"We'd better be getting back—there's the music," he said. "See the women get something to eat, Whiston, will you, there's a good chap."

And he began to draw away. Elsie was drifting helplessly with him. But Whiston put himself beside them, and went along with them. In silence they passed through to the dancing-room. There Adams hesitated, and looked round the room. It was as if he could not see.

A man came hurrying forward, claiming Elsie, and Adams went to his other partner. Whiston stood watching during the dance. She was conscious of him standing there observant of her, like a ghost, or a judgment, or a guardian angel. She was also conscious, much more intimately and impersonally, of the body of the other man moving somewhere in the room. She still belonged to him, but a feeling of distraction possessed her, and helplessness. Adams danced on, adhering to Elsie, waiting his time, with the persistence of cynicism.

The dance was over. Adams was detained. Elsie found herself beside Whiston. There was something shapely about him as he sat, about his knees and his distinct figure, that she clung to. It was as if he had enduring form. She put her hand on his knee.

"Are you enjoying yourself?" he asked.

"*Ever* so," she replied, with a fervent, yet detached tone.

"It's going on for one o'clock," he said.

"Is it?" she answered. It meant nothing to her.

"Should we be going?" he said.

She was silent. For the first time for an hour or more an inkling of her normal consciousness returned. She resented it.

"What for?" she said.

"I thought you might have had enough," he said.

A slight soberness came over her, an irritation at being frustrated of her illusion.

"Why?" she said.

"We've been here since nine," he said.

That was no answer, no reason. It conveyed nothing to her. She sat detached from him. Across the room Sam Adams glanced at her. She sat there exposed for him.

"You don't want to be too free with Sam Adams," said Whiston cautiously, suffering. "You know what he is."

"How, free?" she asked.

"Why—you don't want to have too much to do with him."

She sat silent. He was forcing her into consciousness of her position. But he could not get hold of her feelings, to change them. She had a curious, perverse desire that he should not.

"I like him," she said.

"What do you find to like in him?" he said, with a hot heart.

"I don't know—but I like him," she said.

She was immutable. He sat feeling heavy and dulled with rage. He was not clear as to what he felt. He sat there unliving whilst she danced. And she, distracted, lost to herself between the opposing forces of the two men, drifted. Between the dances, Whiston kept near to her. She was scarcely conscious. She glanced repeatedly at her card, to see when she would dance again with Adams, half in desire, half in dread. Sometimes she met his steady, glaucous eye as she passed him in the dance. Sometimes she saw the steadiness of his flank as he danced. And it was always as if she rested on his arm, were borne along, upborne by him, away from herself. And always there was present the other's antagonism. She was divided.

The time came for her to dance with Adams. Oh, the delicious closing of contact with him, of his limbs touching her limbs, his arm supporting her. She seemed to resolve. Whiston had not made himself real to her. He was only a heavy place in her consciousness.

But she breathed heavily, beginning to suffer from the closeness of strain. She was nervous. Adams also was constrained. A tightness, a tension was coming over them all. And he was exasperated, feeling something counteracting physical magnetism, feeling a will stronger with her than his own, intervening in what was becoming a vital necessity to him.

Elsie was almost lost to her own control. As she went forward with him to take her place at the dance, she stooped for her pocket-handkerchief. The music sounded for quadrilles. Everybody was ready. Adams stood with his body near her, exerting his attraction over her. He was tense and fighting. She stooped for her pocket-handkerchief, and shook it as she rose. It shook out and fell from her hand. With agony, she saw she had taken a white stocking instead of a handkerchief. For a second it lay on the floor, a twist of white stocking. Then, in an instant, Adams picked it up, with a little, surprised laugh of triumph.

"That'll do for me," he whispered—seeming to take possession of her. And he stuffed the stocking in his trousers pocket, and quickly offered her his handkerchief.

The dance began. She felt weak and faint, as if her will were turned to water. A heavy sense of loss came over her. She could not help herself anymore. But it was peace.

When the dance was over, Adams yielded her up. Whiston came to her.

"What was it as you dropped?" Whiston asked.

"I thought it was my handkerchief—I'd taken a stocking by mistake," she said, detached and muted.

"And he's got it?"

"Yes."

"What does he mean by that?"

She lifted her shoulders.

"Are you going to let him keep it?" he asked.

"I don't let him."

There was a long pause.

"Am I to go and have it out with him?" he asked, his face flushed, his blue eyes going hard with opposition.

"No," she said, pale.

"Why?"

"No—I don't want to say anything about it."

He sat exasperated and nonplussed.

"You'll let him keep it, then?" he asked.

She sat silent and made no form of answer.

"What do you mean by it?" he said, dark with fury. And he started up.

"No!" she cried. "Ted!" And she caught hold of him, sharply detaining him.

It made him black with rage.

"Why?" he said.

Then something about her mouth was pitiful to him. He did not understand, but he felt she must have her reasons.

"Then I'm not stopping here," he said. "Are you coming with me?"

She rose mutely, and they went out of the room. Adams had not noticed.

In a few moments they were in the street.

"What the hell do you mean?" he said, in a black fury.

She went at his side, in silence, neutral.

"That great hog, an' all," he added.

Then they went a long time in silence through the frozen, deserted darkness of the town. She felt she could not go indoors. They were drawing near her house.

"I don't want to go home," she suddenly cried in distress and anguish. "I don't want to go home."

He looked at her.

"Why don't you?" he said.

"I don't want to go home," was all she could sob.

He heard somebody coming.

"Well, we can walk a bit further," he said.

She was silent again. They passed out of the town into the fields. He held her by the arm—they could not speak.

"What's a-matter?" he asked at length, puzzled.

She began to cry again.

At last he took her in his arms, to soothe her. She sobbed by herself, almost unaware of him.

"Tell me what's a-matter, Elsie," he said. "Tell me what's a-matter—my dear—tell me, then—"

He kissed her wet face, and caressed her. She made no response. He was puzzled and tender and miserable.

At length she became quiet. Then he kissed her, and she put her arms round him, and clung to him very tight, as if for fear and anguish. He held her in his arms, wondering.

"Ted!" she whispered, frantic. "Ted!"

"What, my love?" he answered, becoming also afraid.

"Be good to me," she cried. "Don't be cruel to me."

"No, my pet," he said, amazed and grieved. "Why?"

"Oh, be good to me," she sobbed.

And he held her very safe, and his heart was white-hot with love for her. His mind was amazed. He could only hold her against his chest that was white-hot with love and belief in her. So she was restored at last.

III

She refused to go to her work at Adams's any more. Her father had to submit and she sent in her notice—she was not well. Sam Adams was ironical. But he had a curious patience. He did not fight.

In a few weeks, she and Whiston were married. She loved him with passion and worship, a fierce little abandon of love that moved him to the depths of his being, and gave him a permanent surety and sense of realness in himself. He did not trouble about himself any more: he felt he was fulfilled and now he had only the many things in the world to busy himself about. Whatever troubled him, at the bottom was surety. He had found himself in this love.

They spoke once or twice of the white stocking.

"Ah!" Whiston exclaimed. "What does it matter?"

He was impatient and angry, and could not bear to consider the matter. So it was left unresolved.

She was quite happy at first, carried away by her adoration of her husband. Then gradually she got used to him. He always was the ground of her happiness, but she got used to him, as to the air she breathed. He never got used to her in the same way.

Inside of marriage she found her liberty. She was rid of the responsibility of herself. Her husband must look after that. She was free to get what she could out of her time.

So that, when, after some months, she met Sam Adams, she was not quite as unkind to him as she might have been. With a young wife's new and exciting knowledge of men, she perceived he was in love with her, she knew he had always kept an unsatisfied desire for her. And, sportive, she could not help playing a little with this, though she cared not one jot for the man himself.

When Valentine's day came, which was near the first anniversary of her wedding day, there arrived a white stocking with a little amethyst brooch. Luckily Whiston did not see it, so she said nothing of it to him. She had not the faintest intention of having anything to do with Sam Adams, but once a little brooch was in her possession, it was hers, and she did not trouble her head for a moment how she had come by it. She kept it.

Now she had the pearl ear-rings. They were a more valuable and a more conspicuous present. She would have to ask her mother to give them to her, to explain their presence. She made a little plan in her head. And she was extraordinarily pleased. As for Sam Adams, even if he saw her wearing them, he would not give her away. What fun, if he saw her wearing his ear-rings! She would pretend she had inherited them from her grandmother, her mother's mother. She laughed to herself as she went down town in the afternoon, the pretty drops dangling in front of her curls. But she saw no one of importance.

Whiston came home tired and depressed. All day the male in him had been uneasy, and this had fatigued him. She was curiously against him, inclined, as she sometimes was nowadays, to make mock of him and jeer at him and cut him off. He did not understand this, and it angered him deeply. She was uneasy before him.

She knew he was in a state of suppressed irritation. The veins stood out on the backs of his hands, his brow was drawn stiffly. Yet she could not help goading him.

"What did you do wi' that white stocking?" he asked, out of a gloomy silence, his voice strong and brutal.

"I put it in a drawer—why?" she replied flippantly.

"Why didn't you put it on the fire back?" he said harshly. "What are you hoarding it up for?"

"I'm not hoarding it up," she said. "I've got a pair."

He relapsed into gloomy silence. She, unable to move him, ran away upstairs, leaving him smoking by the fire. Again she tried on the earrings. Then another little inspiration came to her. She drew on the white stockings, both of them.

Presently she came down in them. Her husband still sat immovable and glowering by the fire.

"Look!" she said. "They'll do beautifully."

And she picked up her skirts to her knees, and twisted round, looking at her pretty legs in the neat stockings.

He filled with unreasonable rage, and took the pipe from his mouth.

"Don't they look nice?" she said. "One from last year and one from this, they just do. Save you buying a pair."

And she looked over her shoulders at her pretty calves, and the dangling frills of her knickers.

"Put your skirts down and don't make a fool of yourself," he said.

"Why a fool of myself?" she asked.

And she began to dance slowly round the room, kicking up her feet half reckless, half jeering, in a ballet-dancer's fashion. Almost fearfully, yet in defiance, she kicked up her legs at him, singing as she did so. She resented him.

"You little fool, ha' done with it," he said. "And you'll backfire them stockings, I'm telling you." He was angry. His face flushed dark, he kept his head bent. She ceased to dance.

"I shan't," she said. "They'll come in very useful."

He lifted his head and watched her, with lighted, dangerous eyes.

"You'll put 'em on the fire back, I tell you," he said.

It was a war now. She bent forward, in a ballet-dancer's fashion, and put her tongue between her teeth.

"I shan't backfire them stockings," she sang, repeating his words, "I shan't, I shan't, I shan't."

And she danced round the room doing a high kick to the tune of her words. There was a real biting indifference in her behaviour.

"We'll see whether you will or not," he said, "trollops! You'd like Sam Adams to know you was wearing 'em, wouldn't you? That's what would please you."

"Yes, I'd like him to see how nicely they fit me, he might give me some more then."

And she looked down at her pretty legs.

He knew somehow that she would like Sam Adams to see how pretty her legs looked in the white stockings. It made his anger go deep, almost to hatred.

"Yer nasty trolley," he cried. "Put yer petticoats down, and stop being so foul-minded."

"I'm not foul-minded," she said. "My legs are my own. And why shouldn't Sam Adams think they're nice?"

There was a pause. He watched her with eyes glittering to a point.

"Have you been havin' owt to do with him?" he asked.

"I've just spoken to him when I've seen him," she said. "He's not as bad as you would make out."

"Isn't he?" he cried, a certain wakefulness in his voice. "Them who has anything to do wi' him is too bad for me, I tell you."

"Why, what are you frightened of him for?" she mocked.

She was rousing all his uncontrollable anger. He sat glowering. Every one of her sentences stirred him up like a red-hot iron. Soon it would be too much. And she was afraid herself; but she was neither conquered nor convinced.

A curious little grin of hate came on his face. He had a long score against her.

"What am I frightened of him for?" he repeated automatically. "What am I frightened of him for? Why, for you, you stray-running little bitch."

She flushed. The insult went deep into her, right home.

"Well, if you're so dull—" she said, lowering her eyelids, and speaking coldly, haughtily.

"If I'm so dull I'll break your neck the first word you speak to him," he said, tense.

"Pf!" she sneered. "Do you think I'm frightened of you?" She spoke coldly, detached.

She was frightened, for all that, white round the mouth.

His heart was getting hotter.

"You *will* be frightened of me, the next time you have anything to do with him," he said.

"Do you think *you'd* ever be told—ha!"

Her jeering scorn made him go white-hot, molten. He knew he was incoherent, scarcely responsible for what he might do. Slowly, unseeing, he rose and went out of doors, stifled, moved to kill her.

He stood leaning against the garden fence, unable either to see or hear. Below him, far off, fumed the lights of the town. He stood still, unconscious with a black storm of rage, his face lifted to the night.

Presently, still unconscious of what he was doing, he went indoors again. She stood, a small stubborn figure with tight-pressed lips and big, sullen, childish eyes, watching him, white with fear. He went heavily across the floor and dropped into his chair.

There was a silence.

"*You're* not going to tell me everything I shall do, and everything I shan't," she broke out at last.

He lifted his head.

"I tell you *this*," he said, low and intense. "Have anything to do with Sam Adams, and I'll break your neck."

She laughed, shrill and false.

"How I hate your word 'break your neck'," she said, with a grimace of the mouth. "It sounds so common and beastly. Can't you say something else—"

There was a dead silence.

"And besides," she said, with a queer chirrup of mocking laughter, "what do you know about anything? He sent me an amethyst brooch and a pair of pearl ear-rings."

"He what?" said Whiston, in a suddenly normal voice. His eyes were fixed on her.

"Sent me a pair of pearl ear-rings, and an amethyst brooch," she repeated, mechanically, pale to the lips.

And her big, black, childish eyes watched him, fascinated, held in her spell.

He seemed to thrust his face and his eyes forward at her, as he rose slowly and came to her. She watched transfixed in terror. Her throat made a small sound, as she tried to scream.

Then, quick as lightning, the back of his hand struck her with a crash across the mouth, and she was flung back blinded against the wall. The shock shook a queer sound out of her. And then she saw him still coming on, his eyes holding her, his fist drawn back, advancing slowly. At any instant the blow might crash into her.

Mad with terror, she raised her hands with a queer clawing movement to cover her eyes and her temples, opening her mouth in a dumb shriek. There was no sound. But the sight of her slowly arrested him. He hung before her, looking at her fixedly, as she stood crouched against the wall with open, bleeding mouth, and wide-staring eyes, and two hands clawing over her temples. And his lust to see her bleed, to break her and destroy her, rose from an old source against her. It carried him. He wanted satisfaction.

But he had seen her standing there, a piteous, horrified thing, and he turned his face aside in shame and nausea. He went and sat heavily in his chair, and a curious ease, almost like sleep, came over his brain.

She walked away from the wall towards the fire, dizzy, white to the lips, mechanically wiping her small, bleeding mouth. He sat motionless. Then, gradually, her breath began to hiss, she shook, and was sobbing silently, in grief for herself. Without looking, he saw. It made his mad desire to destroy her come back.

At length he lifted his head. His eyes were glowing again, fixed on her.

"And what did he give them you for?" he asked, in a steady, unyielding voice.

Her crying dried up in a second. She also was tense.

"They came as valentines," she replied, still not subjugated, even if beaten.

"When, to-day?"

"The pearl ear-rings to-day—the amethyst brooch last year."

"You've had it a year?"

"Yes."

She felt that now nothing would prevent him if he rose to kill her. She could not prevent him any more. She was yielded up to him. They both trembled in the balance, unconscious.

"What have you had to do with him?" he asked, in a barren voice.

"I've not had anything to do with him," she quavered.

"You just kept 'em because they were jewellery?" he said.

A weariness came over him. What was the worth of speaking any more of it? He did not care any more. He was dreary and sick.

She began to cry again, but he took no notice. She kept wiping her mouth on her handkerchief. He could see it, the blood-mark. It made him only more sick and tired of the responsibility of it, the violence, the shame.

When she began to move about again, he raised his head once more from his dead, motionless position.

"Where are the things?" he said.

"They are upstairs," she quavered. She knew the passion had gone down in him.

"Bring them down," he said.

"I won't," she wept, with rage. "You're not going to bully me and hit me like that on the mouth."

And she sobbed again. He looked at her in contempt and compassion and in rising anger.

"Where are they?" he said.

"They're in the little drawer under the looking-glass," she sobbed.

He went slowly upstairs, struck a match, and found the trinkets. He brought them downstairs in his hand.

"These?" he said, looking at them as they lay in his palm.

She looked at them without answering. She was not interested in them any more.

He looked at the little jewels. They were pretty.

"It's none of their fault," he said to himself.

And he searched round slowly, persistently, for a box. He tied the things up and addressed them to Sam Adams. Then he went out in his slippers to post the little package.

When he came back she was still sitting crying.

"You'd better go to bed," he said.

She paid no attention. He sat by the fire. She still cried.

"I'm sleeping down here," he said. "Go you to bed."

In a few moments she lifted her tear-stained, swollen face and looked at him with eyes all forlorn and pathetic. A great flash of anguish went over his body. He went over, slowly, and very gently took her in his hands. She let herself be taken. Then as she lay against his shoulder, she sobbed aloud:

"I never meant—"

"My love—my little love—" he cried, in anguish of spirit, holding her in his arms.

A SICK COLLIER

She was too good for him, everybody said. Yet still she did not regret marrying him. He had come courting her when he was only nineteen, and she twenty. He was in build what they call a tight little fellow; short, dark, with a warm colour, and that upright set of the head and chest, that flaunting way in movement recalling a mating bird, which denotes a body taut and compact with life. Being a good worker he had earned decent money in the mine, and having a good home had saved a little.

She was a cook at "Uplands", a tall, fair girl, very quiet. Having seen her walk down the street, Horsepool had followed her from a distance. He was taken with her, he did not drink, and he was not lazy. So, although he seemed a bit simple, without much intelligence, but having a sort of physical brightness, she considered, and accepted him.

When they were married they went to live in Scargill Street, in a highly respectable six-roomed house which they had furnished between them. The street was built up the side of a long, steep hill. It was narrow and rather tunnel-like. Nevertheless, the back looked out over the adjoining pasture, across a wide valley of fields and woods, in the bottom of which the mine lay snugly.

He made himself gaffer in his own house. She was unacquainted with a collier's mode of life. They were married on a Saturday. On the Sunday night he said:

"Set th' table for my breakfast, an' put my pit-things afront o' th' fire. I s'll be gettin' up at ha'ef pas' five. Tha nedna shift thysen not till when ter likes."

He showed her how to put a newspaper on the table for a cloth. When she demurred:

"I want none o' your white cloths i' th' mornin'. I like ter be able to slobber if I feel like it," he said.

He put before the fire his moleskin trousers, a clean singlet, or sleeveless vest of thick flannel, a pair of stockings and his pit boots, arranging them all to be warm and ready for morning.

"Now tha sees. That wants doin' ivery night."

Punctually at half past five he left her, without any form of leave-taking, going downstairs in his shirt.

When he arrived home at four o'clock in the afternoon his dinner was ready to be dished up. She was startled when he came in, a short, sturdy figure, with a face indescribably black and streaked. She stood before the fire in her white blouse and white apron, a fair girl, the picture of beautiful cleanliness. He "clommaxed" in, in his heavy boots.

"Well, how 'as ter gone on?" he asked.

"I was ready for you to come home," she replied tenderly. In his black face the whites of his brown eyes flashed at her.

"An' I wor ready for comin'," he said. He planked his tin bottle and snap-bag on the dresser, took off his coat and scarf and waistcoat, dragged his arm-chair nearer the fire and sat down.

"Let's ha'e a bit o' dinner, then—I'm about clammed," he said.

"Aren't you goin' to wash yourself first?"

"What am I to wesh mysen for?"

"Well, you can't eat your dinner—"

"Oh, strike a daisy, Missis! Dunna I eat my snap i' th' pit wi'out weshin'?—forced to."

She served the dinner and sat opposite him. His small bullet head was quite black, save for the whites of his eyes and his scarlet lips. It gave her a queer sensation to see him open his red mouth and bare his white teeth as he ate. His arms and hands were mottled black; his bare, strong neck got a little fairer as it settled towards his shoulders, reassuring her. There was the faint indescribable odour of the pit in the room, an odour of damp, exhausted air.

"Why is your vest so black on the shoulders?" she asked.

"My singlet? That's wi' th' watter droppin' on us from th' roof. This is a dry un as I put on afore I come up. They ha'e gre't clothes-'osses, and' as we change us things, we put 'em on theer ter dry."

When he washed himself, kneeling on the hearth-rug stripped to the waist, she felt afraid of him again. He was so muscular, he seemed so intent on what he was doing, so intensely himself, like a vigorous animal. And as he stood wiping himself, with his naked breast towards her, she felt rather sick, seeing his thick arms bulge their muscles.

They were nevertheless very happy. He was at a great pitch of pride because of her. The men in the pit might chaff him, they might try to entice him away, but nothing could reduce his self-assured pride because of her, nothing could unsettle his almost infantile satisfaction. In the evening he sat in his armchair chattering to her, or listening as she read the newspaper to him. When it was fine, he would go into the street, squat on his heels as colliers do, with his back against the wall of his parlour, and call to the passers-by, in greeting, one after another. If no one were passing, he was content just to squat and smoke, having such a fund of sufficiency and satisfaction in his heart. He was well married.

They had not been wed a year when all Brent and Wellwood's men came out on strike. Willy was in the Union, so with a pinch they scrambled through. The furniture was not all paid for, and other debts were incurred. She worried and contrived, he left it to her. But he was a good husband; he gave her all he had.

The men were out fifteen weeks. They had been back just over a year when Willy had an accident in the mine, tearing his bladder. At the pit head the doctor talked of the hospital. Losing his head entirely, the young collier raved like a madman, what with pain and fear of hospital.

"Tha s'lt go whoam, Willy, tha s'lt go whoam," the deputy said.

A lad warned the wife to have the bed ready. Without speaking or hesitating she prepared. But when the ambulance came, and she heard him shout with pain at being moved, she was afraid lest she should sink down. They carried him in.

"Yo' should 'a' had a bed i' th' parlour, Missis," said the deputy, "then we shouldn'a ha' had to hawkse 'im upstairs, an' it 'ud 'a' saved your legs."

But it was too late now. They got him upstairs.

"They let me lie, Lucy," he was crying, "they let me lie two mortal hours on th' sleck afore they took me outer th' stall. Th' peen, Lucy, th' peen; oh, Lucy, th' peen, th' peen!"

"I know th' pain's bad, Willy, I know. But you must try an' bear it a bit."

"Tha manna carry on in that form, lad, thy missis'll niver be able ter stan' it," said the deputy.

"I canna 'elp it, it's th' peen, it's th' peen," he cried again. He had never been ill in his life. When he had smashed a finger he could look at the wound. But this pain came from inside, and terrified him. At last he was soothed and exhausted.

It was some time before she could undress him and wash him. He would let no other woman do for him, having that savage modesty usual in such men.

For six weeks he was in bed, suffering much pain. The doctors were not quite sure what was the matter with him, and scarcely knew what to do. He could eat, he did not lose flesh, nor strength, yet the pain continued, and he could hardly walk at all.

In the sixth week the men came out in the national strike. He would get up quite early in the morning and sit by the window. On Wednesday, the second week of the strike, he sat gazing out on the street as usual, a bullet-headed young man, still vigorous-looking, but with a peculiar expression of hunted fear in his face.

"Lucy," he called, "Lucy!"

She, pale and worn, ran upstairs at his bidding.

"Gi'e me a han'kercher," he said.

"Why, you've got one," she replied, coming near.

"Tha nedna touch me," he cried. Feeling his pocket, he produced a white handkerchief.

"I non want a white un, gi'e me a red un," he said.

"An' if anybody comes to see you," she answered, giving him a red handkerchief.

"Besides," she continued, "you needn't ha' brought me upstairs for that."

"I b'lieve th' peen's commin' on again," he said, with a little horror in his voice.

"It isn't, you know, it isn't," she replied. "The doctor says you imagine it's there when it isn't."

"Canna I feel what's inside me?" he shouted.

"There's a traction-engine coming downhill," she said. "That'll scatter them. I'll just go an' finish your pudding."

She left him. The traction-engine went by, shaking the houses. Then the street was quiet, save for the men. A gang of youths from fifteen to twenty-five years old were playing marbles in the middle of the road. Other little groups of men were playing on the pavement. The street was gloomy. Willy could hear the endless calling and shouting of men's voices.

"Tha'rt skinchin'!"

"I arena!"

"Come 'ere with that blood-alley."

"Swop us four for't."

"Shonna, gie's hold on't."

He wanted to be out, he wanted to be playing marbles. The pain had weakened his mind, so that he hardly knew any self-control.

Presently another gang of men lounged up the street. It was pay morning. The Union was paying the men in the Primitive Chapel. They were returning with their half-sovereigns.

"Sorry!" bawled a voice. "Sorry!"

The word is a form of address, corruption probably of 'Sirrah'. Willy started almost out of his chair.

"Sorry!" again bawled a great voice. "Art goin' wi' me to see Notts play Villa?"

Many of the marble players started up.

"What time is it? There's no treens, we s'll ha'e ter walk."

The street was alive with men.

"Who's goin' ter Nottingham ter see th' match?" shouted the same big voice. A very large, tipsy man, with his cap over his eyes, was calling.

"Com' on—aye, com' on!" came many voices. The street was full of the shouting of men. They split up in excited cliques and groups.

"Play up, Notts!" the big man shouted.

"Plee up, Notts!" shouted the youths and men. They were at kindling pitch. It only needed a shout to rouse them. Of this the careful authorities were aware.

"I'm goin', I'm goin'!" shouted the sick man at his window.

Lucy came running upstairs.

"I'm goin' ter see Notts play Villa on th' Meadows ground," he declared.

"You—_you_ can't go. There are no trains. You can't walk nine miles."

"I'm goin' ter see th' match," he declared, rising.

"You know you can't. Sit down now an' be quiet."

She put her hand on him. He shook it off.

"Leave me alone, leave me alone. It's thee as ma'es th' peen come, it's thee. I'm goin' ter Nottingham to see th' football match."

"Sit down—folks'll hear you, and what will they think?"

"Come off'n me. Com' off. It's her, it's her as does it. Com' off."

He seized hold of her. His little head was bristling with madness, and he was strong as a lion.

"Oh, Willy!" she cried.

"It's 'er, it's 'er. Kill her!" he shouted, "kill her."

"Willy, folks'll hear you."

"Th' peen's commin' on again, I tell yer. I'll kill her for it."

He was completely out of his mind. She struggled with him to prevent his going to the stairs. When she escaped from him, he was shouting and raving, she beckoned to her neighbour, a girl of twenty-four, who was cleaning the window across the road.

Ethel Mellor was the daughter of a well-to-do check-weighman. She ran across in fear to Mrs. Horsepool. Hearing the man raving, people were running out in the street and listening. Ethel hurried upstairs. Everything was clean and pretty in the young home.

Willy was staggering round the room, after the slowly retreating Lucy, shouting:

"Kill her! Kill her!"

"Mr. Horsepool!" cried Ethel, leaning against the bed, white as the sheets, and trembling. "Whatever are you saying?"

"I tell yer it's 'er fault as th' peen comes on—I tell yer it is! Kill 'er—kill 'er!"

"Kill Mrs. Horsepool!" cried the trembling girl. "Why, you're ever so fond of her, you know you are."

"The peen—I ha'e such a lot o' peen—I want to kill 'er."

He was subsiding. When he sat down his wife collapsed in a chair, weeping noiselessly. The tears ran down Ethel's face. He sat staring out of the window; then the old, hurt look came on his face.

"What 'ave I been sayin'?" he asked, looking piteously at his wife.

"Why!" said Ethel, "you've been carrying on something awful, saying, 'Kill her, kill her!'"

"Have I, Lucy?" he faltered.

"You didn't know what you was saying," said his young wife gently but coldly.

His face puckered up. He bit his lip, then broke into tears, sobbing uncontrollably, with his face to the window.

There was no sound in the room but of three people crying bitterly, breath caught in sobs. Suddenly Lucy put away her tears and went over to him.

"You didn't know what you was sayin', Willy, I know you didn't. I knew you didn't, all the time. It doesn't matter, Willy. Only don't do it again."

In a little while, when they were calmer, she went downstairs with Ethel.

"See if anybody is looking in the street," she said.

Ethel went into the parlour and peeped through the curtains.

"Aye!" she said. "You may back your life Lena an' Mrs. Severn'll be out gorping, and that clat-fartin' Mrs. Allsop."

"Oh, I hope they haven't heard anything! If it gets about as he's out of his mind, they'll stop his compensation, I know they will."

"They'd never stop his compensation for *that*," protested Ethel.

"Well, they *have* been stopping some—"

"It'll not get about. I s'll tell nobody."

"Oh, but if it does, whatever shall we do? . . ."

THE CHRISTENING

The mistress of the British School stepped down from her school gate, and instead of turning to the left as usual, she turned to the right. Two women who were hastening home to scramble their husbands' dinners together—it was five minutes to four—stopped to look at her. They stood gazing after her for a moment; then they glanced at each other with a woman's little grimace.

To be sure, the retreating figure was ridiculous: small and thin, with a black straw hat, and a rusty cashmere dress hanging full all round the skirt. For so small and frail and rusty a creature to sail with slow, deliberate stride was also absurd. Hilda Rowbotham was less than thirty, so it was not years that set the measure of her pace; she had heart disease. Keeping her face, that was small with sickness, but not uncomely, firmly lifted and fronting ahead, the young woman sailed on past the market-place, like a black swan of mournful, disreputable plumage.

She turned into Berryman's, the baker's. The shop displayed bread and cakes, sacks of flour and oatmeal, flitches of bacon, hams, lard and sausages. The combination of scents was not unpleasing. Hilda Rowbotham stood for some minutes nervously tapping and pushing a large knife that lay on the counter, and looking at the tall, glittering brass scales. At last a morose man with sandy whiskers came down the step from the house-place.

"What is it?" he asked, not apologizing for his delay.

"Will you give me six-pennyworth of assorted cakes and pastries—and put in some macaroons, please?" she asked, in remarkably rapid and nervous speech. Her lips fluttered like two leaves in a wind, and her words crowded and rushed like a flock of sheep at a gate.

"We've got no macaroons," said the man churlishly.

He had evidently caught that word. He stood waiting.

"Then I can't have any, Mr. Berryman. Now I do feel disappointed. I like those macaroons, you know, and it's not often I treat myself. One gets so tired of trying to spoil oneself, don't you think? It's less profitable even than trying to spoil somebody else." She laughed a quick little nervous laugh, putting her hand to her face.

"Then what'll you have?" asked the man, without the ghost of an answering smile. He evidently had not followed, so he looked more glum than ever.

"Oh, anything you've got," replied the schoolmistress, flushing slightly. The man moved slowly about, dropping the cakes from various dishes one by one into a paper bag.

"How's that sister o' yours getting on?" he asked, as if he were talking to the flour scoop.

"Whom do you mean?" snapped the schoolmistress.

"The youngest," answered the stooping, pale-faced man, with a note of sarcasm.

"Emma! Oh, she's very well, thank you!" The schoolmistress was very red, but she spoke with sharp, ironical defiance. The man grunted. Then he handed her the bag and watched her out of the shop without bidding her "Good afternoon".

She had the whole length of the main street to traverse, a half-mile of slow-stepping torture, with shame flushing over her neck. But she carried her white bag with an appearance of steadfast unconcern. When she turned into the field she seemed to droop a little. The wide valley opened out from her, with the far woods withdrawing into twilight, and away in the centre the great pit streaming its white smoke and chuffing as the men were being turned up. A full, rose-coloured moon, like a flamingo flying low under the far, dusky east, drew out of the mist. It was beautiful, and it made her irritable sadness soften, diffuse.

Across the field, and she was at home. It was a new, substantial cottage, built with unstinted hand, such a house as an old miner could build himself out of his savings. In the rather small kitchen a woman of dark, saturnine complexion sat nursing a baby in a long white gown; a young woman of heavy, brutal cast stood at the table, cutting bread and butter. She had a downcast, humble mien that sat unnaturally on her, and was strangely irritating. She did not look round when her sister entered. Hilda put down the bag of cakes and left the room, not having spoken to Emma, nor to the baby, not to Mrs. Carlin, who had come in to help for the afternoon.

Almost immediately the father entered from the yard with a dustpan full of coals. He was a large man, but he was going to pieces. As he passed through, he gripped the door with his free hand to steady himself, but turning, he lurched and swayed. He began putting the coals on the fire, piece by piece. One lump fell from his hand and smashed on the white hearth. Emma Rowbotham looked round, and began in a rough, loud voice of anger: "Look at you!" Then she consciously moderated her tones. "I'll sweep it up in a minute—don't you bother; you'll only be going head first into the fire."

Her father bent down nevertheless to clear up the mess he had made, saying, articulating his words loosely and slavering in his speech:

"The lousy bit of a thing, it slipped between my fingers like a fish."

As he spoke he went tilting towards the fire. The dark-browed woman cried out: he put his hand on the hot stove to save himself: Emma swung round and dragged him off.

"Didn't I tell you!" she cried roughly. "Now, have you burnt yourself?"

She held tight hold of the big man, and pushed him into his chair.

"What's the matter?" cried a sharp voice from the other room. The speaker appeared, a hard well-favoured woman of twenty-eight. "Emma, don't speak like that to father." Then, in a tone not so cold, but just as sharp: "Now, father, what have you been doing?"

Emma withdrew to her table sullenly.

"It's nöwt," said the old man, vainly protesting. "It's nöwt, at a'. Get on wi' what you're doin'."

"I'm afraid 'e's burnt 'is 'and," said the black-browed woman, speaking of him with a kind of hard pity, as if he were a cumbersome child. Bertha took the old man's hand and looked at it, making a quick tut-tutting noise of impatience.

"Emma, get that zinc ointment—and some white rag," she commanded sharply. The younger sister put down her loaf with the knife in it, and went. To a sensitive observer, this obedience was more intolerable than the most hateful discord. The dark woman bent over the baby and made silent, gentle movements of motherliness to it. The little one smiled and moved on her lap. It continued to move and twist.

"I believe this child's hungry," she said. "How long is it since he had anything?"

"Just afore dinner," said Emma dully.

"Good gracious!" exclaimed Bertha. "You needn't starve the child now you've got it. Once every two hours it ought to be fed, as I've told you; and now it's three. Take him, poor little mite—I'll cut the bread." She bent and looked at the bonny baby. She could not help herself: she smiled, and pressed its cheek with her finger, and nodded to it, making little noises. Then she turned and took the loaf from her sister. The woman rose and gave the child to its mother. Emma bent over the little sucking mite. She hated it when she looked at it, and saw it as a symbol, but when she felt it, her love was like fire in her blood.

"I should think 'e canna be comin'," said the father uneasily, looking up at the clock.

"Nonsense, father—the clock's fast! It's but half-past four! Don't fidget!" Bertha continued to cut the bread and butter.

"Open a tin of pears," she said to the woman, in a much milder tone. Then she went into the next room. As soon as she was gone, the old man said again: "I should ha'e thought he'd 'a' been 'ere by now, if he means comin'."

Emma, engrossed, did not answer. The father had ceased to consider her, since she had become humbled.

"'E'll come—'e'll come!" assured the stranger.

A few minutes later Bertha hurried into the kitchen, taking off her apron. The dog barked furiously. She opened the door, commanded the dog to silence, and said: "He will be quiet now, Mr. Kendal."

"Thank you," said a sonorous voice, and there was the sound of a bicycle being propped against a wall. A clergyman entered, a big-boned, thin, ugly man of nervous manner. He went straight to the father.

"Ah—how are you?" he asked musically, peering down on the great frame of the miner, ruined by locomotor ataxy.

His voice was full of gentleness, but he seemed as if he could not see distinctly, could not get things clear.

"Have you hurt you hand?" he said comfortingly, seeing the white rag.

"It wor nöwt but a pestered bit o' coal as dropped, an' I put my hand on th' hub. I thought tha worna commin'."

The familiar 'tha', and the reproach, were unconscious retaliation on the old man's part. The minister smiled, half wistfully, half indulgently. He was full of vague tenderness. Then he turned to the young mother, who flushed sullenly because her dishonoured breast was uncovered.

"How are *you*?" he asked, very softly and gently, as if she were ill and he were mindful of her.

"I'm all right," she replied, awkwardly taking his hand without rising, hiding her face and the anger that rose in her.

"Yes—yes"—he peered down at the baby, which sucked with distended mouth upon the firm breast. "Yes, yes." He seemed lost in a dim musing.

Coming to, he shook hands unseeingly with the woman.

Presently they all went into the next room, the minister hesitating to help his crippled old deacon.

"I can go by myself, thank yer," testily replied the father.

Soon all were seated. Everybody was separated in feeling and isolated at table. High tea was spread in the middle kitchen, a large, ugly room kept for special occasions.

Hilda appeared last, and the clumsy, raw-boned clergyman rose to meet her. He was afraid of this family, the well-to-do old collier, and the brutal, self-willed children. But Hilda was queen among them. She was the clever one, and had been to college. She felt responsible for the keeping up of a high standard of conduct in all the members of the family. There *was* a difference between the Rowbothams and the common collier folk. Woodbine Cottage was a superior house to most—and was built in pride by the old man. She, Hilda, was a college-trained schoolmistress; she meant to keep up the prestige of her house in spite of blows.

She had put on a dress of green voile for this special occasion. But she was very thin; her neck protruded painfully. The clergyman, however, greeted her almost with reverence, and, with some assumption of dignity, she sat down before the tray. At the far end of the table sat the broken, massive frame of her father. Next to him was the youngest daughter, nursing the restless baby. The minister sat between Hilda and Bertha, hulking his bony frame uncomfortably.

There was a great spread on the table, of tinned fruits and tinned salmon, ham and cakes. Miss Rowbotham kept a keen eye on everything: she felt the importance of the occasion. The young mother who had given rise to all this solemnity ate in sulky discomfort, snatching sullen little smiles at her child, smiles which came, in spite of her, when she felt its little limbs stirring vigorously on her lap. Bertha, sharp and abrupt, was chiefly concerned with the baby. She scorned her sister, and treated her like dirt. But the infant was a streak of light to her. Miss Rowbotham concerned herself with the function and the conversation. Her hands fluttered; she talked in little volleys exceedingly nervous. Towards the end of the meal, there came a pause. The old man wiped his mouth with his red handkerchief, then, his blue eyes going fixed and staring, he began to speak, in a loose, slobbering fashion, charging his words at the clergyman.

"Well, mester—we'n axed you to come her ter christen this childt, an' you'n come, an' I'm sure we're very thankful. I can't see lettin' the poor blessed childt miss baptizing, an' they aren't for goin' to church wi't—" He seemed to lapse into a muse. "So," he resumed, "we'v axed you to come here to do the job. I'm not sayin' as it's not 'ard on us, it is. I'm breakin' up, an' mother's gone. I don't like leavin' a girl o' mine in a situation like 'ers is, but what the Lord's done, He's done, an' it's no matter murmuring. . . . There's one thing to be thankful for, an' we *are* thankful for it: they never need know the want of bread."

Miss Rowbotham, the lady of the family, sat very stiff and pained during this discourse. She was sensitive to so many things that she was bewildered. She felt her young sister's shame, then a kind of swift protecting love for the baby, a feeling that included the mother; she was at a loss before her father's religious sentiment, and she felt and resented bitterly the mark upon the family, against which the common folk could lift their fingers. Still she winced from the sound of her father's words. It was a painful ordeal.

"It is hard for you," began the clergyman in his soft, lingering, unworldly voice. "It is hard for you today, but the Lord gives comfort in His time. A man child is born unto us, therefore let us rejoice and be glad. If sin has entered in among us, let us purify out hearts before the Lord. . . ."

He went on with his discourse. The young mother lifted the whimpering infant, till its face was hid in her loose hair. She was hurt, and a little glowering anger shone in her face. But nevertheless her fingers clasped the body of the child beautifully. She was stupefied with anger against this emotion let loose on her account.

Miss Bertha rose and went to the little kitchen, returning with water in a china bowl. She placed it there among the tea-things.

"Well, we're all ready," said the old man, and the clergyman began to read the service. Miss Bertha was godmother, the two men godfathers. The old man sat with bent head. The scene became impressive. At last Miss Bertha took the child and put it in the arms of the clergyman. He, big and ugly, shone with a kind of unreal love. He had never mixed with life, and women were all unliving, Biblical things to him. When he asked for the name, the old man lifted his head fiercely. "Joseph William, after me," he said, almost out of breath.

"Joseph William, I baptize thee. . . ." resounded the strange, full, chanting voice of the clergyman. The baby was quite still.

"Let us pray!" It came with relief to them all. They knelt before their chairs, all but the young mother, who bent and hid herself over her baby. The clergyman began his hesitating, struggling prayer.

Just then heavy footsteps were heard coming up the path, ceasing at the window. The young mother, glancing up, saw her brother, black in his pit dirt, grinning in through the panes. His red mouth curved in a sneer; his fair hair shone above his blackened skin. He caught the eye of his sister and grinned. Then his black face disappeared. He had gone on into the kitchen. The girl with the child sat still and anger filled her heart. She herself hated now the praying clergyman and the whole emotional business; she hated her brother bitterly. In anger and bondage she sat and listened.

Suddenly her father began to pray. His familiar, loud, rambling voice made her shut herself up and become even insentient. Folks said his mind was weakening. She believed it to be true, and kept herself always disconnected from him.

"We ask Thee, Lord," the old man cried, "to look after this childt. Fatherless he is. But what does the earthly father matter before Thee? The childt is Thine, he is Thy childt. Lord, what father has a man but Thee? Lord, when a man says he is a father, he is wrong from the first word. For Thou art the Father, Lord. Lord, take away from us the conceit that our children are ours. Lord, Thou art Father of this childt as is fatherless here. O God, Thou bring him up. For I have stood between Thee and my children; I've had my way with them, Lord; I've stood between Thee and my children; I've cut 'em off from Thee because they were mine. And they've grown twisted, because of me. Who is their father, Lord, but Thee? But I put myself in the way, they've been plants under a stone, because of me. Lord, if it hadn't been for me, they might ha' been trees in the sunshine. Let me own it, Lord, I've done 'em mischief. It could ha' been better if they'd never known no father. No man is a father, Lord: only Thou art. They can never grow beyond Thee, but I hampered them. Lift 'em up again, and undo what I've done to my children. And let this young childt be like a willow tree beside the waters, with no father but Thee, O God. Aye an' I wish it had been so with my children, that they'd had no father but

Thee. For I've been like a stone upon them, and they rise up and curse me in their wickedness. But let me go, an' lift Thou them up, Lord . . ."

The minister, unaware of the feelings of a father, knelt in trouble, hearing without understanding the special language of fatherhood. Miss Rowbotham alone felt and understood a little. Her heart began to flutter; she was in pain. The two younger daughters kneeled unhearing, stiffened and impervious. Bertha was thinking of the baby; and the younger mother thought of the father of her child, whom she hated. There was a clatter in the scullery. There the youngest son made as much noise as he could, pouring out the water for his wash, muttering in deep anger:

"Blortin', slaverin' old fool!"

And while the praying of his father continued, his heart was burning with rage. On the table was a paper bag. He picked it up and read, "John Berryman—Bread, Pastries, etc." Then he grinned with a grimace. The father of the baby was baker's man at Berryman's. The prayer went on in the middle kitchen. Laurie Rowbotham gathered together the mouth of the bag, inflated it, and burst it with his fist. There was a loud report. He grinned to himself. But he writhed at the same time with shame and fear of his father.

The father broke off from his prayer; the party shuffled to their feet. The young mother went into the scullery.

"What art doin', fool?" she said.

The collier youth tipped the baby under the chin, singing:

> "Pat-a-cake, pat-a-cake, baker's man,
> Bake me a cake as fast as you can. . . ."

The mother snatched the child away. "Shut thy mouth," she said, the colour coming into her cheek.

> "Prick it and stick it and mark it with P,
> And put it i' th' oven for baby an' me. . . ."

He grinned, showing a grimy, and jeering and unpleasant red mouth and white teeth.

"I s'll gi'e thee a dab ower th' mouth," said the mother of the baby grimly. He began to sing again, and she struck out at him.

"Now what's to do?" said the father, staggering in.

The youth began to sing again. His sister stood sullen and furious.

"Why, does *that* upset you?" asked the eldest Miss Rowbotham, sharply, of Emma the mother. "Good gracious, it hasn't improved your temper."

Miss Bertha came in, and took the bonny baby.

The father sat big and unheeding in his chair, his eyes vacant, his physique wrecked. He let them do as they would, he fell to pieces. And yet some power, involuntary, like a curse, remained in him. The very ruin of him was like a lodestone that held them in its control. The wreck of him still dominated the house, in his dissolution even he compelled their being. They had never lived; his life, his will had always been upon them and contained them. They were only half-individuals.

The day after the christening he staggered in at the doorway declaring, in a loud voice, with joy in life still: "The daisies light up the earth, they clap their hands in multitudes, in praise of the morning." And his daughters shrank, sullen.

ODOUR OF CHRYSANTHEMUMS

I

The small locomotive engine, Number 4, came clanking, stumbling down from Selston—with seven full waggons. It appeared round the corner with loud threats of speed, but the colt that it startled from among the gorse, which still flickered indistinctly in the raw afternoon, outdistanced it at a canter. A woman, walking up the railway line to Underwood, drew back into the hedge, held her basket aside, and watched the footplate of the engine advancing. The trucks thumped heavily past, one by one, with slow inevitable movement, as she stood insignificantly trapped between the jolting black waggons and the hedge; then they curved away towards the coppice where the withered oak leaves dropped noiselessly, while the birds, pulling at the scarlet hips beside the track, made off into the dusk that had already crept into the spinney. In the open, the smoke from the engine sank and cleaved to the rough grass. The fields were dreary and forsaken, and in the marshy strip that led to the whimsey, a reedy pit-pond, the fowls had already abandoned their run among the alders, to roost in the tarred fowl-house. The pit-bank loomed up beyond the pond, flames like red sores licking its ashy sides, in the afternoon's stagnant light. Just beyond rose the tapering chimneys and the clumsy black head-stocks of Brinsley Colliery. The two wheels were spinning fast up against the sky, and the winding-engine rapped out its little spasms. The miners were being turned up.

The engine whistled as it came into the wide bay of railway lines beside the colliery, where rows of trucks stood in harbour.

Miners, single, trailing and in groups, passed like shadows diverging home. At the edge of the ribbed level of sidings squat a low cottage, three steps down from the cinder track. A large bony vine clutched at the house, as if to claw down the tiled roof. Round the bricked yard grew a few wintry primroses. Beyond, the long garden sloped down to a bush-covered brook course. There were some twiggy apple trees, winter-crack trees, and ragged cabbages. Beside the path hung dishevelled pink chrysanthemums, like pink cloths hung on bushes. A woman came stooping out of the felt-covered fowl-house, half-way down the garden. She closed and padlocked the door, then drew herself erect, having brushed some bits from her white apron.

She was a till woman of imperious mien, handsome, with definite black eyebrows. Her smooth black hair was parted exactly. For a few moments she stood steadily watching the miners as they passed along the railway: then she turned towards the brook course. Her face was calm and set, her mouth was closed with disillusionment. After a moment she called:

"John!" There was no answer. She waited, and then said distinctly:

"Where are you?"

"Here!" replied a child's sulky voice from among the bushes. The woman looked piercingly through the dusk.

"Are you at that brook?" she asked sternly.

For answer the child showed himself before the raspberry-canes that rose like whips. He was a small, sturdy boy of five. He stood quite still, defiantly.

"Oh!" said the mother, conciliated. "I thought you were down at that wet brook—and you remember what I told you—"

The boy did not move or answer.

126

"Come, come on in," she said more gently, "it's getting dark. There's your grandfather's engine coming down the line!"

The lad advanced slowly, with resentful, taciturn movement. He was dressed in trousers and waistcoat of cloth that was too thick and hard for the size of the garments. They were evidently cut down from a man's clothes.

As they went slowly towards the house he tore at the ragged wisps of chrysanthemums and dropped the petals in handfuls along the path.

"Don't do that—it does look nasty," said his mother. He refrained, and she, suddenly pitiful, broke off a twig with three or four wan flowers and held them against her face. When mother and son reached the yard her hand hesitated, and instead of laying the flower aside, she pushed it in her apron-band. The mother and son stood at the foot of the three steps looking across the bay of lines at the passing home of the miners. The trundle of the small train was imminent. Suddenly the engine loomed past the house and came to a stop opposite the gate.

The engine-driver, a short man with round grey beard, leaned out of the cab high above the woman.

"Have you got a cup of tea?" he said in a cheery, hearty fashion.

It was her father. She went in, saying she would mash. Directly, she returned.

"I didn't come to see you on Sunday," began the little grey-bearded man.

"I didn't expect you," said his daughter.

The engine-driver winced; then, reassuming his cheery, airy manner, he said:

"Oh, have you heard then? Well, and what do you think—?"

"I think it is soon enough," she replied.

At her brief censure the little man made an impatient gesture, and said coaxingly, yet with dangerous coldness:

"Well, what's a man to do? It's no sort of life for a man of my years, to sit at my own hearth like a stranger. And if I'm going to marry again it may as well be soon as late—what does it matter to anybody?"

The woman did not reply, but turned and went into the house. The man in the engine-cab stood assertive, till she returned with a cup of tea and a piece of bread and butter on a plate. She went up the steps and stood near the footplate of the hissing engine.

"You needn't 'a' brought me bread an' butter," said her father. "But a cup of tea"—he sipped appreciatively—"it's very nice." He sipped for a moment or two, then: "I hear as Walter's got another bout on," he said.

"When hasn't he?" said the woman bitterly.

"I heered tell of him in the 'Lord Nelson' braggin' as he was going to spend that b—— afore he went: half a sovereign that was."

"When?" asked the woman.

"A' Sat'day night—I know that's true."

"Very likely," she laughed bitterly. "He gives me twenty-three shillings."

"Aye, it's a nice thing, when a man can do nothing with his money but make a beast of himself!" said the grey-whiskered man. The woman turned her head away. Her father swallowed the last of his tea and handed her the cup.

"Aye," he sighed, wiping his mouth. "It's a settler, it is—"

He put his hand on the lever. The little engine strained and groaned, and the train rumbled towards the crossing. The woman again looked across the metals. Darkness was settling over the spaces of the railway and trucks: the miners, in grey sombre groups, were still passing home. The winding-engine pulsed hurriedly, with brief pauses.

Elizabeth Bates looked at the dreary flow of men, then she went indoors. Her husband did not come.

The kitchen was small and full of firelight; red coals piled glowing up the chimney mouth. All the life of the room seemed in the white, warm hearth and the steel fender reflecting the red fire. The cloth was laid for tea; cups glinted in the shadows. At the back, where the lowest stairs protruded into the room, the boy sat struggling with a knife and a piece of whitewood. He was almost hidden in the shadow. It was half-past four. They had but to await the father's coming to begin tea. As the mother watched her son's sullen little struggle with the wood, she saw herself in his silence and pertinacity; she saw the father in her child's indifference to all but himself. She seemed to be occupied by her husband. He had probably gone past his home, slunk past his own door, to drink before he came in, while his dinner spoiled and wasted in waiting. She glanced at the clock, then took the potatoes to strain them in the yard. The garden and fields beyond the brook were closed in uncertain darkness. When she rose with the saucepan, leaving the drain steaming into the night behind her, she saw the yellow lamps were lit along the high road that went up the hill away beyond the space of the railway lines and the field.

Then again she watched the men trooping home, fewer now and fewer.

Indoors the fire was sinking and the room was dark red. The woman put her saucepan on the hob, and set a batter pudding near the mouth of the oven. Then she stood unmoving. Directly, gratefully, came quick young steps to the door. Someone hung on the latch a moment, then a little girl entered and began pulling off her outdoor things, dragging a mass of curls, just ripening from gold to brown, over her eyes with her hat.

Her mother chid her for coming late from school, and said she would have to keep her at home the dark winter days.

"Why, mother, it's hardly a bit dark yet. The lamp's not lighted, and my father's not home."

"No, he isn't. But it's a quarter to five! Did you see anything of him?"

The child became serious. She looked at her mother with large, wistful blue eyes.

"No, mother, I've never seen him. Why? Has he come up an' gone past, to Old Brinsley? He hasn't, mother, 'cos I never saw him."

"He'd watch that," said the mother bitterly, "he'd take care as you didn't see him. But you may depend upon it, he's seated in the 'Prince o' Wales'. He wouldn't be this late."

The girl looked at her mother piteously.

"Let's have our teas, mother, should we?" said she.

The mother called John to table. She opened the door once more and looked out across the darkness of the lines. All was deserted: she could not hear the winding-engines.

"Perhaps," she said to herself, "he's stopped to get some ripping done."

They sat down to tea. John, at the end of the table near the door, was almost lost in the darkness. Their faces were hidden from each other. The girl crouched against the fender slowly moving a thick piece of bread before the fire. The lad, his face a dusky mark on the shadow, sat watching her who was transfigured in the red glow.

"I do think it's beautiful to look in the fire," said the child.

"Do you?" said her mother. "Why?"

"It's so red, and full of little caves—and it feels so nice, and you can fair smell it."

"It'll want mending directly," replied her mother, "and then if your father comes he'll carry on and say there never is a fire when a man comes home sweating from the pit.—A public-house is always warm enough."

There was silence till the boy said complainingly: "Make haste, our Annie."

"Well, I am doing! I can't make the fire do it no faster, can I?"

"She keeps wafflin' it about so's to make 'er slow," grumbled the boy.

"Don't have such an evil imagination, child," replied the mother.

Soon the room was busy in the darkness with the crisp sound of crunching. The mother ate very little. She drank her tea determinedly, and sat thinking. When she rose her anger was evident in the stern unbending of her head. She looked at the pudding in the fender, and broke out:

"It is a scandalous thing as a man can't even come home to his dinner! If it's crozzled up to a cinder I don't see why I should care. Past his very door he goes to get to a public-house, and here I sit with his dinner waiting for him—"

She went out. As she dropped piece after piece of coal on the red fire, the shadows fell on the walls, till the room was almost in total darkness.

"I canna see," grumbled the invisible John. In spite of herself, the mother laughed.

"You know the way to your mouth," she said. She set the dustpan outside the door. When she came again like a shadow on the hearth, the lad repeated, complaining sulkily:

"I canna see."

"Good gracious!" cried the mother irritably, "you're as bad as your father if it's a bit dusk!"

Nevertheless she took a paper spill from a sheaf on the mantelpiece and proceeded to light the lamp that hung from the ceiling in the middle of the room. As she reached up, her figure displayed itself just rounding with maternity.

"Oh, mother—!" exclaimed the girl.

"What?" said the woman, suspended in the act of putting the lamp glass over the flame. The copper reflector shone handsomely on her, as she stood with uplifted arm, turning to face her daughter.

"You've got a flower in your apron!" said the child, in a little rapture at this unusual event.

"Goodness me!" exclaimed the woman, relieved. "One would think the house was afire." She replaced the glass and waited a moment before turning up the wick. A pale shadow was seen floating vaguely on the floor.

"Let me smell!" said the child, still rapturously, coming forward and putting her face to her mother's waist.

"Go along, silly!" said the mother, turning up the lamp. The light revealed their suspense so that the woman felt it almost unbearable. Annie was still bending at her waist. Irritably, the mother took the flowers out from her apron-band.

"Oh, mother—don't take them out!" Annie cried, catching her hand and trying to replace the sprig.

"Such nonsense!" said the mother, turning away. The child put the pale chrysanthemums to her lips, murmuring:

"Don't they smell beautiful!"

Her mother gave a short laugh.

"No," she said, "not to me. It was chrysanthemums when I married him, and chrysanthemums when you were born, and the first time they ever brought him home drunk, he'd got brown chrysanthemums in his button-hole."

She looked at the children. Their eyes and their parted lips were wondering. The mother sat rocking in silence for some time. Then she looked at the clock.

"Twenty minutes to six!" In a tone of fine bitter carelessness she continued: "Eh, he'll not come now till they bring him. There he'll stick! But he needn't come rolling in here in his pit-dirt, for I won't wash him. He can lie on the floor—Eh, what a fool I've been, what a fool! And this is what I came here for, to this dirty hole, rats and all, for him to slink past his very door. Twice last week—he's begun now-"

She silenced herself, and rose to clear the table.

While for an hour or more the children played, subduedly intent, fertile of imagination, united in fear of the mother's wrath, and in dread of their father's home-coming, Mrs. Bates sat in her rocking-chair making a 'singlet' of thick cream-coloured flannel, which gave a dull wounded sound as she tore off the grey edge. She worked at her sewing with energy, listening to the children, and her anger wearied itself, lay down to rest, opening its eyes from time to time and steadily watching, its ears raised to listen. Sometimes even her anger quailed and shrank, and the mother suspended her sewing, tracing the footsteps that thudded along the sleepers outside; she would lift her head sharply to bid the children 'hush', but she recovered herself in time, and the footsteps went past the gate, and the children were not flung out of their playing world.

But at last Annie sighed, and gave in. She glanced at her waggon of slippers, and loathed the game. She turned plaintively to her mother.

"Mother!"—but she was inarticulate.

John crept out like a frog from under the sofa. His mother glanced up.

"Yes," she said, "just look at those shirt-sleeves!"

The boy held them out to survey them, saying nothing. Then somebody called in a hoarse voice away down the line, and suspense bristled in the room, till two people had gone by outside, talking.

"It is time for bed," said the mother.

"My father hasn't come," wailed Annie plaintively. But her mother was primed with courage.

"Never mind. They'll bring him when he does come—like a log." She meant there would be no scene. "And he may sleep on the floor till he wakes himself. I know he'll not go to work tomorrow after this!"

The children had their hands and faces wiped with a flannel. They were very quiet. When they had put on their nightdresses, they said their prayers, the boy mumbling. The mother looked down at them, at the brown silken bush of intertwining curls in the nape of the girl's neck, at the little black head of the lad, and her heart burst with anger at their father who caused all three such distress. The children hid their faces in her skirts for comfort.

When Mrs. Bates came down, the room was strangely empty, with a tension of expectancy. She took up her sewing and stitched for some time without raising her head. Meantime her anger was tinged with fear.

II

The clock struck eight and she rose suddenly, dropping her sewing on her chair. She went to the stairfoot door, opened it, listening. Then she went out, locking the door behind her.

Something scuffled in the yard, and she started, though she knew it was only the rats with which the place was overrun. The night was very dark. In the great bay of railway lines, bulked with trucks, there was no trace of light, only away back she could see a few yellow lamps at the pit-top, and the red smear of the burning pit-bank on the night. She hurried along the edge of the track, then, crossing the converging lines, came to the stile by the white gates, whence she emerged on the road. Then the fear which had led her shrank. People were walking up to New Brinsley; she saw the lights in the houses; twenty yards further on were the broad windows of the 'Prince of Wales', very warm and bright, and the loud voices of men could be heard distinctly. What a fool she had been to imagine that anything had happened to him! He was merely drinking over there at the 'Prince of Wales'. She faltered. She had never yet been to fetch him, and she never would go. So she continued her walk towards the long straggling line of houses, standing blank on the highway. She entered a passage between the dwellings.

"Mr. Rigley?—Yes! Did you want him? No, he's not in at this minute."

The raw-boned woman leaned forward from her dark scullery and peered at the other, upon whom fell a dim light through the blind of the kitchen window.

"Is it Mrs. Bates?" she asked in a tone tinged with respect.

"Yes. I wondered if your Master was at home. Mine hasn't come yet."

"'Asn't 'e! Oh, Jack's been 'ome an 'ad 'is dinner an' gone out. E's just gone for 'alf an hour afore bedtime. Did you call at the 'Prince of Wales'?"

"No—"

"No, you didn't like—! It's not very nice." The other woman was indulgent. There was an awkward pause. "Jack never said nothink about—about your Mester," she said.

"No!—I expect he's stuck in there!"

Elizabeth Bates said this bitterly, and with recklessness. She knew that the woman across the yard was standing at her door listening, but she did not care. As she turned:

"Stop a minute! I'll just go an' ask Jack if e' knows anythink," said Mrs. Rigley.

"Oh, no—I wouldn't like to put—!"

"Yes, I will, if you'll just step inside an' see as th' childer doesn't come downstairs and set theirselves afire."

Elizabeth Bates, murmuring a remonstrance, stepped inside. The other woman apologized for the state of the room.

The kitchen needed apology. There were little frocks and trousers and childish undergarments on the squab and on the floor, and a litter of playthings everywhere. On the black American cloth of the table were pieces of bread and cake, crusts, slops, and a teapot with cold tea.

"Eh, ours is just as bad," said Elizabeth Bates, looking at the woman, not at the house. Mrs. Rigley put a shawl over her head and hurried out, saying:

"I shanna be a minute."

The other sat, noting with faint disapproval the general untidiness of the room. Then she fell to counting the shoes of various sizes scattered over the floor. There were twelve. She sighed and said to herself, "No wonder!"—glancing at the litter. There came the scratching of two pairs of feet on the yard, and the Rigleys entered. Elizabeth Bates rose. Rigley was a big man, with very large bones. His head looked particularly bony. Across his temple was a blue scar, caused by a wound got in the pit, a wound in which the coal-dust remained blue like tattooing.

"Asna 'e come whoam yit?" asked the man, without any form of greeting, but with deference and sympathy. "I couldna say wheer he is—'e's non ower theer!"—he jerked his head to signify the 'Prince of Wales'.

"'E's 'appen gone up to th' 'Yew'," said Mrs. Rigley.

There was another pause. Rigley had evidently something to get off his mind:

"Ah left 'im finishin' a stint," he began. "Loose-all 'ad bin gone about ten minutes when we com'n away, an' I shouted, 'Are ter comin', Walt?' an' 'e said, 'Go on, Ah shanna be but a'ef a minnit,' so we com'n ter th' bottom, me an' Bowers, thinkin' as 'e wor just behint, an' 'ud come up i' th' next bantle—"

He stood perplexed, as if answering a charge of deserting his mate. Elizabeth Bates, now again certain of disaster, hastened to reassure him:

"I expect 'e's gone up to th' 'Yew Tree', as you say. It's not the first time. I've fretted myself into a fever before now. He'll come home when they carry him."

"Ay, isn't it too bad!" deplored the other woman.

"I'll just step up to Dick's an' see if 'e is theer," offered the man, afraid of appearing alarmed, afraid of taking liberties.

"Oh, I wouldn't think of bothering you that far," said Elizabeth Bates, with emphasis, but he knew she was glad of his offer.

As they stumbled up the entry, Elizabeth Bates heard Rigley's wife run across the yard and open her neighbour's door. At this, suddenly all the blood in her body seemed to switch away from her heart.

"Mind!" warned Rigley. "Ah've said many a time as Ah'd fill up them ruts in this entry, sumb'dy 'll be breakin' their legs yit."

She recovered herself and walked quickly along with the miner.

"I don't like leaving the children in bed, and nobody in the house," she said.

"No, you dunna!" he replied courteously. They were soon at the gate of the cottage.

"Well, I shanna be many minnits. Dunna you be frettin' now, 'e'll be all right," said the butty.

"Thank you very much, Mr. Rigley," she replied.

"You're welcome!" he stammered, moving away. "I shanna be many minnits."

The house was quiet. Elizabeth Bates took off her hat and shawl, and rolled back the rug. When she had finished, she sat down. It was a few minutes past nine. She was startled by the rapid chuff of the winding-engine at the pit, and the sharp whirr of the brakes on the rope as it descended. Again she felt the painful sweep of her blood, and she put her hand to her side, saying aloud, "Good gracious!—it's only the nine o'clock deputy going down," rebuking herself.

She sat still, listening. Half an hour of this, and she was wearied out.

"What am I working myself up like this for?" she said pitiably to herself, "I s'll only be doing myself some damage."

She took out her sewing again.

At a quarter to ten there were footsteps. One person! She watched for the door to open. It was an elderly woman, in a black bonnet and a black woollen shawl—his mother. She was about sixty years old, pale, with blue eyes, and her face all wrinkled and lamentable. She shut the door and turned to her daughter-in-law peevishly.

"Eh, Lizzie, whatever shall we do, whatever shall we do!" she cried.

Elizabeth drew back a little, sharply.

"What is it, mother?" she said.

The elder woman seated herself on the sofa.

"I don't know, child, I can't tell you!"—she shook her head slowly. Elizabeth sat watching her, anxious and vexed.

"I don't know," replied the grandmother, sighing very deeply. "There's no end to my troubles, there isn't. The things I've gone through, I'm sure it's enough—!" She wept without wiping her eyes, the tears running.

"But, mother," interrupted Elizabeth, "what do you mean? What is it?"

The grandmother slowly wiped her eyes. The fountains of her tears were stopped by Elizabeth's directness. She wiped her eyes slowly.

"Poor child! Eh, you poor thing!" she moaned. "I don't know what we're going to do, I don't—and you as you are—it's a thing, it is indeed!"

Elizabeth waited.

"Is he dead?" she asked, and at the words her heart swung violently, though she felt a slight flush of shame at the ultimate extravagance of the question. Her words sufficiently frightened the old lady, almost brought her to herself.

"Don't say so, Elizabeth! We'll hope it's not as bad as that; no, may the Lord spare us that, Elizabeth. Jack Rigley came just as I was sittin' down to a glass afore going to bed, an' 'e said, "Appen you'll go down th' line, Mrs. Bates. Walt's had an accident. 'Appen you'll go an' sit wi' 'er till we can get him home.' I hadn't time to ask him a word afore he was gone. An' I put my bonnet on an' come straight down, Lizzie. I thought to myself, 'Eh, that poor blessed child, if anybody should come an' tell her of a sudden, there's no knowin' what'll 'appen to 'er.' You mustn't let it upset you, Lizzie—or you know what to expect. How long is it, six months—or is it five, Lizzie? Ay!"—the old woman shook her head—"time slips on, it slips on! Ay!"

Elizabeth's thoughts were busy elsewhere. If he was killed—would she be able to manage on the little pension and what she could earn?—she counted up rapidly. If he was hurt—they wouldn't take him to the hospital—how tiresome he would be to nurse!—but perhaps she'd be able to get him away from the drink and his hateful ways. She would—while he was ill. The tears offered to come to her eyes at the picture. But what sentimental luxury was this she was beginning?—She turned to consider the children. At any rate she was absolutely necessary for them. They were her business.

"Ay!" repeated the old woman, "it seems but a week or two since he brought me his first wages. Ay—he was a good lad, Elizabeth, he was, in his way. I don't know why he got to be such a trouble, I don't. He was a happy lad at home, only full of spirits. But there's no mistake he's been a handful of trouble, he has! I hope the Lord'll spare him to mend his ways. I hope so, I hope so. You've had a sight o' trouble with him, Elizabeth, you have indeed. But he was a jolly enough lad wi' me, he was, I can assure you. I don't know how it is . . ."

The old woman continued to muse aloud, a monotonous irritating sound, while Elizabeth thought concentratedly, startled once, when she heard the winding-engine chuff quickly, and the brakes skirr with a shriek. Then she heard the engine more slowly, and the brakes made no sound. The old woman did not notice. Elizabeth waited in suspense. The mother-in-law talked, with lapses into silence.

"But he wasn't your son, Lizzie, an' it makes a difference. Whatever he was, I remember him when he was little, an' I learned to understand him and to make allowances. You've got to make allowances for them—"

It was half-past ten, and the old woman was saying: "But it's trouble from beginning to end; you're never too old for trouble, never too old for that—" when the gate banged back, and there were heavy feet on the steps.

"I'll go, Lizzie, let me go," cried the old woman, rising. But Elizabeth was at the door. It was a man in pit-clothes.

"They're bringin' 'im, Missis," he said. Elizabeth's heart halted a moment. Then it surged on again, almost suffocating her.

"Is he—is it bad?" she asked.

The man turned away, looking at the darkness:

"The doctor says 'e'd been dead hours. 'E saw 'im i' th' lamp-cabin."

The old woman, who stood just behind Elizabeth, dropped into a chair, and folded her hands, crying: "Oh, my boy, my boy!"

"Hush!" said Elizabeth, with a sharp twitch of a frown. "Be still, mother, don't waken th' children: I wouldn't have them down for anything!"

The old woman moaned softly, rocking herself. The man was drawing away. Elizabeth took a step forward.

"How was it?" she asked.

"Well, I couldn't say for sure," the man replied, very ill at ease. "'E wor finishin' a stint an' th' butties 'ad gone, an' a lot o' stuff come down atop 'n 'im."

"And crushed him?" cried the widow, with a shudder.

"No," said the man, "it fell at th' back of 'im. 'E wor under th' face, an' it niver touched 'im. It shut 'im in. It seems 'e wor smothered."

Elizabeth shrank back. She heard the old woman behind her cry:

"What?—what did 'e say it was?"

The man replied, more loudly: "'E wor smothered!"

Then the old woman wailed aloud, and this relieved Elizabeth.

"Oh, mother," she said, putting her hand on the old woman, "don't waken th' children, don't waken th' children."

She wept a little, unknowing, while the old mother rocked herself and moaned. Elizabeth remembered that they were bringing him home, and she must be ready. "They'll lay him in the parlour," she said to herself, standing a moment pale and perplexed.

Then she lighted a candle and went into the tiny room. The air was cold and damp, but she could not make a fire, there was no fireplace. She set down the candle and looked round. The candle-light glittered on the lustre-glasses, on the two vases that held some of the pink chrysanthemums, and on the dark mahogany. There was a cold, deathly smell of chrysanthemums in the room. Elizabeth stood looking at the flowers. She turned away, and calculated whether there would be room to lay him on the floor, between the couch and the chiffonier. She pushed the chairs aside. There would be room to lay him down and to step round him. Then she fetched the old red tablecloth, and another old cloth, spreading them down to save her bit of carpet. She shivered on leaving the parlour; so, from the dresser-drawer she took a clean shirt and put it at the fire to air. All the time her mother-in-law was rocking herself in the chair and moaning.

"You'll have to move from there, mother," said Elizabeth. "They'll be bringing him in. Come in the rocker."

The old mother rose mechanically, and seated herself by the fire, continuing to lament. Elizabeth went into the pantry for another candle, and there, in the little penthouse under the naked tiles, she heard them coming. She stood still in the pantry doorway, listening. She heard them pass the end of the house, and come awkwardly down the three steps, a jumble of shuffling footsteps and muttering voices. The old woman was silent. The men were in the yard.

Then Elizabeth heard Matthews, the manager of the pit, say: "You go in first, Jim. Mind!"

The door came open, and the two women saw a collier backing into the room, holding one end of a stretcher, on which they could see the nailed pit-boots of the dead man. The two carriers halted, the man at the head stooping to the lintel of the door.

"Wheer will you have him?" asked the manager, a short, white-bearded man.

Elizabeth roused herself and came from the pantry carrying the unlighted candle.

"In the parlour," she said.

"In there, Jim!" pointed the manager, and the carriers backed round into the tiny room. The coat with which they had covered the body fell off as they awkwardly turned through the two doorways, and the women saw their man, naked to the waist, lying stripped for work. The old woman began to moan in a low voice of horror.

"Lay th' stretcher at th' side," snapped the manager, "an' put 'im on th' cloths. Mind now, mind! Look you now—!"

One of the men had knocked off a vase of chrysanthemums. He stared awkwardly, then they set down the stretcher. Elizabeth did not look at her husband. As soon as she could get in the room, she went and picked up the broken vase and the flowers.

"Wait a minute!" she said.

The three men waited in silence while she mopped up the water with a duster.

"Eh, what a job, what a job, to be sure!" the manager was saying, rubbing his brow with trouble and perplexity. "Never knew such a thing in my life, never! He'd no business to ha' been left. I never knew such a thing in my life! Fell over him clean as a whistle, an' shut him in. Not four foot of space, there wasn't—yet it scarce bruised him."

He looked down at the dead man, lying prone, half naked, all grimed with coal-dust.

"'Sphyxiated,' the doctor said. It is the most terrible job I've ever known. Seems as if it was done o' purpose. Clean over him, an' shut 'im in, like a mouse-trap"—he made a sharp, descending gesture with his hand.

The colliers standing by jerked aside their heads in hopeless comment.

The horror of the thing bristled upon them all.

Then they heard the girl's voice upstairs calling shrilly: "Mother, mother—who is it? Mother, who is it?"

Elizabeth hurried to the foot of the stairs and opened the door:

"Go to sleep!" she commanded sharply. "What are you shouting about? Go to sleep at once—there's nothing—"

Then she began to mount the stairs. They could hear her on the boards, and on the plaster floor of the little bedroom. They could hear her distinctly:

"What's the matter now?—what's the matter with you, silly thing?"—her voice was much agitated, with an unreal gentleness.

"I thought it was some men come," said the plaintive voice of the child. "Has he come?"

"Yes, they've brought him. There's nothing to make a fuss about. Go to sleep now, like a good child."

They could hear her voice in the bedroom, they waited whilst she covered the children under the bedclothes.

"Is he drunk?" asked the girl, timidly, faintly.

"No! No—he's not! He—he's asleep."

"Is he asleep downstairs?"

"Yes—and don't make a noise."

There was silence for a moment, then the men heard the frightened child again:

"What's that noise?"

"It's nothing, I tell you, what are you bothering for?"

The noise was the grandmother moaning. She was oblivious of everything, sitting on her chair rocking and moaning. The manager put his hand on her arm and bade her "Sh—sh!!"

The old woman opened her eyes and looked at him. She was shocked by this interruption, and seemed to wonder.

"What time is it?"—the plaintive thin voice of the child, sinking back unhappily into sleep, asked this last question.

"Ten o'clock," answered the mother more softly. Then she must have bent down and kissed the children.

Matthews beckoned to the men to come away. They put on their caps and took up the stretcher. Stepping over the body, they tiptoed out of the house. None of them spoke till they were far from the wakeful children.

When Elizabeth came down she found her mother alone on the parlour floor, leaning over the dead man, the tears dropping on him.

"We must lay him out," the wife said. She put on the kettle, then returning knelt at the feet, and began to unfasten the knotted leather laces. The room was clammy and dim with only one candle, so that she had to bend her face almost to the floor. At last she got off the heavy boots and put them away.

"You must help me now," she whispered to the old woman. Together they stripped the man.

When they arose, saw him lying in the naïve dignity of death, the women stood arrested in fear and respect. For a few moments they remained still, looking down, the old mother whimpering. Elizabeth felt countermanded. She saw him, how utterly inviolable he lay in himself. She had nothing to do with him. She could not accept it. Stooping, she laid her hand on him, in claim. He was still warm, for the mine was hot where he had died. His mother had his face between her hands, and was murmuring incoherently. The old tears fell in succession as drops from wet leaves; the mother was not weeping, merely her tears flowed. Elizabeth embraced the body of her husband, with cheek and lips. She seemed to be listening, inquiring, trying to get some connection. But she could not. She was driven away. He was impregnable.

She rose, went into the kitchen, where she poured warm water into a bowl, brought soap and flannel and a soft towel.

"I must wash him," she said.

Then the old mother rose stiffly, and watched Elizabeth as she carefully washed his face, carefully brushing the big blond moustache from his mouth with the flannel. She was afraid with a bottomless fear, so she ministered to him. The old woman, jealous, said:

"Let me wipe him!"—and she kneeled on the other side drying slowly as Elizabeth washed, her big black bonnet sometimes brushing the dark head of her daughter. They worked thus in silence for a long time. They never forgot it was death, and the touch of the man's dead body gave them strange emotions, different in each of the women; a great dread possessed them both, the mother felt the lie was given to her womb, she was denied; the wife felt the utter isolation of the human soul, the child within her was a weight apart from her.

At last it was finished. He was a man of handsome body, and his face showed no traces of drink. He was blonde, full-fleshed, with fine limbs. But he was dead.

"Bless him," whispered his mother, looking always at his face, and speaking out of sheer terror. "Dear lad—bless him!" She spoke in a faint, sibilant ecstasy of fear and mother love.

Elizabeth sank down again to the floor, and put her face against his neck, and trembled and shuddered. But she had to draw away again. He was dead, and her living flesh had no place against his. A great dread and weariness held her: she was so unavailing. Her life was gone like this.

"White as milk he is, clear as a twelve-month baby, bless him, the darling!" the old mother murmured to herself. "Not a mark on him, clear and clean and white, beautiful as ever a child was made," she murmured with pride. Elizabeth kept her face hidden.

"He went peaceful, Lizzie—peaceful as sleep. Isn't he beautiful, the lamb? Ay—he must ha' made his peace, Lizzie. 'Appen he made it all right, Lizzie, shut in there. He'd have time. He wouldn't look like this if he hadn't made his peace. The lamb, the dear lamb. Eh, but he had a hearty laugh. I loved to hear it. He had the heartiest laugh, Lizzie, as a lad—"

Elizabeth looked up. The man's mouth was fallen back, slightly open under the cover of the moustache. The eyes, half shut, did not show glazed in the obscurity. Life with its smoky burning gone from him, had left him apart and utterly alien to her. And she knew what a stranger he was to her. In her womb was ice of fear, because of this separate stranger with whom she had been living as one flesh. Was this what it all meant—utter, intact separateness, obscured by heat of living? In dread she turned her face away. The fact was too deadly. There had been nothing between them, and yet they had come together, exchanging their nakedness repeatedly. Each time he had taken her, they had been two isolated beings, far apart as now. He was no more responsible than she. The child was like ice in her womb. For as she looked at the dead man, her mind, cold and detached, said clearly: "Who am I? What have I been doing? I have been fighting a husband who did not exist. He existed all the time. What wrong have I done? What was that I have been living with? There lies the reality, this man."—And her soul died in her for fear: she knew she had never seen him, he had never seen her, they had met in the dark and had fought in the dark, not knowing whom they met nor whom they fought. And now she saw, and turned silent in seeing. For she had been wrong. She had said he was something he was not; she had felt familiar with him. Whereas he was apart all the while, living as she never lived, feeling as she never felt.

In fear and shame she looked at his naked body, that she had known falsely. And he was the father of her children. Her soul was torn from her body and stood apart. She looked at his naked body and was ashamed, as if she had denied it. After all, it was itself. It seemed awful to her. She looked at his face, and she turned her own face to the wall. For his look was other than hers, his way was not her way. She had denied him what he was—she saw it now. She had refused him as himself.—And this had been her life, and his life.—She was grateful to death, which restored the truth. And she knew she was not dead.

And all the while her heart was bursting with grief and pity for him. What had he suffered? What stretch of horror for this helpless man! She was rigid with agony. She had not been able to help him. He had been cruelly injured, this naked man, this other being, and she could make no reparation. There were the children—but the children belonged to life. This dead man had nothing to do with them. He and she were only channels through which life had flowed to issue in the children. She was a mother—but how awful she knew it now to have been a wife. And he, dead now, how awful he must have felt it to be a husband. She felt that in the next world he would be a stranger to her. If they met there, in the beyond, they would only be ashamed of what had been before. The children had come, for some mysterious reason, out of both of them. But the children did not unite them. Now he was dead, she knew how eternally he was apart from her, how eternally he had nothing more to do with her. She saw this episode of her life closed. They had denied each other in life. Now he had withdrawn. An anguish came over her. It was finished then: it had become hopeless between them long before he died. Yet he had been her husband. But how little!—

"Have you got his shirt, 'Lizabeth?"

Elizabeth turned without answering, though she strove to weep and behave as her mother-in-law expected. But she could not, she was silenced. She went into the kitchen and returned with the garment.

"It is aired," she said, grasping the cotton shirt here and there to try. She was almost ashamed to handle him; what right had she or anyone to lay hands on him; but her touch was humble on his body. It was hard work to clothe him. He was so heavy and inert. A terrible dread gripped her all the while: that he could be so heavy and utterly inert, unresponsive, apart. The horror of the distance between them was almost too much for her—it was so infinite a gap she must look across.

At last it was finished. They covered him with a sheet and left him lying, with his face bound. And she fastened the door of the little parlour, lest the children should see what was lying there. Then, with peace sunk heavy on her heart, she went about making tidy the kitchen. She knew she submitted to life, which was her immediate master. But from death, her ultimate master, she winced with fear and shame.

ENGLAND, MY ENGLAND

He was working on the edge of the common, beyond the small brook that ran in the dip at the bottom of the garden, carrying the garden path in continuation from the plank bridge on to the common. He had cut the rough turf and bracken, leaving the grey, dryish soil bare. But he was worried because he could not get the path straight, there was a pleat between his brows. He had set up his sticks, and taken the sights between the big pine trees, but for some reason everything seemed wrong. He looked again, straining his keen blue eyes, that had a touch of the Viking in them, through the shadowy pine trees as through a doorway, at the green-grassed garden-path rising from the shadow of alders by the log bridge up to the sunlit flowers. Tall white and purple columbines, and the butt-end of the old Hampshire cottage that crouched near the earth amid flowers, blossoming in the bit of shaggy wildness round about.

There was a sound of children's voices calling and talking: high, childish, girlish voices, slightly didactic and tinged with domineering: 'If you don't come quick, nurse, I shall run out there to where there are snakes.' And nobody had the *sang-froid* to reply: 'Run then, little fool.' It was always, 'No, darling. Very well, darling. In a moment, darling. Darling, you *must* be patient.'

His heart was hard with disillusion: a continual gnawing and resistance. But he worked on. What was there to do but submit!

The sunlight blazed down upon the earth, there was a vividness of flamy vegetation, of fierce seclusion amid the savage peace of the commons. Strange how the savage England lingers in patches: as here, amid these shaggy gorse commons, and marshy, snake infested places near the foot of the south downs. The spirit of place lingering on primeval, as when the Saxons came, so long ago.

Ah, how he had loved it! The green garden path, the tufts of flowers, purple and white columbines, and great oriental red poppies with their black chaps and mulleins tall and yellow, this flamy garden which had been a garden for a thousand years, scooped out in the little hollow among the snake-infested commons. He had made it flame with flowers, in a sun cup under its hedges and trees. So old, so old a place! And yet he had recreated it.

The timbered cottage with its sloping, cloak-like roof was old and forgotten. It belonged to the old England of hamlets and yeomen. Lost all alone on the edge of the common, at the end of a wide, grassy, briar-entangled lane shaded with oak, it had never known the world of today. Not till Egbert came with his bride. And he had come to fill it with flowers.

The house was ancient and very uncomfortable. But he did not want to alter it. Ah, marvellous to sit there in the wide, black, time-old chimney, at night when the wind roared overhead, and the wood which he had chopped himself sputtered on the hearth! Himself on one side the angle, and Winifred on the other.

Ah, how he had wanted her: Winifred! She was young and beautiful and strong with life, like a flame in sunshine. She moved with a slow grace of energy like a blossoming, red-flowered bush in motion. She, too, seemed to come out of the old England, ruddy, strong, with a certain crude, passionate quiescence and a hawthorn robustness. And he, he was tall and slim and agile, like an English archer with his long supple legs and fine movements. Her hair was nut-brown and all in energic curls and tendrils. Her eyes were nut-brown, too, like a robin's for brightness. And he was white-skinned with fine, silky hair that had darkened from fair, and a slightly arched nose of an old country family. They were a beautiful couple.

The house was Winifred's. Her father was a man of energy, too. He had come from the north poor. Now he was moderately rich. He had bought this fair stretch of inexpensive land, down in Hampshire. Not far from the tiny church of the almost extinct hamlet stood his own house, a commodious old farmhouse standing back from the road across a bare grassed yard. On one side of this quadrangle was the long, long barn or shed which he had made into a cottage for his youngest daughter Priscilla. One saw little blue-and-white check curtains at the long windows, and inside, overhead, the grand old timbers of the high-pitched shed. This was Prissy's house. Fifty yards away was the pretty little new cottage which he had built for his daughter Magdalen, with the vegetable garden stretching away to the oak copse. And then away beyond the lawns and rose trees of the house-garden went the track across a shaggy, wild grass space, towards the ridge of tall black pines that grew on a dyke-bank, through the pines and above the sloping little bog, under the wide, desolate oak trees, till there was Winifred's cottage crouching unexpectedly in front, so much alone, and so primitive.

It was Winifred's own house, and the gardens and the bit of common and the boggy slope were hers: her tiny domain. She had married just at the time when her father had bought the estate, about ten years before the war, so she had been able to come to Egbert with this for a marriage portion. And who was more delighted, he or she, it would be hard to say. She was only twenty at the time, and he was only twenty-one. He had about a hundred and fifty pounds a year of his own—and nothing else but his very considerable personal attractions. He had no profession: he earned nothing. But he talked of literature and music, he had a passion for old folk-music, collecting folk-songs and folk-dances, studying the Morris-dance and the old customs. Of course in time he would make money in these ways.

Meanwhile youth and health and passion and promise. Winifred's father was always generous: but still, he was a man from the north with a hard head and a hard skin too, having received a good many knocks. At home he kept the hard head out of sight, and played at poetry and romance with his literary wife and his sturdy, passionate girls. He was a man of courage, not given to complaining, bearing his burdens by himself. No, he did not let the world intrude far into his home. He had a delicate, sensitive wife whose poetry won some fame in the narrow world of letters. He himself, with his tough old barbarian fighting spirit, had an almost child-like delight in verse, in sweet poetry, and in the delightful game of a cultured home. His blood was strong even to coarseness. But that only made the home more vigorous, more robust and Christmassy. There was always a touch of Christmas about him, now he was well off. If there was poetry after dinner, there were also chocolates and nuts, and good little out-of-the-way things to be munching.

Well then, into this family came Egbert. He was made of quite a different paste. The girls and the father were strong-limbed, thick-blooded people, true English, as holly-trees and hawthorn are English. Their culture was grafted on to them, as one might perhaps graft a common pink rose on to a thorn-stem. It flowered oddly enough, but it did not alter their blood.

And Egbert was a born rose. The age-long breeding had left him with a delightful spontaneous passion. He was not clever, nor even 'literary'. No, but the intonation of his voice, and the movement of his supple, handsome body, and the fine texture of his flesh and his hair, the slight arch of his nose, the quickness of his blue eyes would easily take the place of poetry. Winifred loved him, loved him, this southerner, as a higher being. A _higher_ being, mind you. Not a deeper. And as for him, he loved her in passion with every fibre of him. She was the very warm stuff of life to him.

Wonderful then, those days at Crockham Cottage, the first days, all alone save for the woman who came to work in the mornings. Marvellous days, when she had all his tall, supple, fine-fleshed youth to herself, for herself, and he had her like a ruddy fire into which he could cast himself for rejuvenation. Ah, that it might never end, this passion, this marriage! The flame of their two bodies burnt again into that old cottage, that was haunted already by so much by-gone, physical desire. You could not be in the dark room for an hour without the influences coming over you. The hot blood-desire of by-gone yeomen, there in this old den where they had lusted and bred for so many generations. The silent house, dark, with thick, timbered walls and the big black chimney-place, and the sense of secrecy. Dark, with low, little windows, sunk into the earth. Dark, like a lair where strong beasts had lurked and mated, lonely at night and lonely by day, left to themselves and their own intensity for so many generations. It seemed to cast a spell on the two young people. They became different. There was a curious secret glow about them, a certain slumbering flame hard to understand, that enveloped them both. They too felt that they did not belong to the London world any more. Crockham had changed their blood: the sense of the snakes that lived and slept even in their own garden, in the sun, so that he, going forward with the spade, would see a curious coiled brownish pile on the black soil, which suddenly would start up, hiss, and dazzle rapidly away, hissing. One day Winifred heard the strangest scream from the flower-bed under the low window of the living room: ah, the strangest scream, like the very soul of the dark past crying aloud. She ran out, and saw a long brown snake on the flower-bed, and in its flat mouth the one hind leg of a frog was striving to escape, and screaming its strange, tiny, bellowing scream. She looked at the snake, and from its sullen flat head it looked at her, obstinately. She gave a cry, and it released the frog and slid angrily away.

That was Crockham. The spear of modern invention had not passed through it, and it lay there secret, primitive, savage as when the Saxons first came. And Egbert and she were caught there, caught out of the world.

He was not idle, nor was she. There were plenty of things to be done, the house to be put into final repair after the workmen had gone, cushions and curtains to sew, the paths to make, the water to fetch and attend to, and then the slope of the deep-soiled, neglected garden to level, to terrace with little terraces and paths, and to fill with flowers. He worked away, in his shirt-sleeves, worked all day intermittently doing this thing and the other. And she, quiet and rich in herself, seeing him stooping and labouring away by himself, would come to help him, to be near him. He of course was an amateur—a born amateur. He worked so hard, and did so little, and nothing he ever did would hold together for long. If he terraced the garden, he held up the earth with a couple of long narrow planks that soon began to bend with the pressure from behind, and would not need many years to rot through and break and let the soil slither all down again in a heap towards the stream-bed. But there you are. He had not been brought up to come to grips with anything, and he thought it would do. Nay, he did not think there was anything else except little temporary contrivances possible, he who had such a passion for his old enduring cottage, and for the old enduring things of the bygone England. Curious that the sense of permanency in the past had such a hold over him, whilst in the present he was all amateurish and sketchy.

Winifred could not criticize him. Town-bred, everything seemed to her splendid, and the very digging and shovelling itself seemed romantic. But neither Egbert nor she yet realized the difference between work and romance.

Godfrey Marshall, her father, was at first perfectly pleased with the ménage down at Crockham Cottage. He thought Egbert was wonderful, the many things he accomplished, and he was gratified by the glow of physical passion between the two young people. To the man who in London still worked hard to keep steady his modest fortune, the thought of this young couple digging away and loving one another down at Crockham Cottage, buried deep among the commons and marshes, near the pale-showing bulk of the downs, was like a chapter of living romance. And they drew the sustenance for their fire of passion from him, from the old man. It was he who fed their flame. He triumphed secretly in the thought. And it was to her father that Winifred still turned, as the one source of all surety and life and support. She loved Egbert with passion. But behind her was the power of her father. It was the power of her father she referred to, whenever she needed to refer. It never occurred to her to refer to Egbert, if she were in difficulty or doubt. No, in all the *serious* matters she depended on her father.

For Egbert had no intention of coming to grips with life. He had no ambition whatsoever. He came from a decent family, from a pleasant country home, from delightful surroundings. He should, of course, have had a profession. He should have studied law or entered business in some way. But no—that fatal three pounds a week would keep him from starving as long as he lived, and he did not want to give himself into bondage. It was not that he was idle. He was always doing something, in his amateurish way. But he had no desire to give himself to the world, and still less had he any desire to fight his way in the world. No, no, the world wasn't worth it. He wanted to ignore it, to go his own way apart, like a casual pilgrim down the forsaken sidetracks. He loved his wife, his cottage and garden. He would make his life there, as a sort of epicurean hermit. He loved the past, the old music and dances and customs of old England. He would try and live in the spirit of these, not in the spirit of the world of business.

But often Winifred's father called her to London: for he loved to have his children round him. So Egbert and she must have a tiny flat in town, and the young couple must transfer themselves from time to time from the country to the city. In town Egbert had plenty of friends, of the same ineffectual sort as himself, tampering with the arts, literature, painting, sculpture, music. He was not bored.

Three pounds a week, however, would not pay for all this. Winifred's father paid. He liked paying. He made her only a very small allowance, but he often gave her ten pounds—or gave Egbert ten pounds. So they both looked on the old man as the mainstay. Egbert didn't mind being patronized and paid for. Only when he felt the family was a little *too* condescending, on account of money, he began to get huffy.

Then of course children came: a lovely little blonde daughter with a head of thistle-down. Everybody adored the child. It was the first exquisite blonde thing that had come into the family, a little mite with the white, slim, beautiful limbs of its father, and as it grew up the dancing, dainty movement of a wild little daisy-spirit. No wonder the Marshalls all loved the child: they called her Joyce. They themselves had their own grace, but it was slow, rather heavy. They had everyone of them strong, heavy limbs and darkish skins, and they were short in stature. And now they had for one of their own this light little cowslip child. She was like a little poem in herself.

But nevertheless, she brought a new difficulty. Winifred must have a nurse for her. Yes, yes, there must be a nurse. It was the family decree. Who was to pay for the nurse? The grandfather—seeing the father himself earned no money. Yes, the grandfather would pay, as he had paid all the lying-in expenses. There came a slight sense of money-strain. Egbert was living on his father-in-law.

After the child was born, it was never quite the same between him and Winifred. The difference was at first hardly perceptible. But it was there. In the first place Winifred had a new centre of interest. She was not going to adore her child. But she had what the modern mother so often has in the place of spontaneous love: a profound sense of duty towards her child. Winifred appreciated her darling little girl, and felt a deep sense of duty towards her. Strange, that this sense of duty should go deeper than the love for her husband. But so it was. And so it often is. The responsibility of motherhood was the prime responsibility in Winifred's heart: the responsibility of wifehood came a long way second.

Her child seemed to link her up again in a circuit with her own family. Her father and mother, herself, and her child, that was the human trinity for her. Her husband—? Yes, she loved him still. But that was like play. She had an almost barbaric sense of duty and of family. Till she married, her first human duty had been towards her father: he was the pillar, the source of life, the everlasting support. Now another link was added to the chain of duty: her father, herself, and her child.

Egbert was out of it. Without anything happening, he was gradually, unconsciously excluded from the circle. His wife still loved him, physically. But, but—he was *almost* the unnecessary party in the affair. He could not complain of Winifred. She still did her duty towards him. She still had a physical passion for him, that physical passion on which he had put all his life and soul. But—but—

It was for a long while an ever-recurring *but*. And then, after the second child, another blonde, winsome touching little thing, not so proud and flame-like as Joyce—after Annabel came, then Egbert began truly to realize how it was. His wife still loved him. But—and now the but had grown enormous—her physical love for him was of secondary importance to her. It became ever less important. After all, she had had it, this physical passion, for two years now. It was not this that one lived from. No, no—something sterner, realer.

She began to resent her own passion for Egbert—just a little she began to despise it. For after all there he was, he was charming, he was lovable, he was terribly desirable.

But—but—oh, the awful looming cloud of that *but!*—he did not stand firm in the landscape of her life like a tower of strength, like a great pillar of significance. No, he was like a cat one has about the house, which will one day disappear and leave no trace. He was like a flower in the garden, trembling in the wind of life, and then gone, leaving nothing to show. As an adjunct, as an accessory, he was perfect. Many a woman would have adored to have him about her all her life, the most beautiful and desirable of all her possessions. But Winifred belonged to another school.

The years went by, and instead of coming more to grips with life, he relaxed more. He was of a subtle, sensitive, passionate nature. But he simply *would* not give himself to what Winifred called life, *Work*. No, he would not go into the world and work for money. No, he just would not. If Winifred liked to live beyond their small income—well, it was her look-out.

And Winifred did not really want him to go out into the world to work for money. Money became, alas, a word like a firebrand between them, setting them both aflame with anger. But that is because we must talk in symbols. Winifred did not really care about money. She did not care whether he earned or did not earn anything. Only she knew she was dependent on her father for three-fourths of the money spent for herself and her children, that she let that be the *casus belli*, the drawn weapon between herself and Egbert.

What did she want—what did she want? Her mother once said to her, with that characteristic touch of irony: 'Well, dear, if it is your fate to consider the lilies, that toil not, neither do they spin, that is one destiny among many others, and perhaps not so unpleasant as most. Why do you take it amiss, my child?'

The mother was subtler than her children, they very rarely knew how to answer her. So Winifred was only more confused. It was not a question of lilies. At least, if it were a question of lilies, then her children were the little blossoms. They at least *grew*. Doesn't Jesus say: 'Consider the lilies *how they grow*.' Good then, she had her growing babies. But as for that other tall, handsome flower of a father of theirs, he was full grown already, so she did not want to spend her life considering him in the flower of his days.

No, it was not that he didn't earn money. It was not that he was idle. He was *not* idle. He was always doing something, always working away, down at Crockham, doing little jobs. But, oh dear, the little jobs—the garden paths—the gorgeous flowers—the chairs to mend, old chairs to mend!

It was that he stood for nothing. If he had done something unsuccessfully, and *lost* what money they had! If he had but striven with something. Nay, even if he had been wicked, a waster, she would have been more free. She would have had something to resist, at least. A waster stands for something, really. He says: 'No, I will not aid and abet society in this business of increase and hanging together, I will upset the apple-cart as much as I can, in my small way.' Or else he says: 'No, I will *not* bother about others. If I have lusts, they are my own, and I prefer them to other people's virtues.' So, a waster, a scamp, takes a sort of stand. He exposes himself to opposition and final castigation: at any rate in story-books.

But Egbert! What are you to do with a man like Egbert? He had no vices. He was really kind, nay generous. And he was not weak. If he had been weak Winifred could have been kind to him. But he did not even give her that consolation. He was not weak, and he did not want her consolation or her kindness. No, thank you. He was of a fine passionate temper, and of a rarer steel than she. He knew it, and she knew it. Hence she was only the more baffled and maddened, poor thing. He, the higher, the finer, in his way the stronger, played with his garden, and his old folk-songs and Morris-dances, just played, and let her support the pillars of the future on her own heart.

And he began to get bitter, and a wicked look began to come on his face. He did not give in to her; not he. There were seven devils inside his long, slim, white body. He was healthy, full of restrained life. Yes, even he himself had to lock up his own vivid life inside himself, now she would not take it from him. Or rather, now that she only took it occasionally. For she had to yield at times. She loved him so, she desired him so, he was so exquisite to her, the fine creature that he was, finer than herself. Yes, with a groan she had to give in to her own unquenched passion for him. And he came to her then—ah, terrible, ah, wonderful, sometimes she wondered how either of them could live after the terror of the passion that swept between them. It was to her as if pure lightning, flash after flash, went through every fibre of her, till extinction came.

But it is the fate of human beings to live on. And it is the fate of clouds that seem nothing but bits of vapour slowly to pile up, to pile up and fill the heavens and blacken the sun entirely.

So it was. The love came back, the lightning of passion flashed tremendously between them. And there was blue sky and gorgeousness for a little while. And then, as inevitably, as inevitably, slowly the clouds began to edge up again above the horizon, slowly, slowly to lurk about the heavens, throwing an occasional cold and hateful shadow: slowly, slowly to congregate, to fill the empyrean space.

And as the years passed, the lightning cleared the sky more and more rarely, less and less the blue showed. Gradually the grey lid sank down upon them, as if it would be permanent.

Why didn't Egbert do something, then? Why didn't he come to grips with life? Why wasn't he like Winifred's father, a pillar of society, even if a slender, exquisite column? Why didn't he go into harness of some sort? Why didn't he take *some* direction?

Well, you can bring an ass to the water, but you cannot make him drink. The world was the water and Egbert was the ass. And he wasn't having any. He couldn't: he just couldn't. Since necessity did not force him to work for his bread and butter, he would not work for work's sake. You can't make the columbine flowers nod in January, nor make the cuckoo sing in England at Christmas. Why? It isn't his season. He doesn't want to. Nay, he *can't* want to.

And there it was with Egbert. He couldn't link up with the world's work, because the basic desire was absent from him. Nay, at the bottom of him he had an even stronger desire: to hold aloof. To hold aloof. To do nobody any damage. But to hold aloof. It was not his season.

Perhaps he should not have married and had children. But you can't stop the waters flowing.

Which held true for Winifred, too. She was not made to endure aloof. Her family tree was a robust vegetation that had to be stirring and believing. In one direction or another her life *had* to go. In her own home she had known nothing of this diffidence which she found in Egbert, and which she could not understand, and which threw her into such dismay. What was she to do, what was she to do, in face of this terrible diffidence?

It was all so different in her own home. Her father may have had his own misgivings, but he kept them to himself. Perhaps he had no very profound belief in this world of ours, this society which we have elaborated with so much effort, only to find ourselves elaborated to death at last. But Godfrey Marshall was of tough, rough fibre, not without a vein of healthy cunning through it all. It was for him a question of winning through, and

F-in-L /daddy

leaving the rest to heaven. Without having many illusions to grace him, he still *did* believe in heaven. In a dark and unquestioning way, he had a sort of faith: an acrid faith like the sap of some not-to-be-exterminated tree. Just a blind acrid faith as sap is blind and acrid, and yet pushes on in growth and in faith. Perhaps he was unscrupulous, but only as a striving tree is unscrupulous, pushing its single way in a jungle of others.

In the end, it is only this robust, sap-like faith which keeps man going. He may live on for many generations inside the shelter of the social establishment which he has erected for himself, as pear-trees and currant bushes would go on bearing fruit for many seasons, inside a walled garden, even if the race of man were suddenly exterminated. But bit by bit the wall-fruit-trees would gradually pull down the very walls that sustained them. Bit by bit every establishment collapses, unless it is renewed or restored by living hands, all the while.

Egbert could not bring himself to any more of this restoring or renewing business. He was not aware of the fact: but awareness doesn't help much, anyhow. He just couldn't. He had the stoic and epicurean quality of his old, fine breeding. His father-in-law, however, though he was not one bit more of a fool than Egbert, realized that since we are here we may as well live. And so he applied himself to his own tiny section of the social work, and to doing the best for his family, and to leaving the rest to the ultimate will of heaven. A certain robustness of blood made him able to go on. But sometimes even from him spurted a sudden gall of bitterness against the world and its make-up. And yet—he had his own will-to-succeed, and this carried him through. He refused to ask himself what the success would amount to. It amounted to the estate down in Hampshire, and his children lacking for nothing, and himself of some importance in the world: and *basta!*— Basta! Basta!

Nevertheless do not let us imagine that he was a common pusher. He was not. He knew as well as Egbert what disillusion meant. Perhaps in his soul he had the same estimation of success. But he had a certain acrid courage, and a certain will-to-power. In his own small circle he would emanate power, the single power of his own blind self. With all his spoiling of his children, he was still the father of the old English type. He was too wise to make laws and to domineer in the abstract. But he had kept, and all honour to him, a certain primitive dominion over the souls of his children, the old, almost magic prestige of paternity. There it was, still burning in him, the old smoky torch or paternal godhead.

And in the sacred glare of this torch his children had been brought up. He had given the girls every liberty, at last. But he had never really let them go beyond his power. And they, venturing out into the hard white light of our fatherless world, learned to see with the eyes of the world. They learned to criticize their father, even, from some effulgence of worldly white light, to see him as inferior. But this was all very well in the head. The moment they forgot their tricks of criticism, the old red glow of his authority came over them again. He was not to be quenched.

Let the psycho-analyst talk about father complex. It is just a word invented. Here was a man who had kept alive the old red flame of fatherhood, fatherhood that had even the right to sacrifice the child to God, like Isaac. Fatherhood that had life-and-death authority over the children: a great natural power. And till his children could be brought under some other great authority as girls; or could arrive at manhood and become themselves centres of the same power, continuing the same male mystery as men; until such time, willy-nilly, Godfrey Marshall would keep his children.

It had seemed as if he might lose Winifred. Winifred had *adored* her husband, and looked up to him as to something wonderful. Perhaps she had expected in him another great authority, a male authority greater, finer than her father's. For having once known the glow of male power, she would not easily turn to the cold white light of feminine independence. She would hunger, hunger all her life for the warmth and shelter of true male strength.

And hunger she might, for Egbert's power lay in the abnegation of power. He was himself the living negative of power. Even of responsibility. For the negation of power at last means the negation of responsibility. As far as these things went, he would confine himself to himself. He would try to confine his own *influence* even to himself. He would try, as far as possible, to abstain from influencing his children by assuming any responsibility for them. 'A little child shall lead them—' His child should lead, then. He would try not to make it go in any direction whatever. He would abstain from influencing it. Liberty!—

Poor Winifred was like a fish out of water in this liberty, gasping for the denser element which should contain her. Till her child came. And then she knew that she must be responsible for it, that she must have authority over it.

But here Egbert silently and negatively stepped in. Silently, negatively, but fatally he neutralized her authority over her children.

There was a third little girl born. And after this Winifred wanted no more children. Her soul was turning to salt.

So she had charge of the children, they were her responsibility. The money for them had come from her father. She would do her very best for them, and have command over their life and death. But no! Egbert would not take the responsibility. He would not even provide the money. But he would not let her have her way. Her dark, silent, passionate authority he would not allow. It was a battle between them, the battle between liberty and the old blood-power. And of course he won. The little girls loved him and adored him. 'Daddy! Daddy!' They could do as they liked with him. Their mother would have ruled them. She would have ruled them passionately, with indulgence, with the old dark magic of parental authority, something looming and unquestioned and, after all, divine: if we believe in divine authority. The Marshalls did, being Catholic.

And Egbert, he turned her old dark, Catholic blood-authority into a sort of tyranny. He would not leave her her children. He stole them from her, and yet without assuming responsibility for them. He stole them from her, in emotion and spirit, and left her only to command their behaviour. A thankless lot for a mother. And her children adored him, adored him, little knowing the empty bitterness they were preparing for themselves when they too grew up to have husbands: husbands such as Egbert, adorable and null.

Joyce, the eldest, was still his favourite. She was now a quicksilver little thing of six years old. Barbara, the youngest, was a toddler of two years. They spent most of their time down at Crockham, because he wanted to be there. And even Winifred loved the place really. But now, in her frustrated and blinded state, it was full of menace for her children. The adders, the poison-berries, the brook, the marsh, the water that might not be pure—one thing and another. From mother and nurse it was a guerilla gunfire of commands, and blithe, quicksilver disobedience from the three blonde, never-still little girls. Behind the girls was the father, against mother and nurse. And so it was.

'If you don't come quick, nurse, I shall run out there to where there are snakes.'

'Joyce, you *must* be patient. I'm just changing Annabel.'

There you are. There it was: always the same. Working away on the common across the brook he heard it. And he worked on, just the same.

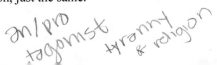

Suddenly he heard a shriek, and he flung the spade from him and started for the bridge, looking up like a startled deer. Ah, there was Winifred—Joyce had hurt herself. He went on up the garden.

'What is it?'

The child was still screaming—now it was—'Daddy! Daddy! Oh—oh, Daddy!' And the mother was saying:

'Don't be frightened, darling. Let mother look.'

But the child only cried:

'Oh, Daddy, Daddy, Daddy!'

She was terrified by the sight of the blood running from her own knee. Winifred crouched down, with her child of six in her lap, to examine the knee. Egbert bent over also.

'Don't make such a noise, Joyce,' he said irritably. 'How did she do it?'

'She fell on that sickle thing which you left lying about after cutting the grass,' said Winifred, looking into his face with bitter accusation as he bent near.

He had taken his handkerchief and tied it round the knee. Then he lifted the still sobbing child in his arms, and carried her into the house and upstairs to her bed. In his arms she became quiet. But his heart was burning with pain and with guilt. He had left the sickle there lying on the edge of the grass, and so his first-born child whom he loved so dearly had come to hurt. But then it was an accident—it was an accident. Why should he feel guilty? It would probably be nothing, better in two or three days. Why take it to heart, why worry? He put it aside.

The child lay on the bed in her little summer frock, her face very white now after the shock, Nurse had come carrying the youngest child: and little Annabel stood holding her skirt. Winifred, terribly serious and wooden-seeming, was bending over the knee, from which she had taken his blood-soaked handkerchief. Egbert bent forward, too, keeping more *sang-froid* in his face than in his heart. Winifred went all of a lump of seriousness, so he had to keep some reserve. The child moaned and whimpered.

The knee was still bleeding profusely—it was a deep cut right in the joint.

'You'd better go for the doctor, Egbert,' said Winifred bitterly.

'Oh, no! Oh, no!' cried Joyce in a panic.

'Joyce, my darling, don't cry!' said Winifred, suddenly catching the little girl to her breast in a strange tragic anguish, the *Mater Dolorata*. Even the child was frightened into silence. Egbert looked at the tragic figure of his wife with the child at her breast, and turned away. Only Annabel started suddenly to cry: 'Joycey, Joycey, don't have your leg bleeding!'

Egbert rode four miles to the village for the doctor. He could not help feeling that Winifred was laying it on rather. Surely the knee itself wasn't hurt! Surely not. It was only a surface cut.

The doctor was out. Egbert left the message and came cycling swiftly home, his heart pinched with anxiety. He dropped sweating off his bicycle and went into the house, looking rather small, like a man who is at fault. Winifred was upstairs sitting by Joyce, who was looking pale and important in bed, and was eating some tapioca pudding. The pale, small, scared face of his child went to Egbert's heart.

'Doctor Wing was out. He'll be here about half past two,' said Egbert.

'I don't want him to come,' whimpered Joyce.

'Joyce, dear, you must be patient and quiet,' said Winifred. 'He won't hurt you. But he will tell us what to do to make your knee better quickly. That is why he must come.'

Winifred always explained carefully to her little girls: and it always took the words off their lips for the moment.

'Does it bleed yet?' said Egbert.

Winifred moved the bedclothes carefully aside.

'I think not,' she said.

Egbert stooped also to look.

'No, it doesn't,' she said. Then he stood up with a relieved look on his face. He turned to the child.

'Eat your pudding, Joyce,' he said. 'It won't be anything. You've only got to keep still for a few days.'

'You haven't had your dinner, have you, Daddy?'

'Not yet.'

'Nurse will give it to you,' said Winifred.

'You'll be all right, Joyce,' he said, smiling to the child and pushing the blonde hair off her brow. She smiled back winsomely into his face.

He went downstairs and ate his meal alone. Nurse served him. She liked waiting on him. All women liked him and liked to do things for him.

The doctor came—a fat country practitioner, pleasant and kind.

'What, little girl, been tumbling down, have you? There's a thing to be doing, for a smart little lady like you! What! And cutting your knee! Tut-tut-tut! That *wasn't* clever of you, now was it? Never mind, never mind, soon be better. Let us look at it. Won't hurt you. Not the least in life. Bring a bowl with a little warm water, nurse. Soon have it all right again, soon have it all right.'

Joyce smiled at him with a pale smile of faint superiority. This was *not* the way in which she was used to being talked to.

He bent down, carefully looking at the little, thin, wounded knee of the child. Egbert bent over him.

'Oh, dear, oh, dear! Quite a deep little cut. Nasty little cut. Nasty little cut. But, never mind. Never mind, little lady. We'll soon have it better. Soon have it better, little lady. What's your name?'

'My name is Joyce,' said the child distinctly.

'Oh, really!' he replied. 'Oh, really! Well, that's a fine name too, in my opinion. Joyce, eh?—And how old might Miss Joyce be? Can she tell me that?'

'I'm six,' said the child, slightly amused and very condescending.

'Six! There now. Add up and count as far as six, can you? Well, that's a clever little girl, a clever little girl. And if she has to drink a spoonful of medicine, she won't make a murmur, I'll be bound. Not like *some* little girls. What? Eh?'

'I take it if mother wishes me to,' said Joyce.

'Ah, there now! That's the style! That's what I like to hear from a little lady in bed because she's cut her knee. That's the style—'

The comfortable and prolix doctor dressed and bandaged the knee and recommended bed and a light diet for the little lady. He thought a week or a fortnight would put it right. No bones or ligatures damaged—fortunately. Only a flesh cut. He would come again in a day or two.

So Joyce was reassured and stayed in bed and had all her toys up. Her father often played with her. The doctor came the third day. He was fairly pleased with the knee. It was healing. It was healing—yes—yes. Let the child continue in bed. He came again after a day or two. Winifred was a trifle uneasy. The wound seemed to be healing on the

148

top, but it hurt the child too much. It didn't look quite right. She said so to Egbert.

'Egbert, I'm sure Joyce's knee isn't healing properly.'

'I think it is,' he said. 'I think it's all right.'

'I'd rather Doctor Wing came again—I don't feel satisfied.'

'Aren't you trying to imagine it worse than it really is?'

'You would say so, of course. But I shall write a post-card to Doctor Wing now.'

The doctor came next day. He examined the knee. Yes, there was inflammation. Yes, there *might* be a little septic poisoning—there might. There might. Was the child feverish?

So a fortnight passed by, and the child *was* feverish, and the knee was more inflamed and grew worse and was painful, painful. She cried in the night, and her mother had to sit up with her. Egbert still insisted it was nothing, really—it would pass. But in his heart he was anxious.

Winifred wrote again to her father. On Saturday the elderly man appeared. And no sooner did Winifred see the thick, rather short figure in its grey suit than a great yearning came over her.

'Father, I'm not satisfied with Joyce. I'm not satisfied with Doctor Wing.'

'Well, Winnie, dear, if you're not satisfied we must have further advice, that is all.'

The sturdy, powerful, elderly man went upstairs, his voice sounding rather grating through the house, as if it cut upon the tense atmosphere.

'How are you, Joyce, darling?' he said to the child. 'Does your knee hurt you? Does it hurt you, dear?'

'It does sometimes.' The child was shy of him, cold towards him.

'Well, dear, I'm sorry for that. I hope you try to bear it, and not trouble mother too much.'

There was no answer. He looked at the knee. It was red and stiff.

'Of course,' he said, 'I think we must have another doctor's opinion. And if we're going to have it, we had better have it at once. Egbert, do you think you might cycle in to Bingham for Doctor Wayne? I found him *very* satisfactory for Winnie's mother.'

'I can go if you think it necessary,' said Egbert.

'Certainly I think it necessary. Even if there if nothing, we can have peace of mind. Certainly I think it necessary. I should like Doctor Wayne to come this evening if possible.'

So Egbert set off on his bicycle through the wind, like a boy sent on an errand, leaving his father-in-law a pillar of assurance, with Winifred.

Doctor Wayne came, and looked grave. Yes, the knee was certainly taking the wrong way. The child might be lame for life.

Up went the fire and fear and anger in every heart. Doctor Wayne came again the next day for a proper examination. And, yes, the knee had really taken bad ways. It should be X-rayed. It was very important.

Godfrey Marshall walked up and down the lane with the doctor, beside the standing motor-car: up and down, up and down in one of those consultations of which he had had so many in his life.

As a result he came indoors to Winifred.

'Well, Winnie, dear, the best thing to do is to take Joyce up to London, to a nursing home where she can have proper treatment. Of course this knee has been allowed to go wrong. And apparently there is a risk that the child may even lose her leg. What do you think, dear? You agree to our taking her up to town and putting her under the best care?'

'Oh, father, you *know* I would do anything on earth for her.'

'I know you would, Winnie darling. The pity is that there has been this unfortunate delay already. I can't think what Doctor Wing was doing. Apparently the child is in danger of losing her leg. Well then, if you will have everything ready, we will take her up to town tomorrow. I will order the large car from Denley's to be here at ten. Egbert, will you take a telegram at once to Doctor Jackson? It is a small nursing home for children and for surgical cases, not far from Baker Street. I'm sure Joyce will be all right there.'

'Oh, father, can't I nurse her myself!'

'Well, darling, if she is to have proper treatment, she had best be in a home. The X-ray treatment, and the electric treatment, and whatever is necessary.'

'It will cost a great deal—' said Winifred.

'We can't think of cost, if the child's leg is in danger—or even her life. No use speaking of cost,' said the elder man impatiently.

And so it was. Poor Joyce, stretched out on a bed in the big closed motor-car—the mother sitting by her head, the grandfather in his short grey beard and a bowler hat, sitting by her feet, thick, and implacable in his responsibility—they rolled slowly away from Crockham, and from Egbert who stood there bareheaded and a little ignominious, left behind. He was to shut up the house and bring the rest of the family back to town, by train, the next day.

Followed a dark and bitter time. The poor child. The poor, poor child, how she suffered, an agony and a long crucifixion in that nursing home. It was a bitter six weeks which changed the soul of Winifred for ever. As she sat by the bed of her poor, tortured little child, tortured with the agony of the knee, and the still worse agony of these diabolic, but perhaps necessary modern treatments, she felt her heart killed and going cold in her breast. Her little Joyce, her frail, brave, wonderful, little Joyce, frail and small and pale as a white flower! Ah, how had she, Winifred, dared to be so wicked, so wicked, so careless, so sensual.

'Let my heart die! Let my woman's heart of flesh die! Saviour, let my heart die. And save my child. Let my heart die from the world and from the flesh. Oh, destroy my heart that is so wayward. Let my heart of pride die. Let my heart die.'

So she prayed beside the bed of her child. And like the Mother with the seven swords in her breast, slowly her heart of pride and passion died in her breast, bleeding away. Slowly it died, bleeding away, and she turned to the Church for comfort, to Jesus, to the Mother of God, but most of all, to that great and enduring institution, the Roman Catholic Church. She withdrew into the shadow of the Church. She was a mother with three children. But in her soul she died, her heart of pride and passion and desire bled to death, her soul belonged to her church, her body belonged to her duty as a mother.

Her duty as a wife did not enter. As a wife she had no sense of duty: only a certain bitterness towards the man with whom she had known such sensuality and distraction. She was purely the *Mater Dolorata*. To the man she was closed as a tomb.

Egbert came to see his child. But Winifred seemed to be always seated there, like the tomb of his manhood and his fatherhood. Poor Winifred: she was still young, still strong and ruddy and beautiful like a ruddy hard flower of the field. Strange—her ruddy, healthy face, so sombre, and her strong, heavy, full-blooded body, so still. She, a nun! Never. And yet the gates of her heart and soul had shut in his face with a slow, resonant clang, shutting him out for ever. There was no need for her to go into a convent. Her will had done it.

And between this young mother and this young father lay the crippled child, like a bit of pale silk floss on the pillow, and a little white pain-quenched face. He could not bear it. He just could not bear it. He turned aside. There was nothing to do but to turn aside. He turned aside, and went hither and thither, desultory. He was still attractive and desirable. But there was a little frown between his brow as if he had been cleft there with a hatchet: cleft right in, for ever, and that was the stigma.

The child's leg was saved: but the knee was locked stiff. The fear now was lest the lower leg should wither, or cease to grow. There must be long-continued massage and treatment, daily treatment, even when the child left the nursing home. And the whole of the expense was borne by the grandfather.

Egbert now had no real home. Winifred with the children and nurse was tied to the little flat in London. He could not live there: he could not contain himself. The cottage was shut-up—or lent to friends. He went down sometimes to work in his garden and keep the place in order. Then with the empty house around him at night, all the empty rooms, he felt his heart go wicked. The sense of frustration and futility, like some slow, torpid snake, slowly bit right through his heart. Futility, futility: the horrible marsh-poison went through his veins and killed him.

As he worked in the garden in the silence of day he would listen for a sound. No sound. No sound of Winifred from the dark inside of the cottage: no sound of children's voices from the air, from the common, from the near distance. No sound, nothing but the old dark marsh-venomous atmosphere of the place. So he worked spasmodically through the day, and at night made a fire and cooked some food alone.

He was alone. He himself cleaned the cottage and made his bed. But his mending he did not do. His shirts were slit on the shoulders, when he had been working, and the white flesh showed through. He would feel the air and the spots of rain on his exposed flesh. And he would look again across the common, where the dark, tufted gorse was dying to seed, and the bits of cat-heather were coming pink in tufts, like a sprinkling of sacrificial blood.

His heart went back to the savage old spirit of the place: the desire for old gods, old, lost passions, the passion of the cold-blooded, darting snakes that hissed and shot away from him, the mystery of blood-sacrifices, all the lost, intense sensations of the primeval people of the place, whose passions seethed in the air still, from those long days before the Romans came. The seethe of a lost, dark passion in the air. The presence of unseen snakes.

A queer, baffled, half-wicked look came on his face. He could not stay long at the cottage. Suddenly he must swing on to his bicycle and go—anywhere. Anywhere, away from the place. He would stay a few days with his mother in the old home. His mother adored him and grieved as a mother would. But the little, baffled, half-wicked smile curled on his face, and he swung away from his mother's solicitude as from everything else.

Always moving on—from place to place, friend to friend: and always swinging away from sympathy. As soon as sympathy, like a soft hand, was reached out to touch him, away he swerved, instinctively, as a harmless snake swerves and swerves and swerves away from an outstretched hand. Away he must go. And periodically he went back to Winifred.

He was terrible to her now, like a temptation. She had devoted herself to her children and her church. Joyce was once more on her feet; but, alas! lame, with iron supports to her leg, and a little crutch. It was strange how she had grown into a long, pallid, wild little thing. Strange that the pain had not made her soft and docile, but had brought out a wild, almost maenad temper in the child. She was seven, and long and white and thin, but by no means subdued. Her blonde hair was darkening. She still had long sufferings to face, and, in her own childish consciousness, the stigma of her lameness to bear.

And she bore it. An almost maenad courage seemed to possess her, as if she were a long, thin, young weapon of life. She acknowledged all her mother's care. She would stand by her mother for ever. But some of her father's fine-tempered desperation flashed in her.

When Egbert saw his little girl limping horribly—not only limping but lurching horribly in crippled, childish way, his heart again hardened with chagrin, like steel that is tempered again. There was a tacit understanding between him and his little girl: not what we would call love, but a weapon-like kinship. There was a tiny touch of irony in his manner towards her, contrasting sharply with Winifred's heavy, unleavened solicitude and care. The child flickered back to him with an answering little smile of irony and recklessness: an odd flippancy which made Winifred only the more sombre and earnest.

The Marshalls took endless thought and trouble for the child, searching out every means to save her limb and her active freedom. They spared no effort and no money, they spared no strength of will. With all their slow, heavy power of will they willed that Joyce should save her liberty of movement, should win back her wild, free grace. Even if it took a long time to recover, it should be recovered.

So the situation stood. And Joyce submitted, week after week, month after month to the tyranny and pain of the treatment. She acknowledged the honourable effort on her behalf. But her flamy reckless spirit was her father's. It was he who had all the glamour for her. He and she were like members of some forbidden secret society who know one another but may not recognize one another. Knowledge they had in common, the same secret of life, the father and the child. But the child stayed in the camp of her mother, honourably, and the father wandered outside like Ishmael, only coming sometimes to sit in the home for an hour or two, an evening or two beside the camp fire, like Ishmael, in a curious silence and tension, with the mocking answer of the desert speaking out of his silence, and annulling the whole convention of the domestic home.

His presence was almost an anguish to Winifred. She prayed against it. That little cleft between his brow, that flickering, wicked, little smile that seemed to haunt his face, and above all, the triumphant loneliness, the Ishmael quality. And then the erectness of his supple body, like a symbol. The very way he stood, so quiet, so insidious, like an erect, supple symbol of life, the living body, confronting her downcast soul, was torture to her. He was like a supple living idol moving before her eyes, and she felt if she watched him she was damned.

And he came and made himself at home in her little home. When he was there, moving in his own quiet way, she felt as if the whole great law of sacrifice, by which she had elected to live, were annulled. He annulled by his very presence the laws of her life. And what did he substitute? Ah, against that question she hardened herself in recoil.

It was awful to her to have to have him about—moving about in his shirt-sleeves, speaking in his tenor, throaty voice to the children. Annabel simply adored him, and he teased the little girl. The baby, Barbara, was not sure of him. She had been born a stranger to him. But even the nurse, when she saw his white shoulder of flesh through the slits of his torn shirt, thought it a shame.

Winifred felt it was only another weapon of his against her.

'You have other shirts—why do you wear that old one that is all torn, Egbert?' she said.

'I may as well wear it out,' he said subtly.

He knew she would not offer to mend it for him. She *could* not. And no, she would not. Had she not her own gods to honour? And could she betray them, submitting to his Baal and Ashtaroth? And it was terrible to her, his unsheathed presence, that seemed to annul her and her faith, like another revelation. Like a gleaming idol evoked against her, a vivid life-idol that might triumph.

He came and he went—and she persisted. And then the great war broke out. He was a man who could not go to the dogs. He could not dissipate himself. He was pure-bred in his Englishness, and even when he would have killed to be vicious, he could not.

So when the war broke out his whole instinct was against it: against war. He had not the faintest desire to overcome any foreigners or to help in their death. He had no conception of Imperial England, and Rule Britannia was just a joke to him. He was a pure-blooded Englishman, perfect in his race, and when he was truly himself he could no more have been aggressive on the score of his Englishness than a rose can be aggressive on the score of its rosiness.

No, he had no desire to defy Germany and to exalt England. The distinction between German and English was not for him the distinction between good and bad. It was the distinction between blue water-flowers and red or white bush-blossoms: just difference. The difference between the wild boar and the wild bear. And a man was good or bad according to his nature, not according to his nationality.

Egbert was well-bred, and this was part of his natural understanding. It was merely unnatural to him to hate a nation *en bloc*. Certain individuals he disliked, and others he liked, and the mass he knew nothing about. Certain deeds he disliked, certain deeds seemed natural to him, and about most deeds he had no particular feeling.

He had, however, the one deepest pure-bred instinct. He recoiled inevitably from having his feelings dictated to him by the mass feeling. His feelings were his own, his understanding was his own, and he would never go back on either, willingly. Shall a man become inferior to his own true knowledge and self, just because the mob expects it of him?

What Egbert felt subtly and without question, his father-in-law felt also in a rough, more combative way. Different as the two men were, they were two real Englishmen, and their instincts were almost the same.

And Godfrey Marshall had the world to reckon with. There was German military aggression, and the English non-military idea of liberty and the 'conquests of peace'— meaning industrialism. Even if the choice between militarism and industrialism were a choice of evils, the elderly man asserted his choice of the latter, perforce. He whose soul was quick with the instinct of power.

Egbert just refused to reckon with the world. He just refused even to decide between German militarism and British industrialism. He chose neither. As for atrocities, he despised the people who committed them as inferior criminal types. There was nothing national about crime.

And yet, war! War! Just war! Not right or wrong, but just war itself. Should he join? Should he give himself over to war? The question was in his mind for some weeks. Not because he thought England was right and Germany wrong. Probably Germany was wrong, but he refused to make a choice. Not because he felt inspired. No. But just—war.

The deterrent was, the giving himself over into the power of other men, and into the power of the mob-spirit of a democratic army. Should he give himself over? Should he make over his own life and body to the control of something which he *knew* was inferior, in spirit, to his own self? Should he commit himself into the power of an inferior control? Should he? Should he betray himself?

He was going to put himself into the power of his inferiors, and he knew it. He was going to subjugate himself. He was going to be ordered about by petty *canaille* of non-commissioned officers—and even commissioned officers. He who was born and bred free. Should he do it?

He went to his wife, to speak to her.

'Shall I join up, Winifred?'

She was silent. Her instinct also was dead against it. And yet a certain profound resentment made her answer:

'You have three children dependent on you. I don't know whether you have thought of that.'

It was still only the third month of the war, and the old pre-war ideas were still alive.

'Of course. But it won't make much difference to them. I shall be earning a shilling a day, at least.'

'You'd better speak to father, I think,' she replied heavily.

Egbert went to his father-in-law. The elderly man's heart was full of resentment.

'I should say,' he said rather sourly, 'it is the best thing you could do.'

Egbert went and joined up immediately, as a private soldier. He was drafted into the light artillery.

Winifred now had a new duty towards him: the duty of a wife towards a husband who is himself performing his duty towards the world. She loved him still. She would always love him, as far as earthly love went. But it was duty she now lived by. When he came back to her in khaki, a soldier, she submitted to him as a wife. It was her duty. But to his passion she could never again fully submit. Something prevented her, for ever: even her own deepest choice.

He went back again to camp. It did not suit him to be a modern soldier. In the thick, gritty, hideous khaki his subtle physique was extinguished as if he had been killed. In the ugly intimacy of the camp his thoroughbred sensibilities were just degraded. But he had chosen, so he accepted. An ugly little look came on to his face, of a man who has accepted his own degradation.

In the early spring Winifred went down to Crockham to be there when primroses were out, and the tassels hanging on the hazel-bushes. She felt something like a reconciliation towards Egbert, now he was a prisoner in camp most of his days. Joyce was wild with delight at seeing the garden and the common again, after the eight or nine months of London and misery. She was still lame. She still had the irons up her leg. But she lurched about with a wild, crippled agility.

Egbert came for a week-end, in his gritty, thick, sand-paper khaki and puttees and the hideous cap. Nay, he looked terrible. And on his face a slightly impure look, a little sore on his lip, as if he had eaten too much or drunk too much or let his blood become a little unclean. He was almost uglily healthy, with the camp life. It did not suit him.

Winifred waited for him in a little passion of duty and sacrifice, willing to serve the soldier, if not the man. It only made him feel a little more ugly inside. The week-end was torment to him: the memory of the camp, the knowledge of the life he led there; even the sight of his own legs in that abhorrent khaki. He felt as if the hideous cloth went into his blood and made it gritty and dirty. Then Winifred so ready to serve the *soldier*, when she repudiated the man. And this made the grit worse between his teeth. And the children running around playing and calling in the rather mincing fashion of children who have nurses and governesses and literature in the family. And Joyce so lame! It had all become unreal to him, after the camp. It only set his soul on edge. He left at dawn on the Monday morning, glad to get back to the realness and vulgarity of the camp.

Winifred would never meet him again at the cottage—only in London, where the world was with them. But sometimes he came alone to Crockham perhaps when friends were staying there. And then he would work awhile in his garden. This summer still it would flame with blue anchusas and big red poppies, the mulleins would sway their soft, downy erections in the air: he loved mulleins: and the honeysuckle would stream out scent like memory, when the owl was whooing. Then he sat by the fire with the friends and with Winifred's sisters, and they sang the folk-songs. He put on thin civilian clothes and his charm and his beauty and the supple dominancy of his body glowed out again. But Winifred was not there.

At the end of the summer he went to Flanders, into action. He seemed already to have gone out of life, beyond the pale of life. He hardly remembered his life any more, being like a man who is going to take a jump from a height, and is only looking to where he must land.

He was twice slightly wounded, in two months. But not enough to put him off duty for more than a day or two. They were retiring again, holding the enemy back. He was in the rear—three machine-guns. The country was all pleasant, war had not yet trampled it. Only the air seemed shattered, and the land awaiting death. It was a small, unimportant action in which he was engaged.

The guns were stationed on a little bushy hillock just outside a village. But occasionally, it was difficult to say from which direction, came the sharp crackle of rifle-fire, and beyond, the far-off thud of cannon. The afternoon was wintry and cold.

A lieutenant stood on a little iron platform at the top of the ladders, taking the sights and giving the aim, calling in a high, tense, mechanical voice. Out of the sky came the sharp cry of the directions, then the warning numbers, then 'Fire!' The shot went, the piston of the gun sprang back, there was a sharp explosion, and a very faint film of smoke in the air. Then the other two guns fired, and there was a lull. The officer was uncertain of the enemy's position. The thick clump of horse-chestnut trees below was without change. Only in the far distance the sound of heavy firing continued, so far off as to give a sense of peace.

The gorse bushes on either hand were dark, but a few sparks of flowers showed yellow. He noticed them almost unconsciously as he waited, in the lull. He was in his shirt-sleeves, and the air came chill on his arms. Again his shirt was slit on the shoulders, and the flesh showed through. He was dirty and unkempt. But his face was quiet. So many things go out of consciousness before we come to the end of consciousness.

Before him, below, was the highroad, running between high banks of grass and gorse. He saw the whitish muddy tracks and deep scores in the road, where the part of the regiment had retired. Now all was still. Sounds that came, came from the outside. The place where he stood was still silent, chill, serene: the white church among the trees beyond seemed like a thought only.

He moved into a lightning-like mechanical response at the sharp cry from the officer overhead. Mechanism, the pure mechanical action of obedience at the guns. Pure mechanical action at the guns. It left the soul unburdened, brooding in dark nakedness. In the end, the soul is alone, brooding on the face of the uncreated flux, as a bird on a dark sea.

Nothing could be seen but the road, and a crucifix knocked slanting and the dark, autumnal fields and woods. There appeared three horsemen on a little eminence, very small, on the crest of a ploughed field. They were our own men. Of the enemy, nothing.

The lull continued. Then suddenly came sharp orders, and a new direction of the guns, and an intense, exciting activity. Yet at the centre the soul remained dark and aloof, alone.

But even so, it was the soul that heard the new sound: the new, deep 'papp!' of a gun that seemed to touch right upon the soul. He kept up the rapid activity at the machine-gun, sweating. But in his soul was the echo of the new, deep sound, deeper than life.

And in confirmation came the awful faint whistling of a shell, advancing almost suddenly into a piercing, tearing shriek that would tear through the membrane of life. He heard it in his ears, but he heard it also in his soul, in tension. There was relief when the thing had swung by and struck, away beyond. He heard the hoarseness of its explosion, and the voice of the soldier calling to the horses. But he did not turn round to look. He only noticed a twig of holly with red berries fall like a gift on to the road below.

Not this time, not this time. Whither thou goest I will go. Did he say it to the shell, or to whom? Whither thou goest I will go. Then, the faint whistling of another shell dawned, and his blood became small and still to receive it. It drew nearer, like some horrible blast of wind; his blood lost consciousness. But in the second of suspension he saw the heavy shell swoop to earth, into the rocky bushes on the right, and earth and stones poured up into the sky. It was as if he heard no sound. The earth and stones and fragments of bush fell to earth again, and there was the same unchanging peace. The Germans had got the aim.

Would they move now? Would they retire? Yes. The officer was giving the last lightning-rapid orders to fire before withdrawing. A shell passed unnoticed in the rapidity of action. And then, into the silence, into the suspense where the soul brooded, finally crashed a noise and a darkness and a moment's flaming agony and horror. Ah, he had seen the dark bird flying towards him, flying home this time. In one instant life and eternity went up in a conflagration of agony, then there was a weight of darkness.

When faintly something began to struggle in the darkness, a consciousness of himself, he was aware of a great load and a clanging sound. To have known the moment of death! And to be forced, before dying, to review it. So, fate, even in death.

There was a resounding of pain. It seemed to sound from the outside of his consciousness: like a loud bell clanging very near. Yet he knew it was himself. He must associate himself with it. After a lapse and a new effort, he identified a pain in his head, a large pain that clanged and resounded. So far he could identify himself with himself. Then there was a lapse.

After a time he seemed to wake up again, and waking, to know that he was at the front, and that he was killed. He did not open his eyes. Light was not yet his. The clanging pain in his head rang out the rest of his consciousness. So he lapsed away from consciousness, in unutterable sick abandon of life.

Bit by bit, like a doom came the necessity to know. He was hit in the head. It was only a vague surmise at first. But in the swinging of the pendulum of pain, swinging ever nearer and nearer, to touch him into an agony of consciousness and a consciousness of agony, gradually the knowledge emerged—he must be hit in the head—hit on the left brow; if so, there would be blood—was there blood?—could he feel blood in his left eye? Then the clanging seemed to burst the membrane of his brain, like death-madness.

Was there blood on his face? Was hot blood flowing? Or was it dry blood congealing down his cheek? It took him hours even to ask the question: time being no more than an agony in darkness, without measurement.

A long time after he had opened his eyes he realized he was seeing something—something, something, but the effort to recall what was too great. No, no; no recall!

Were they the stars in the dark sky? Was it possible it was stars in the dark sky? Stars? The world? Ah, no, he could not know it! Stars and the world were gone for him, he closed his eyes. No stars, no sky, no world. No, No! The thick darkness of blood alone. It should be one great lapse into the thick darkness of blood in agony.

Death, oh, death! The world all blood, and the blood all writhing with death. The soul like the tiniest little light out on a dark sea, the sea of blood. And the light guttering, beating, pulsing in a windless storm, wishing it could go out, yet unable.

There had been life. There had been Winifred and his children. But the frail death-agony effort to catch at straws of memory, straws of life from the past, brought on too great a nausea. No, No! No Winifred, no children. No world, no people. Better the agony of dissolution ahead than the nausea of the effort backwards. Better the terrible work should go forward, the dissolving into the black sea of death, in the extremity of dissolution, than that there should be any reaching back towards life. To forget! To forget! Utterly, utterly to forget, in the great forgetting of death. To break the core and the unit of life, and to lapse out on the great darkness. Only that. To break the clue, and mingle and commingle with the one darkness, without afterwards or forwards. Let the black sea of death itself solve the problem of futurity. Let the will of man break and give up.

What was that? A light! A terrible light! Was it figures? Was it legs of a horse colossal—colossal above him: huge, huge?

The Germans heard a slight noise, and started. Then, in the glare of a light-bomb, by the side of the heap of earth thrown up by the shell, they saw the dead face.

TICKETS, PLEASE

There is in the Midlands a single-line tramway system which boldly leaves the county town and plunges off into the black, industrial countryside, up hill and down dale, through the long ugly villages of workmen's houses, over canals and railways, past churches perched high and nobly over the smoke and shadows, through stark, grimy cold little market-places, tilting away in a rush past cinemas and shops down to the hollow where the collieries are, then up again, past a little rural church, under the ash trees, on in a rush to the terminus, the last little ugly place of industry, the cold little town that shivers on the edge of the wild, gloomy country beyond. There the green and creamy coloured tram-car seems to pause and purr with curious satisfaction. But in a few minutes—the clock on the turret of the Co-operative Wholesale Society's Shops gives the time—away it starts once more on the adventure. Again there are the reckless swoops downhill, bouncing the loops: again the chilly wait in the hill-top market-place: again the breathless slithering round the precipitous drop under the church: again the patient halts at the loops, waiting for the outcoming car: so on and on, for two long hours, till at last the city looms beyond the fat gas-works, the narrow factories draw near, we are in the sordid streets of the great town, once more we sidle to a standstill at our terminus, abashed by the great crimson and cream-coloured city cars, but still perky, jaunty, somewhat dare-devil, green as a jaunty sprig of parsley out of a black colliery garden.

To ride on these cars is always an adventure. Since we are in war-time, the drivers are men unfit for active service: cripples and hunchbacks. So they have the spirit of the devil in them. The ride becomes a steeple-chase. Hurray! we have leapt in a clear jump over the canal bridges—now for the four-lane corner. With a shriek and a trail of sparks we are clear again. To be sure, a tram often leaps the rails—but what matter! It sits in a ditch till other trams come to haul it out. It is quite common for a car, packed with one solid mass of living people, to come to a dead halt in the midst of unbroken blackness, the heart of nowhere on a dark night, and for the driver and the girl conductor to call, 'All get off—car's on fire!' Instead, however, of rushing out in a panic, the passengers stolidly reply: 'Get on—get on! We're not coming out. We're stopping where we are. Push on, George.' So till flames actually appear.

The reason for this reluctance to dismount is that the nights are howlingly cold, black, and windswept, and a car is a haven of refuge. From village to village the miners travel, for a change of cinema, of girl, of pub. The trams are desperately packed. Who is going to risk himself in the black gulf outside, to wait perhaps an hour for another tram, then to see the forlorn notice 'Depot Only', because there is something wrong! Or to greet a unit of three bright cars all so tight with people that they sail past with a howl of derision. Trams that pass in the night.

This, the most dangerous tram-service in England, as the authorities themselves declare, with pride, is entirely conducted by girls, and driven by rash young men, a little crippled, or by delicate young men, who creep forward in terror. The girls are fearless young hussies. In their ugly blue uniform, skirts up to their knees, shapeless old peaked caps on their heads, they have all the *sang-froid* of an old non-commissioned officer. With a tram packed with howling colliers, roaring hymns downstairs and a sort of antiphony of obscenities upstairs, the lasses are perfectly at their ease. They pounce on the youths who try to evade their ticket-machine. They push off the men at the end of their distance. They are not going to be done in the eye—not they. They fear nobody— and everybody fears them.

'Hello, Annie!'

'Hello, Ted!'

'Oh, mind my corn, Miss Stone. It's my belief you've got a heart of stone, for you've trod on it again.'

'You should keep it in your pocket,' replies Miss Stone, and she goes sturdily upstairs in her high boots.

'Tickets, please.'

She is peremptory, suspicious, and ready to hit first. She can hold her own against ten thousand. The step of that tram-car is her Thermopylae.

Therefore, there is a certain wild romance aboard these cars—and in the sturdy bosom of Annie herself. The time for soft romance is in the morning, between ten o'clock and one, when things are rather slack: that is, except market-day and Saturday. Thus Annie has time to look about her. Then she often hops off her car and into a shop where she has spied something, while the driver chats in the main road. There is very good feeling between the girls and the drivers. Are they not companions in peril, shipments aboard this careering vessel of a tram-car, for ever rocking on the waves of a stormy land?

Then, also, during the easy hours, the inspectors are most in evidence. For some reason, everybody employed in this tram-service is young: there are no grey heads. It would not do. Therefore the inspectors are of the right age, and one, the chief, is also good-looking. See him stand on a wet, gloomy morning, in his long oil-skin, his peaked cap well down over his eyes, waiting to board a car. His face is ruddy, his small brown moustache is weathered, he has a faint impudent smile. Fairly tall and agile, even in his waterproof, he springs aboard a car and greets Annie.

'Hello, Annie! Keeping the wet out?'

'Trying to.'

There are only two people in the car. Inspecting is soon over. Then for a long and impudent chat on the foot-board, a good, easy, twelve-mile chat.

The inspector's name is John Thomas Raynor—always called John Thomas, except sometimes, in malice, Coddy. His face sets in fury when he is addressed, from a distance, with this abbreviation. There is considerable scandal about John Thomas in half a dozen villages. He flirts with the girl conductors in the morning, and walks out with them in the dark night, when they leave their tram-car at the depot. Of course, the girls quit the service frequently. Then he flirts and walks out with the newcomer: always providing she is sufficiently attractive, and that she will consent to walk. It is remarkable, however, that most of the girls are quite comely, they are all young, and this roving life aboard the car gives them a sailor's dash and recklessness. What matter how they behave when the ship is in port. Tomorrow they will be aboard again.

Annie, however, was something of a Tartar, and her sharp tongue had kept John Thomas at arm's length for many months. Perhaps, therefore, she liked him all the more: for he always came up smiling, with impudence. She watched him vanquish one girl, then another. She could tell by the movement of his mouth and eyes, when he flirted with her in the morning, that he had been walking out with this lass, or the other, the night before. A fine cock-of-the-walk he was. She could sum him up pretty well.

In this subtle antagonism they knew each other like old friends, they were as shrewd with one another almost as man and wife. But Annie had always kept him sufficiently at arm's length. Besides, she had a boy of her own.

The Statutes fair, however, came in November, at Bestwood. It happened that Annie had the Monday night off. It was a drizzling ugly night, yet she dressed herself up and went to the fair ground. She was alone, but she expected soon to find a pal of some sort.

The roundabouts were veering round and grinding out their music, the side shows were making as much commotion as possible. In the coco-nut shies there were no coco-nuts, but artificial war-time substitutes, which the lads declared were fastened into the irons. There was a sad decline in brilliance and luxury. None the less, the ground was muddy as ever, there was the same crush, the press of faces lighted up by the flares and the electric lights, the same smell of naphtha and a few fried potatoes, and of electricity.

Who should be the first to greet Miss Annie on the showground but John Thomas? He had a black overcoat buttoned up to his chin, and a tweed cap pulled down over his brows, his face between was ruddy and smiling and handy as ever. She knew so well the way his mouth moved.

She was very glad to have a 'boy'. To be at the Statutes without a fellow was no fun. Instantly, like the gallant he was, he took her on the dragons, grim-toothed, round-about switchbacks. It was not nearly so exciting as a tram-car actually. But, then, to be seated in a shaking, green dragon, uplifted above the sea of bubble faces, careering in a rickety fashion in the lower heavens, whilst John Thomas leaned over her, his cigarette in his mouth, was after all the right style. She was a plump, quick, alive little creature. So she was quite excited and happy.

John Thomas made her stay on for the next round. And therefore she could hardly for shame repulse him when he put his arm round her and drew her a little nearer to him, in a very warm and cuddly manner. Besides, he was fairly discreet, he kept his movement as hidden as possible. She looked down, and saw that his red, clean hand was out of sight of the crowd. And they knew each other so well. So they warmed up to the fair.

After the dragons they went on the horses. John Thomas paid each time, so she could but be complaisant. He, of course, sat astride on the outer horse—named 'Black Bess'—and she sat sideways, towards him, on the inner horse—named 'Wildfire'. But of course John Thomas was not going to sit discreetly on 'Black Bess', holding the brass bar. Round they spun and heaved, in the light. And round he swung on his wooden steed, flinging one leg across her mount, and perilously tipping up and down, across the space, half lying back, laughing at her. He was perfectly happy; she was afraid her hat was on one side, but she was excited.

He threw quoits on a table, and won for her two large, pale-blue hat-pins. And then, hearing the noise of the cinemas, announcing another performance, they climbed the boards and went in.

Of course, during these performances pitch darkness falls from time to time, when the machine goes wrong. Then there is a wild whooping, and a loud smacking of simulated kisses. In these moments John Thomas drew Annie towards him. After all, he had a wonderfully warm, cosy way of holding a girl with his arm, he seemed to make such a nice fit. And, after all, it was pleasant to be so held: so very comforting and cosy and nice. He leaned over her and she felt his breath on her hair; she knew he wanted to kiss her on the lips. And, after all, he was so warm and she fitted in to him so softly. After all, she wanted him to touch her lips.

But the light sprang up; she also started electrically, and put her hat straight. He left his arm lying nonchalantly behind her. Well, it was fun, it was exciting to be at the Statutes with John Thomas.

When the cinema was over they went for a walk across the dark, damp fields. He had all the arts of love-making. He was especially good at holding a girl, when he sat with her on a stile in the black, drizzling darkness. He seemed to be holding her in space, against his own warmth and gratification. And his kisses were soft and slow and searching.

So Annie walked out with John Thomas, though she kept her own boy dangling in the distance. Some of the tram-girls chose to be huffy. But there, you must take things as you find them, in this life.

There was no mistake about it, Annie liked John Thomas a good deal. She felt so rich and warm in herself whenever he was near. And John Thomas really liked Annie, more than usual. The soft, melting way in which she could flow into a fellow, as if she melted into his very bones, was something rare and good. He fully appreciated this.

But with a developing acquaintance there began a developing intimacy. Annie wanted to consider him a person, a man; she wanted to take an intelligent interest in him, and to have an intelligent response. She did not want a mere nocturnal presence, which was what he was so far. And she prided herself that he could not leave her.

Here she made a mistake. John Thomas intended to remain a nocturnal presence; he had no idea of becoming an all-round individual to her. When she started to take an intelligent interest in him and his life and his character, he sheered off. He hated intelligent interest. And he knew that the only way to stop it was to avoid it. The possessive female was aroused in Annie. So he left her.

It is no use saying she was not surprised. She was at first startled, thrown out of her count. For she had been so *very* sure of holding him. For a while she was staggered, and everything became uncertain to her. Then she wept with fury, indignation, desolation, and misery. Then she had a spasm of despair. And then, when he came, still impudently, on to her car, still familiar, but letting her see by the movement of his head that he had gone away to somebody else for the time being, and was enjoying pastures new, then she determined to have her own back.

She had a very shrewd idea what girls John Thomas had taken out. She went to Nora Purdy. Nora was a tall, rather pale, but well-built girl, with beautiful yellow hair. She was rather secretive.

'Hey!' said Annie, accosting her; then softly, 'Who's John Thomas on with now?'

'I don't know,' said Nora.

'Why tha does,' said Annie, ironically lapsing into dialect. 'Tha knows as well as I do.'

'Well, I do, then,' said Nora. 'It isn't me, so don't bother.'

'It's Cissy Meakin, isn't it?'

'It is, for all I know.'

'Hasn't he got a face on him!' said Annie. 'I don't half like his cheek. I could knock him off the foot-board when he comes round at me.'

'He'll get dropped-on one of these days,' said Nora.

'Ay, he will, when somebody makes up their mind to drop it on him. I should like to see him taken down a peg or two, shouldn't you?'

'I shouldn't mind,' said Nora.

'You've got quite as much cause to as I have,' said Annie. 'But we'll drop on him one of these days, my girl. What? Don't you want to?'

'I don't mind,' said Nora.

But as a matter of fact, Nora was much more vindictive than Annie.

One by one Annie went the round of the old flames. It so happened that Cissy Meakin left the tramway service in quite a short time. Her mother made her leave. Then John Thomas was on the *qui vive*. He cast his eyes over his old flock. And his eyes lighted on Annie. He thought she would be safe now. Besides, he liked her.

She arranged to walk home with him on Sunday night. It so happened that her car would be in the depot at half past nine: the last car would come in at 10.15. So John Thomas was to wait for her there.

At the depot the girls had a little waiting-room of their own. It was quite rough, but cosy, with a fire and an oven and a mirror, and table and wooden chairs. The half dozen girls who knew John Thomas only too well had arranged to take service this Sunday afternoon. So, as the cars began to come in, early, the girls dropped into the waiting-room. And instead of hurrying off home, they sat around the fire and had a cup of tea. Outside was the darkness and lawlessness of wartime.

John Thomas came on the car after Annie, at about a quarter to ten. He poked his head easily into the girls' waiting-room.

'Prayer-meeting?' he asked.

'Ay,' said Laura Sharp. 'Ladies only.'

'That's me!' said John Thomas. It was one of his favourite exclamations.

'Shut the door, boy,' said Muriel Baggaley.

'On which side of me?' said John Thomas.

'Which tha likes,' said Polly Birkin.

He had come in and closed the door behind him. The girls moved in their circle, to make a place for him near the fire. He took off his great-coat and pushed back his hat.

'Who handles the teapot?' he said.

Nora Purdy silently poured him out a cup of tea.

'Want a bit o' my bread and drippin'?' said Muriel Baggaley to him.

'Ay, give us a bit.'

And he began to eat his piece of bread.

'There's no place like home, girls,' he said.

They all looked at him as he uttered this piece of impudence. He seemed to be sunning himself in the presence of so many damsels.

'Especially if you're not afraid to go home in the dark,' said Laura Sharp.

'Me! By myself I am.'

They sat till they heard the last tram come in. In a few minutes Emma Houselay entered.

'Come on, my old duck!' cried Polly Birkin.

'It *is* perishing,' said Emma, holding her fingers to the fire.

'But—I'm afraid to, go home in, the dark,' sang Laura Sharp, the tune having got into her mind.

'Who're you going with tonight, John Thomas?' asked Muriel Baggaley, coolly.

'Tonight?' said John Thomas. 'Oh, I'm going home by myself tonight—all on my lonely-O.'

'That's me!' said Nora Purdy, using his own ejaculation.

The girls laughed shrilly.

'Me as well, Nora,' said John Thomas.

'Don't know what you mean,' said Laura.

'Yes, I'm toddling,' said he, rising and reaching for his overcoat.

'Nay,' said Polly. 'We're all here waiting for you.'

'We've got to be up in good time in the morning,' he said, in the benevolent official manner.

They all laughed.

'Nay,' said Muriel. 'Don't leave us all lonely, John Thomas. Take one!'

'I'll take the lot, if you like,' he responded gallantly.

'That you won't either,' said Muriel, 'Two's company; seven's too much of a good thing.'

'Nay—take one,' said Laura. 'Fair and square, all above board, and say which.'

'Ay,' cried Annie, speaking for the first time. 'Pick, John Thomas; let's hear thee.'

'Nay,' he said. 'I'm going home quiet tonight. Feeling good, for once.'

'Whereabouts?' said Annie. 'Take a good 'un, then. But tha's got to take one of us!'

'Nay, how can I take one,' he said, laughing uneasily. 'I don't want to make enemies.'

'You'd only make *one*' said Annie.

'The chosen *one*,' added Laura.

'Oh, my! Who said girls!' exclaimed John Thomas, again turning, as if to escape. 'Well—good-night.'

'Nay, you've got to make your pick,' said Muriel. 'Turn your face to the wall, and say which one touches you. Go on—we shall only just touch your back—one of us. Go on—turn your face to the wall, and don't look, and say which one touches you.'

He was uneasy, mistrusting them. Yet he had not the courage to break away. They pushed him to a wall and stood him there with his face to it. Behind his back they all grimaced, tittering. He looked so comical. He looked around uneasily.

'Go on!' he cried.

'You're looking—you're looking!' they shouted.

He turned his head away. And suddenly, with a movement like a swift cat, Annie went forward and fetched him a box on the side of the head that sent his cap flying and himself staggering. He started round.

But at Annie's signal they all flew at him, slapping him, pinching him, pulling his hair, though more in fun than in spite or anger. He, however, saw red. His blue eyes flamed with strange fear as well as fury, and he butted through the girls to the door. It was locked. He wrenched at it. Roused, alert, the girls stood round and looked at him. He faced them, at bay. At that moment they were rather horrifying to him, as they stood in their short uniforms. He was distinctly afraid.

'Come on, John Thomas! Come on! Choose!' said Annie.

'What are you after? Open the door,' he said.

'We shan't—not till you've chosen!' said Muriel.

'Chosen what?' he said.

'Chosen the one you're going to marry,' she replied.

He hesitated a moment.

'Open the blasted door,' he said, 'and get back to your senses.' He spoke with official authority.

'You've got to choose!' cried the girls.

'Come on!' cried Annie, looking him in the eye.' Come on! Come on!'

He went forward, rather vaguely. She had taken off her belt, and swinging it, she fetched him a sharp blow over the head with the buckle end. He sprang and seized her. But immediately the other girls rushed upon him, pulling and tearing and beating him. Their blood was now thoroughly up. He was their sport now. They were going to have their own back, out of him. Strange, wild creatures, they hung on him and rushed at him to bear him down. His tunic was torn right up the back, Nora had hold at the back of his collar, and was actually strangling him. Luckily the button burst. He struggled in a wild frenzy of fury and terror, almost mad terror. His tunic was simply torn off his back, his shirt-sleeves were torn away, his arms were naked. The girls rushed at him, clenched their hands on him and pulled at him: or they rushed at him and pushed him, butted him with all their might: or they struck him wild blows. He ducked and cringed and struck sideways. They became more intense.

At last he was down. They rushed on him, kneeling on him. He had neither breath nor strength to move. His face was bleeding with a long scratch, his brow was bruised.

Annie knelt on him, the other girls knelt and hung on to him. Their faces were flushed, their hair wild, their eyes were all glittering strangely. He lay at last quite still, with face averted, as an animal lies when it is defeated and at the mercy of the captor. Sometimes his eye glanced back at the wild faces of the girls. His breast rose heavily, his wrists were torn.

'Now, then, my fellow!' gasped Annie at length. 'Now then—now—'

At the sound of her terrifying, cold triumph, he suddenly started to struggle as an animal might, but the girls threw themselves upon him with unnatural strength and power, forcing him down.

'Yes—now, then!' gasped Annie at length.

And there was a dead silence, in which the thud of heart-beating was to be heard. It was a suspense of pure silence in every soul.

'Now you know where you are,' said Annie.

The sight of his white, bare arm maddened the girls. He lay in a kind of trance of fear and antagonism. They felt themselves filled with supernatural strength.

Suddenly Polly started to laugh—to giggle wildly—helplessly—and Emma and

Muriel joined in. But Annie and Nora and Laura remained the same, tense, watchful, with gleaming eyes. He winced away from these eyes.

'Yes,' said Annie, in a curious low tone, secret and deadly. 'Yes! You've got it now! You know what you've done, don't you? You know what you've done.'

He made no sound nor sign, but lay with bright, averted eyes, and averted, bleeding face.

'You ought to be *killed*, that's what you ought,' said Annie, tensely. 'You ought to be *killed*.' And there was a terrifying lust in her voice.

Polly was ceasing to laugh, and giving long-drawn Oh-h-hs and sighs as she came to herself.

'He's got to choose,' she said vaguely.

'Oh, yes, he has,' said Laura, with vindictive decision.

'Do you hear—do you hear?' said Annie. And with a sharp movement, that made him wince, she turned his face to her.

'Do you hear?' she repeated, shaking him.

But he was quite dumb. She fetched him a sharp slap on the face. He started, and his eyes widened. Then his face darkened with defiance, after all.

'Do you hear?' she repeated.

He only looked at her with hostile eyes.

'Speak!' she said, putting her face devilishly near his.

'What?' he said, almost overcome.

'You've got to *choose*!' she cried, as if it were some terrible menace, and as if it hurt her that she could not exact more.

'What?' he said, in fear.

'Choose your girl, Coddy. You've got to choose her now. And you'll get your neck broken if you play any more of your tricks, my boy. You're settled now.'

There was a pause. Again he averted his face. He was cunning in his overthrow. He did not give in to them really—no, not if they tore him to bits.

'All right, then,' he said, 'I choose Annie.' His voice was strange and full of malice. Annie let go of him as if he had been a hot coal.

'He's chosen Annie!' said the girls in chorus.

'Me!' cried Annie. She was still kneeling, but away from him. He was still lying prostrate, with averted face. The girls grouped uneasily around.

'Me!' repeated Annie, with a terrible bitter accent.

Then she got up, drawing away from him with strange disgust and bitterness.

'I wouldn't touch him,' she said.

But her face quivered with a kind of agony, she seemed as if she would fall. The other girls turned aside. He remained lying on the floor, with his torn clothes and bleeding, averted face.

'Oh, if he's chosen—' said Polly.

'I don't want him—he can choose again,' said Annie, with the same rather bitter hopelessness.

'Get up,' said Polly, lifting his shoulder. 'Get up.'

He rose slowly, a strange, ragged, dazed creature. The girls eyed him from a distance, curiously, furtively, dangerously.

'Who wants him?' cried Laura, roughly.

'Nobody,' they answered, with contempt. Yet each one of them waited for him to look at her, hoped he would look at her. All except Annie, and something was broken in her.

He, however, kept his face closed and averted from them all. There was a silence of the end. He picked up the torn pieces of his tunic, without knowing what to do with them. The girls stood about uneasily, flushed, panting, tidying their hair and their dress unconsciously, and watching him. He looked at none of them. He espied his cap in a corner, and went and picked it up. He put it on his head, and one of the girls burst into a shrill, hysteric laugh at the sight he presented. He, however, took no heed, but went straight to where his overcoat hung on a peg. The girls moved away from contact with him as if he had been an electric wire. He put on his coat and buttoned it down. Then he rolled his tunic-rags into a bundle, and stood before the locked door, dumbly.

'Open the door, somebody,' said Laura.

'Annie's got the key,' said one.

Annie silently offered the key to the girls. Nora unlocked the door.

'Tit for tat, old man,' she said. 'Show yourself a man, and don't bear a grudge.'

But without a word or sign he had opened the door and gone, his face closed, his head dropped.

'That'll learn him,' said Laura.

'Coddy!' said Nora.

'Shut up, for God's sake!' cried Annie fiercely, as if in torture.

'Well, I'm about ready to go, Polly. Look sharp!' said Muriel.

The girls were all anxious to be off. They were tidying themselves hurriedly, with mute, stupefied faces.

THE BLIND MAN

Isabel Pervin was listening for two sounds—for the sound of wheels on the drive outside and for the noise of her husband's footsteps in the hall. Her dearest and oldest friend, a man who seemed almost indispensable to her living, would drive up in the rainy dusk of the closing November day. The trap had gone to fetch him from the station. And her husband, who had been blinded in Flanders, and who had a disfiguring mark on his brow, would be coming in from the outhouses.

He had been home for a year now. He was totally blind. Yet they had been very happy. The Grange was Maurice's own place. The back was a farmstead, and the Wernhams, who occupied the rear premises, acted as farmers. Isabel lived with her husband in the handsome rooms in front. She and he had been almost entirely alone together since he was wounded. They talked and sang and read together in a wonderful and unspeakable intimacy. Then she reviewed books for a Scottish newspaper, carrying on her old interest, and he occupied himself a good deal with the farm. Sightless, he could still discuss everything with Wernham, and he could also do a good deal of work about the place—menial work, it is true, but it gave him satisfaction. He milked the cows, carried in the pails, turned the separator, attended to the pigs and horses. Life was still very full and strangely serene for the blind man, peaceful with the almost incomprehensible peace of immediate contact in darkness. With his wife he had a whole world, rich and real and invisible.

They were newly and remotely happy. He did not even regret the loss of his sight in these times of dark, palpable joy. A certain exultance swelled his soul.

But as time wore on, sometimes the rich glamour would leave them. Sometimes, after months of this intensity, a sense of burden overcame Isabel, a weariness, a terrible *ennui*, in that silent house approached between a colonnade of tall-shafted pines. Then she felt she would go mad, for she could not bear it. And sometimes he had devastating fits of depression, which seemed to lay waste his whole being. It was worse than depression—a black misery, when his own life was a torture to him, and when his presence was unbearable to his wife. The dread went down to the roots of her soul as these black days recurred. In a kind of panic she tried to wrap herself up still further in her husband. She forced the old spontaneous cheerfulness and joy to continue. But the effort it cost her was almost too much. She knew she could not keep it up. She felt she would scream with the strain, and would give anything, anything, to escape. She longed to possess her husband utterly; it gave her inordinate joy to have him entirely to herself. And yet, when again he was gone in a black and massive misery, she could not bear him, she could not bear herself; she wished she could be snatched away off the earth altogether, anything rather than live at this cost.

Dazed, she schemed for a way out. She invited friends, she tried to give him some further connection with the outer world. But it was no good. After all their joy and suffering, after their dark, great year of blindness and solitude and unspeakable nearness, other people seemed to them both shallow, prattling, rather impertinent. Shallow prattle seemed presumptuous. He became impatient and irritated, she was wearied. And so they lapsed into their solitude again. For they preferred it.

But now, in a few weeks' time, her second baby would be born. The first had died, an infant, when her husband first went out to France. She looked with joy and relief to the coming of the second. It would be her salvation. But also she felt some anxiety. She was thirty years old, her husband was a year younger. They both wanted the child very much. Yet she could not help feeling afraid. She had her husband on her hands, a terrible joy to her, and a terrifying burden. The child would occupy her love and attention. And then, what of Maurice? What would he do? If only she could feel that he, too, would be at peace and happy when the child came! She did so want to luxuriate in a rich, physical satisfaction of maternity. But the man, what would he do? How could she provide for him, how avert those shattering black moods of his, which destroyed them both?

She sighed with fear. But at this time Bertie Reid wrote to Isabel. He was her old friend, a second or third cousin, a Scotchman, as she was a Scotchwoman. They had been brought up near to one another, and all her life he had been her friend, like a brother, but better than her own brothers. She loved him—though not in the marrying sense. There was a sort of kinship between them, an affinity. They understood one another instinctively. But Isabel would never have thought of marrying Bertie. It would have seemed like marrying in her own family.

Bertie was a barrister and a man of letters, a Scotchman of the intellectual type, quick, ironical, sentimental, and on his knees before the woman he adored but did not want to marry. Maurice Pervin was different. He came of a good old country family—the Grange was not a very great distance from Oxford. He was passionate, sensitive, perhaps over-sensitive, wincing—a big fellow with heavy limbs and a forehead that flushed painfully. For his mind was slow, as if drugged by the strong provincial blood that beat in his veins. He was very sensitive to his own mental slowness, his feelings being quick and acute. So that he was just the opposite to Bertie, whose mind was much quicker than his emotions, which were not so very fine.

From the first the two men did not like each other. Isabel felt that they *ought* to get on together. But they did not. She felt that if only each could have the clue to the other there would be such a rare understanding between them. It did not come off, however.

Bertie adopted a slightly ironical attitude, very offensive to Maurice, who returned the Scotch irony with English resentment, a resentment which deepened sometimes into stupid hatred.

This was a little puzzling to Isabel. However, she accepted it in the course of things. Men were made freakish and unreasonable. Therefore, when Maurice was going out to France for the second time, she felt that, for her husband's sake, she must discontinue her friendship with Bertie. She wrote to the barrister to this effect. Bertram Reid simply replied that in this, as in all other matters, he must obey her wishes, if these were indeed her wishes.

For nearly two years nothing had passed between the two friends. Isabel rather gloried in the fact; she had no compunction. She had one great article of faith, which was, that husband and wife should be so important to one another, that the rest of the world simply did not count. She and Maurice were husband and wife. They loved one another. They would have children. Then let everybody and everything else fade into insignificance outside this connubial felicity. She professed herself quite happy and ready to receive Maurice's friends. She was happy and ready: the happy wife, the ready woman in possession. Without knowing why, the friends retired abashed and came no more. Maurice, of course, took as much satisfaction in this connubial absorption as Isabel did.

He shared in Isabel's literary activities, she cultivated a real interest in agriculture and cattle-raising. For she, being at heart perhaps an emotional enthusiast, always cultivated the practical side of life, and prided herself on her mastery of practical affairs. Thus the husband and wife had spent the five years of their married life. The last had been one of blindness and unspeakable intimacy. And now Isabel felt a great indifference coming over her, a sort of lethargy. She wanted to be allowed to bear her child in peace, to nod by the fire and drift vaguely, physically, from day to day. Maurice was like an ominous thunder-cloud. She had to keep waking up to remember him.

When a little note came from Bertie, asking if he were to put up a tombstone to their dead friendship, and speaking of the real pain he felt on account of her husband's loss of sight, she felt a pang, a fluttering agitation of re-awakening. And she read the letter to Maurice.

'Ask him to come down,' he said.

'Ask Bertie to come here!' she re-echoed.

'Yes—if he wants to.'

Isabel paused for a few moments.

'I know he wants to—he'd only be too glad,' she replied. 'But what about you, Maurice? How would you like it?'

'I should like it.'

'Well—in that case—But I thought you didn't care for him—'

'Oh, I don't know. I might think differently of him now,' the blind man replied. It was rather abstruse to Isabel.

'Well, dear,' she said, 'if you're quite sure—'

'I'm sure enough. Let him come,' said Maurice.

So Bertie was coming, coming this evening, in the November rain and darkness. Isabel was agitated, racked with her old restlessness and indecision. She had always suffered from this pain of doubt, just an agonizing sense of uncertainty. It had begun to pass off, in the lethargy of maternity. Now it returned, and she resented it. She struggled as usual to maintain her calm, composed, friendly bearing, a sort of mask she wore over all her body.

A woman had lighted a tall lamp beside the table, and spread the cloth. The long dining-room was dim, with its elegant but rather severe pieces of old furniture. Only the round table glowed softly under the light. It had a rich, beautiful effect. The white cloth glistened and dropped its heavy, pointed lace corners almost to the carpet, the china was old and handsome, creamy-yellow, with a blotched pattern of harsh red and deep blue, the cups large and bell-shaped, the teapot gallant. Isabel looked at it with superficial appreciation.

Her nerves were hurting her. She looked automatically again at the high, uncurtained windows. In the last dusk she could just perceive outside a huge fir-tree swaying its boughs: it was as if she thought it rather than saw it. The rain came flying on the window panes. Ah, why had she no peace? These two men, why did they tear at her? Why did they not come—why was there this suspense?

She sat in a lassitude that was really suspense and irritation. Maurice, at least, might come in—there was nothing to keep him out. She rose to her feet. Catching sight of her reflection in a mirror, she glanced at herself with a slight smile of recognition, as if she were an old friend to herself. Her face was oval and calm, her nose a little arched. Her neck made a beautiful line down to her shoulder. With hair knotted loosely behind, she had something of a warm, maternal look. Thinking this of herself, she arched her eyebrows and her rather heavy eyelids, with a little flicker of a smile, and for a moment her grey eyes looked amused and wicked, a little sardonic, out of her transfigured Madonna face.

Then, resuming her air of womanly patience—she was really fatally self-determined—she went with a little jerk towards the door. Her eyes were slightly reddened.

She passed down the wide hall, and through a door at the end. Then she was in the farm premises. The scent of dairy, and of farm-kitchen, and of farm-yard and of leather almost overcame her: but particularly the scent of dairy. They had been scalding out the pans. The flagged passage in front of her was dark, puddled and wet. Light came out from the open kitchen door. She went forward and stood in the doorway. The farm-people were at tea, seated at a little distance from her, round a long, narrow table, in the centre of which stood a white lamp. Ruddy faces, ruddy hands holding food, red mouths working, heads bent over the tea-cups: men, land-girls, boys: it was tea-time, feeding-time. Some faces caught sight of her. Mrs. Wernham, going round behind the chairs with a large black teapot, halting slightly in her walk, was not aware of her for a moment. Then she turned suddenly.

'Oh, is it Madam!' she exclaimed. 'Come in, then, come in! We're at tea.' And she dragged forward a chair.

'No, I won't come in,' said Isabel, 'I'm afraid I interrupt your meal.'

'No—no—not likely, Madam, not likely.'

'Hasn't Mr. Pervin come in, do you know?'

'I'm sure I couldn't say! Missed him, have you, Madam?'

'No, I only wanted him to come in,' laughed Isabel, as if shyly.

'Wanted him, did ye? Get you, boy—get up, now—'

Mrs. Wernham knocked one of the boys on the shoulder. He began to scrape to his feet, chewing largely.

'I believe he's in top stable,' said another face from the table.

'Ah! No, don't get up. I'm going myself,' said Isabel.

'Don't you go out of a dirty night like this. Let the lad go. Get along wi' ye, boy,' said

Mrs. Wernham.

'No, no,' said Isabel, with a decision that was always obeyed. 'Go on with your tea, Tom. I'd like to go across to the stable, Mrs. Wernham.'

'Did ever you hear tell!' exclaimed the woman.

'Isn't the trap late?' asked Isabel.

'Why, no,' said Mrs. Wernham, peering into the distance at the tall, dim clock. 'No, Madam—we can give it another quarter or twenty minutes yet, good—yes, every bit of a quarter.'

'Ah! It seems late when darkness falls so early,' said Isabel.

'It do, that it do. Bother the days, that they draw in so,' answered Mrs. Wernham.' Proper miserable!'

'They are,' said Isabel, withdrawing.

She pulled on her overshoes, wrapped a large tartan shawl around her, put on a man's felt hat, and ventured out along the causeways of the first yard. It was very dark. The wind was roaring in the great elms behind the outhouses. When she came to the second yard the darkness seemed deeper. She was unsure of her footing. She wished she had brought a lantern. Rain blew against her. Half she liked it, half she felt unwilling to battle.

She reached at last the just visible door of the stable. There was no sign of a light anywhere. Opening the upper half, she looked in: into a simple well of darkness. The smell of horses, and ammonia, and of warmth was startling to her, in that full night. She listened with all her ears, but could hear nothing save the night, and the stirring of a horse.

'Maurice!' she called, softly and musically, though she was afraid. 'Maurice—are you there?'

Nothing came from the darkness. She knew the rain and wind blew in upon the horses, the hot animal life. Feeling it wrong, she entered the stable, and drew the lower half of the door shut, holding the upper part close. She did not stir, because she was aware of the presence of the dark hindquarters of the horses, though she could not see them, and she was afraid. Something wild stirred in her heart.

She listened intensely. Then she heard a small noise in the distance—far away, it seemed—the chink of a pan, and a man's voice speaking a brief word. It would be Maurice, in the other part of the stable. She stood motionless, waiting for him to come through the partition door. The horses were so terrifyingly near to her, in the invisible.

The loud jarring of the inner door-latch made her start; the door was opened. She could hear and feel her husband entering and invisibly passing among the horses near to her, in darkness as they were, actively intermingled. The rather low sound of his voice as he spoke to the horses came velvety to her nerves. How near he was, and how invisible! The darkness seemed to be in a strange swirl of violent life, just upon her. She turned giddy.

Her presence of mind made her call, quietly and musically:

'Maurice! Maurice—dea-ar!'

'Yes,' he answered. 'Isabel?'

She saw nothing, and the sound of his voice seemed to touch her.

'Hello!' she answered cheerfully, straining her eyes to see him. He was still busy, attending to the horses near her, but she saw only darkness. It made her almost desperate.

'Won't you come in, dear?' she said.

'Yes, I'm coming. Just half a minute. *Stand over—now!* Trap's not come, has it?'

'Not yet,' said Isabel.

His voice was pleasant and ordinary, but it had a slight suggestion of the stable to her. She wished he would come away. Whilst he was so utterly invisible she was afraid of him.

'How's the time?' he asked.

'Not yet six,' she replied. She disliked to answer into the dark. Presently he came very near to her, and she retreated out of doors.

'The weather blows in here,' he said, coming steadily forward, feeling for the doors. She shrank away. At last she could dimly see him.

'Bertie won't have much of a drive,' he said, as he closed the doors.

'He won't indeed!' said Isabel calmly, watching the dark shape at the door.

'Give me your arm, dear,' she said.

She pressed his arm close to her, as she went. But she longed to see him, to look at him. She was nervous. He walked erect, with face rather lifted, but with a curious tentative movement of his powerful, muscular legs. She could feel the clever, careful, strong contact of his feet with the earth, as she balanced against him. For a moment he was a tower of darkness to her, as if he rose out of the earth.

In the house-passage he wavered, and went cautiously, with a curious look of silence about him as he felt for the bench. Then he sat down heavily. He was a man with rather sloping shoulders, but with heavy limbs, powerful legs that seemed to know the earth. His head was small, usually carried high and light. As he bent down to unfasten his gaiters and boots he did not look blind. His hair was brown and crisp, his hands were large, reddish, intelligent, the veins stood out in the wrists; and his thighs and knees seemed massive. When he stood up his face and neck were surcharged with blood, the veins stood out on his temples. She did not look at his blindness.

Isabel was always glad when they had passed through the dividing door into their own regions of repose and beauty. She was a little afraid of him, out there in the animal grossness of the back. His bearing also changed, as he smelt the familiar, indefinable odour that pervaded his wife's surroundings, a delicate, refined scent, very faintly spicy. Perhaps it came from the pot-pourri bowls.

He stood at the foot of the stairs, arrested, listening. She watched him, and her heart sickened. He seemed to be listening to fate.

'He's not here yet,' he said. 'I'll go up and change.'

'Maurice,' she said, 'you're not wishing he wouldn't come, are you?'

'I couldn't quite say,' he answered. 'I feel myself rather on the *qui vive*.'

'I can see you are,' she answered. And she reached up and kissed his cheek. She saw his mouth relax into a slow smile.

'What are you laughing at?' she said roguishly.

'You consoling me,' he answered.

'Nay,' she answered. 'Why should I console you? You know we love each other—you know *how* married we are! What does anything else matter?'

'Nothing at all, my dear.'

He felt for her face, and touched it, smiling.

'*You're* all right, aren't you?' he asked, anxiously.

'I'm wonderfully all right, love,' she answered. 'It's you I am a little troubled about, at times.'

'Why me?' he said, touching her cheeks delicately with the tips of his fingers. The touch had an almost hypnotizing effect on her.

He went away upstairs. She saw him mount into the darkness, unseeing and unchanging. He did not know that the lamps on the upper corridor were unlighted. He went on into the darkness with unchanging step. She heard him in the bathroom.

Pervin moved about almost unconsciously in his familiar surroundings, dark though everything was. He seemed to know the presence of objects before he touched them. It was a pleasure to him to rock thus through a world of things, carried on the flood in a sort of blood-prescience. He did not think much or trouble much. So long as he kept this sheer immediacy of blood-contact with the substantial world he was happy, he wanted no intervention of visual consciousness. In this state there was a certain rich positivity, bordering sometimes on rapture. Life seemed to move in him like a tide lapping, and advancing, enveloping all things darkly. It was a pleasure to stretch forth the hand and meet the unseen object, clasp it, and possess it in pure contact. He did not try to remember, to visualize. He did not want to. The new way of consciousness substituted itself in him.

The rich suffusion of this state generally kept him happy, reaching its culmination in the consuming passion for his wife. But at times the flow would seem to be checked and thrown back. Then it would beat inside him like a tangled sea, and he was tortured in the shattered chaos of his own blood. He grew to dread this arrest, this throw-back, this chaos inside himself, when he seemed merely at the mercy of his own powerful and conflicting elements. How to get some measure of control or surety, this was the question. And when the question rose maddening in him, he would clench his fists as if he would *compel* the whole universe to submit to him. But it was in vain. He could not even compel himself.

Tonight, however, he was still serene, though little tremors of unreasonable exasperation ran through him. He had to handle the razor very carefully, as he shaved, for it was not at one with him, he was afraid of it. His hearing also was too much sharpened. He heard the woman lighting the lamps on the corridor, and attending to the fire in the visitor's room. And then, as he went to his room he heard the trap arrive. Then came Isabel's voice, lifted and calling, like a bell ringing:

'Is it you, Bertie? Have you come?'

And a man's voice answered out of the wind:

'Hello, Isabel! There you are.'

'Have you had a miserable drive? I'm so sorry we couldn't send a closed carriage. I can't see you at all, you know.'

'I'm coming. No, I liked the drive—it was like Perthshire. Well, how are you? You're looking fit as ever, as far as I can see.'

'Oh, yes,' said Isabel. 'I'm wonderfully well. How are you? Rather thin, I think—'

'Worked to death—everybody's old cry. But I'm all right, Ciss. How's Pervin?—isn't he here?'

'Oh, yes, he's upstairs changing. Yes, he's awfully well. Take off your wet things; I'll send them to be dried.'

'And how are you both, in spirits? He doesn't fret?'

'No—no, not at all. No, on the contrary, really. We've been wonderfully happy, incredibly. It's more than I can understand—so wonderful: the nearness, and the peace—'

'Ah! Well, that's awfully good news—'

They moved away. Pervin heard no more. But a childish sense of desolation had come over him, as he heard their brisk voices. He seemed shut out—like a child that is left out. He was aimless and excluded, he did not know what to do with himself. The helpless desolation came over him. He fumbled nervously as he dressed himself, in a state almost of childishness. He disliked the Scotch accent in Bertie's speech, and the slight response it found on Isabel's tongue. He disliked the slight purr of complacency in the Scottish speech. He disliked intensely the glib way in which Isabel spoke of their happiness and nearness. It made him recoil. He was fretful and beside himself like a child, he had almost a childish nostalgia to be included in the life circle. And at the same time he was a man, dark and powerful and infuriated by his own weakness. By some fatal flaw, he could not be by himself, he had to depend on the support of another. And this very dependence enraged him. He hated Bertie Reid, and at the same time he knew the hatred was nonsense, he knew it was the outcome of his own weakness.

He went downstairs. Isabel was alone in the dining-room. She watched him enter, head erect, his feet tentative. He looked so strong-blooded and healthy, and, at the same time, cancelled. Cancelled—that was the word that flew across her mind. Perhaps it was his scars suggested it.

'You heard Bertie come, Maurice?' she said.

'Yes—isn't he here?'

'He's in his room. He looks very thin and worn.'

'I suppose he works himself to death.'

A woman came in with a tray—and after a few minutes Bertie came down. He was a little dark man, with a very big forehead, thin, wispy hair, and sad, large eyes. His expression was inordinately sad—almost funny. He had odd, short legs.

Isabel watched him hesitate under the door, and glance nervously at her husband. Pervin heard him and turned.

'Here you are, now,' said Isabel. 'Come, let us eat.'

Bertie went across to Maurice.

'How are you, Pervin,' he said, as he advanced.

The blind man stuck his hand out into space, and Bertie took it.

'Very fit. Glad you've come,' said Maurice.

Isabel glanced at them, and glanced away, as if she could not bear to see them.

'Come,' she said. 'Come to table. Aren't you both awfully hungry? I am, tremendously.'

'I'm afraid you waited for me,' said Bertie, as they sat down.

Maurice had a curious monolithic way of sitting in a chair, erect and distant. Isabel's heart always beat when she caught sight of him thus.

'No,' she replied to Bertie. 'We're very little later than usual. We're having a sort of high tea, not dinner. Do you mind? It gives us such a nice long evening, uninterrupted.'

'I like it,' said Bertie.

Maurice was feeling, with curious little movements, almost like a cat kneading her bed, for his place, his knife and fork, his napkin. He was getting the whole geography of his cover into his consciousness. He sat erect and inscrutable, remote-seeming Bertie watched the static figure of the blind man, the delicate tactile discernment of the large, ruddy hands, and the curious mindless silence of the brow, above the scar. With difficulty he looked away, and without knowing what he did, picked up a little crystal bowl of violets from the table, and held them to his nose.

'They are sweet-scented,' he said. 'Where do they come from?'

'From the garden—under the windows,' said Isabel.

'So late in the year—and so fragrant! Do you remember the violets under Aunt Bell's south wall?'

The two friends looked at each other and exchanged a smile, Isabel's eyes lighting up.

172

'Don't I?' she replied. '*Wasn't* she queer!'

'A curious old girl,' laughed Bertie. 'There's a streak of freakishness in the family, Isabel.'

'Ah—but not in you and me, Bertie,' said Isabel. 'Give them to Maurice, will you?' she added, as Bertie was putting down the flowers. 'Have you smelled the violets, dear? Do!—they are so scented.'

Maurice held out his hand, and Bertie placed the tiny bowl against his large, warm-looking fingers. Maurice's hand closed over the thin white fingers of the barrister. Bertie carefully extricated himself. Then the two watched the blind man smelling the violets. He bent his head and seemed to be thinking. Isabel waited.

'Aren't they sweet, Maurice?' she said at last, anxiously.

'Very,' he said. And he held out the bowl. Bertie took it. Both he and Isabel were a little afraid, and deeply disturbed.

The meal continued. Isabel and Bertie chatted spasmodically. The blind man was silent. He touched his food repeatedly, with quick, delicate touches of his knife-point, then cut irregular bits. He could not bear to be helped. Both Isabel and Bertie suffered: Isabel wondered why. She did not suffer when she was alone with Maurice. Bertie made her conscious of a strangeness.

After the meal the three drew their chairs to the fire, and sat down to talk. The decanters were put on a table near at hand. Isabel knocked the logs on the fire, and clouds of brilliant sparks went up the chimney. Bertie noticed a slight weariness in her bearing.

'You will be glad when your child comes now, Isabel?' he said.

She looked up to him with a quick wan smile.

'Yes, I shall be glad,' she answered. 'It begins to seem long. Yes, I shall be very glad. So will you, Maurice, won't you?' she added.

'Yes, I shall,' replied her husband.

'We are both looking forward so much to having it,' she said.

'Yes, of course,' said Bertie.

He was a bachelor, three or four years older than Isabel. He lived in beautiful rooms overlooking the river, guarded by a faithful Scottish man-servant. And he had his friends among the fair sex—not lovers, friends. So long as he could avoid any danger of courtship or marriage, he adored a few good women with constant and unfailing homage, and he was chivalrously fond of quite a number. But if they seemed to encroach on him, he withdrew and detested them.

Isabel knew him very well, knew his beautiful constancy, and kindness, also his incurable weakness, which made him unable ever to enter into close contact of any sort. He was ashamed of himself, because he could not marry, could not approach women physically. He wanted to do so. But he could not. At the centre of him he was afraid, helplessly and even brutally afraid. He had given up hope, had ceased to expect any more that he could escape his own weakness. Hence he was a brilliant and successful barrister, also *littérateur* of high repute, a rich man, and a great social success. At the centre he felt himself neuter, nothing.

Isabel knew him well. She despised him even while she admired him. She looked at his sad face, his little short legs, and felt contempt of him. She looked at his dark grey eyes, with their uncanny, almost childlike intuition, and she loved him. He understood amazingly—but she had no fear of his understanding. As a man she patronized him.

And she turned to the impassive, silent figure of her husband. He sat leaning back, with folded arms, and face a little uptilted. His knees were straight and massive. She sighed, picked up the poker, and again began to prod the fire, to rouse the clouds of soft, brilliant sparks.

'Isabel tells me,' Bertie began suddenly, 'that you have not suffered unbearably from the loss of sight.'

Maurice straightened himself to attend, but kept his arms folded.

'No,' he said, 'not unbearably. Now and again one struggles against it, you know. But there are compensations.'

'They say it is much worse to be stone deaf,' said Isabel.

'I believe it is,' said Bertie. 'Are there compensations?' he added, to Maurice.

'Yes. You cease to bother about a great many things.' Again Maurice stretched his figure, stretched the strong muscles of his back, and leaned backwards, with uplifted face.

'And that is a relief,' said Bertie. 'But what is there in place of the bothering? What replaces the activity?'

There was a pause. At length the blind man replied, as out of a negligent, unattentive thinking:

'Oh, I don't know. There's a good deal when you're not active.'

'Is there?' said Bertie. 'What, exactly? It always seems to me that when there is no thought and no action, there is nothing.'

Again Maurice was slow in replying.

'There is something,' he replied. 'I couldn't tell you what it is.'

And the talk lapsed once more, Isabel and Bertie chatting gossip and reminiscence, the blind man silent.

At length Maurice rose restlessly, a big, obtrusive figure. He felt tight and hampered. He wanted to go away.

'Do you mind,' he said, 'if I go and speak to Wernham?'

'No—go along, dear,' said Isabel.

And he went out. A silence came over the two friends. At length Bertie said:

'Nevertheless, it is a great deprivation, Cissie.'

'It is, Bertie. I know it is.'

'Something lacking all the time,' said Bertie.

'Yes, I know. And yet—and yet—Maurice is right. There is something else, something *there*, which you never knew was there, and which you can't express.'

'What is there?' asked Bertie.

'I don't know—it's awfully hard to define it—but something strong and immediate. There's something strange in Maurice's presence—indefinable—but I couldn't do without it. I agree that it seems to put one's mind to sleep. But when we're alone I miss nothing; it seems awfully rich, almost splendid, you know.'

'I'm afraid I don't follow,' said Bertie.

They talked desultorily. The wind blew loudly outside, rain chattered on the window-panes, making a sharp, drum-sound, because of the closed, mellow-golden shutters inside. The logs burned slowly, with hot, almost invisible small flames. Bertie seemed uneasy, there were dark circles round his eyes. Isabel, rich with her approaching maternity, leaned looking into the fire. Her hair curled in odd, loose strands, very pleasing to the man. But she had a curious feeling of old woe in her heart, old, timeless night-woe.

'I suppose we're all deficient somewhere,' said Bertie.

'I suppose so,' said Isabel wearily.

'Damned, sooner or later.'

blind english soldier
lawyer scotchman

'I don't know,' she said, rousing herself. 'I feel quite all right, you know. The child coming seems to make me indifferent to everything, just placid. I can't feel that there's anything to trouble about, you know.'

'A good thing, I should say,' he replied slowly.

'Well, there it is. I suppose it's just Nature. If only I felt I needn't trouble about Maurice, I should be perfectly content—'

'But you feel you must trouble about him?'

'Well—I don't know—' She even resented this much effort.

The evening passed slowly. Isabel looked at the clock. 'I say,' she said. 'It's nearly ten o'clock. Where can Maurice be? I'm sure they're all in bed at the back. Excuse me a moment.'

She went out, returning almost immediately.

'It's all shut up and in darkness,' she said. 'I wonder where he is. He must have gone out to the farm—'

Bertie looked at her.

'I suppose he'll come in,' he said.

'I suppose so,' she said. 'But it's unusual for him to be out now.'

'Would you like me to go out and see?'

'Well—if you wouldn't mind. I'd go, but—' She did not want to make the physical effort.

Bertie put on an old overcoat and took a lantern. He went out from the side door. He shrank from the wet and roaring night. Such weather had a nervous effect on him: too much moisture everywhere made him feel almost imbecile. Unwilling, he went through it all. A dog barked violently at him. He peered in all the buildings. At last, as he opened the upper door of a sort of intermediate barn, he heard a grinding noise, and looking in, holding up his lantern, saw Maurice, in his shirt-sleeves, standing listening, holding the handle of a turnip-pulper. He had been pulping sweet roots, a pile of which lay dimly heaped in a corner behind him.

'That you, Wernham?' said Maurice, listening.

'No, it's me,' said Bertie.

A large, half-wild grey cat was rubbing at Maurice's leg. The blind man stooped to rub its sides. Bertie watched the scene, then unconsciously entered and shut the door behind him, He was in a high sort of barn-place, from which, right and left, ran off the corridors in front of the stalled cattle. He watched the slow, stooping motion of the other man, as he caressed the great cat.

Maurice straightened himself.

'You came to look for me?' he said.

'Isabel was a little uneasy,' said Bertie.

'I'll come in. I like messing about doing these jobs.'

The cat had reared her sinister, feline length against his leg, clawing at his thigh affectionately. He lifted her claws out of his flesh.

'I hope I'm not in your way at all at the Grange here,' said Bertie, rather shy and stiff.

'My way? No, not a bit. I'm glad Isabel has somebody to talk to. I'm afraid it's I who am in the way. I know I'm not very lively company. Isabel's all right, don't you think? She's not unhappy, is she?'

'I don't think so.'

'What does she say?'

'She says she's very content—only a little troubled about you.'

'Why me?'

'Perhaps afraid that you might brood,' said Bertie, cautiously.

'She needn't be afraid of that.' He continued to caress the flattened grey head of the cat with his fingers. 'What I am a bit afraid of,' he resumed, 'is that she'll find me a dead weight, always alone with me down here.'

'I don't think you need think that,' said Bertie, though this was what he feared himself.

'I don't know,' said Maurice. 'Sometimes I feel it isn't fair that she's saddled with me.' Then he dropped his voice curiously. 'I say,' he asked, secretly struggling, 'is my face much disfigured? Do you mind telling me?'

'There is the scar,' said Bertie, wondering. 'Yes, it is a disfigurement. But more pitiable than shocking.'

'A pretty bad scar, though,' said Maurice.

'Oh, yes.'

There was a pause.

'Sometimes I feel I am horrible,' said Maurice, in a low voice, talking as if to himself. And Bertie actually felt a quiver of horror.

'That's nonsense,' he said.

Maurice again straightened himself, leaving the cat.

'There's no telling,' he said. Then again, in an odd tone, he added: 'I don't really know you, do I?'

'Probably not,' said Bertie.

'Do you mind if I touch you?' Intimacy

The lawyer shrank away instinctively. And yet, out of very philanthropy, he said, in a small voice: 'Not at all.'

But he suffered as the blind man stretched out a strong, naked hand to him. Maurice accidentally knocked off Bertie's hat. lol

'I thought you were taller,' he said, starting. Then he laid his hand on Bertie Reid's head, closing the dome of the skull in a soft, firm grasp, gathering it, as it were; then, shifting his grasp and softly closing again, with a fine, close pressure, till he had covered the skull and the face of the smaller man, tracing the brows, and touching the full, closed eyes, touching the small nose and the nostrils, the rough, short moustache, the mouth, the rather strong chin. The hand of the blind man grasped the shoulder, the arm, the hand of the other man. He seemed to take him, in the soft, travelling grasp.

'You seem young,' he said quietly, at last.

The lawyer stood almost annihilated, unable to answer.

'Your head seems tender, as if you were young,' Maurice repeated. 'So do your hands. Touch my eyes, will you?—touch my scar.'

Now Bertie quivered with revulsion. Yet he was under the power of the blind man, as if hypnotized. He lifted his hand, and laid the fingers on the scar, on the scarred eyes. Maurice suddenly covered them with his own hand, pressed the fingers of the other man upon his disfigured eye-sockets, trembling in every fibre, and rocking slightly, slowly, from side to side. He remained thus for a minute or more, whilst Bertie stood as if in a swoon, unconscious, imprisoned. intensity

Then suddenly Maurice removed the hand of the other man from his brow, and stood holding it in his own.

'Oh, my God' he said, 'we shall know each other now, shan't we? We shall know each other now.'

Bertie could not answer. He gazed mute and terror-struck, overcome by his own weakness. He knew he could not answer. He had an unreasonable fear, lest the other man should suddenly destroy him. Whereas Maurice was actually filled with hot, poignant love, the passion of friendship. Perhaps it was this very passion of friendship which Bertie shrank from most.

'We're all right together now, aren't we?' said Maurice. 'It's all right now, as long as we live, so far as we're concerned?'

'Yes,' said Bertie, trying by any means to escape.

Maurice stood with head lifted, as if listening. The new delicate fulfilment of mortal friendship had come as a revelation and surprise to him, something exquisite and unhoped-for. He seemed to be listening to hear if it were real.

Then he turned for his coat.

'Come,' he said, 'we'll go to Isabel.'

Bertie took the lantern and opened the door. The cat disappeared. The two men went in silence along the causeways. Isabel, as they came, thought their footsteps sounded strange. She looked up pathetically and anxiously for their entrance. There seemed a curious elation about Maurice. Bertie was haggard, with sunken eyes.

'What is it?' she asked.

'We've become friends,' said Maurice, standing with his feet apart, like a strange colossus.

'Friends!' re-echoed Isabel. And she looked again at Bertie. He met her eyes with a furtive, haggard look; his eyes were as if glazed with misery.

'I'm so glad,' she said, in sheer perplexity.

'Yes,' said Maurice.

He was indeed so glad. Isabel took his hand with both hers, and held it fast.

'You'll be happier now, dear,' she said.

But she was watching Bertie. She knew that he had one desire—to escape from this intimacy, this friendship, which had been thrust upon him. He could not bear it that he had been touched by the blind man, his insane reserve broken in. He was like a mollusk whose shell is broken.

MONKEY NUTS

At first Joe thought the job O.K. He was loading hay on the trucks, along with Albert, the corporal. The two men were pleasantly billeted in a cottage not far from the station: they were their own masters, for Joe never thought of Albert as a master. And the little sidings of the tiny village station was as pleasant a place as you could wish for. On one side, beyond the line, stretched the woods: on the other, the near side, across a green smooth field red houses were dotted among flowering apple trees. The weather being sunny, work being easy, Albert, a real good pal, what life could be better! After Flanders, it was heaven itself.

Albert, the corporal, was a clean-shaven, shrewd-looking fellow of about forty. He seemed to think his one aim in life was to be full of fun and nonsense. In repose, his face looked a little withered, old. He was a very good pal to Joe, steady, decent and grave under all his 'mischief'; for his mischief was only his laborious way of skirting his own *ennui*.

Joe was much younger than Albert—only twenty-three. He was a tallish, quiet youth, pleasant looking. He was of a slightly better class than his corporal, more personable.

Careful about his appearance, he shaved every day. 'I haven't got much of a face,' said Albert. 'If I was to shave every day like you, Joe, I should have none.'

There was plenty of life in the little goods-yard: three porter youths, a continual come and go of farm wagons bringing hay, wagons with timber from the woods, coal carts loading at the trucks. The black coal seemed to make the place sleepier, hotter. Round the big white gate the station-master's children played and his white chickens walked, whilst the stationmaster himself, a young man getting too fat, helped his wife to peg out the washing on the clothes line in the meadow.

The great boat-shaped wagons came up from Playcross with the hay. At first the farm-men waggoned it. On the third day one of the land-girls appeared with the first load, drawing to a standstill easily at the head of her two great horses. She was a buxom girl, young, in linen overalls and gaiters. Her face was ruddy, she had large blue eyes.

'Now that's the waggoner for us, boys,' said the corporal loudly.

'Whoa!' she said to her horses; and then to the corporal: 'Which boys do you mean?'

'We are the pick of the bunch. That's Joe, my pal. Don't you let on that my name's Albert,' said the corporal to his private. 'I'm the corporal.'

'And I'm Miss Stokes,' said the land-girl coolly, 'if that's all the boys you are.'

'You know you couldn't want more, Miss Stokes,' said Albert politely. Joe, who was bare-headed, whose grey flannel sleeves were rolled up to the elbow, and whose shirt was open at the breast, looked modestly aside as if he had no part in the affair.

'Are you on this job regular, then?' said the corporal to Miss Stokes.

'I don't know for sure,' she said, pushing a piece of hair under her hat, and attending to her splendid horses.

'Oh, make it a certainty,' said Albert.

She did not reply. She turned and looked over the two men coolly. She was pretty, moderately blonde, with crisp hair, a good skin, and large blue eyes. She was strong, too, and the work went on leisurely and easily.

'Now!' said the corporal, stopping as usual to look round, 'pleasant company makes work a pleasure—don't hurry it, boys.' He stood on the truck surveying the world. That was one of his great and absorbing occupations: to stand and look out on things in general. Joe, also standing on the truck, also turned round to look what was to be seen. But he could not become blankly absorbed, as Albert could.

Miss Stokes watched the two men from under her broad felt hat. She had seen hundreds of Alberts, khaki soldiers standing in loose attitudes, absorbed in watching nothing in particular. She had seen also a good many Joes, quiet, good-looking young soldiers with half-averted faces. But there was something in the turn of Joe's head, and something in his quiet, tender-looking form, young and fresh—which attracted her eye. As she watched him closely from below, he turned as if he felt her, and his dark-blue eye met her straight, light-blue gaze. He faltered and turned aside again and looked as if he were going to fall off the truck. A slight flush mounted under the girl's full, ruddy face. She liked him.

Always, after this, when she came into the sidings with her team, it was Joe she looked for. She acknowledged to herself that she was sweet on him. But Albert did all the talking. He was so full of fun and nonsense. Joe was a very shy bird, very brief and remote in his answers. Miss Stokes was driven to indulge in repartee with Albert, but she fixed her magnetic attention on the younger fellow. Joe would talk with Albert, and laugh at his jokes. But Miss Stokes could get little out of him. She had to depend on her silent forces. They were more effective than might be imagined.

Suddenly, on Saturday afternoon, at about two o'clock, Joe received a bolt from the blue—a telegram: 'Meet me Belbury Station 6.00 p.m. today. M.S.' He knew at once who M.S. was. His heart melted, he felt weak as if he had had a blow.

'What's the trouble, boy?' asked Albert anxiously.

'No—no trouble—it's to meet somebody.' Joe lifted his dark-blue eyes in confusion towards his corporal.

'Meet somebody!' repeated the corporal, watching his young pal with keen blue eyes. 'It's all right, then; nothing wrong?'

'No—nothing wrong. I'm not going,' said Joe.

Albert was old and shrewd enough to see that nothing more should be said before the housewife. He also saw that Joe did not want to take him into confidence. So he held his peace, though he was piqued.

The two soldiers went into town, smartened up. Albert knew a fair number of the boys round about; there would be plenty of gossip in the market-place, plenty of lounging in groups on the Bath Road, watching the Saturday evening shoppers. Then a modest drink or two, and the movies. They passed an agreeable, casual, nothing-in-particular evening, with which Joe was quite satisfied. He thought of Belbury Station, and of M.S. waiting there. He had not the faintest intention of meeting her. And he had not the faintest intention of telling Albert.

And yet, when the two men were in their bedroom, half undressed, Joe suddenly held out the telegram to his corporal, saying: 'What d'you think of that?'

Albert was just unbuttoning his braces. He desisted, took the telegram form, and turned towards the candle to read it.

'*Meet me Belbury Station 6.00 p.m. today. M.S.*,' he read, *sotto voce*. His face took on its fun-and-nonsense look.

'Who's M.S.?' he asked, looking shrewdly at Joe.

'You know as well as I do,' said Joe, non-committal.

'*M.S.*,' repeated Albert. 'Blamed if I know, boy. Is it a woman?'

The conversation was carried on in tiny voices, for fear of disturbing the householders.

'I don't know,' said Joe, turning. He looked full at Albert, the two men looked straight into each other's eyes. There was a lurking grin in each of them.

'Well, I'm—*blamed*!' said Albert at last, throwing the telegram down emphatically on the bed.

'Wha-at?' said Joe, grinning rather sheepishly, his eyes clouded none the less.

Albert sat on the bed and proceeded to undress, nodding his head with mock gravity all the while. Joe watched him foolishly.

'What?' he repeated faintly.

Albert looked up at him with a knowing look.

'If that isn't coming it quick, boy!' he said. 'What the blazes! What ha' you bin doing?'

'Nothing!' said Joe.

Albert slowly shook his head as he sat on the side of the bed.

'Don't happen to me when *I've* bin doin' nothing,' he said. And he proceeded to pull off his stockings.

Joe turned away, looking at himself in the mirror as he unbuttoned his tunic.

'You didn't want to keep the appointment?' Albert asked, in a changed voice, from the bedside.

Joe did not answer for a moment. Then he said:

'I made no appointment.'

'I'm not saying you did, boy. Don't be nasty about it. I mean you didn't want to answer the—unknown person's summons—shall I put it that way?'

'No,' said Joe.

'What was the deterring motive?' asked Albert, who was now lying on his back in bed.

'Oh,' said Joe, suddenly looking round rather haughtily. 'I didn't want to.' He had a well-balanced head, and could take on a sudden distant bearing.

'Didn't want to—didn't cotton on, like. Well—*they be artful, the women*—' he mimicked his landlord. 'Come on into bed, boy. Don't loiter about as if you'd lost something.'

Albert turned over, to sleep.

On Monday Miss Stokes turned up as usual, striding beside her team. Her 'whoa!' was resonant and challenging, she looked up at the truck as her steeds came to a standstill. Joe had turned aside, and had his face averted from her. She glanced him over—save for his slender succulent tenderness she would have despised him. She sized him up in a steady look. Then she turned to Albert, who was looking down at her and smiling in his mischievous turn. She knew his aspects by now. She looked straight back at him, though her eyes were hot. He saluted her.

'Beautiful morning, Miss Stokes.'

'Very!' she replied.

'Handsome is as handsome looks,' said Albert.

Which produced no response.

'Now, Joe, come on here,' said the corporal. 'Don't keep the ladies waiting—it's the sign of a weak heart.'

Joe turned, and the work began. Nothing more was said for the time being. As the week went on all parties became more comfortable. Joe remained silent, averted, neutral, a little on his dignity. Miss Stokes was off-hand and masterful. Albert was full of mischief.

The great theme was a circus, which was coming to the market town on the following Saturday.

'You'll go to the circus, Miss Stokes?' said Albert.

'I may go. Are you going?'

'Certainly. Give us the pleasure of escorting you.'

'No, thanks.'

'That's what I call a flat refusal—what, Joe? You don't mean that you have no liking for our company, Miss Stokes?'

'Oh, I don't know,' said Miss Stokes. 'How many are there of you?'

'Only me and Joe.'

'Oh, is that all?' she said, satirically.

Albert was a little nonplussed.

'Isn't that enough for you?' he asked.

'Too many by half,' blurted out Joe, jeeringly, in a sudden fit of uncouth rudeness that made both the others stare.

'Oh, I'll stand out of the way, boy, if that's it,' said Albert to Joe. Then he turned mischievously to Miss Stokes. 'He wants to know what M. stands for,' he said, confidentially.

'Monkeys,' she replied, turning to her horses.

'What's M.S.?' said Albert.

'Monkey nuts,' she retorted, leading off her team.

Albert looked after her a little discomfited. Joe had flushed dark, and cursed Albert in his heart.

On the Saturday afternoon the two soldiers took the train into town. They would have to walk home. They had tea at six o'clock, and lounged about till half past seven. The circus was in a meadow near the river—a great red-and-white striped tent. Caravans stood at the side. A great crowd of people was gathered round the ticket-caravan.

Inside the tent the lamps were lighted, shining on a ring of faces, a great circular bank of faces round the green grassy centre. Along with some comrades, the two soldiers packed themselves on a thin plank seat, rather high. They were delighted with the flaring lights, the wild effect. But the circus performance did not affect them deeply. They admired the lady in black velvet with rose-purple legs who leapt so neatly on to the galloping horse; they watched the feats of strength and laughed at the clown. But they felt a little patronizing, they missed the sensational drama of the cinema.

Half-way through the performance Joe was electrified to see the face of Miss Stokes not very far from him. There she was, in her khaki and her felt hat, as usual; he pretended not to see her. She was laughing at the clown; she also pretended not to see him. It was a blow to him, and it made him angry. He would not even mention it to Albert. Least said, soonest mended. He liked to believe she had not seen him. But he knew, fatally, that she had.

When they came out it was nearly eleven o'clock; a lovely night, with a moon and tall, dark, noble trees: a magnificent May night. Joe and Albert laughed and chaffed with the boys. Joe looked round frequently to see if he were safe from Miss Stokes. It seemed so.

But there were six miles to walk home. At last the two soldiers set off, swinging their canes. The road was white between tall hedges, other stragglers were passing out of the town towards the villages; the air was full of pleased excitement.

They were drawing near to the village when they saw a dark figure ahead. Joe's heart sank with pure fear. It was a figure wheeling a bicycle; a land girl; Miss Stokes. Albert was ready with his nonsense. Miss Stokes had a puncture.

'Let me wheel the rattler,' said Albert.

'Thank you,' said Miss Stokes. 'You *are* kind.'

'Oh, I'd be kinder than that, if you'd show me how,' said Albert.

'Are you sure?' said Miss Stokes.

'Doubt my words?' said Albert. 'That's cruel of you, Miss Stokes.'

Miss Stokes walked between them, close to Joe.

'Have you been to the circus?' she asked him.

'Yes,' he replied, mildly.

'Have *you* been?' Albert asked her.

'Yes. I didn't see you,' she replied.

'What!—you say so! Didn't see us! Didn't think us worth looking at,' began Albert. 'Aren't I as handsome as the clown, now? And you didn't as much as glance in our direction? I call it a downright oversight.'

'I never *saw* you,' reiterated Miss Stokes. 'I didn't know you saw me.'

'That makes it worse,' said Albert.

The road passed through a belt of dark pine-wood. The village, and the branch road, was very near. Miss Stokes put out her fingers and felt for Joe's hand as it swung at his side. To say he was staggered is to put it mildly. Yet he allowed her softly to clasp his fingers for a few moments. But he was a mortified youth.

At the cross-road they stopped—Miss Stokes should turn off. She had another mile to go.

'You'll let us see you home,' said Albert.

'Do me a kindness,' she said. 'Put my bike in your shed, and take it to Baker's on Monday, will you?'

'I'll sit up all night and mend it for you, if you like.'

'No thanks. And Joe and I'll walk on.'

'Oh—ho! Oh—ho!' sang Albert. 'Joe! Joe! What do you say to that, now, boy? Aren't you in luck's way. And I get the bloomin' old bike for my pal. Consider it again, Miss Stokes.'

Joe turned aside his face, and did not speak.

'Oh, well! I wheel the grid, do I? I leave you, boy—'

'I'm not keen on going any further,' barked out Joe, in an uncouth voice. 'She hain't my choice.'

The girl stood silent, and watched the two men.

'There now!' said Albert. 'Think o' that! If it was *me* now—' But he was uncomfortable. 'Well, Miss Stokes, have me,' he added.

Miss Stokes stood quite still, neither moved nor spoke. And so the three remained for some time at the lane end. At last Joe began kicking the ground—then he suddenly lifted his face. At that moment Miss Stokes was at his side. She put her arm delicately round his waist.

'Seems I'm the one extra, don't you think?' Albert inquired of the high bland moon.

Joe had dropped his head and did not answer. Miss Stokes stood with her arm lightly round his waist. Albert bowed, saluted, and bade good-night. He walked away, leaving the two standing.

Miss Stokes put a light pressure on Joe's waist, and drew him down the road. They walked in silence. The night was full of scent—wild cherry, the first bluebells. Still they walked in silence. A nightingale was singing. They approached nearer and nearer, till they stood close by his dark bush. The powerful notes sounded from the cover, almost like flashes of light—then the interval of silence—then the moaning notes, almost like a dog faintly howling, followed by the long, rich trill, and flashing notes. Then a short silence again.

Miss Stokes turned at last to Joe. She looked up at him, and in the moonlight he saw her faintly smiling. He felt maddened, but helpless. Her arm was round his waist, she drew him closely to her with a soft pressure that made all his bones rotten.

Meanwhile Albert was waiting at home. He put on his overcoat, for the fire was out, and he had had malarial fever. He looked fitfully at the *Daily Mirror* and the *Daily Sketch*, but he saw nothing. It seemed a long time. He began to yawn widely, even to nod. At last Joe came in.

Albert looked at him keenly. The young man's brow was black, his face sullen.

'All right, boy?' asked Albert.

Joe merely grunted for a reply. There was nothing more to be got out of him. So they went to bed.

Next day Joe was silent, sullen. Albert could make nothing of him. He proposed a walk after tea.

'I'm going somewhere,' said Joe.

'Where—Monkey nuts?' asked the corporal. But Joe's brow only became darker.

So the days went by. Almost every evening Joe went off alone, returning late. He was sullen, taciturn and had a hang-dog look, a curious way of dropping his head and looking dangerously from under his brows. And he and Albert did not get on so well any more with one another. For all his fun and nonsense, Albert was really irritable, soon made angry. And Joe's stand-offish sulkiness and complete lack of confidence riled him, got on his nerves. His fun and nonsense took a biting, sarcastic turn, at which Joe's eyes glittered occasionally, though the young man turned unheeding aside. Then again Joe would be full of odd, whimsical fun, outshining Albert himself.

Miss Stokes still came to the station with the wain: Monkey-nuts, Albert called her, though not to her face. For she was very clear and good-looking, almost she seemed to gleam. And Albert was a tiny bit afraid of her. She very rarely addressed Joe whilst the hay-loading was going on, and that young man always turned his back to her. He seemed thinner, and his limber figure looked more slouching. But still it had the tender, attractive appearance, especially from behind. His tanned face, a little thinned and darkened, took a handsome, slightly sinister look.

'Come on, Joe!' the corporal urged sharply one day. 'What're you doing, boy? Looking for beetles on the bank?'

Joe turned round swiftly, almost menacing, to work.

'He's a different fellow these days, Miss Stokes,' said Albert to the young woman. 'What's got him? Is it Monkey nuts that don't suit him, do you think?'

'Choked with chaff, more like,' she retorted. 'It's as bad as feeding a threshing machine, to have to listen to some folks.'

'As bad as what?' said Albert. 'You don't mean me, do you, Miss Stokes?'

'No,' she cried. 'I don't mean you.'

Joe's face became dark red during these sallies, but he said nothing. He would eye the young woman curiously, as she swung so easily at the work, and he had some of the look of a dog which is going to bite.

Albert, with his nerves on edge, began to find the strain rather severe. The next Saturday evening, when Joe came in more black-browed than ever, he watched him, determined to have it out with him.

When the boy went upstairs to bed, the corporal followed him. He closed the door behind him carefully, sat on the bed and watched the younger man undressing. And for once he spoke in a natural voice, neither chaffing nor commanding.

'What's gone wrong, boy?'

Joe stopped a moment as if he had been shot. Then he went on unwinding his puttees, and did not answer or look up.

'You can hear, can't you?' said Albert, nettled.

'Yes, I can hear,' said Joe, stooping over his puttees till his face was purple.

'Then why don't you answer?'

Joe sat up. He gave a long, sideways look at the corporal. Then he lifted his eyes and stared at a crack in the ceiling.

The corporal watched these movements shrewdly.

'And *then* what?' he asked, ironically.

Again Joe turned and stared him in the face. The corporal smiled very slightly, but kindly.

'There'll be murder done one of these days,' said Joe, in a quiet, unimpassioned voice.

'So long as it's by daylight—' replied Albert. Then he went over, sat down by Joe, put his hand on his shoulder affectionately, and continued, 'What is it, boy? What's gone wrong? You can trust me, can't you?'

Joe turned and looked curiously at the face so near to his.

'It's nothing, that's all,' he said laconically.

Albert frowned.

'Then who's going to be murdered?—and who's going to do the murdering?—me or you—which is it, boy?' He smiled gently at the stupid youth, looking straight at him all the while, into his eyes. Gradually the stupid, hunted, glowering look died out of Joe's eyes. He turned his head aside, gently, as one rousing from a spell.

'I don't want her,' he said, with fierce resentment.

'Then you needn't have her,' said Albert. 'What do you go for, boy?'

But it wasn't as simple as all that. Joe made no remark.

'She's a smart-looking girl. What's wrong with her, my boy? I should have thought you were a lucky chap, myself.'

'I don't want 'er,' Joe barked, with ferocity and resentment.

'Then tell her so and have done,' said Albert. He waited awhile. There was no response. 'Why don't you?' he added.

'Because I don't,' confessed Joe, sulkily.

Albert pondered—rubbed his head.

'You're too soft-hearted, that's where it is, boy. You want your mettle dipping in cold water, to temper it. You're too soft-hearted—'

He laid his arm affectionately across the shoulders of the younger man. Joe seemed to yield a little towards him.

'When are you going to see her again?' Albert asked. For a long time there was no answer.

'When is it, boy?' persisted the softened voice of the corporal.

'Tomorrow,' confessed Joe.

'Then let me go,' said Albert. 'Let me go, will you?'

The morrow was Sunday, a sunny day, but a cold evening. The sky was grey, the new foliage very green, but the air was chill and depressing. Albert walked briskly down the white road towards Beeley. He crossed a larch plantation, and followed a narrow by-road, where blue speedwell flowers fell from the banks into the dust. He walked swinging his cane, with mixed sensations. Then having gone a certain length, he turned and began to walk in the opposite direction.

So he saw a young woman approaching him. She was wearing a wide hat of grey straw, and a loose, swinging dress of nigger-grey velvet. She walked with slow inevitability. Albert faltered a little as he approached her. Then he saluted her, and his roguish, slightly withered skin flushed. She was staring straight into his face.

He fell in by her side, saying impudently:

'Not so nice for a walk as it was, is it?'

She only stared at him. He looked back at her.

'You've seen me before, you know,' he said, grinning slightly. 'Perhaps you never noticed me. Oh, I'm quite nice looking, in a quiet way, you know. What—?'

But Miss Stokes did not speak: she only stared with large, icy blue eyes at him. He became self-conscious, lifted up his chin, walked with his nose in the air, and whistled at random. So they went down the quiet, deserted grey lane. He was whistling the air: 'I'm Gilbert, the filbert, the colonel of the nuts.'

At last she found her voice:

'Where's Joe?'

'He thought you'd like a change: they say variety's the salt of life—that's why I'm mostly in pickle.'

'Where is he?'

'Am I my brother's keeper? He's gone his own ways.'

'Where?'

'Nay, how am I to know? Not so far but he'll be back for supper.'

She stopped in the middle of the lane. He stopped facing her.

'Where's Joe?' she asked.

He struck a careless attitude, looked down the road this way and that, lifted his eyebrows, pushed his khaki cap on one side, and answered:

'He is not conducting the service tonight: he asked me if I'd officiate.'

'Why hasn't he come?'

'Didn't want to, I expect. *I* wanted to.'

She stared him up and down, and he felt uncomfortable in his spine, but maintained his air of nonchalance. Then she turned slowly on her heel, and started to walk back. The corporal went at her side.

'You're not going back, are you?' he pleaded. 'Why, me and you, we should get on like a house on fire.'

She took no heed, but walked on. He went uncomfortably at her side, making his funny remarks from time to time. But she was as if stone deaf. He glanced at her, and to his dismay saw the tears running down her cheeks. He stopped suddenly, and pushed back his cap.

'I say, you know—' he began.

But she was walking on like an automaton, and he had to hurry after her.

She never spoke to him. At the gate of her farm she walked straight in, as if he were not there. He watched her disappear. Then he turned on his heel, cursing silently, puzzled, lifting off his cap to scratch his head.

That night, when they were in bed, he remarked: 'Say, Joe, boy; strikes me you're well-off without Monkey nuts. Gord love us, beans ain't in it.'

So they slept in amity. But they waited with some anxiety for the morrow.

It was a cold morning, a grey sky shifting in a cold wind, and threatening rain. They watched the wagon come up the road and through the yard gates. Miss Stokes was with her team as usual; her 'Whoa!' rang out like a war-whoop.

She faced up at the truck where the two men stood.

'Joe!' she called, to the averted figure which stood up in the wind.

'What?' he turned unwillingly.

She made a queer movement, lifting her head slightly in a sipping, half-inviting, half-commanding gesture. And Joe was crouching already to jump off the truck to obey her, when Albert put his hand on his shoulder.

'Half a minute, boy! Where are you off? Work's work, and nuts is nuts. You stop here.'

Joe slowly straightened himself.

'Joe!' came the woman's clear call from below.

Again Joe looked at her. But Albert's hand was on his shoulder, detaining him. He stood half averted, with his tail between his legs.

'Take your hand off him, you!' said Miss Stokes.

'Yes, Major,' retorted Albert satirically.

She stood and watched.

'Joe!' Her voice rang for the third time.

Joe turned and looked at her, and a slow, jeering smile gathered on his face.

'Monkey nuts!' he replied, in a tone mocking her call.

She turned white—dead white. The men thought she would fall. Albert began yelling to the porters up the line to come and help with the load. He could yell like any non-commissioned officer upon occasion.

Some way or other the wagon was unloaded, the girl was gone. Joe and his corporal looked at one another and smiled slowly. But they had a weight on their minds, they were afraid.

They were reassured, however, when they found that Miss Stokes came no more with the hay. As far as they were concerned, she had vanished into oblivion. And Joe felt more relieved even than he had felt when he heard the firing cease, after the news had come that the armistice was signed.

WINTRY PEACOCK

There was thin, crisp snow on the ground, the sky was blue, the wind very cold, the air clear. Farmers were just turning out the cows for an hour or so in the midday, and the smell of cow-sheds was unendurable as I entered Tible. I noticed the ash-twigs up in the sky were pale and luminous, passing into the blue. And then I saw the peacocks. There they were in the road before me, three of them, and tailless, brown, speckled birds, with dark-blue necks and ragged crests. They stepped archly over the filigree snow, and their bodies moved with slow motion, like small, light, flat-bottomed boats. I admired them, they were curious. Then a gust of wind caught them, heeled them over as if they were three frail boats opening their feathers like ragged sails. They hopped and skipped with discomfort, to get out of the draught of the wind. And then, in the lee of the walls, they resumed their arch, wintry motion, light and unballasted now their tails were gone, indifferent. They were indifferent to my presence. I might have touched them. They turned off to the shelter of an open shed.

As I passed the end of the upper house, I saw a young woman just coming out of the back door. I had spoken to her in the summer. She recognized me at once, and waved to me. She was carrying a pail, wearing a white apron that was longer than her preposterously short skirt, and she had on the cotton bonnet. I took off my hat to her and was going on. But she put down her pail and darted with a swift, furtive movement after me.

'Do you mind waiting a minute?' she said. 'I'll be out in a minute.'

She gave me a slight, odd smile, and ran back. Her face was long and sallow and her nose rather red. But her gloomy black eyes softened caressively to me for a moment, with that momentary humility which makes a man lord of the earth.

I stood in the road, looking at the fluffy, dark-red young cattle that mooed and seemed to bark at me. They seemed happy, frisky cattle, a little impudent, and either determined to go back into the warm shed, or determined not to go back, I could not decide which.

Presently the woman came forward again, her head rather ducked. But she looked up at me and smiled, with that odd, immediate intimacy, something witch-like and impossible.

'Sorry to keep you waiting,' she said. 'Shall we stand in this cart-shed—it will be more out of the wind.'

So we stood among the shafts of the open cart-shed that faced the road. Then she looked down at the ground, a little sideways, and I noticed a small black frown on her brows. She seemed to brood for a moment. Then she looked straight into my eyes, so that I blinked and wanted to turn my face aside. She was searching me for something and her look was too near. The frown was still on her keen, sallow brow.

'Can you speak French?' she asked me abruptly.

'More or less,' I replied.

'I was supposed to learn it at school,' she said. 'But I don't know a word.' She ducked her head and laughed, with a slightly ugly grimace and a rolling of her black eyes.

'No good keeping your mind full of scraps,' I answered.

But she had turned aside her sallow, long face, and did not hear what I said. Suddenly again she looked at me. She was searching. And at the same time she smiled at me, and her eyes looked softly, darkly, with infinite trustful humility into mine. I was being cajoled.

'Would you mind reading a letter for me, in French,' she said, her face immediately black and bitter-looking. She glanced at me, frowning.

'Not at all,' I said.

'It's a letter to my husband,' she said, still scrutinizing.

I looked at her, and didn't quite realize. She looked too far into me, my wits were gone. She glanced round. Then she looked at me shrewdly. She drew a letter from her pocket, and handed it to me. It was addressed from France to Lance-Corporal Goyte, at Tible. I took out the letter and began to read it, as mere words. '*Mon cher Alfred*'—it might have been a bit of a torn newspaper. So I followed the script: the trite phrases of a letter from a French-speaking girl to an English soldier. 'I think of you always, always. Do you think sometimes of me?' And then I vaguely realized that I was reading a man's private correspondence. And yet, how could one consider these trivial, facile French phrases private! Nothing more trite and vulgar in the world, than such a love-letter—no newspaper more obvious.

Therefore I read with a callous heart the effusions of the Belgian damsel. But then I gathered my attention. For the letter went on, '*Notre cher petit bébé*—our dear little baby was born a week ago. Almost I died, knowing you were far away, and perhaps forgetting the fruit of our perfect love. But the child comforted me. He has the smiling eyes and virile air of his English father. I pray to the Mother of Jesus to send me the dear father of my child, that I may see him with my child in his arms, and that we may be united in holy family love. Ah, my Alfred, can I tell you how I miss you, how I weep for you. My thoughts are with you always, I think of nothing but you, I live for nothing but you and our dear baby. If you do not come back to me soon, I shall die, and our child will die. But no, you cannot come back to me. But I can come to you, come to England with our child. If you do not wish to present me to your good mother and father, you can meet me in some town, some city, for I shall be so frightened to be alone in England with my child, and no one to take care of us. Yet I must come to you, I must bring my child, my little Alfred to his father, the big, beautiful Alfred that I love so much. Oh, write and tell me where I shall come. I have some money, I am not a penniless creature. I have money for myself and my dear baby—'

I read to the end. It was signed: 'Your very happy and still more unhappy Élise.' I suppose I must have been smiling.

'I can see it makes you laugh,' said Mrs. Goyte, sardonically. I looked up at her.

'It's a love-letter, I know that,' she said. 'There's too many "Alfreds" in it.'

'One too many,' I said.

'Oh, yes—And what does she say—Eliza? We know her name's Eliza, that's another thing.' She grimaced a little, looking up at me with a mocking laugh.

'Where did you get this letter?' I said.

'Postman gave it me last week.'

'And is your husband at home?'

'I expect him home tonight. He's been wounded, you know, and we've been applying for him home. He was home about six weeks ago—he's been in Scotland since then. Oh, he was wounded in the leg. Yes, he's all right, a great strapping fellow. But he's lame, he limps a bit. He expects he'll get his discharge—but I don't think he will. We married? We've been married six years—and he joined up the first day of the war. Oh, he thought he'd like the life. He'd been through the South African War. No, he was sick of it, fed up. I'm living with his father and mother—I've no home of my own now. My people had a big farm—over a thousand acres—in Oxfordshire. Not like here—no. Oh, they're very good to me, his father and mother. Oh, yes, they couldn't be better. They think more of me than of their own daughters. But it's not like being in a place of your own, is it? You can't *really* do as you like. No, there's only me and his father and mother at home. Before the war? Oh, he was anything. He's had a good education—but he liked the farming better. Then he was a chauffeur. That's how he knew French. He was driving a gentleman in France for a long time—'

At this point the peacocks came round the corner on a puff of wind.

'Hello, Joey!' she called, and one of the birds came forward, on delicate legs. Its grey speckled back was very elegant, it rolled its full, dark-blue neck as it moved to her. She crouched down. 'Joey, dear,' she said, in an odd, saturnine caressive voice, 'you're bound to find me, aren't you?' She put her face forward, and the bird rolled his neck, almost touching her face with his beak, as if kissing her.

'He loves you,' I said.

She twisted her face up at me with a laugh.

'Yes,' she said, 'he loves me, Joey does,'—then, to the bird—'and I love Joey, don't I. I *do* love Joey.' And she smoothed his feathers for a moment. Then she rose, saying: 'He's an affectionate bird.'

I smiled at the roll of her 'bir-rrd'.

'Oh, yes, he is,' she protested. 'He came with me from my home seven years ago. Those others are his descendants—but they're not like Joey—*are they, dee-urr?*' Her voice rose at the end with a witch-like cry.

Then she forgot the birds in the cart-shed and turned to business again.

'Won't you read that letter?' she said. 'Read it, so that I know what it says.'

'It's rather behind his back,' I said.

'Oh, never mind him,' she cried. 'He's been behind my back long enough—all these four years. If he never did no worse things behind my back than I do behind his, he wouldn't have cause to grumble. You read me what it says.'

Now I felt a distinct reluctance to do as she bid, and yet I began—'My dear Alfred.'

'I guessed that much,' she said. 'Eliza's dear Alfred.' She laughed. 'How do you say it in French? *Eliza?*'

I told her, and she repeated the name with great contempt—*Élise*.

'Go on,' she said. 'You're not reading.'

So I began—'I have been thinking of you sometimes—have you been thinking of me?'—

'Of several others as well, beside her, I'll wager,' said Mrs. Goyte.

'Probably not,' said I, and continued. 'A dear little baby was born here a week ago. Ah, can I tell you my feelings when I take my darling little brother into my arms—'

'I'll bet it's *his*,' cried Mrs. Goyte.

'No,' I said. 'It's her mother's.'

'Don't you believe it,' she cried. 'It's a blind. You mark, it's her own right enough—and his.'

'No,' I said, 'it's her mother's.' 'He has sweet smiling eyes, but not like your beautiful English eyes—'

She suddenly struck her hand on her skirt with a wild motion, and bent down, doubled with laughter. Then she rose and covered her face with her hand.

'I'm forced to laugh at the beautiful English eyes,' she said.

'Aren't his eyes beautiful?' I asked.

'Oh, yes—*very!* Go on!—*Joey, dear, dee-urr, Joey!*'—this to the peacock.

—'Er—We miss you very much. We all miss you. We wish you were here to see the darling baby. Ah, Alfred, how happy we were when you stayed with us. We all loved you so much. My mother will call the baby Alfred so that we shall never forget you—'

'Of course it's his right enough,' cried Mrs. Goyte.

'No,' I said. 'It's the mother's.' Er—'My mother is very well. My father came home yesterday—on leave. He is delighted with his son, my little brother, and wishes to have him named after you, because you were so good to us all in that terrible time, which I shall never forget. I must weep now when I think of it. Well, you are far away in England, and perhaps I shall never see you again. How did you find your dear mother and father? I am so happy that your wound is better, and that you can nearly walk—'

'How did he find his dear *wife!*' cried Mrs. Goyte. 'He never told her he had one. Think of taking the poor girl in like that!'

'We are so pleased when you write to us. Yet now you are in England you will forget the family you served so well—'

'A bit too well—eh, *Joey!*' cried the wife.

'If it had not been for you we should not be alive now, to grieve and to rejoice in this life, that is so hard for us. But we have recovered some of our losses, and no longer feel the burden of poverty. The little Alfred is a great comfort to me. I hold him to my breast and think of the big, good Alfred, and I weep to think that those times of suffering were perhaps the times of a great happiness that is gone for ever.'

'Oh, but isn't it a shame, to take a poor girl in like that!' cried Mrs. Goyte. 'Never to let on that he was married, and raise her hopes—I call it beastly, I do.'

'You don't know,' I said. 'You know how anxious women are to fall in love, wife or no wife. How could he help it, if she was determined to fall in love with him?'

'He could have helped it if he'd wanted.'

'Well,' I said, 'we aren't all heroes.'

'Oh, but that's different! The big, good Alfred!—did ever you hear such tommy-rot in your life! Go on—what does she say at the end?'

'Er—We shall be pleased to hear of your life in England. We all send many kind regards to your good parents. I wish you all happiness for your future days. Your very affectionate and ever-grateful Élise.'

There was silence for a moment, during which Mrs. Goyte remained with her head dropped, sinister and abstracted. Suddenly she lifted her face, and her eyes flashed.

'Oh, but I call it beastly, I call it mean, to take a girl in like that.'

'Nay,' I said. 'Probably he hasn't taken her in at all. Do you think those French girls are such poor innocent things? I guess she's a great deal more downy than he.'

'Oh, he's one of the biggest fools that ever walked,' she cried.

'There you are!' said I.

'But it's his child right enough,' she said.

'I don't think so,' said I.

'I'm sure of it.'

'Oh, well,' I said, 'if you prefer to think that way.'

'What other reason has she for writing like that—'

I went out into the road and looked at the cattle.

'Who is this driving the cows?' I said. She too came out.

'It's the boy from the next farm,' she said.

'Oh, well,' said I, 'those Belgian girls! You never know where their letters will end. And, after all, it's his affair—you needn't bother.'

'Oh—!' she cried, with rough scorn—'it's not *me* that bothers. But it's the nasty meanness of it—me writing him such loving letters'—she put her hand before her face and laughed malevolently—'and sending him parcels all the time. You bet he fed that gurrl on my parcels—I know he did. It's just like him. I'll bet they laughed together over my letters. I bet anything they did—'

'Nay,' said I. 'He'd burn your letters for fear they'd give him away.'

There was a black look on her yellow face. Suddenly a voice was heard calling. She poked her head out of the shed, and answered coolly:

'All right!' Then turning to me: 'That's his mother looking after me.'

She laughed into my face, witch-like, and we turned down the road.

When I awoke, the morning after this episode, I found the house darkened with deep, soft snow, which had blown against the large west windows, covering them with a screen. I went outside, and saw the valley all white and ghastly below me, the trees beneath black and thin looking like wire, the rock-faces dark between the glistening shroud, and the sky above sombre, heavy, yellowish-dark, much too heavy for this world below of hollow bluey whiteness figured with black. I felt I was in a valley of the dead. And I sensed I was a prisoner, for the snow was everywhere deep, and drifted in places. So all the morning I remained indoors, looking up the drive at the shrubs so heavily plumed with snow, at the gateposts raised high with a foot or more of extra whiteness. Or I looked down into the white-and-black valley that was utterly motionless and beyond life, a hollow sarcophagus.

Nothing stirred the whole day—no plume fell off the shrubs, the valley was as abstracted as a grove of death. I looked over at the tiny, half-buried farms away on the bare uplands beyond the valley hollow, and I thought of Tible in the snow, of the black witch-like little Mrs. Goyte. And the snow seemed to lay me bare to influences I wanted to escape.

In the faint glow of the half-clear light that came about four o'clock in the afternoon, I was roused to see a motion in the snow away below, near where the thorn trees stood very black and dwarfed, like a little savage group, in the dismal white. I watched closely. Yes, there was a flapping and a struggle—a big bird, it must be, labouring in the snow. I wondered. Our biggest birds, in the valley, were the large hawks that often hung flickering opposite my windows, level with me, but high above some prey on the steep valleyside. This was much too big for a hawk—too big for any known bird. I searched in my mind for the largest English wild birds, geese, buzzards.

Still it laboured and strove, then was still, a dark spot, then struggled again. I went out of the house and down the steep slope, at risk of breaking my leg between the rocks. I knew the ground so well—and yet I got well shaken before I drew near the thorn-trees.

Yes, it was a bird. It was Joey. It was the grey-brown peacock with a blue neck. He was snow-wet and spent.

'Joey—Joey, de-urr!' I said, staggering unevenly towards him. He looked so pathetic, rowing and struggling in the snow, too spent to rise, his blue neck stretching out and lying sometimes on the snow, his eye closing and opening quickly, his crest all battered.

'Joey dee-uur! Dee-urr!' I said caressingly to him. And at last he lay still, blinking, in the surged and furrowed snow, whilst I came near and touched him, stroked him, gathered him under my arm. He stretched his long, wetted neck away from me as I held him, none the less he was quiet in my arm, too tired, perhaps, to struggle. Still he held his poor, crested head away from me, and seemed sometimes to droop, to wilt, as if he might suddenly die.

He was not so heavy as I expected, yet it was a struggle to get up to the house with him again. We set him down, not too near the fire, and gently wiped him with cloths. He submitted, only now and then stretched his soft neck away from us, avoiding us helplessly. Then we set warm food by him. I *put* it to his beak, tried to make him eat. But he ignored it. He seemed to be ignorant of what we were doing, recoiled inside himself inexplicably. So we put him in a basket with cloths, and left him crouching oblivious. His food we put near him. The blinds were drawn, the house was warm, it was night. Sometimes he stirred, but mostly he huddled still, leaning his queer crested head on one side. He touched no food, and took no heed of sounds or movements. We talked of brandy or stimulants. But I realized we had best leave him alone.

In the night, however, we heard him thumping about. I got up anxiously with a candle. He had eaten some food, and scattered more, making a mess. And he was perched on the back of a heavy arm-chair. So I concluded he was recovered, or recovering.

The next day was clear, and the snow had frozen, so I decided to carry him back to Tible. He consented, after various flappings, to sit in a big fish-bag with his battered head peeping out with wild uneasiness. And so I set off with him, slithering down into the valley, making good progress down in the pale shadow beside the rushing waters, then climbing painfully up the arrested white valleyside, plumed with clusters of young pine trees, into the paler white radiance of the snowy, upper regions, where the wind cut fine. Joey seemed to watch all the time with wide anxious, unseeing eye, brilliant and inscrutable. As I drew near to Tible township he stirred violently in the bag, though I do not know if he had recognized the place. Then, as I came to the sheds, he looked sharply from side to side, and stretched his neck out long. I was a little afraid of him. He gave a loud, vehement yell, opening his sinister beak, and I stood still, looking at him as he struggled in the bag, shaken myself by his struggles, yet not thinking to release him.

Mrs. Goyte came darting past the end of the house, her head sticking forward in sharp scrutiny. She saw me, and came forward.

'Have you got Joey?' she cried sharply, as if I were a thief.

I opened the bag, and he flopped out, flapping as if he hated the touch of the snow now. She gathered him up, and put her lips to his beak. She was flushed and handsome, her eyes bright, her hair slack, thick, but more witch-like than ever. She did not speak.

She had been followed by a grey-haired woman with a round, rather sallow face and a slightly hostile bearing.

'Did you bring him with you, then?' she asked sharply. I answered that I had rescued him the previous evening.

From the background slowly approached a slender man with a grey moustache and large patches on his trousers.

'You've got 'im back 'gain, ah see,' he said to his daughter-in-law. His wife explained how I had found Joey.

'Ah,' went on the grey man. 'It wor our Alfred scared him off, back your life. He must'a flyed ower t'valley. Tha ma' thank thy stars as 'e wor fun, Maggie. 'E'd a bin froze. They a bit nesh, you know,' he concluded to me.

'They are,' I answered. 'This isn't their country.'

'No, it isna,' replied Mr. Goyte. He spoke very slowly and deliberately, quietly, as if the soft pedal were always down in his voice. He looked at his daughter-in-law as she crouched, flushed and dark, before the peacock, which would lay its long blue neck for a moment along her lap. In spite of his grey moustache and thin grey hair, the elderly man had a face young and almost delicate, like a young man's. His blue eyes twinkled with some inscrutable source of pleasure, his skin was fine and tender, his nose delicately arched. His grey hair being slightly ruffled, he had a debonair look, as of a youth who is in love.

'We mun tell 'im it's come,' he said slowly, and turning he called: 'Alfred—Alfred! Wheer's ter gotten to?'

Then he turned again to the group.

'Get up then, Maggie, lass, get up wi' thee. Tha ma'es too much o' th' bod.'

A young man approached, wearing rough khaki and kneebreeches. He was Danish looking, broad at the loins.

'I's come back then,' said the father to the son; 'leastwise, he's bin browt back, flyed ower the Griff Low.'

The son looked at me. He had a devil-may-care bearing, his cap on one side, his hands stuck in the front pockets of his breeches. But he said nothing.

'Shall you come in a minute, Master,' said the elderly woman, to me.

'Ay, come in an' ha'e a cup o' tea or summat. You'll do wi' summat, carrin' that bod. Come on, Maggie wench, let's go in.'

So we went indoors, into the rather stuffy, overcrowded living-room, that was too cosy, and too warm. The son followed last, standing in the doorway. The father talked to me.

Maggie put out the tea-cups. The mother went into the dairy again.

'Tha'lt rouse thysen up a bit again, now, Maggie,' the father-in-law said—and then to me: "ers not bin very bright sin' Alfred came whoam, an' the bod flyed awee. 'E come whoam a Wednesday night, Alfred did. But ay, you knowed, didna yer. Ay, 'e comed 'a Wednesday—an' I reckon there wor a bit of a to-do between 'em, worn't there, Maggie?'

He twinkled maliciously to his daughter-in-law, who was flushed, brilliant and handsome.

'Oh, be quiet, father. You're wound up, by the sound of you,' she said to him, as if crossly. But she could never be cross with him.

"Ers got 'er colour back this mornin',' continued the father-in-law slowly. 'It's bin heavy weather wi' 'er this last two days. Ay—'er's bin northeast sin 'er seed you a Wednesday.'

'Father, do stop talking. You'd wear the leg off an iron pot. I can't think where you've found your tongue, all of a sudden,' said Maggie, with caressive sharpness.

'Ah've found it wheer I lost it. Aren't goin' ter come in an' sit thee down, Alfred?'

But Alfred turned and disappeared.

"E's got th' monkey on 'is back ower this letter job,' said the father secretly to me. 'Mother, 'er knows nowt about it. Lot o' tom-foolery, isn't it? Ay! What's good o' makkin' a peck o' trouble over what's far enough off, an' ned niver come no nigher. No—not a smite o' use. That's what I tell 'er. 'Er should ta'e no notice on't. Ty, what can y' expect.'

The mother came in again, and the talk became general. Maggie flashed her eyes at me from time to time, complacent and satisfied, moving among the men. I paid her little compliments, which she did not seem to hear. She attended to me with a kind of sinister, witch-like graciousness, her dark head ducked between her shoulders, at once humble and powerful. She was happy as a child attending to her father-in-law and to me. But there was something ominous between her eyebrows, as if a dark moth were settled there—and something ominous in her bent, hulking bearing.

She sat on a low stool by the fire, near her father-in-law. Her head was dropped, she seemed in a state of abstraction. From time to time she would suddenly recover, and look up at us, laughing and chatting. Then she would forget again. Yet in her hulked black forgetting she seemed very near to us.

The door having been opened, the peacock came slowly in, prancing calmly. He went near to her and crouched down, coiling his blue neck. She glanced at him, but almost as if she did not observe him. The bird sat silent, seeming to sleep, and the woman also sat hulked and silent, seemingly oblivious. Then once more there was a heavy step, and Alfred entered. He looked at his wife, and he looked at the peacock crouching by her. He stood large in the doorway, his hands stuck in front of him, in his breeches pockets. Nobody spoke. He turned on his heel and went out again.

I rose also to go. Maggie started as if coming to herself.

'Must you go?' she asked, rising and coming near to me, standing in front of me, twisting her head sideways and looking up at me. 'Can't you stop a bit longer? We can all be cosy today, there's nothing to do outdoors.' And she laughed, showing her teeth oddly. She had a long chin.

I said I must go. The peacock uncoiled and coiled again his long blue neck, as he lay on the hearth. Maggie still stood close in front of me, so that I was acutely aware of my waistcoat buttons.

'Oh, well,' she said, 'you'll come again, won't you? Do come again.'

I promised.

'Come to tea one day—yes, do!'

I promised—one day.

The moment I went out of her presence I ceased utterly to exist for her—as utterly as I ceased to exist for Joey. With her curious abstractedness she forgot me again immediately. I knew it as I left her. Yet she seemed almost in physical contact with me while I was with her.

The sky was all pallid again, yellowish. When I went out there was no sun; the snow was blue and cold. I hurried away down the hill, musing on Maggie. The road made a loop down the sharp face of the slope. As I went crunching over the laborious snow I became aware of a figure striding down the steep scarp to intercept me. It was a man with his hands in front of him, half stuck in his breeches pockets, and his shoulders square—a real farmer of the hills; Alfred, of course. He waited for me by the stone fence.

'Excuse me,' he said as I came up.

I came to a halt in front of him and looked into his sullen blue eyes. He had a certain odd haughtiness on his brows. But his blue eyes stared insolently at me.

'Do you know anything about a letter—in French—that my wife opened—a letter of mine—?'

'Yes,' said I. 'She asked me to read it to her.'

He looked square at me. He did not know exactly how to feel.

'What was there in it?' he asked.

'Why?' I said. 'Don't you know?'

'She makes out she's burnt it,' he said.

'Without showing it you?' I asked.

He nodded slightly. He seemed to be meditating as to what line of action he should take. He wanted to know the contents of the letter: he must know: and therefore he must ask me, for evidently his wife had taunted him. At the same time, no doubt, he would like to wreak untold vengeance on my unfortunate person. So he eyed me, and I eyed him, and neither of us spoke. He did not want to repeat his request to me. And yet I only looked at him, and considered.

Suddenly he threw back his head and glanced down the valley. Then he changed his position—he was a horse-soldier. Then he looked at me confidentially.

'She burnt the blasted thing before I saw it,' he said.

'Well,' I answered slowly, 'she doesn't know herself what was in it.'

He continued to watch me narrowly. I grinned to myself.

'I didn't like to read her out what there was in it,' I continued.

He suddenly flushed so that the veins in his neck stood out, and he stirred again uncomfortably.

'The Belgian girl said her baby had been born a week ago, and that they were going to call it Alfred,' I told him.

He met my eyes. I was grinning. He began to grin, too.

'Good luck to her,' he said.

'Best of luck,' said I.

'And what did you tell *her*?' he asked.

'That the baby belonged to the old mother—that it was brother to your girl, who was writing to you as a friend of the family.'

He stood smiling, with the long, subtle malice of a farmer.

'And did she take it in?' he asked.

'As much as she took anything else.'

He stood grinning fixedly. Then he broke into a short laugh.

'Good for *her*' he exclaimed cryptically.

And then he laughed aloud once more, evidently feeling he had won a big move in his contest with his wife.

'What about the other woman?' I asked.

'Who?'

'Élise.'

'Oh'—he shifted uneasily—'she was all right—'

'You'll be getting back to her,' I said.

He looked at me. Then he made a grimace with his mouth.

'Not me,' he said. 'Back your life it's a plant.'

'You don't think the *cher petit bébé* is a little Alfred?'

'It might be,' he said.

'Only might?'

'Yes—an' there's lots of mites in a pound of cheese.' He laughed boisterously but uneasily.

'What did she say, exactly?' he asked.

I began to repeat, as well as I could, the phrases of the letter:

'*Mon cher Alfred—Figure-toi comme je suis desolée—*'

He listened with some confusion. When I had finished all I could remember, he said:

'They know how to pitch you out a letter, those Belgian lasses.'

'Practice,' said I.

'They get plenty,' he said.

There was a pause.

'Oh, well,' he said. 'I've never got that letter, anyhow.'

The wind blew fine and keen, in the sunshine, across the snow. I blew my nose and prepared to depart.

'And *she* doesn't know anything?' he continued, jerking his head up the hill in the direction of Tible.

'She knows nothing but what I've said—that is, if she really burnt the letter.'

'I believe she burnt it,' he said, 'for spite. She's a little devil, she is. But I shall have it out with her.' His jaw was stubborn and sullen. Then suddenly he turned to me with a new note.

'Why?' he said. 'Why didn't you wring that b—— peacock's neck-that b—— Joey?'

'Why?' I said. 'What for?'

'I hate the brute,' he said. 'I had a shot at him—'

I laughed. He stood and mused.

'Poor little Elise,' he murmured.

'Was she small—*petite*?' I asked. He jerked up his head.

'No,' he said. 'Rather tall.'

'Taller than your wife, I suppose.'

Again he looked into my eyes. And then once more he went into a loud burst of laughter that made the still, snow-deserted valley clap again.

'God, it's a knockout!' he said, thoroughly amused. Then he stood at ease, one foot out, his hands in his breeches pockets, in front of him, his head thrown back, a handsome figure of a man.

'But I'll do that blasted Joey in—' he mused.

I ran down the hill, shouting with laughter.

YOU TOUCHED ME

The Pottery House was a square, ugly, brick house girt in by the wall that enclosed the whole grounds of the pottery itself. To be sure, a privet hedge partly masked the house and its ground from the pottery-yard and works: but only partly. Through the hedge could be seen the desolate yard, and the many-windowed, factory-like pottery, over the hedge could be seen the chimneys and the outhouses. But inside the hedge, a pleasant garden and lawn sloped down to a willow pool, which had once supplied the works.

The Pottery itself was now closed, the great doors of the yard permanently shut. No more the great crates with yellow straw showing through, stood in stacks by the packing shed. No more the drays drawn by great horses rolled down the hill with a high load. No more the pottery-lasses in their clay-coloured overalls, their faces and hair splashed with grey fine mud, shrieked and larked with the men. All that was over.

'We like it much better—oh, much better—quieter,' said Matilda Rockley.

'Oh, yes,' assented Emmie Rockley, her sister.

'I'm sure you do,' agreed the visitor.

But whether the two Rockley girls really liked it better, or whether they only imagined they did, is a question. Certainly their lives were much more grey and dreary now that the grey clay had ceased to spatter its mud and silt its dust over the premises. They did not quite realize how they missed the shrieking, shouting lasses, whom they had known all their lives and disliked so much.

Matilda and Emmie were already old maids. In a thorough industrial district, it is not easy for the girls who have expectations above the common to find husbands. The ugly industrial town was full of men, young men who were ready to marry. But they were all colliers or pottery-hands, mere workmen. The Rockley girls would have about ten thousand pounds each when their father died: ten thousand pounds' worth of profitable house-property. It was not to be sneezed at: they felt so themselves, and refrained from sneezing away such a fortune on any mere member of the proletariat. Consequently, bank-clerks or nonconformist clergymen or even school-teachers having failed to come forward, Matilda had begun to give up all idea of ever leaving the Pottery House.

Matilda was a tall, thin, graceful fair girl, with a rather large nose. She was the Mary to Emmie's Martha: that is, Matilda loved painting and music, and read a good many novels, whilst Emmie looked after the house-keeping. Emmie was shorter, plumper than her sister, and she had no accomplishments. She looked up to Matilda, whose mind was naturally refined and sensible.

In their quiet, melancholy way, the two girls were happy. Their mother was dead. Their father was ill also. He was an intelligent man who had had some education, but preferred to remain as if he were one with the rest of the working people. He had a passion for music and played the violin pretty well. But now he was getting old, he was very ill, dying of a kidney disease. He had been rather a heavy whisky-drinker.

This quiet household, with one servant-maid, lived on year after year in the Pottery House. Friends came in, the girls went out, the father drank himself more and more ill. Outside in the street there was a continual racket of the colliers and their dogs and children. But inside the pottery wall was a deserted quiet.

In all this ointment there was one little fly. Ted Rockley, the father of the girls, had had four daughters, and no son. As his girls grew, he felt angry at finding himself always in a house-hold of women. He went off to London and adopted a boy out of a Charity Institution. Emmie was fourteen years old, and Matilda sixteen, when their father arrived home with his prodigy, the boy of six, Hadrian.

Hadrian was just an ordinary boy from a Charity Home, with ordinary brownish hair and ordinary bluish eyes and of ordinary rather cockney speech. The Rockley girls—there were three at home at the time of his arrival—had resented his being sprung on them. He, with his watchful, charity-institution instinct, knew this at once. Though he was only six years old, Hadrian had a subtle, jeering look on his face when he regarded the three young women. They insisted he should address them as Cousin: Cousin Flora, Cousin Matilda, Cousin Emmie. He complied, but there seemed a mockery in his tone.

The girls, however, were kind-hearted by nature. Flora married and left home. Hadrian did very much as he pleased with Matilda and Emmie, though they had certain strictnesses. He grew up in the Pottery House and about the Pottery premises, went to an elementary school, and was invariably called Hadrian Rockley. He regarded Cousin Matilda and Cousin Emmie with a certain laconic indifference, was quiet and reticent in his ways. The girls called him sly, but that was unjust. He was merely cautious, and without frankness. His Uncle, Ted Rockley, understood him tacitly, their natures were somewhat akin. Hadrian and the elderly man had a real but unemotional regard for one another.

When he was thirteen years old the boy was sent to a High School in the County town. He did not like it. His Cousin Matilda had longed to make a little gentleman of him, but he refused to be made. He would give a little contemptuous curve to his lip, and take on a shy, charity-boy grin, when refinement was thrust upon him. He played truant from the High School, sold his books, his cap with its badge, even his very scarf and pocket-handkerchief, to his school-fellows, and went raking off heaven knows where with the money. So he spent two very unsatisfactory years.

When he was fifteen he announced that he wanted to leave England and go to the Colonies. He had kept touch with the Home. The Rockleys knew that, when Hadrian made a declaration, in his quiet, half-jeering manner, it was worse than useless to oppose him. So at last the boy departed, going to Canada under the protection of the Institution to which he had belonged. He said good-bye to the Rockleys without a word of thanks, and parted, it seemed, without a pang. Matilda and Emmie wept often to think of how he left them: even on their father's face a queer look came. But Hadrian wrote fairly regularly from Canada. He had entered some electricity works near Montreal, and was doing well.

At last, however, the war came. In his turn, Hadrian joined up and came to Europe. The Rockleys saw nothing of him. They lived on, just the same, in the Pottery House. Ted Rockley was dying of a sort of dropsy, and in his heart he wanted to see the boy. When the armistice was signed, Hadrian had a long leave, and wrote that he was coming home to the Pottery House.

The girls were terribly fluttered. To tell the truth, they were a little afraid of Hadrian. Matilda, tall and thin, was frail in her health, both girls were worn with nursing their father. To have Hadrian, a young man of twenty-one, in the house with them, after he had left them so coldly five years before, was a trying circumstance.

They were in a flutter. Emmie persuaded her father to have his bed made finally in the morning-room downstairs, whilst his room upstairs was prepared for Hadrian. This was done, and preparations were going on for the arrival, when, at ten o'clock in the morning the young man suddenly turned up, quite unexpectedly. Cousin Emmie, with her hair bobbed up in absurd little bobs round her forehead, was busily polishing the stair-rods, while Cousin Matilda was in the kitchen washing the drawing-room ornaments in a lather, her sleeves rolled back on her thin arms, and her head tied up oddly and coquettishly in a duster.

Cousin Matilda blushed deep with mortification when the self-possessed young man walked in with his kit-bag, and put his cap on the sewing machine. He was little and self-confident, with a curious neatness about him that still suggested the Charity Institution. His face was brown, he had a small moustache, he was vigorous enough in his smallness.

'*Well*, is it Hadrian!' exclaimed Cousin Matilda, wringing the lather off her hand. 'We didn't expect you till tomorrow.'

'I got off Monday night,' said Hadrian, glancing round the room.

'Fancy!' said Cousin Matilda. Then, having dried her hands, she went forward, held out her hand, and said:

'How are you?'

'Quite well, thank you,' said Hadrian.

'You're quite a man,' said Cousin Matilda.

Hadrian glanced at her. She did not look her best: so thin, so large-nosed, with that pink-and-white checked duster tied round her head. She felt her disadvantage. But she had had a good deal of suffering and sorrow, she did not mind any more.

The servant entered—one that did not know Hadrian.

'Come and see my father,' said Cousin Matilda.

In the hall they roused Cousin Emmie like a partridge from cover. She was on the stairs pushing the bright stair-rods into place. Instinctively her hand went to the little knobs, her front hair bobbed on her forehead.

'Why!' she exclaimed, crossly. 'What have you come today for?'

'I got off a day earlier,' said Hadrian, and his man's voice so deep and unexpected was like a blow to Cousin Emmie.

'Well, you've caught us in the midst of it,' she said, with resentment. Then all three went into the middle room.

Mr. Rockley was dressed—that is, he had on his trousers and socks—but he was resting on the bed, propped up just under the window, from whence he could see his beloved and resplendent garden, where tulips and apple-trees were ablaze. He did not look as ill as he was, for the water puffed him up, and his face kept its colour. His stomach was much swollen. He glanced round swiftly, turning his eyes without turning his head. He was the wreck of a handsome, well-built man.

Seeing Hadrian, a queer, unwilling smile went over his face. The young man greeted him sheepishly.

'You wouldn't make a life-guardsman,' he said. 'Do you want something to eat?'

Hadrian looked round—as if for the meal.

'I don't mind,' he said.

'What shall you have—egg and bacon?' asked Emmie shortly.

'Yes, I don't mind,' said Hadrian.

The sisters went down to the kitchen, and sent the servant to finish the stairs.

'Isn't he *altered*?' said Matilda, *sotto voce*.

'Isn't he!' said Cousin Emmie. '*What* a little man!'

They both made a grimace, and laughed nervously.

'Get the frying-pan,' said Emmie to Matilda.

'But he's as cocky as ever,' said Matilda, narrowing her eyes and shaking her head knowingly, as she handed the frying-pan.

'Mannie!' said Emmie sarcastically. Hadrian's new-fledged, cock-sure manliness evidently found no favour in her eyes.

'Oh, he's not bad,' said Matilda. 'You don't want to be prejudiced against him.'

I'm not prejudiced against him, I think he's all right for looks,' said Emmie, 'but there's too much of the little mannie about him.'

'Fancy catching us like this,' said Matilda.

'They've no thought for anything,' said Emmie with contempt. 'You go up and get dressed, our Matilda. I don't care about him. I can see to things, and you can talk to him. I shan't.'

'He'll talk to my father,' said Matilda, meaningful.

'*Sly—!*' exclaimed Emmie, with a grimace.

The sisters believed that Hadrian had come hoping to get something out of their father—hoping for a legacy. And they were not at all sure he would not get it.

Matilda went upstairs to change. She had thought it all out how she would receive Hadrian, and impress him. And he had caught her with her head tied up in a duster, and her thin arms in a basin of lather. But she did not care. She now dressed herself most scrupulously, carefully folded her long, beautiful, blonde hair, touched her pallor with a little rouge, and put her long string of exquisite crystal beads over her soft green dress. Now she looked elegant, like a heroine in a magazine illustration, and almost as unreal.

She found Hadrian and her father talking away. The young man was short of speech as a rule, but he could find his tongue with his 'uncle'. They were both sipping a glass of brandy, and smoking, and chatting like a pair of old cronies. Hadrian was telling about Canada. He was going back there when his leave was up.

'You wouldn't like to stop in England, then?' said Mr. Rockley.

'No, I wouldn't stop in England,' said Hadrian.

'How's that? There's plenty of electricians here,' said Mr. Rockley.

'Yes. But there's too much difference between the men and the employers over here—too much of that for me,' said Hadrian.

The sick man looked at him narrowly, with oddly smiling eyes.

'That's it, is it?' he replied.

Matilda heard and understood. 'So that's your big idea, is it, my little man,' she said to herself. She had always said of Hadrian that he had no proper *respect* for anybody or anything, that he was sly and *common*. She went down to the kitchen for a *sotto voce* confab with Emmie.

'He thinks a rare lot of himself!' she whispered.

'He's somebody, he is!' said Emmie with contempt.

'He thinks there's too much difference between masters and men, over here,' said Matilda.

'Is it any different in Canada?' asked Emmie.

'Oh, yes—democratic,' replied Matilda, 'He thinks they're all on a level over there.'

'Ay, well he's over here now,' said Emmie dryly, 'so he can keep his place.'

As they talked they saw the young man sauntering down the garden, looking casually at the flowers. He had his hands in his pockets, and his soldier's cap neatly on his head. He looked quite at his ease, as if in possession. The two women, fluttered, watched him through the window.

'We know what he's come for,' said Emmie, churlishly. Matilda looked a long time at the neat khaki figure. It had something of the charity-boy about it still; but now it was a man's figure, laconic, charged with plebeian energy. She thought of the derisive passion in his voice as he had declaimed against the propertied classes, to her father.

'You don't know, Emmie. Perhaps he's not come for that,' she rebuked her sister. They were both thinking of the money.

They were still watching the young soldier. He stood away at the bottom of the garden, with his back to them, his hands in his pockets, looking into the water of the willow pond. Matilda's dark-blue eyes had a strange, full look in them, the lids, with the faint blue veins showing, dropped rather low. She carried her head light and high, but she had a look of pain. The young man at the bottom of the garden turned and looked up the path. Perhaps he saw them through the window. Matilda moved into shadow.

That afternoon their father seemed weak and ill. He was easily exhausted. The doctor came, and told Matilda that the sick man might die suddenly at any moment—but then he might not. They must be prepared.

So the day passed, and the next. Hadrian made himself at home. He went about in the morning in his brownish jersey and his khaki trousers, collarless, his bare neck showing. He explored the pottery premises, as if he had some secret purpose in so doing, he talked with Mr. Rockley, when the sick man had strength. The two girls were always angry when the two men sat talking together like cronies. Yet it was chiefly a kind of politics they talked.

On the second day after Hadrian's arrival, Matilda sat with her father in the evening. She was drawing a picture which she wanted to copy. It was very still, Hadrian was gone out somewhere, no one knew where, and Emmie was busy. Mr. Rockley reclined on his bed, looking out in silence over his evening-sunny garden.

'If anything happens to me, Matilda,' he said, 'you won't sell this house—you'll stop here—'

Matilda's eyes took their slightly haggard look as she stared at her father.

'Well, we couldn't do anything else,' she said.

'You don't know what you might do,' he said. 'Everything is left to you and Emmie, equally. You do as you like with it—only don't sell this house, don't part with it.'

'No,' she said.

'And give Hadrian my watch and chain, and a hundred pounds out of what's in the bank—and help him if he ever wants helping. I haven't put his name in the will.'

'Your watch and chain, and a hundred pounds—yes. But you'll be here when he goes back to Canada, father.'

'You never know what'll happen,' said her father.

Matilda sat and watched him, with her full, haggard eyes, for a long time, as if tranced. She saw that he knew he must go soon—she saw like a clairvoyant.

Later on she told Emmie what her father had said about the watch and chain and the money.

'What right has *he'*—he—meaning Hadrian—'to my father's watch and chain—what has it to do with him? Let him have the money, and get off,' said Emmie. She loved her father.

That night Matilda sat late in her room. Her heart was anxious and breaking, her mind seemed entranced. She was too much entranced even to weep, and all the time she thought of her father, only her father. At last she felt she must go to him.

It was near midnight. She went along the passage and to his room. There was a faint light from the moon outside. She listened at his door. Then she softly opened and entered. The room was faintly dark. She heard a movement on the bed.

'Are you asleep?' she said softly, advancing to the side of the bed.

'Are you asleep?' she repeated gently, as she stood at the side of the bed. And she reached her hand in the darkness to touch his forehead. Delicately, her fingers met the nose and the eyebrows, she laid her fine, delicate hand on his brow. It seemed fresh and smooth—very fresh and smooth. A sort of surprise stirred her, in her entranced state. But it could not waken her. Gently, she leaned over the bed and stirred her fingers over the low-growing hair on his brow.

'Can't you sleep tonight?' she said.

There was a quick stirring in the bed. 'Yes, I can,' a voice answered. It was Hadrian's voice. She started away. Instantly, she was wakened from her late-at-night trance. She remembered that her father was downstairs, that Hadrian had his room. She stood in the darkness as if stung.

'It is you, Hadrian?' she said. 'I thought it was my father.' She was so startled, so shocked, that she could not move. The young man gave an uncomfortable laugh, and turned in his bed.

At last she got out of the room. When she was back in her own room, in the light, and her door was closed, she stood holding up her hand that had touched him, as if it were hurt. She was almost too shocked, she could not endure.

'Well,' said her calm and weary mind, 'it was only a mistake, why take any notice of it.'

But she could not reason her feelings so easily. She suffered, feeling herself in a false position. Her right hand, which she had laid so gently on his face, on his fresh skin, ached now, as if it were really injured. She could not forgive Hadrian for the mistake: it made her dislike him deeply.

Hadrian too slept badly. He had been awakened by the opening of the door, and had not realized what the question meant. But the soft, straying tenderness of her hand on his face startled something out of his soul. He was a charity boy, aloof and more or less at bay. The fragile exquisiteness of her caress startled him most, revealed unknown things to him.

In the morning she could feel the consciousness in his eyes, when she came downstairs. She tried to bear herself as if nothing at all had happened, and she succeeded. She had the calm self-control, self-indifference, of one who has suffered and borne her suffering. She looked at him from her darkish, almost drugged blue eyes, she met the spark of consciousness in his eyes, and quenched it. And with her long, fine hand she put the sugar in his coffee.

But she could not control him as she thought she could. He had a keen memory stinging his mind, a new set of sensations working in his consciousness. Something new was alert in him. At the back of his reticent, guarded mind he kept his secret alive and vivid. She was at his mercy, for he was unscrupulous, his standard was not her standard.

He looked at her curiously. She was not beautiful, her nose was too large, her chin was too small, her neck was too thin. But her skin was clear and fine, she had a high-bred sensitiveness. This queer, brave, high-bred quality she shared with her father. The charity boy could see it in her tapering fingers, which were white and ringed. The same glamour that he knew in the elderly man he now saw in the woman. And he wanted to possess himself of it, he wanted to make himself master of it. As he went about through the old pottery-yard, his secretive mind schemed and worked. To be master of that strange soft delicacy such as he had felt in her hand upon his face,—this was what he set himself towards. He was secretly plotting.

He watched Matilda as she went about, and she became aware of his attention, as of some shadow following her. But her pride made her ignore it. When he sauntered near her, his hands in his pockets, she received him with that same commonplace kindliness which mastered him more than any contempt. Her superior breeding seemed to control him. She made herself feel towards him exactly as she had always felt: he was a young boy who lived in the house with them, but was a stranger. Only, she dared not remember his face under her hand. When she remembered that, she was bewildered. Her hand had offended her, she wanted to cut it off. And she wanted, fiercely, to cut off the memory in him. She assumed she had done so.

One day, when he sat talking with his 'uncle', he looked straight into the eyes of the sick man, and said:

'But I shouldn't like to live and die here in Rawsley.'

'No—well—you needn't,' said the sick man.

'Do you think Cousin Matilda likes it?'

'I should think so.'

'I don't call it much of a life,' said the youth. 'How much older is she than me, Uncle?'

The sick man looked at the young soldier.

'A good bit,' he said.

'Over thirty?' said Hadrian.

'Well, not so much. She's thirty-two.'

Hadrian considered a while.

'She doesn't look it,' he said.

Again the sick father looked at him.

'Do you think she'd like to leave here?' said Hadrian.

'Nay, I don't know,' replied the father, restive.

Hadrian sat still, having his own thoughts. Then in a small, quiet voice, as if he were speaking from inside himself, he said:

'I'd marry her if you wanted me to.'

The sick man raised his eyes suddenly, and stared. He stared for a long time. The youth looked inscrutably out of the window.

'*You!*' said the sick man, mocking, with some contempt. Hadrian turned and met his eyes. The two men had an inexplicable understanding.

'If you wasn't against it,' said Hadrian.

'Nay,' said the father, turning aside, 'I don't think I'm against it. I've never thought of it. But—But Emmie's the youngest.'

He had flushed, and looked suddenly more alive. Secretly he loved the boy.

'You might ask her,' said Hadrian.

The elder man considered.

'Hadn't you better ask her yourself?' he said.

'She'd take more notice of you,' said Hadrian.

They were both silent. Then Emmie came in.

For two days Mr. Rockley was excited and thoughtful. Hadrian went about quietly, secretly, unquestioning. At last the father and daughter were alone together. It was very early morning, the father had been in much pain. As the pain abated, he lay still, thinking.

'Matilda!' he said suddenly, looking at his daughter.

'Yes, I'm here,' she said.

'Ay! I want you to do something—'

She rose in anticipation.

'Nay, sit still. I want you to marry Hadrian—'

She thought he was raving. She rose, bewildered and frightened.

'Nay, sit you still, sit you still. You hear what I tell you.'

'But you don't know what you're saying, father.'

'Ay, I know well enough. I want you to marry Hadrian, I tell you.'

She was dumbfounded. He was a man of few words.

'You'll do what I tell you,' he said.

She looked at him slowly.

'What put such an idea in your mind?' she said proudly.

'He did.'

Matilda almost looked her father down, her pride was so offended.

'Why, it's disgraceful,' she said.

'Why?'

She watched him slowly.

'What do you ask me for?' she said. 'It's disgusting.'

'The lad's sound enough,' he replied, testily.

'You'd better tell him to clear out,' she said, coldly.

He turned and looked out of the window. She sat flushed and erect for a long time. At length her father turned to her, looking really malevolent.

'If you won't,' he said, 'you're a fool, and I'll make you pay for your foolishness, do you see?'

Suddenly a cold fear gripped her. She could not believe her senses. She was terrified and bewildered. She stared at her father, believing him to be delirious, or mad, or drunk. What could she do?

'I tell you,' he said. 'I'll send for Whittle tomorrow if you don't. You shall neither of you have anything of mine.'

Whittle was the solicitor. She understood her father well enough: he would send for his solicitor, and make a will leaving all his property to Hadrian: neither she nor Emmie should have anything. It was too much. She rose and went out of the room, up to her own room, where she locked herself in.

She did not come out for some hours. At last, late at night, she confided in Emmie.

'The sliving demon, he wants the money,' said Emmie. 'My father's out of his mind.'

The thought that Hadrian merely wanted the money was another blow to Matilda. She did not love the impossible youth—but she had not yet learned to think of him as a thing of evil. He now became hideous to her mind.

Emmie had a little scene with her father next day.

'You don't mean what you said to our Matilda yesterday, do you, father?' she asked aggressively.

'Yes,' he replied.

'What, that you'll alter your will?'

'Yes.'

'You won't,' said his angry daughter.

But he looked at her with a malevolent little smile.

'Annie!' he shouted. 'Annie!'

He had still power to make his voice carry. The servant maid came in from the kitchen.

'Put your things on, and go down to Whittle's office, and say I want to see Mr. Whittle as soon as he can, and will he bring a will-form.'

The sick man lay back a little—he could not lie down. His daughter sat as if she had been struck. Then she left the room.

Hadrian was pottering about in the garden. She went straight down to him.

'Here,' she said. 'You'd better get off. You'd better take your things and go from here, quick.'

Hadrian looked slowly at the infuriated girl.

'Who says so?' he asked.

'*We* say so—get off, you've done enough mischief and damage.'

'Does Uncle say so?'

'Yes, he does.'

'I'll go and ask him.'

But like a fury Emmie barred his way.

'No, you needn't. You needn't ask him nothing at all. We don't want you, so you can go.'

'Uncle's boss here.'

'A man that's dying, and you crawling round and working on him for his money!—you're not fit to live.'

'Oh!' he said. 'Who says I'm working for his money?'

'I say. But my father told our Matilda, and *she* knows what you are. *She* knows what you're after. So you might as well clear out, for all you'll get—guttersnipe!'

He turned his back on her, to think. It had not occurred to him that they would think he was after the money. He *did* want the money—badly. He badly wanted to be an employer himself, not one of the employed. But he knew, in his subtle, calculating way, that it was not for money he wanted Matilda. He wanted both the money and Matilda. But he told himself the two desires were separate, not one. He could not do with Matilda, *without* the money. But he did not want her *for* the money.

When he got this clear in his mind, he sought for an opportunity to tell it her, lurking and watching. But she avoided him. In the evening the lawyer came. Mr. Rockley seemed to have a new access of strength—a will was drawn up, making the previous arrangements wholly conditional. The old will held good, if Matilda would consent to marry Hadrian. If she refused then at the end of six months the whole property passed to Hadrian.

Mr. Rockley told this to the young man, with malevolent satisfaction. He seemed to have a strange desire, quite unreasonable, for revenge upon the women who had surrounded him for so long, and served him so carefully.

'Tell her in front of me,' said Hadrian.

So Mr. Rockley sent for his daughters.

At last they came, pale, mute, stubborn. Matilda seemed to have retired far off, Emmie seemed like a fighter ready to fight to the death. The sick man reclined on the bed, his eyes bright, his puffed hand trembling. But his face had again some of its old, bright handsomeness. Hadrian sat quiet, a little aside: the indomitable, dangerous charity boy.

'There's the will,' said their father, pointing them to the paper.

The two women sat mute and immovable, they took no notice.

'Either you marry Hadrian, or he has everything,' said the father with satisfaction.

'Then let him have everything,' said Matilda boldly.

'He's not! He's not!' cried Emmie fiercely. 'He's not going to have it. The guttersnipe!'

An amused look came on her father's face.

'You hear that, Hadrian,' he said.

'I didn't offer to marry Cousin Matilda for the money,' said Hadrian, flushing and moving on his seat.

Matilda looked at him slowly, with her dark-blue, drugged eyes. He seemed a strange little monster to her.

'Why, you liar, you know you did,' cried Emmie.

The sick man laughed. Matilda continued to gaze strangely at the young man.

'She knows I didn't,' said Hadrian.

He too had his courage, as a rat has indomitable courage in the end. Hadrian had some of the neatness, the reserve, the underground quality of the rat. But he had perhaps the ultimate courage, the most unquenchable courage of all.

Emmie looked at her sister.

'Oh, well,' she said. 'Matilda—don't bother. Let him have everything, we can look after ourselves.'

'I know he'll take everything,' said Matilda, abstractedly.

Hadrian did not answer. He knew in fact that if Matilda refused him he would take everything, and go off with it.

'A clever little mannie—!' said Emmie, with a jeering grimace.

The father laughed noiselessly to himself. But he was tired....

'Go on, then,' he said. 'Go on, let me be quiet.'

Emmie turned and looked at him.

'You deserve what you've got,' she said to her father bluntly.

'Go on,' he answered mildly. 'Go on.'

Another night passed—a night nurse sat up with Mr. Rockley. Another day came. Hadrian was there as ever, in his woollen jersey and coarse khaki trousers and bare neck. Matilda went about, frail and distant, Emmie black-browed in spite of her blondness. They were all quiet, for they did not intend the mystified servant to learn anything.

Mr. Rockley had very bad attacks of pain, he could not breathe. The end seemed near. They all went about quiet and stoical, all unyielding. Hadrian pondered within himself. If he did not marry Matilda he would go to Canada with twenty thousand pounds. This was itself a very satisfactory prospect. If Matilda consented he would have nothing—she would have her own money.

Emmie was the one to act. She went off in search of the solicitor and brought him with her. There was an interview, and Whittle tried to frighten the youth into withdrawal—but without avail. The clergyman and relatives were summoned—but Hadrian stared at them and took no notice. It made him angry, however.

He wanted to catch Matilda alone. Many days went by, and he was not successful: she avoided him. At last, lurking, he surprised her one day as she came to pick gooseberries, and he cut off her retreat. He came to the point at once.

'You don't want me, then?' he said, in his subtle, insinuating voice.

'I don't want to speak to you,' she said, averting her face.

'You put your hand on me, though,' he said. 'You shouldn't have done that, and then I should never have thought of it. You shouldn't have touched me.'

'If you were anything decent, you'd know that was a mistake, and forget it,' she said.

'I know it was a mistake—but I shan't forget it. If you wake a man up, he can't go to sleep again because he's told to.'

'If you had any decent feeling in you, you'd have gone away,' she replied.

'I didn't want to,' he replied.

She looked away into the distance. At last she asked:

'What do you persecute me for, if it isn't for the money. I'm old enough to be your mother. In a way I've been your mother.'

'Doesn't matter,' he said. 'You've been no mother to me. Let us marry and go out to Canada—you might as well—you've touched me.'

She was white and trembling. Suddenly she flushed with anger.

'It's so *indecent*,' she said.

'How?' he retorted. 'You touched me.'

But she walked away from him. She felt as if he had trapped her. He was angry and depressed, he felt again despised.

That same evening she went into her father's room.

'Yes,' she said suddenly. 'I'll marry him.'

Her father looked up at her. He was in pain, and very ill.

'You like him now, do you?' he said, with a faint smile.

She looked down into his face, and saw death not far off. She turned and went coldly out of the room.

The solicitor was sent for, preparations were hastily made. In all the interval Matilda did not speak to Hadrian, never answered him if he addressed her. He approached her in the morning.

'You've come round to it, then?' he said, giving her a pleasant look from his twinkling, almost kindly eyes. She looked down at him and turned aside. She looked down on him both literally and figuratively. Still he persisted, and triumphed.

Emmie raved and wept, the secret flew abroad. But Matilda was silent and unmoved, Hadrian was quiet and satisfied, and nipped with fear also. But he held out against his fear. Mr. Rockley was very ill, but unchanged.

On the third day the marriage took place. Matilda and Hadrian drove straight home from the registrar, and went straight into the room of the dying man. His face lit up with a clear twinkling smile.

'Hadrian—you've got her?' he said, a little hoarsely.

'Yes,' said Hadrian, who was pale round the gills.

'Ay, my lad, I'm glad you're mine,' replied the dying man. Then he turned his eyes closely on Matilda.

'Let's look at you, Matilda,' he said. Then his voice went strange and unrecognizable. 'Kiss me,' he said.

She stooped and kissed him. She had never kissed him before, not since she was a tiny child. But she was quiet, very still.

'Kiss him,' the dying man said.

Obediently, Matilda put forward her mouth and kissed the young husband.

'That's right! That's right!' murmured the dying man.

SAMSON AND DELILAH

A man got down from the motor-omnibus that runs from Penzance to St Just-in-Penwith, and turned northwards, uphill towards the Polestar. It was only half past six, but already the stars were out, a cold little wind was blowing from the sea, and the crystalline, three-pulse flash of the lighthouse below the cliffs beat rhythmically in the first darkness.

The man was alone. He went his way unhesitating, but looked from side to side with cautious curiosity. Tall, ruined power-houses of tin-mines loomed in the darkness from time to time, like remnants of some by-gone civilization. The lights of many miners' cottages scattered on the hilly darkness twinkled desolate in their disorder, yet twinkled with the lonely homeliness of the Celtic night.

He tramped steadily on, always watchful with curiosity. He was a tall, well-built man, apparently in the prime of life. His shoulders were square and rather stiff, he leaned forwards a little as he went, from the hips, like a man who must stoop to lower his height. But he did not stoop his shoulders: he bent his straight back from the hips.

Now and again short, stump, thick-legged figures of Cornish miners passed him, and he invariably gave them goodnight, as if to insist that he was on his own ground. He spoke with the west-Cornish intonation. And as he went along the dreary road, looking now at the lights of the dwellings on land, now at the lights away to sea, vessels veering round in sight of the Longships Lighthouse, the whole of the Atlantic Ocean in darkness and space between him and America, he seemed a little excited and pleased with himself, watchful, thrilled, veering along in a sense of mastery and of power in conflict.

The houses began to close on the road, he was entering the straggling, formless, desolate mining village, that he knew of old. On the left was a little space set back from the road, and cosy lights of an inn. There it was. He peered up at the sign: 'The Tinners' Rest'. But he could not make out the name of the proprietor. He listened. There was excited talking and laughing, a woman's voice laughing shrilly among the men's.

Stooping a little, he entered the warmly-lit bar. The lamp was burning, a buxom woman rose from the white-scrubbed deal table where the black and white and red cards were scattered, and several men, miners, lifted their faces from the game.

The stranger went to the counter, averting his face. His cap was pulled down over his brow.

'Good-evening!' said the landlady, in her rather ingratiating voice.

'Good-evening. A glass of ale.'

'A glass of ale,' repeated the landlady suavely. 'Cold night—but bright.'

'Yes,' the man assented, laconically. Then he added, when nobody expected him to say any more: 'Seasonable weather.'

'Quite seasonable, quite,' said the landlady. 'Thank you.'

The man lifted his glass straight to his lips, and emptied it. He put it down again on the zinc counter with a click.

'Let's have another,' he said.

The woman drew the beer, and the man went away with his glass to the second table, near the fire. The woman, after a moment's hesitation, took her seat again at the table with the card-players. She had noticed the man: a big fine fellow, well dressed, a stranger.

But he spoke with that Cornish-Yankee accent she accepted as the natural twang among the miners.

The stranger put his foot on the fender and looked into the fire. He was handsome, well coloured, with well-drawn Cornish eyebrows, and the usual dark, bright, mindless Cornish eyes. He seemed abstracted in thought. Then he watched the card-party.

The woman was buxom and healthy, with dark hair and small, quick brown eyes. She was bursting with life and vigour, the energy she threw into the game of cards excited all the men, they shouted, and laughed, and the woman held her breast, shrieking with laughter.

'Oh, my, it'll be the death o' me,' she panted. 'Now, come on, Mr. Trevorrow, play fair. Play fair, I say, or I s'll put the cards down.'

'Play fair! Why who's played unfair?' ejaculated Mr. Trevorrow. 'Do you mean t'accuse me, as I haven't played fair, Mrs. Nankervis?'

'I do. I say it, and I mean it. Haven't you got the queen of spades? Now, come on, no dodging round me. I know you've got that queen, as well as I know my name's Alice.'

'Well—if your name's Alice, you'll have to have it—'

'Ay, now—what did I say? Did you ever see such a man? My word, but your missus must be easy took in, by the looks of things.'

And off she went into peals of laughter. She was interrupted by the entrance of four men in khaki, a short, stumpy sergeant of middle age, a young corporal, and two young privates. The woman leaned back in her chair.

'Oh, my!' she cried. 'If there isn't the boys back: looking perished, I believe—'

'Perished, Ma!' exclaimed the sergeant. 'Not yet.'

'Near enough,' said a young private, uncouthly.

The woman got up.

'I'm sure you are, my dears. You'll be wanting your suppers, I'll be bound.'

'We could do with 'em.'

'Let's have a wet first,' said the sergeant.

The woman bustled about getting the drinks. The soldiers moved to the fire, spreading out their hands.

'Have your suppers in here, will you?' she said. 'Or in the kitchen?'

'Let's have it here,' said the sergeant. 'More cosier—*if* you don't mind.'

'You shall have it where you like, boys, where you like.'

She disappeared. In a minute a girl of about sixteen came in. She was tall and fresh, with dark, young, expressionless eyes, and well-drawn brows, and the immature softness and mindlessness of the sensuous Celtic type.

'Ho, Maryann! Evenin', Maryann! How's Maryann, now?' came the multiple greeting.

She replied to everybody in a soft voice, a strange, soft *aplomb* that was very attractive. And she moved round with rather mechanical, attractive movements, as if her thoughts were elsewhere. But she had always this dim far-awayness in her bearing: a sort of modesty. The strange man by the fire watched her curiously. There was an alert, inquisitive, mindless curiosity on his well-coloured face.

'I'll have a bit of supper with you, if I might,' he said.

She looked at him, with her clear, unreasoning eyes, just like the eyes of some non-human creature.

'I'll ask mother,' she said. Her voice was soft-breathing, gently singsong.

When she came in again:

'Yes,' she said, almost whispering. 'What will you have?'

'What have you got?' he said, looking up into her face.

'There's cold meat—'

'That's for me, then.'

The stranger sat at the end of the table and ate with the tired, quiet soldiers. Now, the landlady was interested in him. Her brow was knit rather tense, there was a look of panic in her large, healthy face, but her small brown eyes were fixed most dangerously. She was a big woman, but her eyes were small and tense. She drew near the stranger. She wore a rather loud-patterned flannelette blouse, and a dark skirt.

'What will you have to drink with your supper?' she asked, and there was a new, dangerous note in her voice.

He moved uneasily.

'Oh, I'll go on with ale.'

She drew him another glass. Then she sat down on the bench at the table with him and the soldiers, and fixed him with her attention.

'You've come from St Just, have you?' she said.

He looked at her with those clear, dark, inscrutable Cornish eyes, and answered at length:

'No, from Penzance.'

'Penzance!—but you're not thinking of going back there tonight?'

'No—no.'

He still looked at her with those wide, clear eyes that seemed like very bright agate. Her anger began to rise. It was seen on her brow. Yet her voice was still suave and deprecating.

'I *thought* not—but you're not living in these parts, are you?'

'No—no, I'm not living here.' He was always slow in answering, as if something intervened between him and any outside question.

'Oh, I see,' she said. 'You've got relations down here.'

Again he looked straight into her eyes, as if looking her into silence.

'Yes,' he said.

He did not say any more. She rose with a flounce. The anger was tight on her brow. There was no more laughing and card-playing that evening, though she kept up her motherly, suave, good-humoured way with the men. But they knew her, they were all afraid of her.

The supper was finished, the table cleared, the stranger did not go. Two of the young soldiers went off to bed, with their cheery:

'Good-night, Ma. Good-night, Maryann.'

The stranger talked a little to the sergeant about the war, which was in its first year, about the new army, a fragment of which was quartered in this district, about America.

The landlady darted looks at him from her small eyes, minute by minute the electric storm welled in her bosom, as still he did not go. She was quivering with suppressed, violent passion, something frightening and abnormal. She could not sit still for a moment. Her heavy form seemed to flash with sudden, involuntary movements as the minutes passed by, and still he sat there, and the tension on her heart grew unbearable. She watched the hands of the dock move on. Three of the soldiers had gone to bed, only the crop-headed, terrier-like old sergeant remained.

The landlady sat behind the bar fidgeting spasmodically with the newspaper. She looked again at the clock. At last it was five minutes to ten.

'Gentlemen—the enemy!' she said, in her diminished, furious voice. 'Time, please. Time, my dears. And good-night all!'

The men began to drop out, with a brief good-night. It was a minute to ten. The landlady rose.

'Come,' she said. 'I'm shutting the door.'

The last of the miners passed out. She stood, stout and menacing, holding the door. Still the stranger sat on by the fire, his black overcoat opened, smoking.

'We're closed now, sir,' came the perilous, narrowed voice of the landlady.

The little, dog-like, hard-headed sergeant touched the arm of the stranger.

'Closing time,' he said.

The stranger turned round in his seat, and his quick-moving, dark, jewel-like eyes went from the sergeant to the landlady.

'I'm stopping here tonight,' he said, in his laconic Cornish-Yankee accent.

The landlady seemed to tower. Her eyes lifted strangely, frightening.

'Oh! indeed!' she cried.' Oh, indeed! And whose orders are those, may I ask?'

He looked at her again.

'My orders,' he said.

Involuntarily she shut the door, and advanced like a great, dangerous bird. Her voice rose, there was a touch of hoarseness in it.

'And what might *your* orders be, if you please?' she cried. 'Who might *you* be, to give orders, in the house?'

He sat still, watching her.

'You know who I am,' he said. 'At least, I know who you are.'

'Oh, you do? Oh, do you? And who am *I* then, if you'll be so good as to tell me?'

He stared at her with his bright, dark eyes.

'You're my Missis, you are,' he said. 'And you know it, as well as I do.'

She started as if something had exploded in her.

Her eyes lifted and flared madly.

'*Do* I know it, indeed!' she cried. 'I know no such thing! I know no such thing! Do you think a man's going to walk into this bar, and tell me off-hand I'm his Missis, and I'm going to believe him?—I say to you, whoever you may be, you're mistaken. I know myself for no Missis of yours, and I'll thank you to go out of this house, this minute, before I get those that will put you out.'

The man rose to his feet, stretching his head towards her a little. He was a handsomely built Cornishman in the prime of life.

'What you say, eh? You don't know me?' he said, in his sing-song voice, emotionless, but rather smothered and pressing: it reminded one of the girl's. 'I should know you anywhere, you see. I should! I shouldn't have to look twice to know you, you see. You see, now, don't you?'

The woman was baffled.

'So you may say,' she replied, staccato. 'So you may say. That's easy enough. My name's known, and respected, by most people for ten miles round. But I don't know *you*.'

Her voice ran to sarcasm. 'I can't say I know *you*. You're a *perfect* stranger to me, and I don't believe I've ever set eyes on you before tonight.'

Her voice was very flexible and sarcastic.

'Yes, you have,' replied the man, in his reasonable way.' Yes, you have. Your name's my name, and that girl Maryann is my girl; she's my daughter. You're my Missis right enough. As sure as I'm Willie Nankervis.'

He spoke as if it were an accepted fact. His face was handsome, with a strange, watchful alertness and a fundamental fixity of intention that maddened her.

'You villain!' she cried. 'You villain, to come to this house and dare to speak to me. You villain, you down-right rascal!'

He looked at her.

'Ay,' he said, unmoved. 'All that.' He was uneasy before her. Only he was not afraid of her. There was something impenetrable about him, like his eyes, which were as bright as agate.

She towered, and drew near to him menacingly.

'You're going out of this house, aren't you?'—She stamped her foot in sudden madness. '*This minute!*'

He watched her. He knew she wanted to strike him.

'No,' he said, with suppressed emphasis. 'I've told you, I'm stopping here.'

He was afraid of her personality, but it did not alter him. She wavered. Her small, tawny-brown eyes concentrated in a point of vivid, sightless fury, like a tiger's. The man was wincing, but he stood his ground. Then she bethought herself. She would gather her forces.

'We'll see whether you're stopping here,' she said. And she turned, with a curious, frightening lifting of her eyes, and surged out of the room. The man, listening, heard her go upstairs, heard her tapping at a bedroom door, heard her saying: 'Do you mind coming down a minute, boys? I want you. I'm in trouble.'

The man in the bar took off his cap and his black overcoat, and threw them on the seat behind him. His black hair was short and touched with grey at the temples. He wore a well-cut, well-fitting suit of dark grey, American in style, and a turn-down collar. He looked well-to-do, a fine, solid figure of a man. The rather rigid look of the shoulders came from his having had his collar-bone twice broken in the mines.

The little terrier of a sergeant, in dirty khaki, looked at him furtively.

'She's your Missis?' he asked, jerking his head in the direction of the departed woman.

'Yes, she is,' barked the man. 'She's that, sure enough.'

'Not seen her for a long time, haven't ye?'

'Sixteen years come March month.'

'Hm!'

And the sergeant laconically resumed his smoking.

The landlady was coming back, followed by the three young soldiers, who entered rather sheepishly, in trousers and shirt and stocking-feet. The woman stood histrionically at the end of the bar, and exclaimed:

'That man refuses to leave the house, claims he's stopping the night here. You know very well I have no bed, don't you? And this house doesn't accommodate travellers. Yet he's going to stop in spite of all! But not while I've a drop of blood in my body, that I declare with my dying breath. And not if you men are worth the name of men, and will help a woman as has no one to help her.'

Her eyes sparkled, her face was flushed pink. She was drawn up like an Amazon.

The young soldiers did not quite know what to do. They looked at the man, they looked at the sergeant, one of them looked down and fastened his braces on the second button.

'What say, sergeant?' asked one whose face twinkled for a little devilment.

'Man says he's husband to Mrs. Nankervis,' said the sergeant.

'He's no husband of mine. I declare I never set eyes on him before this night. It's a dirty trick, nothing else, it's a dirty trick.'

'Why, you're a liar, saying you never set eyes on me before,' barked the man near the hearth. 'You're married to me, and that girl Maryann you had by me—well enough you know it.'

The young soldiers looked on in delight, the sergeant smoked imperturbed.

'Yes,' sang the landlady, slowly shaking her head in supreme sarcasm, 'it sounds very pretty, doesn't it? But you see we don't believe a word of it, and *how* are you going to prove it?' She smiled nastily.

The man watched in silence for a moment, then he said:

'It wants no proof.'

'Oh, yes, but it does! Oh, yes, but it does, sir, it wants a lot of proving!' sang the lady's sarcasm. 'We're not such gulls as all that, to swallow your words whole.'

But he stood unmoved near the fire. She stood with one hand resting on the zinc-covered bar, the sergeant sat with legs crossed, smoking, on the seat halfway between them, the three young soldiers in their shirts and braces stood wavering in the gloom behind the bar. There was silence.

'Do you know anything of the whereabouts of your husband, Mrs. Nankervis? Is he still living?' asked the sergeant, in his judicious fashion.

Suddenly the landlady began to cry, great scalding tears, that left the young men aghast.

'I know nothing of him,' she sobbed, feeling for her pocket handkerchief. 'He left me when Maryann was a baby, went mining to America, and after about six months never wrote a line nor sent me a penny bit. I can't say whether he's alive or dead, the villain. All

I've heard of him's to the bad—and I've heard nothing for years an' all, now.' She sobbed violently.

The golden-skinned, handsome man near the fire watched her as she wept. He was frightened, he was troubled, he was bewildered, but none of his emotions altered him underneath.

There was no sound in the room but the violent sobbing of the landlady. The men, one and all, were overcome.

'Don't you think as you'd better go, for tonight?' said the sergeant to the man, with sweet reasonableness. 'You'd better leave it a bit, and arrange something between you. You can't have much claim on a woman, I should imagine, if it's how she says. And you've come down on her a bit too sudden-like.'

The landlady sobbed heart-brokenly. The man watched her large breasts shaken. They seemed to cast a spell over his mind.

'How I've treated her, that's no matter,' he replied. 'I've come back, and I'm going to stop in my own home—for a bit, anyhow. There you've got it.'

'A dirty action,' said the sergeant, his face flushing dark. 'A dirty action, to come, after deserting a woman for that number of years, and want to force yourself on her! A dirty action—as isn't allowed by the law.'

The landlady wiped her eyes.

'Never you mind about law nor nothing,' cried the man, in a strange, strong voice. 'I'm not moving out of this public tonight.'

The woman turned to the soldiers behind her, and said in a wheedling, sarcastic tone:

'Are we going to stand it, boys?—Are we going to be done like this, Sergeant Thomas, by a scoundrel and a bully as has led a life beyond *mention*, in those American mining-camps, and then wants to come back and make havoc of a poor woman's life and savings, after having left her with a baby in arms to struggle as best she might? It's a crying shame if nobody will stand up for me—a crying shame—!'

The soldiers and the little sergeant were bristling. The woman stooped and rummaged under the counter for a minute. Then, unseen to the man away near the fire, she threw out a plaited grass rope, such as is used for binding bales, and left it lying near the feet of the young soldiers, in the gloom at the back of the bar.

Then she rose and fronted the situation.

'Come now,' she said to the man, in a reasonable, coldly-coaxing tone, 'put your coat on and leave us alone. Be a man, and not worse than a brute of a German. You can get a bed easy enough in St Just, and if you've nothing to pay for it sergeant would lend you a couple of shillings, I'm sure he would.'

All eyes were fixed on the man. He was looking down at the woman like a creature spell-bound or possessed by some devil's own intention.

'I've got money of my own,' he said. 'Don't you be frightened for your money, I've plenty of that, for the time.'

'Well, then,' she coaxed, in a cold, almost sneering propitiation, 'put your coat on and go where you're wanted—be a *man*, not a brute of a German.'

She had drawn quite near to him, in her challenging coaxing intentness. He looked down at her with his bewitched face.

'No, I shan't,' he said. 'I shan't do no such thing. *You'll* put me up for tonight.'

'Shall I!' she cried. And suddenly she flung her arms round him, hung on to him with all her powerful weight, calling to the soldiers: 'Get the rope, boys, and fasten him up. Alfred—John, quick now—'

The man reared, looked round with maddened eyes, and heaved his powerful body. But the woman was powerful also, and very heavy, and was clenched with the determination of death. Her face, with its exulting, horribly vindictive look, was turned up to him from his own breast; he reached back his head frantically, to get away from it. Meanwhile the young soldiers, after having watched this frightful Laocoon swaying for a moment, stirred, and the malicious one darted swiftly with the rope. It was tangled a little.

'Give me the end here,' cried the sergeant.

Meanwhile the big man heaved and struggled, swung the woman round against the seat and the table, in his convulsive effort to get free. But she pinned down his arms like a cuttlefish wreathed heavily upon him. And he heaved and swayed, and they crashed about the room, the soldiers hopping, the furniture bumping.

The young soldier had got the rope once round, the brisk sergeant helping him. The woman sank heavily lower, they got the rope round several times. In the struggle the victim fell over against the table. The ropes tightened till they cut his arms. The woman clung to his knees. Another soldier ran in a flash of genius, and fastened the strange man's feet with the pair of braces. Seats had crashed over, the table was thrown against the wall, but the man was bound, his arms pinned against his sides, his feet tied. He lay half fallen, sunk against the table, still for a moment.

The woman rose, and sank, faint, on to the seat against the wall. Her breast heaved, she could not speak, she thought she was going to die. The bound man lay against the overturned table, his coat all twisted and pulled up beneath the ropes, leaving the loins exposed. The soldiers stood around, a little dazed, but excited with the row.

The man began to struggle again, heaving instinctively against the ropes, taking great, deep breaths. His face, with its golden skin, flushed dark and surcharged, he heaved again. The great veins in his neck stood out. But it was no good, he went relaxed. Then again, suddenly, he jerked his feet.

'Another pair of braces, William,' cried the excited soldier. He threw himself on the legs of the bound man, and managed to fasten the knees. Then again there was stillness. They could hear the clock tick.

The woman looked at the prostrate figure, the strong, straight limbs, the strong back bound in subjection, the wide-eyed face that reminded her of a calf tied in a sack in a cart, only its head stretched dumbly backwards. And she triumphed.

The bound-up body began to struggle again. She watched fascinated the muscles working, the shoulders, the hips, the large, clean thighs. Even now he might break the ropes. She was afraid. But the lively young soldier sat on the shoulders of the bound man, and after a few perilous moments, there was stillness again.

'Now,' said the judicious sergeant to the bound man, 'if we untie you, will you promise to go off and make no more trouble.'

'You'll not untie him in here,' cried the woman. 'I wouldn't trust him as far as I could blow him.'

There was silence.

'We might carry him outside, and undo him there,' said the soldier. 'Then we could get the policeman, if he made any bother.'

'Yes,' said the sergeant. 'We could do that.' Then again, in an altered, almost severe tone, to the prisoner. 'If we undo you outside, will you take your coat and go without creating any more disturbance?'

But the prisoner would not answer, he only lay with wide, dark, bright, eyes, like a bound animal. There was a space of perplexed silence.

'Well, then, do as you say,' said the woman irritably. 'Carry him out amongst you, and let us shut up the house.'

They did so. Picking up the bound man, the four soldiers staggered clumsily into the silent square in front of the inn, the woman following with the cap and the overcoat. The young soldiers quickly unfastened the braces from the prisoner's legs, and they hopped indoors. They were in their stocking-feet, and outside the stars flashed cold. They stood in the doorway watching. The man lay quite still on the cold ground.

'Now,' said the sergeant, in a subdued voice, 'I'll loosen the knot, and he can work himself free, if you go in, Missis.'

She gave a last look at the dishevelled, bound man, as he sat on the ground. Then she went indoors, followed quickly by the sergeant. Then they were heard locking and barring the door.

The man seated on the ground outside worked and strained at the rope. But it was not so easy to undo himself even now. So, with hands bound, making an effort, he got on his feet, and went and worked the cord against the rough edge of an old wall. The rope, being of a kind of plaited grass, soon frayed and broke, and he freed himself. He had various contusions. His arms were hurt and bruised from the bonds. He rubbed them slowly. Then he pulled his clothes straight, stooped, put on his cap, struggled into his overcoat, and walked away.

The stars were very brilliant. Clear as crystal, the beam from the lighthouse under the cliffs struck rhythmically on the night. Dazed, the man walked along the road past the churchyard. Then he stood leaning up against a wall, for a long time.

He was roused because his feet were so cold. So he pulled himself together, and turned again in the silent night, back towards the inn.

The bar was in darkness. But there was a light in the kitchen. He hesitated. Then very quietly he tried the door.

He was surprised to find it open. He entered, and quietly closed it behind him. Then he went down the step past the bar-counter, and through to the lighted doorway of the kitchen. There sat his wife, planted in front of the range, where a furze fire was burning. She sat in a chair full in front of the range, her knees wide apart on the fender. She looked over her shoulder at him as he entered, but she did not speak. Then she stared in the fire again.

It was a small, narrow kitchen. He dropped his cap on the table that was covered with yellowish American cloth, and took a seat with his back to the wall, near the oven. His wife still sat with her knees apart, her feet on the steel fender and stared into the fire, motionless. Her skin was smooth and rosy in the firelight. Everything in the house was very clean and bright. The man sat silent, too, his head dropped. And thus they remained.

It was a question who would speak first. The woman leaned forward and poked the ends of the sticks in between the bars of the range. He lifted his head and looked at her.

'Others gone to bed, have they?' he asked.

But she remained closed in silence.

"S a cold night, out,' he said, as if to himself.

And he laid his large, yet well-shapen workman's hand on the top of the stove, that was polished black and smooth as velvet. She would not look at him, yet she glanced out of the corners of her eyes.

His eyes were fixed brightly on her, the pupils large and electric like those of a cat.

'I should have picked you out among thousands,' he said. 'Though you're bigger than

I'd have believed. Fine flesh you've made.'

She was silent for some time. Then she turned in her chair upon him.

'What do you think of yourself,' she said, 'coming back on me like this after over fifteen years? You don't think I've not heard of you, neither, in Butte City and elsewhere?'

He was watching her with his clear, translucent, unchallenged eyes.

'Yes,' he said. 'Chaps comes an' goes—I've heard tell of you from time to time.'

She drew herself up.

'And what lies have you heard about *me*?' she demanded superbly.

'I dunno as I've heard any lies at all—'cept as you was getting on very well, like.'

His voice ran warily and detached. Her anger stirred again in her violently. But she subdued it, because of the danger there was in him, and more, perhaps, because of the beauty of his head and his level drawn brows, which she could not bear to forfeit.

'That's more than I can say of *you*,' she said. 'I've heard more harm than good about *you*.'

'Ay, I dessay,' he said, looking in the fire. It was a long time since he had seen the furze burning, he said to himself. There was a silence, during which she watched his face.

'Do you call yourself a *man*?' she said, more in contemptuous reproach than in anger. 'Leave a woman as you've left me, you don't care to what!—and then to turn up in *this* fashion, without a word to say for yourself.'

He stirred in his chair, planted his feet apart, and resting his arms on his knees, looked steadily into the fire, without answering. So near to her was his head, and the close black hair, she could scarcely refrain from starting away, as if it would bite her.

'Do you call that the action of a *man*?' she repeated.

'No,' he said, reaching and poking the bits of wood into the fire with his fingers. 'I didn't call it anything, as I know of. It's no good calling things by any names whatsoever, as I know of.'

She watched him in his actions. There was a longer and longer pause between each speech, though neither knew it.

'I *wonder* what you think of yourself!' she exclaimed, with vexed emphasis. 'I *wonder* what sort of a fellow you take yourself to be!' She was really perplexed as well as angry.

'Well,' he said, lifting his head to look at her, 'I guess I'll answer for my own faults, if everybody else'll answer for theirs.'

Her heart beat fiery hot as he lifted his face to her. She breathed heavily, averting her face, almost losing her self-control.

'And what do you take *me* to be?' she cried, in real helplessness.

His face was lifted watching her, watching her soft, averted face, and the softly heaving mass of her breasts.

'I take you,' he said, with that laconic truthfulness which exercised such power over her, 'to be the deuce of a fine woman—darn me if you're not as fine a built woman as I've seen, handsome with it as well. I shouldn't have expected you to put on such handsome flesh: 'struth I shouldn't.'

Her heart beat fiery hot, as he watched her with those bright agate eyes, fixedly.

'Been very handsome to *you*, for fifteen years, my sakes!' she replied.

He made no answer to this, but sat with his bright, quick eyes upon her.

Then he rose. She started involuntarily. But he only said, in his laconic, measured way:

'It's warm in here now.'

And he pulled off his overcoat, throwing it on the table. She sat as if slightly cowed, whilst he did so.

'Them ropes has given my arms something, by Ga-ard,' he drawled, feeling his arms with his hands.

Still she sat in her chair before him, slightly cowed.

'You was sharp, wasn't you, to catch me like that, eh?' he smiled slowly. 'By Ga-ard, you had me fixed proper, proper you had. Darn me, you fixed me up proper—proper, you did.'

He leaned forwards in his chair towards her.

'I don't think no worse of you for it, no, darned if I do. Fine pluck in a woman's what I admire. That I do, indeed.'

She only gazed into the fire.

'We fet from the start, we did. And, my word, you begin again quick the minute you see me, you did. Darn me, you was too sharp for me. A darn fine woman, puts up a darn good fight. Darn me if I could find a woman in all the darn States as could get me down like that. Wonderful fine woman you be, truth to say, at this minute.'

She only sat glowering into the fire.

'As grand a pluck as a man could wish to find in a woman, true as I'm here,' he said, reaching forward his hand and tentatively touching her between her full, warm breasts, quietly.

She started, and seemed to shudder. But his hand insinuated itself between her breasts, as she continued to gaze in the fire.

'And don't you think I've come back here a-begging,' he said. 'I've more than *one* thousand pounds to my name, I have. And a bit of a fight for a how-de-do pleases me, that it do. But that doesn't mean as you're going to deny as you're my Missis....'

THE PRIMROSE PATH

A young man came out of the Victoria station, looking undecidedly at the taxi-cabs, dark-red and black, pressing against the kerb under the glass-roof. Several men in greatcoats and brass buttons jerked themselves erect to catch his attention, at the same time keeping an eye on the other people as they filtered through the open doorways of the station. Berry, however, was occupied by one of the men, a big, burly fellow whose blue eyes glared back and whose red-brown moustache bristled in defiance.

'Do you *want* a cab, sir?' the man asked, in a half-mocking, challenging voice.

Berry hesitated still.

'Are you Daniel Sutton?' he asked.

'Yes,' replied the other defiantly, with uneasy conscience.

'Then you are my uncle,' said Berry.

They were alike in colouring, and somewhat in features, but the taxi driver was a powerful, well-fleshed man who glared at the world aggressively, being really on the defensive against his own heart. His nephew, of the same height, was thin, well-dressed, quiet and indifferent in his manner. And yet they were obviously kin.

'And who the devil are you?' asked the taxi driver.

'I'm Daniel Berry,' replied the nephew.

'Well, I'm damned—never saw you since you were a kid.'

Rather awkwardly at this late hour the two shook hands.

'How are you, lad?'

'All right. I thought you were in Australia.'

'Been back three months—bought a couple of these damned things'—he kicked the tyre of his taxi-cab in affectionate disgust. There was a moment's silence.

'Oh, but I'm going back out there. I can't stand this cankering, rotten-hearted hell of a country any more; you want to come out to Sydney with me, lad. That's the place for you—beautiful place, oh, you could wish for nothing better. And money in it, too.— How's your mother?'

'She died at Christmas,' said the young man.

'Dead! What!—our Anna!' The big man's eyes stared, and he recoiled in fear. 'God, lad,' he said, 'that's three of 'em gone!'

The two men looked away at the people passing along the pale grey pavements, under the wall of Trinity Church.

'Well, strike me lucky!' said the taxi driver at last, out of breath. 'She wor th' best o' th' bunch of 'em. I see nowt nor hear nowt from any of 'em—they're not worth it, I'll be damned if they are—our sermon-lapping Adela and Maud,' he looked scornfully at his nephew. 'But she was the best of 'em, our Anna was, that's a fact.'

He was talking because he was afraid.

'An' after a hard life like she'd had. How old was she, lad?'

'Fifty-five.'

'Fifty-five ...' He hesitated. Then, in a rather hushed voice, he asked the question that frightened him:

'And what was it, then?'

'Cancer.'

'Cancer again, like Julia! I never knew there was cancer in our family. Oh, my good God, our poor Anna, after the life she'd had!—What, lad, do you see any God at the back of that?—I'm damned if I do.'

He was glaring, very blue-eyed and fierce, at his nephew. Berry lifted his shoulders slightly.

'God?' went on the taxi driver, in a curious intense tone, 'You've only to look at the folk in the street to know there's nothing keeps it going but gravitation. Look at 'em. Look at him!'—A mongrel-looking man was nosing past. 'Wouldn't *he* murder you for your watch-chain, but that he's afraid of society. He's got it *in* him.... Look at 'em.'

Berry watched the towns-people go by, and, sensitively feeling his uncle's antipathy, it seemed he was watching a sort of *danse macabre* of ugly criminals.

'Did you ever see such a God-forsaken crew creeping about! It gives you the very horrors to look at 'em. I sit in this damned car and watch 'em till, I can tell you, I feel like running the cab amuck among 'em, and running myself to kingdom come—'

Berry wondered at this outburst. He knew his uncle was the black-sheep, the youngest, the darling of his mother's family. He knew him to be at outs with respectability, mixing with the looser, sporting type, all betting and drinking and showing dogs and birds, and racing. As a critic of life, however, he did not know him. But the young man felt curiously understanding. 'He uses words like I do, he talks nearly as I talk, except that I shouldn't say those things. But I might feel like that, in myself, if I went a certain road.'

'I've got to go to Watmore,' he said. 'Can you take me?'

'When d'you want to go?' asked the uncle fiercely.

'Now.'

'Come on, then. What d'yer stand gassin' on th' causeway for?'

The nephew took his seat beside the driver. The cab began to quiver, then it started forward with a whirr. The uncle, his hands and feet acting mechanically, kept his blue eyes fixed on the highroad into whose traffic the car was insinuating its way. Berry felt curiously as if he were sitting beside an older development of himself. His mind went back to his mother. She had been twenty years older than this brother of hers whom she had loved so dearly. 'He was one of the most affectionate little lads, and such a curly head! I could never have believed he would grow into the great, coarse bully he is—for he's nothing else. My father made a god of him—well, it's a good thing his father is dead. He got in with that sporting gang, that's what did it. Things were made too easy for him, and so he thought of no one but himself, and this is the result.'

Not that 'Joky' Sutton was so very black a sheep. He had lived idly till he was eighteen, then had suddenly married a young, beautiful girl with clear brows and dark grey eyes, a factory girl. Having taken her to live with his parents he, lover of dogs and pigeons, went on to the staff of a sporting paper. But his wife was without uplift or warmth. Though they made money enough, their house was dark and cold and uninviting. He had two or three dogs, and the whole attic was turned into a great pigeon-house. He and his wife lived together roughly, with no warmth, no refinement, no touch of beauty anywhere, except that she was beautiful. He was a blustering, impetuous man, she was rather cold in her soul, did not care about anything very much, was rather capable and close with money. And she had a common accent in her speech. He outdid her a thousand times in coarse language, and yet that cold twang in her voice tortured him with shame that he stamped down in bullying and in becoming more violent in his own speech.

Only his dogs adored him, and to them, and to his pigeons, he talked with rough, yet curiously tender caresses while they leaped and fluttered for joy.

After he and his wife had been married for seven years a little girl was born to them, then later, another. But the husband and wife drew no nearer together. She had an affection for her children almost like a cool governess. He had an emotional man's fear of sentiment, which helped to nip his wife from putting out any shoots. He treated his children roughly, and pretended to think it a good job when one was adopted by a well-to-do maternal aunt. But in his soul he hated his wife that she could give away one of his children. For after her cool fashion, she loved him. With a chaos of a man such as he, she had no chance of being anything but cold and hard, poor thing. For she did love him.

In the end he fell absurdly and violently in love with a rather sentimental young woman who read Browning. He made his wife an allowance and established a new ménage with the young lady, shortly after emigrating with her to Australia. Meanwhile his wife had gone to live with a publican, a widower, with whom she had had one of those curious, tacit understandings of which quiet women are capable, something like an arrangement for provision in the future.

This was as much as the nephew knew. He sat beside his uncle, wondering how things stood at the present. They raced lightly out past the cemetery and along the boulevard, then turned into the rather grimy country. The mud flew out on either side, there was a fine mist of rain which blew in their faces. Berry covered himself up.

In the lanes the high hedges shone black with rain. The silvery grey sky, faintly dappled, spread wide over the low, green land. The elder man glanced fiercely up the road, then turned his red face to his nephew.

'And how're you going on, lad?' he said loudly. Berry noticed that his uncle was slightly uneasy of him. It made him also uncomfortable. The elder man had evidently something pressing on his soul.

'Who are you living with in town?' asked the nephew. 'Have you gone back to Aunt Maud?'

'No,' barked the uncle. 'She wouldn't have me. I offered to—I want to—but she wouldn't.'

'You're alone, then?'

'No, I'm not alone.'

He turned and glared with his fierce blue eyes at his nephew, but said no more for some time. The car ran on through the mud, under the wet wall of the park.

'That other devil tried to poison me,' suddenly shouted the elder man. 'The one I went to Australia with.' At which, in spite of himself, the younger smiled in secret.

'How was that?' he asked.

'Wanted to get rid of me. She got in with another fellow on the ship.... By Jove, I was bad.'

'Where?—on the ship?'

'No,' bellowed the other. 'No. That was in Wellington, New Zealand. I was bad, and got lower an' lower—couldn't think what was up. I could hardly crawl about. As certain as I'm here, she was poisoning me, to get to th' other chap—I'm certain of it.'

'And what did you do?'

'I cleared out—went to Sydney—'

'And left her?'

'Yes, I thought begod, I'd better clear out if I wanted to live.'

'And you were all right in Sydney?'

'Better in no time—I *know* she was putting poison in my coffee.'

'Hm!'

There was a glum silence. The driver stared at the road ahead, fixedly, managing the car as if it were a live thing. The nephew felt that his uncle was afraid, quite stupefied with fear, fear of life, of death, of himself.

'You're in rooms, then?' asked the nephew.

'No, I'm in a house of my own,' said the uncle defiantly, 'wi' th' best little woman in th' Midlands. She's a marvel.—Why don't you come an' see us?'

'I will. Who is she?'

'Oh, she's a good girl—a beautiful little thing. I was clean gone on her first time I saw her. An' she was on me. Her mother lives with us—respectable girl, none o' your....'

'And how old is she?'

'—how old is she?—she's twenty-one.'

'Poor thing.'

'*She's* right enough.'

'You'd marry her—getting a divorce—?'

'I shall marry her.'

There was a little antagonism between the two men.

'Where's Aunt Maud?' asked the younger.

'She's at the Railway Arms—we passed it, just against Rollin's Mill Crossing.... They sent me a note this morning to go an' see her when I can spare time. She's got consumption.'

'Good Lord! Are you going?'

'Yes—'

But again Berry felt that his uncle was afraid.

The young man got through his commission in the village, had a drink with his uncle at the inn, and the two were returning home. The elder man's subject of conversation was Australia. As they drew near the town they grew silent, thinking both of the public-house. At last they saw the gates of the railway crossing were closed before them.

'Shan't you call?' asked Berry, jerking his head in the direction of the inn, which stood at the corner between two roads, its sign hanging under a bare horse-chestnut tree in front.

'I might as well. Come in an' have a drink,' said the uncle.

It had been raining all the morning, so shallow pools of water lay about. A brewer's wagon, with wet barrels and warm-smelling horses, stood near the door of the inn. Everywhere seemed silent, but for the rattle of trains at the crossing. The two men went uneasily up the steps and into the bar. The place was paddled with wet feet, empty. As the bar-man was heard approaching, the uncle asked, his usual bluster slightly hushed by fear:

'What yer goin' ta have, lad? Same as last time?'

A man entered, evidently the proprietor. He was good-looking, with a long, heavy face and quick, dark eyes. His glance at Sutton was swift, a start, a recognition, and a withdrawal, into heavy neutrality.

'How are yer, Dan?' he said, scarcely troubling to speak.

'Are yer, George?' replied Sutton, hanging back. 'My nephew, Dan Berry. Give us Red Seal, George.'

The publican nodded to the younger man, and set the glasses on the bar. He pushed forward the two glasses, then leaned back in the dark corner behind the door, his arms folded, evidently preferring to get back from the watchful eyes of the nephew.

'—'s luck,' said Sutton.

The publican nodded in acknowledgement. Sutton and his nephew drank.

'Why the hell don't you get that road mended in Cinder Hill—,' said Sutton fiercely, pushing back his driver's cap and showing his short-cut, bristling hair.

'They can't find it in their hearts to pull it up,' replied the publican, laconically.

'Find in their hearts! They want settin' in barrows an' runnin' up an' down it till they cried for mercy.'

Sutton put down his glass. The publican renewed it with a sure hand, at ease in whatsoever he did. Then he leaned back against the bar. He wore no coat. He stood with arms folded, his chin on his chest, his long moustache hanging. His back was round and slack, so that the lower part of his abdomen stuck forward, though he was not stout. His cheek was healthy, brown-red, and he was muscular. Yet there was about him this physical slackness, a reluctance in his slow, sure movements. His eyes were keen under his dark brows, but reluctant also, as if he were gloomily apathetic.

There was a halt. The publican evidently would say nothing. Berry looked at the mahogany bar-counter, slopped with beer, at the whisky-bottles on the shelves. Sutton, his cap pushed back, showing a white brow above a weather-reddened face, rubbed his cropped hair uneasily.

The publican glanced round suddenly. It seemed that only his dark eyes moved.

'Going up?' he asked.

And something, perhaps his eyes, indicated the unseen bed-chamber.

'Ay—that's what I came for,' replied Sutton, shifting nervously from one foot to the other. 'She's been asking for me?'

'This morning,' replied the publican, neutral.

Then he put up a flap of the bar, and turned away through the dark doorway behind.

Sutton, pulling off his cap, showing a round, short-cropped head which now was ducked forward, followed after him, the buttons holding the strap of his great-coat behind glittering for a moment.

They climbed the dark stairs, the husband placing his feet carefully, because of his big boots. Then he followed down the passage, trying vaguely to keep a grip on his bowels, which seemed to be melting away, and definitely wishing for a neat brandy. The publican opened a door. Sutton, big and burly in his great-coat, went past him.

The bedroom seemed light and warm after the passage. There was a red eider-down on the bed. Then, making an effort, Sutton turned his eyes to see the sick woman. He met her eyes direct, dark, dilated. It was such a shock he almost started away. For a second he remained in torture, as if some invisible flame were playing on him to reduce his bones and fuse him down. Then he saw the sharp white edge of her jaw, and the black hair beside the hollow cheek. With a start he went towards the bed.

'Hello, Maud!' he said. 'Why, what ye been doin'?'

The publican stood at the window with his back to the bed. The husband, like one condemned but on the point of starting away, stood by the bedside staring in horror at his wife, whose dilated grey eyes, nearly all black now, watched him wearily, as if she were looking at something a long way off.

Going exceedingly pale, he jerked up his head and stared at the wall over the pillows. There was a little coloured picture of a bird perched on a bell, and a nest among ivy leaves beneath. It appealed to him, made him wonder, roused a feeling of childish magic in him. They were wonderfully fresh, green ivy leaves, and nobody had seen the nest among them save him.

Then suddenly he looked down again at the face on the bed, to try and recognize it. He knew the white brow and the beautiful clear eyebrows. That was his wife, with whom he had passed his youth, flesh of his flesh, his, himself. Then those tired eyes, which met his again from a long way off, disturbed him until he did not know where he was. Only the sunken cheeks, and the mouth that seemed to protrude now were foreign to him, and filled him with horror. It seemed he lost his identity. He was the young husband of the woman with the clear brows; he was the married man fighting with her whose eyes watched him, a little indifferently, from a long way off; and he was a child in horror of that protruding mouth.

There came a crackling sound of her voice. He knew she had consumption of the throat, and braced himself hard to bear the noise.

'What was it, Maud?' he asked in panic.

Then the broken, crackling voice came again. He was too terrified of the sound of it to hear what was said. There was a pause.

'You'll take Winnie?' the publican's voice interpreted from the window.

'Don't you bother, Maud, I'll take her,' he said, stupefying his mind so as not to understand.

He looked curiously round the room. It was not a bad bedroom, light and warm. There were many medicine bottles aggregated in a corner of the washstand—and a bottle of Three Star brandy, half full. And there were also photographs of strange people on the chest of drawers. It was not a bad room.

Again he started as if he were shot. She was speaking. He bent down, but did not look at her.

'Be good to her,' she whispered.

When he realized her meaning, that he should be good to their child when the mother was gone, a blade went through his flesh.

'I'll be good to her, Maud, don't you bother,' he said, beginning to feel shaky.

He looked again at the picture of the bird. It perched cheerfully under a blue sky, with robust, jolly ivy leaves near. He was gathering his courage to depart. He looked down, but struggled hard not to take in the sight of his wife's face.

'I s'll come again, Maud,' he said. 'I hope you'll go on all right. Is there anything as you want?'

There was an almost imperceptible shake of the head from the sick woman, making his heart melt swiftly again. Then, dragging his limbs, he got out of the room and down the stairs.

The landlord came after him.

'I'll let you know if anything happens,' the publican said, still laconic, but with his eyes dark and swift.

'Ay, a' right,' said Button blindly. He looked round for his cap, which he had all the time in his hand. Then he got out of doors.

In a moment the uncle and nephew were in the car jolting on the level crossing. The elder man seemed as if something tight in his brain made him open his eyes wide, and stare. He held the steering wheel firmly. He knew he could steer accurately, to a hair's breadth. Glaring fixedly ahead, he let the car go, till it bounded over the uneven road. There were three coal-carts in a string. In an instant the car grazed past them, almost biting the kerb on the other side. Sutton aimed his car like a projectile, staring ahead. He did not want to know, to think, to realize, he wanted to be only the driver of that quick taxi.

The town drew near, suddenly. There were allotment-gardens with dark-purple twiggy fruit-trees and wet alleys between the hedges. Then suddenly the streets of dwelling-houses whirled close, and the car was climbing the hill, with an angry whirr,—up—up—till they rode out on to the crest and could see the tram-cars, dark-red and yellow, threading their way round the corner below, and all the traffic roaring between the shops.

'Got anywhere to go?' asked Sutton of his nephew.

'I was going to see one or two people.'

'Come an' have a bit o' dinner with us,' said the other.

Berry knew that his uncle wanted to be distracted, so that he should not think nor realize. The big man was running hard away from the horror of realization.

'All right,' Berry agreed.

The car went quickly through the town. It ran up a long street nearly into the country again. Then it pulled up at a house that stood alone, below the road.

'I s'll be back in ten minutes,' said the uncle.

The car went on to the garage. Berry stood curiously at the top of the stone stairs that led from the highroad down to the level of the house, an old stone place. The garden was dilapidated. Broken fruit-trees leaned at a sharp angle down the steep bank. Right across the dim grey atmosphere, in a kind of valley on the edge of the town, new suburb-patches showed pinkish on the dark earth. It was a kind of unresolved borderland.

Berry went down the steps. Through the broken black fence of the orchard, long grass showed yellow. The place seemed deserted. He knocked, then knocked again. An elderly woman appeared. She looked like a housekeeper. At first she said suspiciously that Mr. Sutton was not in.

'My uncle just put me down. He'll be in in ten minutes,' replied the visitor.

'Oh, are you the Mr. Berry who is related to him?' exclaimed the elderly woman. 'Come in—come in.'

She was at once kindly and a little bit servile. The young man entered. It was an old house, rather dark, and sparsely furnished. The elderly woman sat nervously on the edge of one of the chairs in a drawing-room that looked as if it were furnished from dismal relics of dismal homes, and there was a little straggling attempt at conversation. Mrs. Greenwell was evidently a working class woman unused to service or to any formality.

Presently she gathered up courage to invite her visitor into the dining-room. There from the table under the window rose a tall, slim girl with a cat in her arms. She was evidently a little more lady-like than was habitual to her, but she had a gentle, delicate, small nature. Her brown hair almost covered her ears, her dark lashes came down in shy awkwardness over her beautiful blue eyes. She shook hands in a frank way, yet she was shrinking. Evidently she was not sure how her position would affect her visitor. And yet she was assured in herself, shrinking and timid as she was.

'She must be a good deal in love with him,' thought Berry.

Both women glanced shamefacedly at the roughly laid table. Evidently they ate in a rather rough and ready fashion.

Elaine—she had this poetic name—fingered her cat timidly, not knowing what to say or to do, unable even to ask her visitor to sit down. He noticed how her skirt hung almost flat on her hips. She was young, scarce developed, a long, slender thing. Her colouring was warm and exquisite.

The elder woman bustled out to the kitchen. Berry fondled the terrier dogs that had come curiously to his heels, and glanced out of the window at the wet, deserted orchard.

This room, too, was not well furnished, and rather dark. But there was a big red fire.

'He always has fox terriers,' he said.

'Yes,' she answered, showing her teeth in a smile.

'Do you like them, too?'

'Yes'—she glanced down at the dogs. 'I like Tam better than Sally—'

Her speech always tailed off into an awkward silence.

'We've been to see Aunt Maud,' said the nephew.

Her eyes, blue and scared and shrinking, met his.

'Dan had a letter,' he explained. 'She's very bad.'

'Isn't it horrible!' she exclaimed, her face crumbling up with fear.

The old woman, evidently a hard-used, rather down-trodden workman's wife, came in with two soup-plates. She glanced anxiously to see how her daughter was progressing with the visitor.

'Mother, Dan's been to see Maud,' said Elaine, in a quiet voice full of fear and trouble.

The old woman looked up anxiously, in question.

'I think she wanted him to take the child. She's very bad, I believe,' explained Berry.

'Oh, we should take Winnie!' cried Elaine. But both women seemed uncertain, wavering in their position. Already Berry could see that his uncle had bullied them, as he bullied everybody. But they were used to unpleasant men, and seemed to keep at a distance.

'Will you have some soup?' asked the mother, humbly.

She evidently did the work. The daughter was to be a lady, more or less, always dressed and nice for when Sutton came in.

They heard him heavily running down the steps outside. The dogs got up. Elaine seemed to forget the visitor. It was as if she came into life. Yet she was nervous and afraid. The mother stood as if ready to exculpate herself.

Sutton burst open the door. Big, blustering, wet in his immense grey coat, he came into the dining-room.

'Hello!' he said to his nephew, 'making yourself at home?'

'Oh, yes,' replied Berry.

'Hello, Jack,' he said to the girl. 'Got owt to grizzle about?'

'What for?' she asked, in a clear, half-challenging voice, that had that peculiar twang, almost petulant, so female and so attractive. Yet she was defiant like a boy.

'It's a wonder if you haven't,' growled Sutton. And, with a really intimate movement, he stooped down and fondled his dogs, though paying no attention to them. Then he stood up, and remained with feet apart on the hearthrug, his head ducked forward, watching the girl. He seemed abstracted, as if he could only watch her. His great-coat hung open, so that she could see his figure, simple and human in the great husk of cloth. She stood nervously with her hands behind her, glancing at him, unable to see anything else. And he was scarcely conscious but of her. His eyes were still strained and staring, and as they followed the girl, when, long-limbed and languid, she moved away, it was as if he saw in her something impersonal, the female, not the woman.

'Had your dinner?' he asked.

'We were just going to have it,' she replied, with the same curious little vibration in her voice, like the twang of a string.

The mother entered, bringing a saucepan from which she ladled soup into three plates.

'Sit down, lad,' said Sutton. 'You sit down, Jack, an' give me mine here.'

'Oh, aren't you coming to table?' she complained.

'No, I tell you,' he snarled, almost pretending to be disagreeable. But she was slightly afraid even of the pretence, which pleased and relieved him. He stood on the hearthrug eating his soup noisily.

'Aren't you going to take your coat off?' she said. 'It's filling the place full of steam.'

He did not answer, but, with his head bent forward over the plate, he ate his soup hastily, to get it done with. When he put down his empty plate, she rose and went to him.

'Do take your coat off, Dan,' she said, and she took hold of the breast of his coat, trying to push it back over his shoulder. But she could not. Only the stare in his eyes changed to a glare as her hand moved over his shoulder. He looked down into her eyes. She became pale, rather frightened-looking, and she turned her face away, and it was drawn slightly with love and fear and misery. She tried again to put off his coat, her thin wrists pulling at it. He stood solidly planted, and did not look at her, but stared straight in front. She was playing with passion, afraid of it, and really wretched because it left her, the person, out of count. Yet she continued. And there came into his bearing, into his eyes, the curious smile of passion, pushing away even the death-horror. It was life stronger than death in him. She stood close to his breast. Their eyes met, and she was carried away.

'Take your coat off, Dan,' she said coaxingly, in a low tone meant for no one but him. And she slid her hands on his shoulder, and he yielded, so that the coat was pushed back. She had flushed, and her eyes had grown very bright. She got hold of the cuff of his coat. Gently, he eased himself, so that she drew it off. Then he stood in a thin suit, which revealed his vigorous, almost mature form.

'What a weight!' she exclaimed, in a peculiar penetrating voice, as she went out hugging the overcoat. In a moment she came back.

He stood still in the same position, a frown over his fiercely staring eyes. The pain, the fear, the horror in his breast were all burning away in the new, fiercest flame of passion.

'Get your dinner,' he said roughly to her.

'I've had all I want,' she said. 'You come an' have yours.'

He looked at the table as if he found it difficult to see things.

'I want no more,' he said.

She stood close to his chest. She wanted to touch him and to comfort him. There was something about him now that fascinated her. Berry felt slightly ashamed that she seemed to ignore the presence of others in the room.

The mother came in. She glanced at Sutton, standing planted on the hearthrug, his head ducked, the heavy frown hiding his eyes. There was a peculiar braced intensity about him that made the elder woman afraid. Suddenly he jerked his head round to his nephew.

'Get on wi' your dinner, lad,' he said, and he went to the door. The dogs, which had continually lain down and got up again, uneasy, now rose and watched. The girl went after him, saying, clearly:

'What did you want, Dan?'

Her slim, quick figure was gone, the door was closed behind her.

There was silence. The mother, still more slave-like in her movement, sat down in a low chair. Berry drank some beer.

'That girl will leave him,' he said to himself. 'She'll hate him like poison. And serve him right. Then she'll go off with somebody else.'

And she did.

THE HORSE DEALER'S DAUGHTER

'Well, Mabel, and what are you going to do with yourself?' asked Joe, with foolish flippancy. He felt quite safe himself. Without listening for an answer, he turned aside, worked a grain of tobacco to the tip of his tongue, and spat it out. He did not care about anything, since he felt safe himself.

The three brothers and the sister sat round the desolate breakfast table, attempting some sort of desultory consultation. The morning's post had given the final tap to the family fortunes, and all was over. The dreary dining-room itself, with its heavy mahogany furniture, looked as if it were waiting to be done away with.

But the consultation amounted to nothing. There was a strange air of ineffectuality about the three men, as they sprawled at table, smoking and reflecting vaguely on their own condition. The girl was alone, a rather short, sullen-looking young woman of twenty-seven. She did not share the same life as her brothers. She would have been good-looking, save for the impassive fixity of her face, 'bull-dog', as her brothers called it.

There was a confused tramping of horses' feet outside. The three men all sprawled round in their chairs to watch. Beyond the dark holly-bushes that separated the strip of lawn from the highroad, they could see a cavalcade of shire horses swinging out of their own yard, being taken for exercise. This was the last time. These were the last horses that would go through their hands. The young men watched with critical, callous look. They were all frightened at the collapse of their lives, and the sense of disaster in which they were involved left them no inner freedom.

Yet they were three fine, well-set fellows enough. Joe, the eldest, was a man of thirty-three, broad and handsome in a hot, flushed way. His face was red, he twisted his black moustache over a thick finger, his eyes were shallow and restless. He had a sensual way of uncovering his teeth when he laughed, and his bearing was stupid. Now he watched the horses with a glazed look of helplessness in his eyes, a certain stupor of downfall.

The great draught-horses swung past. They were tied head to tail, four of them, and they heaved along to where a lane branched off from the highroad, planting their great hoofs floutingly in the fine black mud, swinging their great rounded haunches sumptuously, and trotting a few sudden steps as they were led into the lane, round the corner. Every movement showed a massive, slumbrous strength, and a stupidity which held them in subjection. The groom at the head looked back, jerking the leading rope. And the calvalcade moved out of sight up the lane, the tail of the last horse, bobbed up tight and stiff, held out taut from the swinging great haunches as they rocked behind the hedges in a motion-like sleep.

Joe watched with glazed hopeless eyes. The horses were almost like his own body to him. He felt he was done for now. Luckily he was engaged to a woman as old as himself, and therefore her father, who was steward of a neighbouring estate, would provide him with a job. He would marry and go into harness. His life was over, he would be a subject animal now.

He turned uneasily aside, the retreating steps of the horses echoing in his ears. Then, with foolish restlessness, he reached for the scraps of bacon-rind from the plates, and making a faint whistling sound, flung them to the terrier that lay against the fender. He watched the dog swallow them, and waited till the creature looked into his eyes. Then a faint grin came on his face, and in a high, foolish voice he said:

'You won't get much more bacon, shall you, you little b——?'

The dog faintly and dismally wagged its tail, then lowered his haunches, circled round, and lay down again.

There was another helpless silence at the table. Joe sprawled uneasily in his seat, not willing to go till the family conclave was dissolved. Fred Henry, the second brother, was erect, clean-limbed, alert. He had watched the passing of the horses with more *sang-froid*. If he was an animal, like Joe, he was an animal which controls, not one which is controlled. He was master of any horse, and he carried himself with a well-tempered air of mastery. But he was not master of the situations of life. He pushed his coarse brown moustache upwards, off his lip, and glanced irritably at his sister, who sat impassive and inscrutable.

'You'll go and stop with Lucy for a bit, shan't you?' he asked. The girl did not answer.

'I don't see what else you can do,' persisted Fred Henry.

'Go as a skivvy,' Joe interpolated laconically.

The girl did not move a muscle.

'If I was her, I should go in for training for a nurse,' said Malcolm, the youngest of them all. He was the baby of the family, a young man of twenty-two, with a fresh, jaunty *museau*.

But Mabel did not take any notice of him. They had talked at her and round her for so many years, that she hardly heard them at all.

The marble clock on the mantel-piece softly chimed the half-hour, the dog rose uneasily from the hearthrug and looked at the party at the breakfast table. But still they

226

sat on in ineffectual conclave.

'Oh, all right,' said Joe suddenly, *à propos* of nothing. 'I'll get a move on.'

He pushed back his chair, straddled his knees with a downward jerk, to get them free, in horsy fashion, and went to the fire. Still he did not go out of the room; he was curious to know what the others would do or say. He began to charge his pipe, looking down at the dog and saying, in a high, affected voice:

'Going wi' me? Going wi' me are ter? Tha'rt goin' further than tha counts on just now, dost hear?'

The dog faintly wagged its tail, the man stuck out his jaw and covered his pipe with his hands, and puffed intently, losing himself in the tobacco, looking down all the while at the dog with an absent brown eye. The dog looked up at him in mournful distrust. Joe stood with his knees stuck out, in real horsy fashion.

'Have you had a letter from Lucy?' Fred Henry asked of his sister.

'Last week,' came the neutral reply.

'And what does she say?'

There was no answer.

'Does she *ask* you to go and stop there?' persisted Fred Henry.

'She says I can if I like.'

'Well, then, you'd better. Tell her you'll come on Monday.'

This was received in silence.

'That's what you'll do then, is it?' said Fred Henry, in some exasperation.

But she made no answer. There was a silence of futility and irritation in the room. Malcolm grinned fatuously.

'You'll have to make up your mind between now and next Wednesday,' said Joe loudly, 'or else find yourself lodgings on the kerbstone.'

The face of the young woman darkened, but she sat on immutable.

'Here's Jack Fergusson!' exclaimed Malcolm, who was looking aimlessly out of the window.

'Where?' exclaimed Joe, loudly.

'Just gone past.'

'Coming in?'

Malcolm craned his neck to see the gate.

'Yes,' he said.

There was a silence. Mabel sat on like one condemned, at the head of the table. Then a whistle was heard from the kitchen. The dog got up and barked sharply. Joe opened the door and shouted:

'Come on.'

After a moment a young man entered. He was muffled up in overcoat and a purple woollen scarf, and his tweed cap, which he did not remove, was pulled down on his head. He was of medium height, his face was rather long and pale, his eyes looked tired.

'Hello, Jack! Well, Jack!' exclaimed Malcolm and Joe. Fred Henry merely said, 'Jack.'

'What's doing?' asked the newcomer, evidently addressing Fred Henry.

'Same. We've got to be out by Wednesday.—Got a cold?'

'I have—got it bad, too.'

'Why don't you stop in?'

'*Me* stop in? When I can't stand on my legs, perhaps I shall have a chance.' The young man spoke huskily. He had a slight Scotch accent.

'It's a knock-out, isn't it,' said Joe, boisterously, 'if a doctor goes round croaking with a cold. Looks bad for the patients, doesn't it?'

The young doctor looked at him slowly.

'Anything the matter with *you*, then?' he asked sarcastically.

'Not as I know of. Damn your eyes, I hope not. Why?'

'I thought you were very concerned about the patients, wondered if you might be one yourself.'

'Damn it, no, I've never been patient to no flaming doctor, and hope I never shall be,' returned Joe.

At this point Mabel rose from the table, and they all seemed to become aware of her existence. She began putting the dishes together. The young doctor looked at her, but did not address her. He had not greeted her. She went out of the room with the tray, her face impassive and unchanged.

'When are you off then, all of you?' asked the doctor.

'I'm catching the eleven-forty,' replied Malcolm. 'Are you goin' down wi' th' trap, Joe?'

'Yes, I've told you I'm going down wi' th' trap, haven't I?'

'We'd better be getting her in then.—So long, Jack, if I don't see you before I go,' said Malcolm, shaking hands.

He went out, followed by Joe, who seemed to have his tail between his legs.

'Well, this is the devil's own,' exclaimed the doctor, when he was left alone with Fred Henry. 'Going before Wednesday, are you?'

'That's the orders,' replied the other.

'Where, to Northampton?'

'That's it.'

'The devil!' exclaimed Fergusson, with quiet chagrin.

And there was silence between the two.

'All settled up, are you?' asked Fergusson.

'About.'

There was another pause.

'Well, I shall miss yer, Freddy, boy,' said the young doctor.

'And I shall miss thee, Jack,' returned the other.

'Miss you like hell,' mused the doctor.

Fred Henry turned aside. There was nothing to say. Mabel came in again, to finish clearing the table.

'What are *you* going to do, then, Miss Pervin?' asked Fergusson. 'Going to your sister's, are you?'

Mabel looked at him with her steady, dangerous eyes, that always made him uncomfortable, unsettling his superficial ease.

'No,' she said.

'Well, what in the name of fortune *are* you going to do? Say what you mean to do,' cried Fred Henry, with futile intensity.

But she only averted her head, and continued her work. She folded the white table-cloth, and put on the chenille cloth.

'The sulkiest bitch that ever trod!' muttered her brother.

But she finished her task with perfectly impassive face, the young doctor watching her interestedly all the while. Then she went out.

Fred Henry stared after her, clenching his lips, his blue eyes fixing in sharp

228

antagonism, as he made a grimace of sour exasperation.

'You could bray her into bits, and that's all you'd get out of her,' he said, in a small, narrowed tone.

The doctor smiled faintly.

'What's she *going* to do, then?' he asked.

'Strike me if I know!' returned the other.

There was a pause. Then the doctor stirred.

'I'll be seeing you tonight, shall I?' he said to his friend.

'Ay—where's it to be? Are we going over to Jessdale?'

'I don't know. I've got such a cold on me. I'll come round to the Moon and Stars, anyway.'

'Let Lizzie and May miss their night for once, eh?'

'That's it—if I feel as I do now.'

'All's one—'.

The two young men went through the passage and down to the back door together. The house was large, but it was servantless now, and desolate. At the back was a small bricked house-yard, and beyond that a big square, gravelled fine and red, and having stables on two sides. Sloping, dank, winter-dark fields stretched away on the open sides.

But the stables were empty. Joseph Pervin, the father of the family, had been a man of no education, who had become a fairly large horse dealer. The stables had been full of horses, there was a great turmoil and come-and-go of horses and of dealers and grooms. Then the kitchen was full of servants. But of late things had declined. The old man had married a second time, to retrieve his fortunes. Now he was dead and everything was gone to the dogs, there was nothing but debt and threatening.

For months, Mabel had been servantless in the big house, keeping the home together in penury for her ineffectual brothers. She had kept house for ten years. But previously, it was with unstinted means. Then, however brutal and coarse everything was, the sense of money had kept her proud, confident. The men might be foul-mouthed, the women in the kitchen might have bad reputations, her brothers might have illegitimate children. But so long as there was money, the girl felt herself established, and brutally proud, reserved.

No company came to the house, save dealers and coarse men. Mabel had no associates of her own sex, after her sister went away. But she did not mind. She went regularly to church, she attended to her father. And she lived in the memory of her mother, who had died when she was fourteen, and whom she had loved. She had loved her father, too, in a different way, depending upon him, and feeling secure in him, until at the age of fifty-four he married again. And then she had set hard against him. Now he had died and left them all hopelessly in debt.

She had suffered badly during the period of poverty. Nothing, however, could shake the curious sullen, animal pride that dominated each member of the family. Now, for Mabel, the end had come. Still she would not cast about her. She would follow her own way just the same. She would always hold the keys of her own situation. Mindless and persistent, she endured from day to day. Why should she think? Why should she answer anybody? It was enough that this was the end, and there was no way out. She need not pass any more darkly along the main street of the small town, avoiding every eye. She need not demean herself any more, going into the shops and buying the cheapest food. This was at an end. She thought of nobody, not even of herself. Mindless and persistent, she seemed in a sort of ecstasy to be coming nearer to her fulfilment, her own glorification, approaching her dead mother, who was glorified.

In the afternoon she took a little bag, with shears and sponge and a small scrubbing brush, and went out. It was a grey, wintry day, with saddened, dark-green fields and an atmosphere blackened by the smoke of foundries not far off. She went quickly, darkly along the causeway, heeding nobody, through the town to the churchyard.

There she always felt secure, as if no one could see her, although as a matter of fact she was exposed to the stare of everyone who passed along under the churchyard wall. Nevertheless, once under the shadow of the great looming church, among the graves, she felt immune from the world, reserved within the thick churchyard wall as in another country. "rapture" - Odour p. 128

Carefully she clipped the grass from the grave, and arranged the pinky-white, small chrysanthemums in the tin cross. When this was done, she took an empty jar from a neighbouring grave, brought water, and carefully, most scrupulously sponged the marble headstone and the coping-stone.

It gave her sincere satisfaction to do this. She felt in immediate contact with the world of her mother. She took minute pains, went through the park in a state bordering on pure happiness, as if in performing this task she came into a subtle, intimate connection with her mother. For the life she followed here in the world was far less real than the world of death she inherited from her mother.

The doctor's house was just by the church. Fergusson, being a mere hired assistant, was slave to the countryside. As he hurried now to attend to the outpatients in the surgery, glancing across the graveyard with his quick eye, he saw the girl at her task at the grave. She seemed so intent and remote, it was like looking into another world. Some mystical element was touched in him. He slowed down as he walked, watching her as if spell-bound. connection

She lifted her eyes, feeling him looking. Their eyes met. And each looked again at once, each feeling, in some way, found out by the other. He lifted his cap and passed on down the road. There remained distinct in his consciousness, like a vision, the memory of her face, lifted from the tombstone in the churchyard, and looking at him with slow, large, portentous eyes. It *was* portentous, her face. It seemed to mesmerize him. There was a heavy power in her eyes which laid hold of his whole being, as if he had drunk some powerful drug. He had been feeling weak and done before. Now the life came back into him, he felt delivered from his own fretted, daily self. eye sex

He finished his duties at the surgery as quickly as might be, hastily filling up the bottles of the waiting people with cheap drugs. Then, in perpetual haste, he set off again to visit several cases in another part of his round, before teatime. At all times he preferred to walk, if he could, but particularly when he was not well. He fancied the motion restored him.

The afternoon was falling. It was grey, deadened, and wintry, with a slow, moist, heavy coldness sinking in and deadening all the faculties. But why should he think or notice? He hastily climbed the hill and turned across the dark-green fields, following the black cinder-track. In the distance, across a shallow dip in the country, the small town was clustered like smouldering ash, a tower, a spire, a heap of low, raw, extinct houses. And on the nearest fringe of the town, sloping into the dip, was Oldmeadow, the Pervins' house. He could see the stables and the outbuildings distinctly, as they lay towards him on the slope. Well, he would not go there many more times! Another resource would be lost to him, another place gone: the only company he cared for in the alien, ugly little town he was losing. Nothing but work, drudgery, constant hastening from dwelling to dwelling among the colliers and the iron-workers. It wore him out, but at the same time he had a craving for it. It was a stimulant to him to be in the homes of the working people, moving as it were through the innermost body of their life. His nerves were excited and gratified. He could come so near, into the very lives of the rough, inarticulate, powerfully emotional men and women. He grumbled, he said he hated the hellish hole. But as a matter of fact it excited him, the contact with the rough, strongly-feeling people was a stimulant applied direct to his nerves.

Below Oldmeadow, in the green, shallow, soddened hollow of fields, lay a square, deep pond. Roving across the landscape, the doctor's quick eye detected a figure in black passing through the gate of the field, down towards the pond. He looked again. It would be Mabel Pervin. His mind suddenly became alive and attentive.

Why was she going down there? He pulled up on the path on the slope above, and stood staring. He could just make sure of the small black figure moving in the hollow of the failing day. He seemed to see her in the midst of such obscurity, that he was like a clairvoyant, seeing rather with the mind's eye than with ordinary sight. Yet he could see her positively enough, whilst he kept his eye attentive. He felt, if he looked away from her, in the thick, ugly falling dusk, he would lose her altogether.

He followed her minutely as she moved, direct and intent, like something transmitted rather than stirring in voluntary activity, straight down the field towards the pond. There she stood on the bank for a moment. She never raised her head. Then she waded slowly into the water.

He stood motionless as the small black figure walked slowly and deliberately towards the centre of the pond, very slowly, gradually moving deeper into the motionless water, and still moving forward as the water got up to her breast. Then he could see her no more in the dusk of the dead afternoon.

'There!' he exclaimed. 'Would you believe it?'

And he hastened straight down, running over the wet, soddened fields, pushing through the hedges, down into the depression of callous wintry obscurity. It took him several minutes to come to the pond. He stood on the bank, breathing heavily. He could see nothing. His eyes seemed to penetrate the dead water. Yes, perhaps that was the dark shadow of her black clothing beneath the surface of the water.

He slowly ventured into the pond. The bottom was deep, soft clay, he sank in, and the water clasped dead cold round his legs. As he stirred he could smell the cold, rotten clay that fouled up into the water. It was objectionable in his lungs. Still, repelled and yet not heeding, he moved deeper into the pond. The cold water rose over his thighs, over his loins, upon his abdomen. The lower part of his body was all sunk in the hideous cold element. And the bottom was so deeply soft and uncertain, he was afraid of pitching with his mouth underneath. He could not swim, and was afraid.

He crouched a little, spreading his hands under the water and moving them round, trying to feel for her. The dead cold pond swayed upon his chest. He moved again, a little deeper, and again, with his hands underneath, he felt all around under the water. And he touched her clothing. But it evaded his fingers. He made a desperate effort to grasp it.

And so doing he lost his balance and went under, horribly, suffocating in the foul earthy water, struggling madly for a few moments. At last, after what seemed an eternity, he got his footing, rose again into the air and looked around. He gasped, and knew he was in the world. Then he looked at the water. She had risen near him. He grasped her clothing, and drawing her nearer, turned to take his way to land again.

He went very slowly, carefully, absorbed in the slow progress. He rose higher, climbing out of the pond. The water was now only about his legs; he was thankful, full of relief to be out of the clutches of the pond. He lifted her and staggered on to the bank, out of the horror of wet, grey clay.

He laid her down on the bank. She was quite unconscious and running with water. He made the water come from her mouth, he worked to restore her. He did not have to work very long before he could feel the breathing begin again in her; she was breathing naturally. He worked a little longer. He could feel her live beneath his hands; she was coming back. He wiped her face, wrapped her in his overcoat, looked round into the dim, dark-grey world, then lifted her and staggered down the bank and across the fields.

It seemed an unthinkably long way, and his burden so heavy he felt he would never get to the house. But at last he was in the stable-yard, and then in the house-yard. He opened the door and went into the house. In the kitchen he laid her down on the hearthrug, and called. The house was empty. But the fire was burning in the grate.

Then again he kneeled to attend to her. She was breathing regularly, her eyes were wide open and as if conscious, but there seemed something missing in her look. She was conscious in herself, but unconscious of her surroundings.

He ran upstairs, took blankets from a bed, and put them before the fire to warm. Then he removed her saturated, earthy-smelling clothing, rubbed her dry with a towel, and wrapped her naked in the blankets. Then he went into the dining-room, to look for spirits. There was a little whisky. He drank a gulp himself, and put some into her mouth.

The effect was instantaneous. She looked full into his face, as if she had been seeing him for some time, and yet had only just become conscious of him.

'Dr. Fergusson?' she said.

'What?' he answered.

He was divesting himself of his coat, intending to find some dry clothing upstairs. He could not bear the smell of the dead, clayey water, and he was mortally afraid for his own health.

'What did I do?' she asked.

'Walked into the pond,' he replied. He had begun to shudder like one sick, and could hardly attend to her. Her eyes remained full on him, he seemed to be going dark in his mind, looking back at her helplessly. The shuddering became quieter in him, his life came back in him, dark and unknowing, but strong again.

'Was I out of my mind?' she asked, while her eyes were fixed on him all the time.

'Maybe, for the moment,' he replied. He felt quiet, because his strength had come back. The strange fretful strain had left him.

'Am I out of my mind now?' she asked.

'Are you?' he reflected a moment. 'No,' he answered truthfully, 'I don't see that you are.' He turned his face aside. He was afraid now, because he felt dazed, and felt dimly that her power was stronger than his, in this issue. And she continued to look at him fixedly all the time. 'Can you tell me where I shall find some dry things to put on?' he asked.

'Did you dive into the pond for me?' she asked.

'No,' he answered. 'I walked in. But I went in overhead as well.'

There was silence for a moment. He hesitated. He very much wanted to go upstairs to get into dry clothing. But there was another desire in him. And she seemed to hold him. His will seemed to have gone to sleep, and left him, standing there slack before her. But he felt warm inside himself. He did not shudder at all, though his clothes were sodden on him.

'Why did you?' she asked.

'Because I didn't want you to do such a foolish thing,' he said. *seduce*

'It wasn't foolish,' she said, still gazing at him as she lay on the floor, with a sofa cushion under her head. 'It was the right thing to do. *I* knew best, then.'

'I'll go and shift these wet things,' he said. But still he had not the power to move out of her presence, until she sent him. It was as if she had the life of his body in her hands, and he could not extricate himself. Or perhaps he did not want to.

Suddenly she sat up. Then she became aware of her own immediate condition. She felt the blankets about her, she knew her own limbs. For a moment it seemed as if her reason were going. She looked round, with wild eye, as if seeking something. He stood still with fear. She saw her clothing lying scattered.

'Who undressed me?' she asked, her eyes resting full and inevitable on his face.

'I did,' he replied, 'to bring you round.'

For some moments she sat and gazed at him awfully, her lips parted.

'Do you love me then?' she asked.

He only stood and stared at her, fascinated. His soul seemed to melt.

She shuffled forward on her knees, and put her arms round him, round his legs, as he stood there, pressing her breasts against his knees and thighs, clutching him with strange, convulsive certainty, pressing his thighs against her, drawing him to her face, her throat, as she looked up at him with flaring, humble eyes, of transfiguration, triumphant in first possession.

'You love me,' she murmured, in strange transport, yearning and triumphant and confident. 'You love me. I know you love me, I know.' ? wtf

And she was passionately kissing his knees, through the wet clothing, passionately and indiscriminately kissing his knees, his legs, as if unaware of every thing.

He looked down at the tangled wet hair, the wild, bare, animal shoulders. He was amazed, bewildered, and afraid. He had never thought of loving her. He had never wanted to love her. When he rescued her and restored her, he was a doctor, and she was a patient. He had had no single personal thought of her. Nay, this introduction of the personal element was very distasteful to him, a violation of his professional honour. It was horrible to have her there embracing his knees. It was horrible. He revolted from it, violently. And yet—and yet—he had not the power to break away.

She looked at him again, with the same supplication of powerful love, and that same transcendent, frightening light of triumph. In view of the delicate flame which seemed to come from her face like a light, he was powerless. And yet he had never intended to love her. He had never intended. And something stubborn in him could not give way.

'You love me,' she repeated, in a murmur of deep, rhapsodic assurance. 'You love me.'

Her hands were drawing him, drawing him down to her. He was afraid, even a little horrified. For he had, really, no intention of loving her. Yet her hands were drawing him towards her. He put out his hand quickly to steady himself, and grasped her bare shoulder. A flame seemed to burn the hand that grasped her soft shoulder. He had no intention of loving her: his whole will was against his yielding. It was horrible. And yet wonderful was the touch of her shoulders, beautiful the shining of her face. Was she perhaps mad? He had a horror of yielding to her. Yet something in him ached also.

He had been staring away at the door, away from her. But his hand remained on her shoulder. She had gone suddenly very still. He looked down at her. Her eyes were now wide with fear, with doubt, the light was dying from her face, a shadow of terrible greyness was returning. He could not bear the touch of her eyes' question upon him, and the look of death behind the question.

With an inward groan he gave way, and let his heart yield towards her. A sudden gentle smile came on his face. And her eyes, which never left his face, slowly, slowly filled with tears. He watched the strange water rise in her eyes, like some slow fountain coming up. And his heart seemed to burn and melt away in his breast.

He could not bear to look at her any more. He dropped on his knees and caught her head with his arms and pressed her face against his throat. She was very still. His heart, which seemed to have broken, was burning with a kind of agony in his breast. And he felt her slow, hot tears wetting his throat. But he could not move.

He felt the hot tears wet his neck and the hollows of his neck, and he remained motionless, suspended through one of man's eternities. Only now it had become indispensable to him to have her face pressed close to him; he could never let her go again. He could never let her head go away from the close clutch of his arm. He wanted to remain like that for ever, with his heart hurting him in a pain that was also life to him. Without knowing, he was looking down on her damp, soft brown hair.

Then, as it were suddenly, he smelt the horrid stagnant smell of that water. And at the same moment she drew away from him and looked at him. Her eyes were wistful and unfathomable. He was afraid of them, and he fell to kissing her, not knowing what he was doing. He wanted her eyes not to have that terrible, wistful, unfathomable look. *development of phenomenon of falling in ♡*

When she turned her face to him again, a faint delicate flush was glowing, and there was again dawning that terrible shining of joy in her eyes, which really terrified him, and yet which he now wanted to see, because he feared the look of doubt still more.

'You love me?' she said, rather faltering.

'Yes.' The word cost him a painful effort. Not because it wasn't true. But because it was too newly true, the *saying* seemed to tear open again his newly-torn heart. And he hardly wanted it to be true, even now.

She lifted her face to him, and he bent forward and kissed her on the mouth, gently, with the one kiss that is an eternal pledge. And as he kissed her his heart strained again in his breast. He never intended to love her. But now it was over. He had crossed over the gulf to her, and all that he had left behind had shrivelled and become void. *truth*

After the kiss, her eyes again slowly filled with tears. She sat still, away from him, with her face drooped aside, and her hands folded in her lap. The tears fell very slowly. There was complete silence. He too sat there motionless and silent on the hearthrug. The strange pain of his heart that was broken seemed to consume him. That he should love her? That this was love! That he should be ripped open in this way!—Him, a doctor!— How they would all jeer if they knew!—It was agony to him to think they might know.

In the curious naked pain of the thought he looked again to her. She was sitting there drooped into a muse. He saw a tear fall, and his heart flared hot. He saw for the first time that one of her shoulders was quite uncovered, one arm bare, he could see one of her small breasts; dimly, because it had become almost dark in the room.

'Why are you crying?' he asked, in an altered voice. *?*

She looked up at him, and behind her tears the consciousness of her situation for the first time brought a dark look of shame to her eyes.

'I'm not crying, really,' she said, watching him half frightened.

He reached his hand, and softly closed it on her bare arm.

'I love you! I love you!' he said in a soft, low vibrating voice, unlike himself.

She shrank, and dropped her head. The soft, penetrating grip of his hand on her arm distressed her. She looked up at him.

"electric type touch" moments   sexual contact

'I want to go,' she said. 'I want to go and get you some dry things.'

'Why?' he said. 'I'm all right.'

'But I want to go,' she said. 'And I want you to change your things.'

He released her arm, and she wrapped herself in the blanket, looking at him rather frightened. And still she did not rise.

'Kiss me,' she said wistfully.

He kissed her, but briefly, half in anger.

Then, after a second, she rose nervously, all mixed up in the blanket. He watched her in her confusion, as she tried to extricate herself and wrap herself up so that she could walk. He watched her relentlessly, as she knew. And as she went, the blanket trailing, and as he saw a glimpse of her feet and her white leg, he tried to remember her as she was when he had wrapped her in the blanket. But then he didn't want to remember, because she had been nothing to him then, and his nature revolted from remembering her as she was when she was nothing to him.

A tumbling, muffled noise from within the dark house startled him. Then he heard her voice:—'There are clothes.' He rose and went to the foot of the stairs, and gathered up the garments she had thrown down. Then he came back to the fire, to rub himself down and dress. He grinned at his own appearance when he had finished.

The fire was sinking, so he put on coal. The house was now quite dark, save for the light of a street-lamp that shone in faintly from beyond the holly trees. He lit the gas with matches he found on the mantel-piece. Then he emptied the pockets of his own clothes, and threw all his wet things in a heap into the scullery. After which he gathered up her sodden clothes, gently, and put them in a separate heap on the copper-top in the scullery.

It was six o'clock on the clock. His own watch had stopped. He ought to go back to the surgery. He waited, and still she did not come down. So he went to the foot of the stairs and called:

'I shall have to go.'

Almost immediately he heard her coming down. She had on her best dress of black voile, and her hair was tidy, but still damp. She looked at him—and in spite of herself, smiled.

'I don't like you in those clothes,' she said.

'Do I look a sight?' he answered.

They were shy of one another.

'I'll make you some tea,' she said.

'No, I must go.'

'Must you?' And she looked at him again with the wide, strained, doubtful eyes. And again, from the pain of his breast, he knew how he loved her. He went and bent to kiss her, gently, passionately, with his heart's painful kiss.

'And my hair smells so horrible,' she murmured in distraction. 'And I'm so awful, I'm so awful! Oh, no, I'm too awful.' And she broke into bitter, heart-broken sobbing. 'You can't want to love me, I'm horrible.'

'Don't be silly, don't be silly,' he said, trying to comfort her, kissing her, holding her in his arms. 'I want you, I want to marry you, we're going to be married, quickly, quickly—to-morrow if I can.'

But she only sobbed terribly, and cried:

'I feel awful. I feel awful. I feel I'm horrible to you.'

'No, I want you, I want you,' was all he answered, blindly, with that terrible intonation which frightened her almost more than her horror lest he should *not* want her.

FANNY AND ANNIE

Flame-lurid his face as he turned among the throng of flame-lit and dark faces upon the platform. In the light of the furnace she caught sight of his drifting countenance, like a piece of floating fire. And the nostalgia, the doom of homecoming went through her veins like a drug. His eternal face, flame-lit now! The pulse and darkness of red fire from the furnace towers in the sky, lighting the desultory, industrial crowd on the wayside station, lit him and went out.

Of course he did not see her. Flame-lit and unseeing! Always the same, with his meeting eyebrows, his common cap, and his red-and-black scarf knotted round his throat. Not even a collar to meet her! The flames had sunk, there was shadow.

She opened the door of her grimy, branch-line carriage, and began to get down her bags. The porter was nowhere, of course, but there was Harry, obscure, on the outer edge of the little crowd, missing her, of course.

'Here! Harry!' she called, waving her umbrella in the twilight. He hurried forward.

'Tha's come, has ter?' he said, in a sort of cheerful welcome. She got down, rather flustered, and gave him a peck of a kiss.

'Two suit-cases!' she said.

Her soul groaned within her, as he clambered into the carriage after her bags. Up shot the fire in the twilight sky, from the great furnace behind the station. She felt the red flame go across her face. She had come back, she had come back for good. And her spirit groaned dismally. She doubted if she could bear it.

There, on the sordid little station under the furnaces, she stood, tall and distinguished, in her well-made coat and skirt and her broad grey velour hat. She held her umbrella, her bead chatelaine, and a little leather case in her grey-gloved hands, while Harry staggered out of the ugly little train with her bags.

'There's a trunk at the back,' she said in her bright voice. But she was not feeling bright. The twin black cones of the iron foundry blasted their sky-high fires into the night. The whole scene was lurid. The train waited cheerfully. It would wait another ten minutes. She knew it. It was all so deadly familiar.

Let us confess it at once. She was a lady's maid, thirty years old, come back to marry her first-love, a foundry worker: after having kept him dangling, off and on, for a dozen years. Why had she come back? Did she love him? No. She didn't pretend to. She had loved her brilliant and ambitious cousin, who had jilted her, and who had died. She had had other affairs which had come to nothing. So here she was, come back suddenly to marry her first-love, who had waited—or remained single—all these years.

'Won't a porter carry those?' she said, as Harry strode with his workman's stride down the platform towards the guard's van.

'I can manage,' he said.

And with her umbrella, her chatelaine, and her little leather case, she followed him.

The trunk was there.

'We'll get Heather's greengrocer's cart to fetch it up,' he said.

'Isn't there a cab?' said Fanny, knowing dismally enough that there wasn't.

'I'll just put it aside o' the penny-in-the-slot, and Heather's greengrocers'll fetch it about half past eight,' he said.

He seized the box by its two handles and staggered with it across the level-crossing, bumping his legs against it as he waddled. Then he dropped it by the red sweet-meats machine.

'Will it be safe there?' she said.

'Ay—safe as houses,' he answered. He returned for the two bags. Thus laden, they started to plod up the hill, under the great long black building of the foundry. She walked beside him—workman of workmen he was, trudging with that luggage. The red lights flared over the deepening darkness. From the foundry came the horrible, slow clang, clang, clang of iron, a great noise, with an interval just long enough to make it unendurable.

Compare this with the arrival at Gloucester: the carriage for her mistress, the dog-cart for herself with the luggage; the drive out past the river, the pleasant trees of the carriage-approach; and herself sitting beside Arthur, everybody so polite to her.

She had come home—for good! Her heart nearly stopped beating as she trudged up that hideous and interminable hill, beside the laden figure. What a come-down! What a come-down! She could not take it with her usual bright cheerfulness. She knew it all too well. It is easy to bear up against the unusual, but the deadly familiarity of an old stale past!

He dumped the bags down under a lamp-post, for a rest. There they stood, the two of them, in the lamplight. Passers-by stared at her, and gave good-night to Harry. Her they hardly knew, she had become a stranger.

'They're too heavy for you, let me carry one,' she said.

'They begin to weigh a bit by the time you've gone a mile,' he answered.

'Let me carry the little one,' she insisted.

'Tha can ha'e it for a minute, if ter's a mind,' he said, handing over the valise.

And thus they arrived in the streets of shops of the little ugly town on top of the hill. How everybody stared at her; my word, how they stared! And the cinema was just going in, and the queues were tailing down the road to the corner. And everybody took full stock of her. 'Night, Harry!' shouted the fellows, in an interested voice.

However, they arrived at her aunt's—a little sweet-shop in a side street. They 'pinged' the door-bell, and her aunt came running forward out of the kitchen.

'There you are, child! Dying for a cup of tea, I'm sure. How are you?'

Fanny's aunt kissed her, and it was all Fanny could do to refrain from bursting into tears, she felt so low. Perhaps it was her tea she wanted.

'You've had a drag with that luggage,' said Fanny's aunt to Harry.

'Ay—I'm not sorry to put it down,' he said, looking at his hand which was crushed and cramped by the bag handle.

Then he departed to see about Heather's greengrocery cart.

When Fanny sat at tea, her aunt, a grey-haired, fair-faced little woman, looked at her with an admiring heart, feeling bitterly sore for her. For Fanny was beautiful: tall, erect, finely coloured, with her delicately arched nose, her rich brown hair, her large lustrous grey eyes. A passionate woman—a woman to be afraid of. So proud, so inwardly violent! She came of a violent race.

It needed a woman to sympathize with her. Men had not the courage. Poor Fanny! She was such a lady, and so straight and magnificent. And yet everything seemed to do her down. Every time she seemed to be doomed to humiliation and disappointment, this handsome, brilliantly sensitive woman, with her nervous, overwrought laugh.

'So you've really come back, child?' said her aunt.

'I really have, Aunt,' said Fanny.

'Poor Harry! I'm not sure, you know, Fanny, that you're not taking a bit of an advantage of him.'

'Oh, Aunt, he's waited so long, he may as well have what he's waited for.' Fanny laughed grimly.

'Yes, child, he's waited so long, that I'm not sure it isn't a bit hard on him. You know, I *like* him, Fanny—though as you know quite well, I don't think he's good enough for you. And I think he thinks so himself, poor fellow.'

'Don't you be so sure of that, Aunt. Harry is common, but he's not humble. He wouldn't think the Queen was any too good for him, if he'd a mind to her.'

'Well—It's as well if he has a proper opinion of himself.'

'It depends what you call proper,' said Fanny. 'But he's got his good points—'

'Oh, he's a nice fellow, and I like him, I do like him. Only, as I tell you, he's not good enough for you.'

'I've made up my mind, Aunt,' said Fanny, grimly.

'Yes,' mused the aunt. 'They say all things come to him who waits—'

'More than he's bargained for, eh, Aunt?' laughed Fanny rather bitterly.

The poor aunt, this bitterness grieved her for her niece.

They were interrupted by the ping of the shop-bell, and Harry's call of 'Right!' But as he did not come in at once, Fanny, feeling solicitous for him presumably at the moment, rose and went into the shop. She saw a cart outside, and went to the door.

And the moment she stood in the doorway, she heard a woman's common vituperative voice crying from the darkness of the opposite side of the road:

'Tha'rt theer, are ter? I'll shame thee, Mester. I'll shame thee, see if I dunna.'

Startled, Fanny stared across the darkness, and saw a woman in a black bonnet go under one of the lamps up the side street.

Harry and Bill Heather had dragged the trunk off the little dray, and she retreated before them as they came up the shop step with it.

'Wheer shalt ha'e it?' asked Harry.

'Best take it upstairs,' said Fanny.

She went up first to light the gas.

When Heather had gone, and Harry was sitting down having tea and pork pie, Fanny asked:

'Who was that woman shouting?'

'Nay, I canna tell thee. To somebody, Is'd think,' replied Harry. Fanny looked at him, but asked no more.

He was a fair-haired fellow of thirty-two, with a fair moustache. He was broad in his speech, and looked like a foundry-hand, which he was. But women always liked him. There was something of a mother's lad about him—something warm and playful and really sensitive.

He had his attractions even for Fanny. What she rebelled against so bitterly was that he had no sort of ambition. He was a moulder, but of very commonplace skill. He was thirty-two years old, and hadn't saved twenty pounds. She would have to provide the money for the home. He didn't care. He just didn't care. He had no initiative at all. He had no vices—no obvious ones. But he was just indifferent, spending as he went, and not caring. Yet he did not look happy. She remembered his face in the fire-glow: something haunted, abstracted about it. As he sat there eating his pork pie, bulging his cheek out, she felt he was like a doom to her. And she raged against the doom of him. It wasn't that he was gross. His way was common, almost on purpose. But he himself wasn't really common. For instance, his food was not particularly important to him, he was not greedy.

He had a charm, too, particularly for women, with his blondness and his sensitiveness and his way of making a woman feel that she was a higher being. But Fanny knew him, knew the peculiar obstinate limitedness of him, that would nearly send her mad.

He stayed till about half past nine. She went to the door with him.

'When are you coming up?' he said, jerking his head in the direction, presumably, of his own home.

'I'll come tomorrow afternoon,' she said brightly. Between Fanny and Mrs. Goodall, his mother, there was naturally no love lost.

Again she gave him an awkward little kiss, and said good-night.

'You can't wonder, you know, child, if he doesn't seem so very keen,' said her aunt. 'It's your own fault.'

'Oh, Aunt, I couldn't stand him when he was keen. I can do with him a lot better as he is.'

The two women sat and talked far into the night. They understood each other. The aunt, too, had married as Fanny was marrying: a man who was no companion to her, a violent man, brother of Fanny's father. He was dead, Fanny's father was dead.

Poor Aunt Lizzie, she cried woefully over her bright niece, when she had gone to bed.

Fanny paid the promised visit to his people the next afternoon. Mrs. Goodall was a large woman with smooth-parted hair, a common, obstinate woman, who had spoiled her four lads and her one vixen of a married daughter. She was one of those old-fashioned powerful natures that couldn't do with looks or education or any form of showing off. She fairly hated the sound of correct English. She *thee'd* and *tha'd* her prospective daughter-in-law, and said:

'I'm none as ormin' as I look, seest ta.'

Fanny did not think her prospective mother-in-law looked at all orming, so the speech was unnecessary.

'I towd him mysen,' said Mrs. Goodall, "'Er's held back all this long, let 'er stop as 'er is. 'E'd none ha' had thee for *my* tellin'—tha hears. No, 'e's a fool, an' I know it. I says to him, 'Tha looks a man, doesn't ter, at thy age, goin' an' openin' to her when ter hears her scrat' at th' gate, after she's done gallivantin' round wherever she'd a mind. That looks rare an' soft.' But it's no use o' any talking: he answered that letter o' thine and made his own bad bargain.'

But in spite of the old woman's anger, she was also flattered at Fanny's coming back to Harry. For Mrs. Goodall was impressed by Fanny—a woman of her own match. And more than this, everybody knew that Fanny's Aunt Kate had left her two hundred pounds: this apart from the girl's savings.

So there was high tea in Princes Street when Harry came home black from work, and a rather acrid odour of cordiality, the vixen Jinny darting in to say vulgar things. Of course Jinny lived in a house whose garden end joined the paternal garden. They were a clan who stuck together, these Goodalls.

It was arranged that Fanny should come to tea again on the Sunday, and the wedding was discussed. It should take place in a fortnight's time at Morley Chapel. Morley was a hamlet on the edge of the real country, and in its little Congregational Chapel Fanny and Harry had first met.

What a creature of habit he was! He was still in the choir of Morley Chapel—not very regular. He belonged just because he had a tenor voice, and enjoyed singing. Indeed his solos were only spoilt to local fame because when he sang he handled his aitches so hopelessly.

> 'And I saw 'eaven hopened
> And be'old, a wite 'orse—'

This was one of Harry's classics, only surpassed by the fine outburst of his heaving:

> 'Hangels—hever bright an' fair-'

It was a pity, but it was inalterable. He had a good voice, and he sang with a certain lacerating fire, but his pronunciation made it all funny. And nothing could alter him.

So he was never heard save at cheap concerts and in the little, poorer chapels. The others scoffed.

Now the month was September, and Sunday was Harvest Festival at Morley Chapel, and Harry was singing solos. So that Fanny was to go to afternoon service, and come home to a grand spread of Sunday tea with him. Poor Fanny! One of the most wonderful afternoons had been a Sunday afternoon service, with her cousin Luther at her side, Harvest Festival in Morley Chapel. Harry had sung solos then—ten years ago. She remembered his pale blue tie, and the purple asters and the great vegetable marrows in which he was framed, and her cousin Luther at her side, young, clever, come down from London, where he was getting on well, learning his Latin and his French and German so brilliantly.

However, once again it was Harvest Festival at Morley Chapel, and once again, as ten years before, a soft, exquisite September day, with the last roses pink in the cottage gardens, the last dahlias crimson, the last sunflowers yellow. And again the little old chapel was a bower, with its famous sheaves of corn and corn-plaited pillars, its great bunches of grapes, dangling like tassels from the pulpit corners, its marrows and potatoes and pears and apples and damsons, its purple asters and yellow Japanese sunflowers. Just as before, the red dahlias round the pillars were dropping, weak-headed among the oats. The place was crowded and hot, the plates of tomatoes seemed balanced perilously on the gallery front, the Rev. Enderby was weirder than ever to look at, so long and emaciated and hairless.

The Rev. Enderby, probably forewarned, came and shook hands with her and welcomed her, in his broad northern, melancholy singsong before he mounted the pulpit. Fanny was handsome in a gauzy dress and a beautiful lace hat. Being a little late, she sat in a chair in the side-aisle wedged in, right in front of the chapel. Harry was in the gallery above, and she could only see him from the eyes upwards. She noticed again how his eyebrows met, blond and not very marked, over his nose. He was attractive too: physically lovable, very. If only—if only her *pride* had not suffered! She felt he dragged her down.

> 'Come, ye thankful people come,
> Raise the song of harvest-home.
> All is safely gathered in
> Ere the winter storms begin—'

Even the hymn was a falsehood, as the season had been wet, and half the crops were still out, and in a poor way.

Poor Fanny! She sang little, and looked beautiful through that inappropriate hymn. Above her stood Harry—mercifully in a dark suit and dark tie, looking almost handsome. And his lacerating, pure tenor sounded well, when the words were drowned in the general commotion. Brilliant she looked, and brilliant she felt, for she was hot and angrily miserable and inflamed with a sort of fatal despair. Because there was about him a physical attraction which she really hated, but which she could not escape from. He was the first man who had ever kissed her. And his kisses, even while she rebelled from them, had lived in her blood and sent roots down into her soul. After all this time she had come back to them. And her soul groaned, for she felt dragged down, dragged down to earth, as a bird which some dog has got down in the dust. She knew her life would be unhappy. She knew that what she was doing was fatal. Yet it was her doom. She had to come back to him.

He had to sing two solos this afternoon: one before the 'address' from the pulpit and one after. Fanny looked at him, and wondered he was not too shy to stand up there in front of all the people. But no, he was not shy. He had even a kind of assurance on his face as he looked down from the choir gallery at her: the assurance of a common man deliberately entrenched in his commonness. Oh, such a rage went through her veins as she saw the air of triumph, laconic, indifferent triumph which sat so obstinately and recklessly on his eyelids as he looked down at her. Ah, she despised him! But there he stood up in that choir gallery like Balaam's ass in front of her, and she could not get beyond him. A certain winsomeness also about him. A certain physical winsomeness, and as if his flesh were new and lovely to touch. The thorn of desire rankled bitterly in her heart.

He, it goes without saying, sang like a canary this particular afternoon, with a certain defiant passion which pleasantly crisped the blood of the congregation. Fanny felt the crisp flames go through her veins as she listened. Even the curious loud-mouthed vernacular had a certain fascination. But, oh, also, it was so repugnant. He would triumph over her, obstinately he would drag her right back into the common people: a doom, a vulgar doom.

The second performance was an anthem, in which Harry sang the solo parts. It was clumsy, but beautiful, with lovely words.

> 'They that sow in tears shall reap in joy,
> He that goeth forth and weepeth, bearing precious seed
> Shall doubtless come again with rejoicing, bringing his sheaves with him—'

'Shall doubtless come, Shall doubtless come—' softly intoned the altos—'Bringing his she-e-eaves with him,' the trebles flourished brightly, and then again began the half-wistful solo:

> 'They that sow in tears shall reap in joy—'

Yes, it was effective and moving.

But at the moment when Harry's voice sank carelessly down to his close, and the choir, standing behind him, were opening their mouths for the final triumphant outburst, a shouting female voice rose up from the body of the congregation. The organ gave one startled trump, and went silent; the choir stood transfixed.

'You look well standing there, singing in God's holy house,' came the loud, angry female shout. Everybody turned electrified. A stoutish, red-faced woman in a black bonnet was standing up denouncing the soloist. Almost fainting with shock, the congregation realized it. 'You look well, don't you, standing there singing solos in God's holy house, you, Goodall. But I said I'd shame you. You look well, bringing your young woman here with you, don't you? I'll let her know who she's dealing with. A scamp as won't take the consequences of what he's done.' The hard-faced, frenzied woman turned in the direction of Fanny. '*That's* what Harry Goodall is, if you want to know.'

And she sat down again in her seat. Fanny, startled like all the rest, had turned to look. She had gone white, and then a burning red, under the attack. She knew the woman: a Mrs. Nixon, a devil of a woman, who beat her pathetic, drunken, red-nosed second husband, Bob, and her two lanky daughters, grown-up as they were. A notorious character. Fanny turned round again, and sat motionless as eternity in her seat.

There was a minute of perfect silence and suspense. The audience was open-mouthed and dumb; the choir stood like Lot's wife; and Harry, with his music-sheet, stood there uplifted, looking down with a dumb sort of indifference on Mrs. Nixon, his face naïve and faintly mocking. Mrs. Nixon sat defiant in her seat, braving them all.

Then a rustle, like a wood when the wind suddenly catches the leaves. And then the tall, weird minister got to his feet, and in his strong, bell-like, beautiful voice—the only beautiful thing about him—he said with infinite mournful pathos:

'Let us unite in singing the last hymn on the hymn-sheet; the last hymn on the hymn-sheet, number eleven.

'Fair waved the golden corn,
In Canaan's pleasant land.'

The organ tuned up promptly. During the hymn the offertory was taken. And after the hymn, the prayer.

Mr. Enderby came from Northumberland. Like Harry, he had never been able to conquer his accent, which was very broad. He was a little simple, one of God's fools, perhaps, an odd bachelor soul, emotional, ugly, but very gentle.

'And if, O our dear Lord, beloved Jesus, there should fall a shadow of sin upon our harvest, we leave it to Thee to judge, for Thou art judge. We lift our spirits and our sorrow, Jesus, to Thee, and our mouths are dumb. O, Lord, keep us from forward speech, restrain us from foolish words and thoughts, we pray Thee, Lord Jesus, who knowest all and judgest all.'

Thus the minister said in his sad, resonant voice, washed his hands before the Lord. Fanny bent forward open-eyed during the prayer. She could see the roundish head of Harry, also bent forward. His face was inscrutable and expressionless. The shock left her bewildered. Anger perhaps was her dominating emotion.

The audience began to rustle to its feet, to ooze slowly and excitedly out of the chapel, looking with wildly-interested eyes at Fanny, at Mrs. Nixon, and at Harry. Mrs. Nixon, shortish, stood defiant in her pew, facing the aisle, as if announcing that, without rolling her sleeves up, she was ready for anybody. Fanny sat quite still. Luckily the people did not have to pass her. And Harry, with red ears, was making his way sheepishly out of the gallery. The loud noise of the organ covered all the downstairs commotion of exit.

The minister sat silent and inscrutable in his pulpit, rather like a death's-head, while the congregation filed out. When the last lingerers had unwillingly departed, craning their necks to stare at the still seated Fanny, he rose, stalked in his hooked fashion down the little country chapel and fastened the door. Then he returned and sat down by the silent young woman.

'This is most unfortunate, most unfortunate!' he moaned. 'I am so sorry, I am so sorry, indeed, indeed, ah, indeed!' he sighed himself to a close.

'It's a sudden surprise, that's one thing,' said Fanny brightly.

'Yes—yes—indeed. Yes, a surprise, yes. I don't know the woman, I don't know her.'

'I know her,' said Fanny. 'She's a bad one.'

'Well! Well!' said the minister. 'I don't know her. I don't understand. I don't understand at all. But it is to be regretted, it is very much to be regretted. I am very sorry.'

Fanny was watching the vestry door. The gallery stairs communicated with the vestry, not with the body of the chapel. She knew the choir members had been peeping for information.

At last Harry came—rather sheepishly—with his hat in his hand.

'Well!' said Fanny, rising to her feet.

'We've had a bit of an extra,' said Harry.

'I should think so,' said Fanny.

'A most unfortunate circumstance—a most *unfortunate* circumstance. Do you understand it, Harry? I don't understand it at all.'

'Ah, I understand it. The daughter's goin' to have a childt, an' 'er lays it on to me.'

'And has she no occasion to?' asked Fanny, rather censorious.

'It's no more mine than it is some other chap's,' said Harry, looking aside.

There was a moment of pause.

'Which girl is it?' asked Fanny.

'Annie—the young one—'

There followed another silence.

'I don't think I know them, do I?' asked the minister.

'I shouldn't think so. Their name's Nixon—mother married old Bob for her second husband. She's a tanger—'s driven the gel to what she is. They live in Manners Road.'

'Why, what's amiss with the girl?' asked Fanny sharply. 'She was all right when I knew her.'

'Ay—she's all right. But she's always in an' out o' th' pubs, wi' th' fellows,' said Harry.

'A nice thing!' said Fanny.

Harry glanced towards the door. He wanted to get out.

'Most distressing, indeed!' The minister slowly shook his head.

'What about tonight, Mr. Enderby?' asked Harry, in rather a small voice. 'Shall you want me?'

Mr. Enderby looked up painedly, and put his hand to his brow. He studied Harry for some time, vacantly. There was the faintest sort of a resemblance between the two men.

'Yes,' he said. 'Yes, I think. I think we must take no notice, and cause as little remark as possible.'

Fanny hesitated. Then she said to Harry.

'But *will* you come?'

He looked at her.

'Ay, I s'll come,' he said.

Then he turned to Mr. Enderby.

'Well, good-afternoon, Mr. Enderby,' he said.

'Good-afternoon, Harry, good-afternoon,' replied the mournful minister. Fanny followed Harry to the door, and for some time they walked in silence through the late afternoon.

'And it's yours as much as anybody else's?' she said.

'Ay,' he answered shortly.

And they went without another word, for the long mile or so, till they came to the corner of the street where Harry lived. Fanny hesitated. Should she go on to her aunt's? Should she? It would mean leaving all this, for ever. Harry stood silent.

Some obstinacy made her turn with him along the road to his own home. When they entered the house-place, the whole family was there, mother and father and Jinny, with Jinny's husband and children and Harry's two brothers.

'You've been having yours ears warmed, they tell me,' said Mrs. Goodall grimly.

'Who telled thee?' asked Harry shortly.

'Maggie and Luke's both been in.'

'You look well, don't you!' said interfering Jinny.

Harry went and hung his hat up, without replying.

'Come upstairs and take your hat off,' said Mrs. Goodall to Fanny, almost kindly. It would have annoyed her very much if Fanny had dropped her son at this moment.

'What's 'er say, then?' asked the father secretly of Harry, jerking his head in the direction of the stairs whence Fanny had disappeared.

'Nowt yet,' said Harry.

'Serve you right if she chucks you now,' said Jinny. 'I'll bet it's right about Annie Nixon an' you.'

'Tha bets so much,' said Harry.

'Yi—but you can't deny it,' said Jinny.

'I can if I've a mind.'

His father looked at him inquiringly.

'It's no more mine than it is Bill Bower's, or Ted Slaney's, or six or seven on 'em,' said Harry to his father.

And the father nodded silently.

'That'll not get you out of it, in court,' said Jinny.

Upstairs Fanny evaded all the thrusts made by his mother, and did not declare her hand. She tidied her hair, washed her hands, and put the tiniest bit of powder on her face, for coolness, there in front of Mrs. Goodall's indignant gaze. It was like a declaration of independence. But the old woman said nothing.

They came down to Sunday tea, with sardines and tinned salmon and tinned peaches, besides tarts and cakes. The chatter was general. It concerned the Nixon family and the scandal.

'Oh, she's a foul-mouthed woman,' said Jinny of Mrs. Nixon. 'She may well talk about God's holy house, *she* had. It's first time she's set foot in it, ever since she dropped off from being converted. She's a devil and she always was one. Can't you remember how she treated Bob's children, mother, when we lived down in the Buildings? I can remember when I was a little girl she used to bathe them in the yard, in the cold, so that they shouldn't splash the house. She'd half kill them if they made a mark on the floor, and the language she'd use! And one Saturday I can remember Garry, that was Bob's own girl, she ran off when her stepmother was going to bathe her—ran off without a rag of clothes on—can you remember, mother? And she hid in Smedley's closes—it was the time of mowing-grass—and nobody could find her. She hid out there all night, didn't she, mother? Nobody could find her. My word, there was a talk. They found her on Sunday morning—'

'Fred Coutts threatened to break every bone in the woman's body, if she touched the children again,' put in the father.

'Anyhow, they frightened her,' said Jinny. 'But she was nearly as bad with her own two. And anybody can see that she's driven old Bob till he's gone soft.'

'Ah, soft as mush,' said Jack Goodall. "E'd never addle a week's wage, nor yet a day's if th' chaps didn't make it up to him.'

'My word, if he didn't bring her a week's wage, she'd pull his head off,' said Jinny.

'But a clean woman, and respectable, except for her foul mouth,' said Mrs. Goodall. 'Keeps to herself like a bull-dog. Never lets anybody come near the house, and neighbours with nobody.'

'Wanted it thrashed out of her,' said Mr. Goodall, a silent, evasive sort of man.

'Where Bob gets the money for his drink from is a mystery,' said Jinny.

'Chaps treats him,' said Harry.

'Well, he's got the pair of frightenedest rabbit-eyes you'd wish to see,' said Jinny.

'Ay, with a drunken man's murder in them, *I* think,' said Mrs. Goodall.

So the talk went on after tea, till it was practically time to start off to chapel again.

'You'll have to be getting ready, Fanny,' said Mrs. Goodall.

'I'm not going tonight,' said Fanny abruptly. And there was a sudden halt in the family. 'I'll stop with *you* tonight, Mother,' she added.

'Best you had, my gel,' said Mrs. Goodall, flattered and assured.

HER TURN

She was his second wife, and so there was between them that truce which is never held between a man and his first woman.

He was one for the women, and as such, an exception among the colliers. In spite of their prudery, the neighbour women liked him; he was big, naïve, and very courteous with them; he was so, even to his second wife.

Being a large man of considerable strength and perfect health, he earned good money in the pit. His natural courtesy saved him from enemies, while his fresh interest in life made his presence always agreeable. So he went his own way, had always plenty of friends, always a good job down pit.

He gave his wife thirty-five shillings a week. He had two grown-up sons at home, and they paid twelve shillings each. There was only one child by the second marriage, so Radford considered his wife did well.

Eighteen months ago, Bryan and Wentworth's men were out on strike for eleven weeks. During that time, Mrs. Radford could neither cajole nor entreat nor nag the ten shillings strike-pay from her husband. So that when the second strike came on, she was prepared for action.

Radford was going, quite inconspicuously, to the publican's wife at the "Golden Horn". She is a large, easy-going lady of forty, and her husband is sixty-three, moreover crippled with rheumatism. She sits in the little bar-parlour of the wayside public-house, knitting for dear life, and sipping a very moderate glass of Scotch. When a decent man arrives at the three-foot width of bar, she rises, serves him, surveys him over, and, if she likes his looks, says:

"Won't you step inside, sir?"

If he steps inside, he will find not more than one or two men present. The room is warm, quite small. The landlady knits. She gives a few polite words to the stranger, then resumes her conversation with the man who interests her most. She is straight, highly-coloured, with indifferent brown eyes.

"What was that you asked me, Mr. Radford?"

"What is the difference between a donkey's tail and a rainbow?" asked Radford, who had a consuming passion for conundrums.

"All the difference in the world," replied the landlady.

"Yes, but what special difference?"

"I s'll have to give it up again. You'll think me a donkey's head, I'm afraid."

"Not likely. But just you consider now, wheer . . ."

The conundrum was still under weigh, when a girl entered. She was swarthy, a fine animal. After she had gone out:

"Do you know who that is?" asked the landlady.

"I can't say as I do," replied Radford.

"She's Frederick Pinnock's daughter, from Stony Ford. She's courting our Willy."

"And a fine lass, too."

"Yes, fine enough, as far as that goes. What sort of a wife'll she make him, think you?"

"You just let me consider a bit," said the man. He took out a pocket-book and a pencil. The landlady continued to talk to the other guests.

Radford was a big fellow, black-haired, with a brown moustache, and darkish blue eyes. His voice, naturally deep, was pitched in his throat, and had a peculiar, tenor quality, rather husky, and disturbing. He modulated it a good deal as he spoke, as men do who talk much with women. Always, there was a certain indolence in his carriage.

"Our mester's lazy," his wife said. "There's many a bit of a jab wants doin', but get him to do it if you can."

But she knew he was merely indifferent to the little jobs, and not lazy.

He sat writing for about ten minutes, at the end of which time, he read:

"I see a fine girl full of life.

I see her just ready for wedlock,

But there's jealousy between her eyebrows

And jealousy on her mouth.

I see trouble ahead.

Willy is delicate.

She would do him no good.

She would never see when he wasn't well,

She would only see what she wanted—"

So, in phrases, he got down his thoughts. He had to fumble for expression, and therefore anything serious he wanted to say he wrote in "poetry", as he called it.

Presently, the landlady rose, saying:

"Well, I s'll have to be looking after our mester. I s'll be in again before we close."

Radford sat quite comfortably on. In a while, he too bade the company good-night.

When he got home, at a quarter-past eleven, his sons were in bed, and his wife sat awaiting him. She was a woman of medium height, fat and sleek, a dumpling. Her black hair was parted smooth, her narrow-opened eyes were sly and satirical, she had a peculiar twang in her rather sleering voice.

"Our missis is a puss-puss," he said easily, of her. Her extraordinarily smooth, sleek face was remarkable. She was very healthy.

He never came in drunk. Having taken off his coat and his cap, he sat down to supper in his shirt-sleeves. Do as he might, she was fascinated by him. He had a strong neck, with the crisp hair growing low. Let her be angry as she would yet she had a passion for that neck of his, particularly when she saw the great vein rib under the skin.

"I think, missis," he said, "I'd rather ha'e a smite o' cheese than this meat."

"Well, can't you get it yourself?"

"Yi, surely I can," he said, and went out to the pantry.

"I think, if yer comin' in at this time of night, you can wait on yourself," she justified herself.

She moved uneasily in her chair. There were several jam-tarts alongside the cheese on the dish he brought.

"Yi, Missis, them tan-tafflins'll go down very nicely," he said.

"Oh, will they! Then you'd better help to pay for them," she said, amiably, but determined.

"Now what art after?"

"What am I after? Why, can't you think?" she said sarcastically.

"I'm not for thinkin', missis."

"No, I know you're not. But wheer's my money? You've been paid the Union to-day. Wheer do I come in?"

"Tha's got money, an' tha mun use it."

"Thank yer. An' 'aven't you none, as well?"

"I hadna, not till we was paid, not a ha'p'ny."

"Then you ought to be ashamed of yourself to say so."

"'Appen so."

"We'll go shares wi' th' Union money," she said. "That's nothing but what's right."

"We shonna. Tha's got plenty o' money as tha can use."

"Oh, all right," she said. "I will do."

She went to bed. It made her feel sharp that she could not get at him.

The next day, she was just as usual. But at eleven o'clock she took her purse and went up town. Trade was very slack. Men stood about in gangs, men were playing marbles everywhere in the streets. It was a sunny morning. Mrs. Radford went into the furnisher-and-upholsterer's shop.

"There's a few things," she said to Mr. Allcock, "as I'm wantin' for the house, and I might as well get them now, while the men's at home, and can shift me the furniture."

She put her fat purse on to the counter with a click. The man should know she was not wanting "strap". She bought linoleum for the kitchen, a new wringer, a breakfast-service, a spring mattress, and various other things, keeping a mere thirty shillings, which she tied in a corner of her handkerchief. In her purse was some loose silver.

Her husband was gardening in a desultory fashion when she got back home. The daffodils were out. The colts in the field at the end of the garden were tossing their velvety brown necks.

"Sithee here, missis," called Radford, from the shed which stood halfway down the path. Two doves in a cage were cooing.

"What have you got?" asked the woman, as she approached. He held out to her in his big, earthy hand a tortoise. The reptile was very, very slowly issuing its head again to the warmth.

"He's wakened up betimes," said Radford.

"He's like th' men, wakened up for a holiday," said the wife. Radford scratched the little beast's scaly head.

"We pleased to see him out," he said.

They had just finished dinner, when a man knocked at the door.

"From Allcock's!" he said.

The plump woman took up the clothes-basket containing the crockery she had bought.

"Whativer hast got theer?" asked her husband.

"We've been wantin' some breakfast-cups for ages, so I went up town an' got 'em this mornin'," she replied.

He watched her taking out the crockery.

"Hm!" he said. "Tha's been on th' spend, seemly."

Again there was a thud at the door. The man had put down a roll of linoleum. Mr. Radford went to look at it.

"They come rolling in!" he exclaimed.

"Who's grumbled more than you about the raggy oilcloth of this kitchen?" said the insidious, cat-like voice of the wife.

"It's all right, it's all right," said Radford.

The carter came up the entry with another roll, which he deposited with a grunt at the door.

"An' how much do you reckon this lot is?" he asked.

"Oh, they're all paid for, don't worry," replied the wife.

"Shall yer gi'e me a hand, mester?" asked the carter.

Radford followed him down the entry, in his easy, slouching way. His wife went after. His waistcoat was hanging loose over his shirt. She watched his easy movement of well-being as she followed him, and she laughed to herself.

The carter took hold of one end of the wire mattress, dragged it forth.

"Well, this is a corker!" said Radford, as he received the burden.

"Now the mangle!" said the carter.

"What dost reckon tha's been up to, missis?" asked the husband.

"I said to myself last wash-day, if I had to turn that mangle again, tha'd ha'e ter wash the clothes thyself."

Radford followed the carter down the entry again. In the street, women were standing watching, and dozens of men were lounging round the cart. One officiously helped with the wringer.

"Gi'e him thrippence," said Mrs. Radford.

"Gi'e him thysen," replied her husband.

"I've no change under half a crown."

Radford tipped the carter, and returned indoors. He surveyed the array of crockery, linoleum, mattress, mangle, and other goods crowding the house and the yard.

"Well, this is a winder!" he repeated.

"We stood in need of 'em enough," she replied.

"I hope tha's got plenty more from wheer they came from," he replied dangerously.

"That's just what I haven't." She opened her purse. "Two half-crowns, that's every copper I've got i' th' world."

He stood very still as he looked.

"It's right," she said.

There was a certain smug sense of satisfaction about her. A wave of anger came over him, blinding him. But he waited and waited. Suddenly his arm leapt up, the fist clenched, and his eyes blazed at her. She shrank away, pale and frightened. But he dropped his fist to his side, turned, and went out, muttering. He went down to the shed that stood in the middle of the garden. There he picked up the tortoise, and stood with bent head, rubbing its horny head.

She stood hesitating, watching him. Her heart was heavy, and yet there was a curious, cat-like look of satisfaction round her eyes. Then she went indoors and gazed at her new cups, admiringly.

The next week he handed her his half-sovereign without a word.

"You'll want some for yourself," she said, and she gave him a shilling. He accepted it.

STRIKE-PAY

Strike-money is paid in the Primitive Methodist Chapel. The crier was round quite early on Wednesday morning to say that paying would begin at ten o'clock.

The Primitive Methodist Chapel is a big barn of a place, built, designed, and paid for by the colliers themselves. But it threatened to fall down from its first form, so that a professional architect had to be hired at last to pull the place together.

It stands in the Square. Forty years ago, when Bryan and Wentworth opened their pits, they put up the "squares" of miners' dwellings. They are two great quadrangles of houses, enclosing a barren stretch of ground, littered with broken pots and rubbish, which forms a square, a great, sloping, lumpy playground for the children, a drying-ground for many women's washing.

Wednesday is still wash-day with some women. As the men clustered round the Chapel, they heard the thud-thud-thud of many pouches, women pounding away at the wash-tub with a wooden pestle. In the Square the white clothes were waving in the wind from a maze of clothes-lines, and here and there women were pegging out, calling to the miners, or to the children who dodged under the flapping sheets.

Ben Townsend, the Union agent, has a bad way of paying. He takes the men in order of his round, and calls them by name. A big, oratorical man with a grey beard, he sat at the table in the Primitive school-room, calling name after name. The room was crowded with colliers, and a great group pushed up outside. There was much confusion. Ben dodged from the Scargill Street list to the Queen Street. For this Queen Street men were not prepared. They were not to the fore.

"Joseph Grooby—Joseph Grooby! Now, Joe, where are you?"

"Hold on a bit, Sorry!" cried Joe from outside. "I'm shovin' up."

There was a great noise from the men.

"I'm takin' Queen Street. All you Queen Street men should be ready. Here you are, Joe," said the Union agent loudly.

"Five children!" said Joe, counting the money suspiciously.

"That's right, I think," came the mouthing voice. "Fifteen shillings, is it not?"

"A bob a kid," said the collier.

"Thomas Sedgwick—How are you, Tom? Missis better?"

"Ay, 'er's shapin' nicely. Tha'rt hard at work to-day, Ben." This was sarcasm on the idleness of a man who had given up the pit to become a Union agent.

"Yes. I rose at four to fetch the money."

"Dunna hurt thysen," was the retort, and the men laughed.

"No—John Merfin!"

But the colliers, tired with waiting, excited by the strike spirit, began to rag. Merfin was young and dandiacal. He was choir-master at the Wesleyan Chapel.

"Does your collar cut, John?" asked a sarcastic voice out of the crowd.

"Hymn Number Nine.

'Diddle-diddle dumpling, my son John
Went to bed with his best suit on,'"

came the solemn announcement.

Mr. Merfin, his white cuffs down to his knuckles, picked up his half-sovereign, and walked away loftily.

"Sam Coutts!" cried the paymaster.

"Now, lad, reckon it up," shouted the voice of the crowd, delighted.

Mr. Coutts was a straight-backed ne'er-do-well. He looked at his twelve shillings sheepishly.

"Another two-bob—he had twins a-Monday night—get thy money, Sam, tha's earned it—tha's addled it, Sam; dunna go be-out it. Let him ha' the two bob for 'is twins, mister," came the clamour from the men around.

Sam Coutts stood grinning awkwardly.

"You should ha' given us notice, Sam," said the paymaster suavely. "We can make it all right for you next week—"

"Nay, nay, nay," shouted a voice. "Pay on delivery—the goods is there right enough."

"Get thy money, Sam, tha's addled it," became the universal cry, and the Union agent had to hand over another florin, to prevent a disturbance. Sam Coutts grinned with satisfaction.

"Good shot, Sam," the men exclaimed.

"Ephraim Wharmby," shouted the pay-man.

A lad came forward.

"Gi' him sixpence for what's on t'road," said a sly voice.

"Nay, nay," replied Ben Townsend; "pay on delivery."

There was a roar of laughter. The miners were in high spirits.

In the town they stood about in gangs, talking and laughing. Many sat on their heels in the market-place. In and out of the public-houses they went, and on every bar the half-sovereigns clicked.

"Comin' ter Nottingham wi' us, Ephraim?" said Sam Coutts to the slender, pale young fellow of about twenty-two.

"I'm non walkin' that far of a gleamy day like this."

"He has na got the strength," said somebody, and a laugh went up.

"How's that?" asked another pertinent voice.

"He's a married man, mind yer," said Chris Smitheringale, "an' it ta'es a bit o' keepin' up."

The youth was teased in this manner for some time.

"Come on ter Nottingham wi's; tha'll be safe for a bit," said Coutts.

A gang set off, although it was only eleven o'clock. It was a nine-mile walk. The road was crowded with colliers travelling on foot to see the match between Notts and Aston Villa. In Ephraim's gang were Sam Coutts, with his fine shoulders and his extra florin, Chris Smitheringale, fat and smiling, and John Wharmby, a remarkable man, tall, erect as a soldier, black-haired and proud; he could play any musical instrument, he declared.

"I can play owt from a comb up'ards. If there's music to be got outer a thing, I back I'll get it. No matter what shape or form of instrument you set before me, it doesn't signify if I niver clapped eyes on it before, I's warrant I'll have a tune out of it in five minutes."

He beguiled the first two miles so. It was true, he had caused a sensation by introducing the mandoline into the townlet, filling the hearts of his fellow-colliers with pride as he sat on the platform in evening dress, a fine soldierly man, bowing his black head, and scratching the mewing mandoline with hands that had only to grasp the "instrument" to crush it entirely.

Chris stood a can round at the "White Bull" at Gilt Brook. John Wharmby took his turn at Kimberley top.

"We wunna drink again," they decided, "till we're at Cinder Hill. We'll non stop i' Nuttall."

They swung along the high-road under the budding trees. In Nuttall churchyard the crocuses blazed with yellow at the brim of the balanced, black yews. White and purple crocuses clipt up over the graves, as if the churchyard were bursting out in tiny tongues of flame.

"Sithee," said Ephraim, who was an ostler down pit, "sithee, here comes the Colonel. Sithee at his 'osses how they pick their toes up, the beauties!"

The Colonel drove past the men, who took no notice of him.

"Hast heard, Sorry," said Sam, "as they're com'n out i' Germany, by the thousand, an' begun riotin'?"

"An' comin' out i' France simbitar," cried Chris.

The men all gave a chuckle.

"Sorry," shouted John Wharmby, much elated, "we oughtna ter go back under a twenty per cent rise."

"We should get it," said Chris.

"An' easy! They can do nowt bi-out us, we'n on'y ter stop out long enough."

"I'm willin'," said Sam, and there was a laugh. The colliers looked at one another. A thrill went through them as if an electric current passed.

"We'n on'y ter stick out, an' we s'll see who's gaffer."

"Us!" cried Sam. "Why, what can they do again' us, if we come out all over th' world?"

"Nowt!" said John Wharmby. "Th' mesters is bobbin' about like corks on a cassivoy a'ready." There was a large natural reservoir, like a lake, near Bestwood, and this supplied the simile.

Again there passed through the men that wave of elation, quickening their pulses. They chuckled in their throats. Beyond all consciousness was this sense of battle and triumph in the hearts of the working-men at this juncture.

It was suddenly suggested at Nuttall that they should go over the fields to Bulwell, and into Nottingham that way. They went single file across the fallow, past the wood, and over the railway, where now no trains were running. Two fields away was a troop of pit ponies. Of all colours, but chiefly of red or brown, they clustered thick in the field, scarcely moving, and the two lines of trodden earth patches showed where fodder was placed down the field.

"Theer's the pit 'osses," said Sam. "Let's run 'em."

"It's like a circus turned out. See them skewbawd 'uns—seven skewbawd," said Ephraim.

The ponies were inert, unused to freedom. Occasionally one walked round. But there they stood, two thick lines of ruddy brown and piebald and white, across the trampled field. It was a beautiful day, mild, pale blue, a "growing day", as the men said, when there was the silence of swelling sap everywhere.

"Let's ha'e a ride," said Ephraim.

The younger men went up to the horses.

"Come on—co-oop, Taffy—co-oop, Ginger."

The horses tossed away. But having got over the excitement of being above-ground, the animals were feeling dazed and rather dreary. They missed the warmth and the life of the pit. They looked as if life were a blank to them.

Ephraim and Sam caught a couple of steeds, on whose backs they went careering round, driving the rest of the sluggish herd from end to end of the field. The horses were good specimens, on the whole, and in fine condition. But they were out of their element.

Performing too clever a feat, Ephraim went rolling from his mount. He was soon up again, chasing his horse. Again he was thrown. Then the men proceeded on their way.

They were drawing near to miserable Bulwell, when Ephraim, remembering his turn was coming to stand drinks, felt in his pocket for his beloved half-sovereign, his strike-pay. It was not there. Through all his pockets he went, his heart sinking like lead.

"Sam," he said, "I believe I'n lost that ha'ef a sovereign."

"Tha's got it somewheer about thee," said Chris.

They made him take off his coat and waistcoat. Chris examined the coat, Sam the waistcoat, whilst Ephraim searched his trousers.

"Well," said Chris, "I'n foraged this coat, an' it's non theer."

"An' I'll back my life as th' on'y bit a metal on this wa'scoat is the buttons," said Sam.

"An' it's non in my breeches," said Ephraim. He took off his boots and his stockings. The half-sovereign was not there. He had not another coin in his possession.

"Well," said Chris, "we mun go back an' look for it."

Back they went, four serious-hearted colliers, and searched the field, but in vain.

"Well," said Chris, "we s'll ha'e ter share wi' thee, that's a'."

"I'm willin'," said John Wharmby.

"An' me," said Sam.

"Two bob each," said Chris.

Ephraim, who was in the depths of despair, shamefully accepted their six shillings.

In Bulwell they called in a small public-house, which had one long room with a brick floor, scrubbed benches and scrubbed tables. The central space was open. The place was full of colliers, who were drinking. There was a great deal of drinking during the strike, but not a vast amount drunk. Two men were playing skittles, and the rest were betting. The seconds sat on either side the skittle-board, holding caps of money, sixpences and coppers, the wagers of the "backers".

Sam, Chris, and John Wharmby immediately put money on the man who had their favour. In the end Sam declared himself willing to play against the victor. He was the Bestwood champion. Chris and John Wharmby backed him heavily, and even Ephraim the Unhappy ventured sixpence.

In the end, Sam had won half a crown, with which he promptly stood drinks and bread and cheese for his comrades. At half-past one they set off again.

It was a good match between Notts and Villa—no goals at half-time, two-none for

Notts at the finish. The colliers were hugely delighted, especially as Flint, the forward for Notts, who was an Underwood man well known to the four comrades, did some handsome work, putting the two goals through.

Ephraim determined to go home as soon as the match was over. He knew John Wharmby would be playing the piano at the "Punch Bowl", and Sam, who had a good tenor voice, singing, while Chris cut in with witticisms, until evening. So he bade them farewell, as he must get home. They, finding him somewhat of a damper on their spirits, let him go.

He was the sadder for having witnessed an accident near the football-ground. A navvy, working at some drainage, carting an iron tip-tub of mud and emptying it, had got with his horse on to the deep deposit of ooze which was crusted over. The crust had broken, the man had gone under the horse, and it was some time before the people had realised he had vanished. When they found his feet sticking out, and hauled him forth, he was dead, stifled dead in the mud. The horse was at length hauled out, after having its neck nearly pulled from the socket.

Ephraim went home vaguely impressed with a sense of death, and loss, and strife. Death was loss greater than his own, the strike was a battle greater than that he would presently have to fight.

He arrived home at seven o'clock, just when it had fallen dark. He lived in Queen Street with his young wife, to whom he had been married two months, and with his mother-in-law, a widow of sixty-four. Maud was the last child remaining unmarried, the last of eleven.

Ephraim went up the entry. The light was burning in the kitchen. His mother-in-law was a big, erect woman, with wrinkled, loose face, and cold blue eyes. His wife was also large, with very vigorous fair hair, frizzy like unravelled rope. She had a quiet way of stepping, a certain cat-like stealth, in spite of her large build. She was five months pregnant.

"Might we ask wheer you've been to?" inquired Mrs. Marriott, very erect, very dangerous. She was only polite when she was very angry.

"I' bin ter th' match."

"Oh, indeed!" said the mother-in-law. "And why couldn't we be told as you thought of jaunting off?"

"I didna know mysen," he answered, sticking to his broad Derbyshire.

"I suppose it popped into your mind, an' so you darted off," said the mother-in-law dangerously.

"I didna. It wor Chris Smitheringale who exed me."

"An' did you take much invitin'?"

"I didna want ter goo."

"But wasn't there enough man beside your jacket to say no?"

He did not answer. Down at the bottom he hated her. But he was, to use his own words, all messed up with having lost his strike-pay and with knowing the man was dead. So he was more helpless before his mother-in-law, whom he feared. His wife neither looked at him nor spoke, but kept her head bowed. He knew she was with her mother.

"Our Maud's been waitin' for some money, to get a few things," said the mother-in-law.

In silence, he put five-and-sixpence on the table.

"Take that up, Maud," said the mother.

Maud did so.

"You'll want it for us board, shan't you?" she asked, furtively, of her mother.

"Might I ask if there's nothing you want to buy yourself, first?"

"No, there's nothink I want," answered the daughter.

Mrs. Marriott took the silver and counted it.

"And do you," said the mother-in-law, towering upon the shrinking son, but speaking slowly and statelily, "do you think I'm going to keep you and your wife for five and sixpence a week?"

"It's a' I've got," he answered sulkily.

"You've had a good jaunt, my sirs, if it's cost four and sixpence. You've started your game early, haven't you?"

He did not answer.

"It's a nice thing! Here's our Maud an' me been sitting since eleven o'clock this morning! Dinner waiting and cleared away, tea waiting and washed up; then in he comes crawling with five and sixpence. Five and sixpence for a man an' wife's board for a week, if you please!"

Still he did not say anything.

"You must think something of yourself, Ephraim Wharmby!" said his mother-in-law. "You must think something of yourself. You suppose, do you, *I'm* going to keep you an' your wife, while you make a holiday, off on the nines to Nottingham, drink an' women."

"I've neither had drink nor women, as you know right well," he said.

"I'm glad we know summat about you. For you're that close, anybody'd think we was foreigners to you. You're a pretty little jockey, aren't you? Oh, it's a gala time for you, the strike is. That's all men strike for, indeed. They enjoy themselves, they do that. Ripping and racing and drinking, from morn till night, my sirs!"

"Is there on'y tea for me?" he asked, in a temper.

"Hark at him! Hark-ye! Should I ask you whose house you think you're in? Kindly order me about, do. Oh, it makes him big, the strike does. See him land home after being out on the spree for hours, and give his orders, my sirs! Oh, strike sets the men up, it does. Nothing have they to do but guzzle and gallivant to Nottingham. Their wives'll keep them, oh yes. So long as they get something to eat at home, what more do they want! What more *should* they want, prithee? Nothing! Let the women and children starve and scrape, but fill the man's belly, and let him have his fling. My sirs, indeed, I think so! Let tradesmen go—what do they matter! Let rent go. Let children get what they can catch. Only the man will see *he's* all right. But not here, though!"

"Are you goin' ter gi'e me ony bloody tea?"

His mother-in-law started up.

"If tha dares ter swear at me, I'll lay thee flat."

"Are yer—goin' ter—gi'e me—any blasted, rotten, còssed, blòody tèa?" he bawled, in a fury, accenting every other word deliberately.

"Maud!" said the mother-in-law, cold and stately, "If you gi'e him any tea after that, you're a trollops." Whereupon she sailed out to her other daughters.

Maud quietly got the tea ready.

"Shall y'ave your dinner warmed up?" she asked.

"Ay."

She attended to him. Not that she was really meek. But—he was *her* man, not her mother's.

A PRELUDE

"Sweet is pleasure after pain..."

In the kitchen of a small farm a little woman sat cutting bread and butter. The glow of the clear, ruddy fire was on her shining cheek and white apron; but grey hair will not take the warm caress of firelight.

She skilfully spread the softened butter, and cut off great slices from the floury loaf in her lap. Already two plates were piled, but she continued to cut.

Outside the naked ropes of the creeper tapped and lashed at the window.

The grey-haired mother looked up, and setting the butter on the hearth, rose and went to look out. The sky was heavy and grey as she saw it in the narrow band over the near black wood. So she turned and went to look through the tiny window which opened from the deep recess on the opposite side of the room. The northern sky was blacker than ever.

She turned away with a little sigh, and took a duster from the red, shining warming-pan to take the bread from the oven. Afterwards she laid the table for five.

There was a rumbling and a whirring in the corner, and the clock struck five. Like clocks in many farmers' kitchens, it was more than half an hour fast. The little woman hurried about, bringing milk and other things from the dairy; lifting the potatoes from the fire, peeping through the window anxiously. Very often her neck ached with watching the gate for a sign of approach. There was a click of the yard gate. She ran to the window, but turned away again, and catching up the blue enamelled teapot, dropped into it a handful of tea from the caddy, and poured on the water. A clinking scrape of iron shod boots sounded outside, then the door opened with a burst as a burly, bearded man entered. He drooped at the shoulders, and leaned forward as a man who has worked heavily all his life.

"Hello, mother," he said, loudly and cheerfully. "Am I first? Aren't any of the lads down yet? Fred will be here in a minute."

"I wish they would come," said his wife, "or else it'll rain before they're here."

"Ay," he assented, "it's beginning, and it's cold rain an' all. Bit of sleet, I think," and he sat down heavily in his armchair, looking at his wife as she knelt and turned the bread, and took a large jar of stewed apples from the oven.

"Well, mother," he said, with a pleasant comfortable little smile, "here's another Christmas for you and me. They keep passing us by."

"Ay," she answered, the effects of her afternoon's brooding now appearing. "They come and go, but they never find us any better off."

"It seems so," he said, a shade of regret appearing momentarily over his cheerfulness. "This year we've certainly had some very bad luck. But we keep straight—and we never regret that Christmas, see, it's twenty-seven years since—twenty-seven years."

"No, perhaps not, but there's Fred as hasn't had above three pounds for the whole year's work, and the other two at the pit."

"Well, what can I do? If I hadn't lost the biggest part of the hay, and them two beast -"

"If... Besides what prospects has he? Here he is working year in year out for you and getting nothing at the end of it. When you were his age, when you were 25, you were married and had two children. How can he ask anybody to marry him?"

"I don't know that he wants to. He's fairly contented. Don't be worrying about him and upsetting him. He's only go and leave us if he got married. Besides, we may have a good year next year, and we can make this up."

"Ay, so you say."

"Don't fret yourself to-night, lass. It's true things haven't gone as we hoped they would. I never thought to see you doing all the work you have to do, but we've been very comfortable, all things considered, haven't we?"

"I never thought to see my first lad a farm labourer at 25, and the other two in the pit. Two of my sons in the pit!"

"I'm sure I've done what I could, and "- but they heard a scraping outside, and he said no more.

The eldest son tramped in, his great boots and his leggings all covered with mud. He took off his wet overcoat, and stood on the hearthrug, his hands spread out behind him in the warmth of the fire. Looking smilingly at his mother, as she moved about the kitchen, he said: "You do look warm and cosy, mother. When I was coming up with the last load, I thought of you trotting about in that big, white apron, getting tea ready, watching the weather. There are the lads. Aren't you quite contented now—perfectly happy?"

She laughed an odd little laugh, and poured out the tea. The boys came in from the pit, wet and dirty, with clean streaks down their faces where the rain had trickled. They changed their clothes and sat at the table. The elder was a big, heavy loosely-made fellow, with a long nose and chin, and comical wrinkling round his eyes. The younger, Arthur, was a handsome lad, dark-haired, with ruddy colour glowing through his dirt, and dark eyes. When he talked and laughed the red of his lips and the whiteness of his teeth and eyeballs stood out in startling contrast to the surrounding black.

"Mother, I'm glad to see thee," he said, looking at her with frank, boyish affection.

"There, mother, what more can you want?" asked her husband.

She took a bite of bread and butter, and looked up with a quaint, comical glance, as if she were given only her just dues, but for all that it pleased and amused her, only she was half shy, and a grain doubtful.

"Lad," said Henry. "it's Christmas Eve. The fire ought to burn its brightest.

"Yes. I will have just another potato, seeing as Christmas is the time for feeding. What are we going to do? Are we going to have a party, mother?

"Yes, if you want one."

"Party," laughed the father, "who'd come?

"We might ask somebody. We could have Nellie Wycherley, who used to come, an' David Garton."

We shall not do for Nellie nowadays, said the father, "I saw her on Sunday morning on the top road. She was drivin' home with another young woman, an' she stopped an' asked me if we'd got any holly with berries on, an I said we hadn't."

Fred looked up from the book he was reading over tea. He had dark brown eyes, something like his mother's, and they always drew attention when he turned them on anyone.

"There is a tree covered in the wood," he said.

"Well," answered the irrepressible Henry, "that's not ours, is it? An' If she's got that proud she won't come near to see us, am I goin' choppin' trees down for her? If she'd come here an' say she wanted a bit, I'd fetch her half the wood in. but when she sits in the trap and looks down on you an' asks, 'Do you happen to hev a bush of berried holly in your hedges? Preston can't find a sprig to decorate the house, and I hev some people coming down from town,' then I tell her we're all crying because we've none to decorate ourselves, and we want it the more 'cause nobody's coming, neither from th' town nor th' country, an' we're likely to forget it's Christmas if we've neither folks nor things to remind us."

"What did she say?" asked the mother.

"She said she was sorry, an' I told her not to bother, it's better lookin' at folks than at bits o' holly. The other lass was laughing, an' she wanted to know what folks. I told her any as hadn't got more pricks than a holly bush to keep you off."

"Ha! ha!" laughed the father; "did she take it?"

"The other girl nudged her, and they both began a laughing. Then Nellie told me to send down the guysers to-night. I said I would, but they're not going now."

"Why not?" asked Fred.

"Billy Simpson's got a gathered face, an' Ward's gone to Nottingham."

"The company down at Ramsley Mill will have nobody to laugh at to-night," said Arthur.

"Tell ye what," exclaimed Henry, "we'll go."

"How can we, three of us?" asked Arthur.

"Well," persisted Henry. "we could dress up so as they'd niver know us, an' hae a bit o' fun. Hey!" he suddenly shouted to Fred, who was reading, and taking no notice, "Hey, we're going to the Mill guysering."

"Who is?" asked the elder brother. somewhat surprised.

"You an' me, an' our Arthur. I'll be Beelzebub."

Here he distorted his face to look diabolic, so that everybody roared.

"Go," said his father, "you'll make our fortunes."

"What!" he exclaimed, "by making a fool of myself? They say fools for luck. What fools wise folk must be. Well, I'll be the devil — are you shocked, mother? What will you be, Arthur?"

"I don't care," was the answer. "We can put some of that red paint on our faces, and some soot, they'd never know us. Shall we go, Fred?"

"I don't know."

"Why, I should like to see her with her company, to see if she has very fine airs. We could leave some holly for her in the scullery."

"All right, then."

After tea all helped with the milking and feeding. Then Fred took a hedge knife and a hurricane lamp and went into the wood to cut some of the richly berried holly. When he got back he found his brothers roaring with laughter before the mirror. They were smeared with red and black, and had fastened on grotesque horsehair moustaches, so that they were entirely unrecognisable.

"Oh, you are hideous," cried their mother. "Oh, it's shameful to disfigure the work of the Almighty like that."

Fred washed and proceeded to dress. They could not persuade him to use paint or soot. He rolled his sleeves up to the shoulder, and wrapped himself in a great striped horse rug. Then be tied a white cloth round his head, as the Bedouins do, and pulled out his moustache to fierce points. He looked at himself with approval, took an old sword from the wall, and held it in one naked, muscular arm.

"Decidedly." he thought, "it is very picturesque, and I look very fine."

"Oh, that is grand" said his mother. as he entered the kitchen. His dark eyes glowed with pleasure to hear her say it. He seemed somewhat excited, this bucolic young man. His tanned skin shone rich and warm under the white cloth, its coarseness hidden by the yellow lamplight. His eyes glittered like a true Arab's, and it was to be noticed that the muscles of his sun-browned arms were tense with the grip of the broad hand.

It was remarkable how the dark folds of the rug and the flowing burnous glorified this young farmer, who, in his best clothes looked awkward and ungainly, and whose face a linen collar showed coarse, owing to exposure to the weather, and long application to heavy labour.

They set out to cross the two of their own fields, and two of their neighbour's, which separated their home from the mill. A few uncertain flakes of snow were eddying down, melting as they settled. The ground was wet, and the night very dark. But they knew. the way well, and were soon at the gate leading to the mill yard. The dog began to bark furiously, but they called to him, "Trip, Trip," and knowing their voices, he was quieted.

Henry gave a thundering knock, and bawled in stentorian tones, "Dun yer want guysers?"

A man came to the door, very tall, very ungainly, very swarthy

"We non want yer." he said, talking down his nose.

"Here comes Beelzebub," banged away Henry thumping a pan which he carried. "Here comes Beelzebub, an' he's come to th' right place."

A big, bonny farm girl came to the door.

"Who is it?" she asked.

"Beelzebub, you know him well." was the answer.

"I'll ask Miss Ellen it she wants you."

Henry winked a red and black wink at the maid, saying, "Never keep Satan on the doorstep," and he stepped into the scullery.

The girl ran away, and soon was heard a laughing, and bright talking of women's voices drawing nearer to the kitchen.

"Tell them to come in." said a voice.

The three trooped in. and glanced round the big kitchen. They could only see Betty, seated as near to them as possible on the squab, her father, black and surly, in his armchair, and two women's figures in the deep shadows of one of the great ingle-nook seats.

"Ah," said Beelzebub, "this is a bit more like it, a bit hotter. The Devils feels at home here."

They began the ludicrous old Christmas play that everyone knows so well. Beelzebub acted with much force, much noise, and some humour. St. George, that is Fred, played his part with zeal and earnestness most amusing, but at one of the most crucial moments he entirely forgot his speech, which, however, was speedily rectified by Beelzebub. Arthur was nervous and awkward, so that Beelzebub supplied him with most of his speeches.

After much horseplay, stabbing, falling on the floor, bangings of dripping-pans, and ludicrous striving to fill in the blanks, they came to an end.

They waited in silence.

"Well what next," asked a voice from the shadows.

"It's your turn," said Beelzebub

"What do you want?"

"As little as you have the heart to give."

"But," said another voice, one they knew well, "We have no heart to give at all."

"You did not know your parts well." said Blanche, the stranger. "The big fellow in the blanket deserves nothing."

258

"What about me?" asked Arthur.

"You," answered the same voice, "oh you're a nice boy, and a lady's; thanks are enough reward for you."

He blushed, and muttered something unintelligible.

"There'll be the Devil to pay," suggested Beelzebub.

"Give the Devil his dues, Nell," said Blanche choking again with laughter. Nellie threw a large silver coin on the flagstone floor, but she was nervous and it rolled to the feet of Preston in his arm-chair.

"'Alf-a-crern!" he exclaimed, "gie em thrippence, an' they're non worth that much."

This was too much for the chivalrous St. George. He could bear no longer to stand in this ridiculous garb before his scornful lady-love and her laughing friend.

He snatched off his burnous and his robe, flung them over one arm, and with the other caught back Beelzebub, who would have gone to pick up the money. There he stood, St. George metamorphosed into a simple young farmer, with ruffled curly black hair, a heavy frown and bare arms.

"Won't you let him have it?" asked Blanche. "Well, what do you want?" she continued,

"Nothing, thanks. I'm sorry we troubled you."

"Come on," he said, drawing the reluctant Beelzebub, and the three made their exit. Blanche laughed and laughed again to see the discomfited knight tramp out, rolling down his shirt sleeves.

Nellie did not laugh. Seeing him turn, she saw him again as a child, before her father had made money by the cattle-dealing, when she was a poor, wild little creature. But her father had grown rich and the mill was a big farm, and when the old cattle dealer had died, she became sole mistress. Then Preston, their chief man, came with Betty and Sarah, to live in, and take charge of the farm.

Nellie had seen little of her old friends since then. She had stayed a long time in town, and when she called on them after her return found them cool and estranged. So she had not been again, and now it was almost a year since she had spoken many words to Fred.

Her brief meditations were disturbed by a scream from Betty in the scullery, followed by the wild rush of that damsel into the kitchen.

"What's up?" asked her father.

"There's somebody there got hold of my legs."

Nellie felt suddenly her own loneliness. Preston struck a match and investigated. He returned with a bunch of glittering holly, thick with scarlet berries.

"Here's yer somebody," said he, flinging the bunch down on the table.

"Oh, that is pretty," exclaimed Blanche. Nellie rose, looked, then hurried down the passage to the sitting-room, followed by her friend. There, to the consternation of Blanche, she sat down and began to cry.

"Whatever is the matter?" asked Blanche.

It was some time before she had a reply, then, "It's so miserable." faltered Nellie, "and so lonely. I do think Will and Harry and Louie and all the others were mean not to com, then this wouldn't have happened. It was such a shame—such a shame."

"What was a shame?" asked Blanche.

"Why, when he had got me that holly, and come down to see —" she ended blushing.

"Whom do you mean—the Bedouin?"

"And I had not seen him for months, and he will think I am Just a mean, proud thing."

"You don't mean to say you care for him?"

Nellie's tears began to flow again. "I do, and I wish this miserable farm and bit of money had never come between us. He'll never come again, never, I know."

"Then," said Blanche. "you must go to him."

"Yes, and I will."

"Come along, then."

In the meantime, the disappointed brothers had reached home. Fred had thrown down his Bedouin wardrobe, and put on his coat, muttering something about having a walk up the village. Then he had gone out, his mother's eyes watching his exit with helpless grief, his father looking over his spectacles in a half-surprised paternal sympathy. However, they heard him tramp down the yard and enter the barn, and they knew he would soon recover. Then the lads went out, and nothing was heard In the kitchen save the beat of the clock and the rustle of the newspaper, or the rattle of the board, as the mother rolled out paste for the mince-pies.

In the pitch-dark barn, the rueful Bedouin told himself that he expected no other than this, and that it was high time he ceased fooling himself with fancies, that he was well-cured, that even if she had invited him to stay, how could he; how could he have asked her; she must think he wanted badly to become master of Ramsley Mill. What a fool he had been to go—what a fool!

"But," he argued, "let her think what she likes. I don't care. She may remember if she can that I used to sole her boots with my father's leather, and she went home in mine. She can remember that my mother taught her how to write and sew decently. I should think she must sometimes."

Then he admitted to himself that he was sure she did not forget. He could feel quite well that she was wishing that this long estrangement might cease.

"But," came the question, "why doesn't she end it? Pah, It's only my conceit; she thinks more of those glib, grinning fellows from the clerk's stools. Let her, what do I care!"

Suddenly he heard voices from the field at the back, and sat up listening.

"Oh, it's a regular slough." said someone. "We can never get through the gate. See, let us climb the stockyard fence. They've put some new rails in. Can you manage, Blanche? Here, just between the lilac bush and the stack. What a blessing they keep Chris at the front! Mind, bend under this plum tree. Dare we go, Blanche?"

"Go on, go on," whispered Blanche, and they crept up to the tiny window, through which the lamplight streamed uninterrupted. Fred stole out of the barn and hid behind the great water-butt. He saw them stoop and creep to the window and peep through.

In the kitchen sat the father, smoking and appearing to read, but really staring into the fire. The mother was putting the top crusts on the little pies, but she was interrupted by the need to wipe her eyes.

"Oh, Blanche," whispered Nellie. "he's gone out."

"It looks like it," assented the other.

"Perhaps he's not, though," resumed the former bravely. "He's very likely only in the parlour."

"That's all right, then." said Blanche. "I thought we should have seen him looking so miserable. But, of course, he wouldn't let his mother see it."

"Certainly not," said Blanche.

Fred chuckled.

"But," she continued doubtfully, "If he has gone out, whatever shall we do? What can we tell his mother?"

"Tell her we came up for fun."

"But if he's out?"

"Stay till he comes home."

"If it's late?"

"It's Christmas Eve."

"Perhaps he doesn't care after all."

"You think he does, so do I; and you're quite sure you want him."

"You know I do, Blanche, and I always have done."

"Let us begin, then."

"What? 'Good King Wenceslas?'"

The mother and father started as the two voices suddenly began to carol outside. She would have run to the door, but her husband waved her excitedly back. "Let them finish," his eyes shining. "Let them finish."

The girls had retired from the window lest they should be seen, and stood near the water-butt. When the old carol was finished, Nellie began the beautiful song of Giordani's:—

> Turn once again, heal thou my pain,
> Parted from thee, my heart is sore.

As she sang she stood holding a bough of the old plum tree, so close to Fred that by leaning forward he could have touched her coat. Carried away by the sweet pathos of her song, he could hardly refrain from rising and flinging his arms around her.

She finished, the door opened, showing a little woman holding out her hands.

Both girls made a motion towards her, but -

"Nell, Nell," he whispered, and caught her in his arms. She gave a little cry of alarm and delight. Blanche stepped into the kitchen, and shut the door, laughing.

She sat in the low rocking-chair swinging to and fro in a delighted excitement, chattering brightly about a hundred things. And with a keen woman's eye, she noticed the mother put her hands on her husband's as she sat on the sofa by his chair, and saw him hold the shining stiffened hand in one of his, and stroke it with old, undiminished affection.

Soon the two came in, Nellie all blushing. Without a word she ran and kissed the little mother, lingering a moment over her before she turned to the quiet embrace of the father. Then she took off her hat, and brushed back the brown tendrils all curled so prettily by the damp.

Already she was at home.

THE MORTAL COIL

I

She stood motionless in the middle of the room, something tense in her reckless bearing. Her gown of reddish stuff fell silkily about her feet; she looked tall and splendid in the candlelight. Her dark-blond hair was gathered loosely in a fold on top of her head, her young, blossom-fresh face was lifted. From her throat to her feet she was clothed in the elegantly-made dress of silky red stuff, the colour of red earth. She looked complete and lovely, only love could make her such a strange, complete blossom. Her cloak and hat were thrown across a table just in front of her.

Quite alone, abstracted, she stood there arrested in a conflict of emotions. Her hand, down against her skirt, worked irritably, the ball of the thumb rubbing, rubbing across the tips of the fingers. There was a slight tension between her lifted brows.

About her the room glowed softly, reflecting the candlelight from its whitewashed walls, and from the great, bowed, whitewashed ceiling. It was a large attic, with two windows, and the ceiling curving down on either side, so that both the far walls were low. Against one, on one side, was a single bed, opened for the night, the white over-bolster piled back. Not far from this was the iron stove. Near the window closest to the bed was a table with writing materials, and a handsome cactus-plant with clear scarlet blossoms threw its bizarre shadow on the wall. There was another table near the second window, and opposite was the door on which hung a military cloak. Along the far wall, were guns and fishing-tackle, and some clothes too, hung on pegs—all men's clothes, all military. It was evidently the room of a man, probably a young lieutenant.

The girl, in her pure red dress that fell about her feet, so that she looked a woman, not a girl, at last broke from her abstraction and went aimlessly to the writing-table. Her mouth was closed down stubbornly, perhaps in anger, perhaps in pain. She picked up a large seal made of agate, looked at the ingraven coat of arms, then stood rubbing her finger across the cut-out stone, time after time. At last she put the seal down, and looked at the other things—a beautiful old beer-mug used as a tobacco-jar, a silver box like an urn, old and of exquisite shape, a bowl of sealing wax. She fingered the pieces of wax. This, the dark-green, had sealed her last letter. Ah, well! She carelessly turned over the blotting book, which again had his arms stamped on the cover. Then she went away to the window. There, in the window-recess, she stood and looked out. She opened the casement and took a deep breath of the cold night air. Ah, it was good! Far below was the street, a vague golden milky way beneath her, its tiny black figures moving and crossing and re-crossing with marionette, insect-like intentness. A small horse-car rumbled along the lines, so belittled, it was an absurdity. So much for the world! . . . he did not come.

She looked overhead. The stars were white and flashing, they looked nearer than the street, more kin to her, more real. She stood pressing her breast on her arms, her face lifted to the stars, in the long, anguished suspense of waiting. Noises came up small from the street, as from some insect-world. But the great stars overhead struck white and invincible, infallible. Her heart felt cold like the stars.

At last she started. There was a noisy knocking at the door, and a female voice calling:

"Anybody there?"

"Come in," replied the girl.

She turned round, shrinking from this intrusion, unable to bear it, after the flashing stars.

There entered a thin, handsome dark girl dressed in an extravagantly-made gown of dark purple silk and dark blue velvet. She was followed by a small swarthy, inconspicuous lieutenant in pale-blue uniform.

"Ah *you!* . . . alone?" cried Teresa, the newcomer, advancing into the room. "Where's the Fritz, then?"

The girl in red raised her shoulders in a shrug, and turned her face aside, but did not speak.

"Not here! You don't know where he is? Ach, the dummy, the lout!" Teresa swung round on her companion.

"Where is he?" she demanded.

He also lifted his shoulders in a shrug.

"He said he was coming in half an hour," the young lieutenant replied.

"Ha!—half an hour! Looks like it! How long is that ago—two hours?"

Again the young man only shrugged. He had beautiful black eye-lashes, and steady eyes. He stood rather deprecatingly, whilst his girl, golden like a young panther, hung over him.

"One knows where he is," said Teresa, going and sitting on the opened bed. A dangerous contraction came between the brows of Marta, the girl in red, at this act.

"Wine, Women and Cards!" said Teresa, in her loud voice. "But they prefer the women on the cards.

> 'My love he has four Queenies,
> Four Queenies has my lo-o-ove,'"

she sang. Then she broke off, and turned to Podewils. "Was he winning when you left him, Karl?"

Again the young baron raised his shoulders.

"Tant pis que mal,' he replied, cryptically.

"Ah, *you!*" cried Teresa, "with your *tant pis que mal!* Are *you* tant pis que mal?" She laughed her deep, strange laugh. "Well," she added, "he'll be coming in with a fortune for you, Marta—"

There was a vague, unhappy silence.

"I know his fortunes," said Marta.

"Yes," said Teresa, in sudden sober irony, "he's a horse-shoe round your neck, is that young jockey.—But what are you going to do, Matzen dearest? You're not going to wait for him any longer?—Don't dream of it! The idea, waiting for that young gentleman as if you were married to him!—Put your hat on, dearest, and come along with us . . . Where are we going, Karl, you pillar of salt?—Eh?—Geier's?—To Geier's, Marta, my dear. Come, quick, up—you've been martyred enough, Marta, my martyr—haw!—haw!!—put your hat on. Up—away!"

Teresa sprang up like an explosion, anxious to be off.

"No, I'll wait for him," said Marta, sullenly.

"Don't be such a fool!" cried Teresa, in her deep voice. "Wait for him! *I'd* give him wait for him. Catch this little bird waiting." She lifted her hand and blew a little puff across the fingers. "Choo-fly!" she sang, as if a bird had just flown.

The young lieutenant stood silent with smiling dark eyes. Teresa was quick, and golden as a panther.

"No, but really, Marta, you're not going to wait any more—really! It's stupid for you to play Gretchen—your eyes are much too green. Put your hat on, there's a darling."

"No," said Marta, her flower-like face strangely stubborn. "I'll wait for him. He'll have to come some time."

There was a moment's uneasy pause.

"Well," said Teresa, holding her long shoulders for her cloak, "so long as you don't wait as long as Lenora-fuhr-ums-Morgenrot—! Adieu, my dear, God be with you."

The young lieutenant bowed a solicitous bow, and the two went out, leaving the girl in red once more alone.

She went to the writing table, and on a sheet of paper began writing her name in stiff Gothic characters, time after time:

Marta Hohenest

Marta Hohenest

Marta Hohenest.

The vague sounds from the street below continued. The wind was cold. She rose and shut the window. Then she sat down again.

At last the door opened, and a young officer entered. He was buttoned up in a dark-blue great-coat, with large silver buttons going down on either side of the breast. He entered quickly, glancing over the room, at Marta, as she sat with her back to him. She was marking with a pencil on paper. He closed the door. Then with fine beautiful movements he divested himself of his coat and went to hang it up. How well Marta knew the sound of his movements, the quick light step! But she continued mechanically making crosses on the paper, her head bent forward between the candles, so that her hair made fine threads and mist of light, very beautiful. He saw this, and it touched him. But he could not afford to be touched any further.

"You have been waiting?" he said formally. The insulting futile question! She made no sign, as if she had not heard. He was absorbed in the tragedy of himself, and hardly heeded her.

He was a slim, good-looking youth, clear-cut and delicate in mould. His features now were pale, there was something evasive in his dilated, vibrating eyes. He was barely conscious of the girl, intoxicated with his own desperation, that held him mindless and distant.

To her, the atmosphere of the room was almost unbreathable, since he had come in. She felt terribly bound, walled up. She rose with a sudden movement that tore his nerves. She looked to him tall and bright and dangerous, as she faced round on him.

"Have you come back with a fortune?" she cried, in mockery, her eyes full of dangerous light.

He was unfastening his belt, to change his tunic. She watched him up and down, all the time. He could not answer, his lips seemed dumb. Besides, silence was his strength.

"Have you come back with a fortune?" she repeated, in her strong, clear voice of mockery.

"No," he said, suddenly turning. "Let it please you that—that I've come back at all."

He spoke desperately, and tailed off into silence. He was a man doomed. She looked at him: he was insignificant in his doom. She turned in ridicule. And yet she was afraid; she loved him.

He had stood long enough exposed, in his helplessness. With difficulty he took a few steps, went and sat down at the writing-table. He looked to her like a dog with its tail between its legs.

He saw the paper, where her name was repeatedly written. She must find great satisfaction in her own name, he thought vaguely. Then he picked up the seal and kept twisting it round in his fingers, doing some little trick. And continually the seal fell on to the table with a sudden rattle that made Marta stiffen cruelly. He was quite oblivious of her.

She stood watching as he sat bent forward in his stupefaction. The fine cloth of his uniform showed the moulding of his back. And something tortured her as she saw him, till she could hardly bear it: the desire of his finely-shaped body, the stupefaction and the abjectness of him now, his immersion in the tragedy of himself, his being unaware of her. All her will seemed to grip him, to bruise some manly nonchalance and attention out of him.

"I suppose you're in a fury with me, for being late?" he said, with impotent irony in his voice. Her fury over trifles, when he was lost in calamity! How great was his real misery, how trivial her small offendedness!

Something in his tone burned her, and made her soul go cold.

"I'm not exactly pleased," she said coldly, turning away to a window.

Still he sat bent over the table, twisting something with his fingers. She glanced round on him. How nervy he was! He had beautiful hands, and the big topaz signet-ring on his finger made yellow lights. Ah, if only his hands were really dare-devil and reckless! They always seemed so guilty, so cowardly.

"I'm done for now," he said suddenly, as if to himself, tilting back his chair a little. In all his physical movement he was so fine and poised, so sensitive! Oh, and it attracted her so much!

"Why?" she said, carelessly.

An anger burned in him. She was so flippant. If he were going to be shot, she would not be moved more than about half a pound of sweets.

"Why!" he repeated laconically. "The same unimportant reason as ever."

"Debts?" she cried, in contempt.

"Exactly."

Her soul burned in anger.

"What have you done now?—lost more money?"

"Three thousand marks."

She was silent in deep wrath.

"More fool you!" she said. Then, in her anger, she was silent for some minutes. "And so you're done for, for three thousand marks?" she exclaimed, jeering at him. "You go pretty cheap."

"Three thousand—and the rest," he said, keeping up a manly *sang froid.*"

"And the rest!" she repeated in contempt. "And for three thousand—and the rest, your life is over!"

"My career," he corrected her.

"Oh," she mocked, "only your career! I thought it was a matter of life and death. Only your career? Oh, only that!"

His eyes grew furious under her mockery.

"My career is my life," he said.

"Oh, is it!—You're not a *man* then, you are only a career?"

"I am a gentleman."

"Oh, are you! How amusing! How very amusing, to be a gentleman, and not a man!—I suppose that's what it means, to be a gentleman, to have no guts outside your career?"

"Outside my honour—none."

"And might I ask what *is* your honour?" She spoke in extreme irony.

"Yes, you may ask," he replied coolly. "But if you don't know without being told, I'm afraid I could never explain it."

"Oh, you couldn't! No, I believe you—you are incapable of explaining it, it wouldn't bear explaining." There was a long, tense pause. "So you've made too many debts, and you're afraid they'll kick you out of the army, therefore your honour is gone, is it?—And what then—what after that?"

She spoke in extreme irony. He winced again at her phrase "kick you out of the army". But he tilted his chair back with assumed nonchalance.

"I've made too many debts, and I *know* they'll kick me out of the army," he repeated, thrusting the thorn right home to the quick. "After that—I can shoot myself. Or I might even be a waiter in a restaurant—or possibly a clerk, with twenty-five shillings a week."

"Really!—All those alternatives!—Well, why not, why not be a waiter in the Germania? It might be awfully jolly."

"Why not?" he repeated ironically. "Because it wouldn't become me."

She looked at him, at his aristocratic fineness of physique, his extreme physical sensitiveness. And all her German worship for his old, proud family rose up in her. No, he could not be a waiter in the Germania: she could not bear it. He was too refined and beautiful a thing.

"Ha!" she cried suddenly. "It wouldn't come to that, either. If they kick you out of the army, you'll find somebody to get round—you're like a cat, you'll land on your feet."

But this was just what he was not. He was not like a cat. His self-mistrust was too deep. Ultimately he had no belief in himself, as a separate isolated being. He knew he was sufficiently clever, an aristocrat, good-looking, the sensitive superior of most men. The trouble was, that apart from the social fabric he belonged to, he felt himself nothing, a cipher. He bitterly envied the common working-men for a certain manly aplomb, a grounded, almost stupid self-confidence he saw in them. Himself—he could lead such men through the gates of hell—for what did he care about danger or hurt to himself, whilst he was leading? But—cut him off from all this, and what was he? A palpitating rag of meaningless human life.

But she, coming from the people, could not fully understand. And it was best to leave her in the dark. The free indomitable self-sufficient being which a man must be in his relation to a woman who loves him—this he could pretend. But he knew he was not it. He knew that the world of man from which he took his value was his mistress beyond any woman. He wished, secretly, cravingly, almost cravenly, in his heart, it was not so. But so it was.

Therefore, he heard her phrase "you're like a cat," with some bitter envy.

"Whom shall I get round?—some woman, who will marry me?" he said.

This was a way out. And it was almost the inevitable thing, for him. But he felt it the last ruin of his manhood, even he.

The speech hurt her mortally, worse than death. She would rather he died, because then her own love would not turn to ash.

"Get married, then, if you want to," she said, in a small broken voice.

"Naturally," he said.

There was a long silence, a foretaste of barren hopelessness.

"Why is it so terrible to you," she asked at length, "to come out of the army and trust to your own resources? Other men are strong enough."

"Other men are not me," he said.

Why would she torture him? She seemed to enjoy torturing him. The thought of his expulsion from the army was an agony to him, really worse than death. He saw himself in the despicable civilian clothes, engaged in some menial occupation. And he could not bear it. It was too heavy a cross.

Who was she to talk? She was herself, an actress, daughter of a tradesman. He was himself. How should one of them speak for the other? It was impossible. He loved her. He loved her far better than men usually loved their mistresses. He really cared.—And he was strangely proud of his love for her, as if it were a distinction to him . . . But there was a limit to her understanding. There was a point beyond which she had nothing to do with him, and she had better leave him alone. Here in this crisis, which was *his* crisis, his downfall, she should not presume to talk, because she did not understand.—But she loved to torture him, that was the truth.

"Why should it hurt you to work?" she reiterated.

He lifted his face, white and tortured, his grey eyes flaring with fear and hate.

"Work!" he cried. "What do you think I am worth?—Twenty-five shillings a week, if I am lucky."

His evident anguish penetrated her. She sat dumbfounded, looking at him with wide eyes. He was white with misery and fear; his hand, that lay loose on the table, was abandoned in nervous ignominy. Her mind filled with wonder, and with deep, cold dread. Did he really care so much? But did it *really* matter so much to him? When he said he was worth twenty-five shillings a week, he was like a man whose soul is pierced. He sat there, annihilated. She looked for him, and he was nothing then. She looked for the man, the free being that loved her. And he was not, he was gone, this blank figure remained. Something with a blanched face sat there in the chair, staring at nothing.

His amazement deepened with intolerable dread. It was as if the world had fallen away into chaos. Nothing remained. She seemed to grasp the air for foothold.

He sat staring in front of him, a dull numbness settled on his brain. He was watching the flame of the candle. And, in his detachment, he realized the flame was a swiftly travelling flood, flowing swiftly from the source of the wick through a white surge and on into the darkness above. It was like a fountain suddenly foaming out, then running on dark and smooth. Could one dam the flood? He took a piece of paper, and cut off the flame for a second.

The girl in red started at the pulse of the light. She seemed to come to, from some trance. She saw his face, clear now, attentive, abstract, absolved. He was quite absolved from his temporal self.

"It isn't true," she said, "is it? It's not so tragic, really?—It's only your pride is hurt, your silly little pride?" She was rather pleading.

He looked at her with clear steady eyes.

"My pride!" he said. "And isn't my pride *me*? What am I without my pride?"

"You are *yourself*," she said. "If they take your uniform off you, and turn you naked into the street, you are still *yourself*."

His eyes grew hot. Then he cried:

"What does it mean, *myself*! It means I put on ready-made civilian clothes and do some dirty drudging elsewhere: that is what myself amounts to."

She knitted her brows.

"But what you are to *me*—that naked self which you are to me—that is something, isn't it?—everything," she said.

"What is it, if it means nothing?" he said: "What is it, more than a pound of chocolate *dragées*?—It stands for nothing—unless as you say, a petty clerkship, at twenty-five shillings a week."

These were all wounds to her, very deep. She looked in wonder for a few moments.

"And what does it stand for now?" she said. "A magnificent second-lieutenant!"

He made a gesture of dismissal with his hand.

She looked at him from under lowered brows.

"And our love!" she said. "It means nothing to you, nothing at all?"

"To me as a menial clerk, what does it mean? What does love mean! Does it mean that a man shall be no more than a dirty rag in the world?—What worth do you think I have in love, if in life I am a wretched inky subordinate clerk?"

"What does it matter?"

"It matters everything."

There was silence for a time, then the anger flashed up in her.

"It doesn't matter to you what *I* feel, whether *I* care or not," she cried, her voice rising. "They'll take his little uniform with buttons off him, and he'll have to be a common little civilian, so all he can do is to shoot himself!—It doesn't matter that I'm there—"

He sat stubborn and silent. He thought her vulgar. And her raving did not alter the situation in the least.

"Don't you see what value you put on *me*, you clever little man?" she cried in fury. "I've loved you, loved you with all my soul, for two years—and you've lied, and said you loved me. And now, what do I get? He'll shoot himself, because his tuppenny vanity is wounded.—Ah, *fool*—!"

He lifted his head and looked at her. His face was fixed and superior.

"All of which," he said, "leaves the facts of the case quite untouched!"

She hated his cool little speeches.

"Then shoot yourself," she cried, "and you'll be worth *less* than twenty-five shillings a week!"

There was a fatal silence.

"*Then* there'll be no question of worth," he said.

"Ha!" she ejaculated in scorn.

She had finished. She had no more to say. At length, after they had both sat motionless and silent, separate, for some time, she rose and went across to her hat and cloak. He shrank in apprehension. Now, he could not bear her to go. He shrank as if he were being whipped. She put her hat on, roughly, then swung her warm plaid cloak over her shoulders. Her hat was of black glossy silk, with a sheeny heap of cocks-feathers, her plaid cloak was dark green and blue, it swung open above her clear harsh-red dress. How beautiful she was, like a fiery Madonna!

"Good-bye," she said, in her voice of mockery. "I'm going now."

He sat motionless, as if loaded with fetters. She hesitated, then moved towards the door.

Suddenly, with a spring like a cat, he was confronting her, his back to the door. His eyes were full and dilated, like a cat's, his face seemed to gleam at her. She quivered, as some subtle fluid ran through her nerves.

"Let me go," she said dumbly. "I've had enough." His eyes, with a wide, dark electric pupil, like a cat's, only watched her objectively. And again a wave of female submissiveness went over her.

"I want to go," she pleaded. "You know it's no good.—You know this is no good."

She stood humbly before him. A flexible little grin quivered round his mouth.

"You know you don't want me," she persisted. "You know you don't really want me.—You only do this to show your power over me—which is a mean trick."

But he did not answer, only his eyes narrowed in a sensual, cruel smile. She shrank, afraid, and yet she was fascinated.

"You won't go yet," he said.

She tried in vain to rouse her real opposition.

"I shall call out," she threatened. "I shall shame you before people."

His eyes narrowed again in the smile of vindictive, mocking indifference.

"Call then," he said.

And at the sound of his still, cat-like voice, an intoxication ran over her veins.

"I *will*," she said, looking defiantly into his eyes. But the smile in the dark, full, dilated pupils made her waver into submission again.

"Won't you let me go?" she pleaded sullenly.

Now the smile went openly over his face.

"Take your hat off," he said.

And with quick, light fingers he reached up and drew out the pins of her hat, unfastened the clasp of her cloak, and laid her things aside.

She sat down in a chair. Then she rose again, and went to the window. In the street below, the tiny figures were moving just the same. She opened the window, and leaned out, and wept.

He looked round at her in irritation as she stood in her long, clear-red dress in the window-recess, leaning out. She was exasperating.

"You will be cold," he said.

She paid no heed. He guessed, by some tension in her attitude, that she was crying. It irritated him exceedingly, like a madness. After a few minutes of suspense, he went across to her, and took her by the arm. His hand was subtle, soft in its touch, and yet rather cruel than gentle.

"Come away," he said. "Don't stand there in the air—come away."

He drew her slowly away to the bed, she sat down, and he beside her.

"What are you crying for?" he said in his strange, penetrating voice, that had a vibration of exultancy in it. But her tears only ran faster.

He kissed her face, that was soft, and fresh, and yet warm, wet with tears. He kissed her again, and again, in pleasure of the soft, wet saltness of her. She turned aside and wiped her face with her handkerchief, and blew her nose. He was disappointed—yet the way she blew her nose pleased him.

Suddenly she slid away to the floor, and hid her face in the side of the bed, weeping and crying loudly:

"You don't love me—Oh, you don't love me—I thought you did, and you let me go on thinking it—but you don't, no, you don't, and I can't bear it.—Oh, I can't bear it."

He sat and listened to the strange, animal sound of her crying. His eyes flickered with exultancy, his body seemed full and surcharged with power. But his brows were knitted in tension. He laid his hand softly on her head, softly touched her face, which was buried against the bed.

She suddenly rubbed her face against the sheets, and looked up once more.

"You've deceived me," she said, as she sat beside him.

"Have I? Then I've deceived myself." His body felt so charged with male vigour, he was almost laughing in his strength.

"Yes," she said enigmatically, fatally. She seemed absorbed in her thoughts. Then her face quivered again.

"And I loved you so much," she faltered, the tears rising. There was a clangor of delight in his heart.

"I love *you*," he said softly, softly touching her, softly kissing her, in a sort of subtle, restrained ecstasy.

She shook her head stubbornly. She tried to draw away. Then she did break away, and turned to look at him, in fear and doubt. The little, fascinating, fiendish lights were hovering in his eyes like laughter.

"Don't hurt me so much," she faltered, in a last protest.

A faint smile came on his face. He took her face between his hands and covered it with soft, blinding kisses, like a soft, narcotic rain. He felt himself such an unbreakable fountain-head of powerful blood. He was trembling finely in all his limbs, with mastery.

When she lifted her face and opened her eyes, her face was wet, and her greenish-golden eyes were shining, it was like sudden sunshine in wet foliage. She smiled at him like a child of knowledge, through the tears, and softly, infinitely softly he dried her tears with his mouth and his soft young moustache.

"You'd never shoot yourself, because you're mine, aren't you!" she said, knowing the fine quivering of his body, in mastery.

"Yes," he said.

"Quite mine?" she said, her voice rising in ecstasy.

"Yes."

"Nobody else but mine—nothing at all—?"

"Nothing at all," he re-echoed.

"But me?" came her last words of ecstasy.

"Yes."

And she seemed to be released free into the infinite of ecstasy.

II

They slept in fulfilment through the long night. But then strange dreams began to fill them both, strange dreams that were neither waking nor sleeping;—only, in curious weariness, through her dreams, she heard at last a continual low rapping. She awoke with difficulty. The rapping began again—she started violently. It was at the door—it would be the orderly rapping for Friedeburg. Everything seemed wild and unearthly. She put her hand on the shoulder of the sleeping man, and pulled him roughly, waited a moment, then pushed him, almost violently, to awake him. He woke with a sense of resentment at her violent handling. Then he heard the knocking of the orderly. He gathered his senses.

"Yes, Heinrich!" he said.

Strange, the sound of a voice! It seemed a far-off tearing sound. Then came the muffled voice of the servant.

"Half past four, Sir."

"Right!" said Friedeburg, and automatically he got up and made a light. She was suddenly as wide awake as if it were daylight. But it was a strange, false day, like a delirium. She saw him put down the match, she saw him moving about, rapidly dressing. And the movement in the room was a trouble to her. He himself was vague and unreal, a thing seen but not comprehended. She watched all the acts of his toilet, saw all the motions, but never saw him. There was only a disturbance about her, which fretted her, she was not aware of any presence. Her mind, in its strange, hectic clarity, wanted to consider things in absolute detachment. For instance, she wanted to consider the cactus plant. It was a curious object with pure scarlet blossoms. Now, how did these scarlet blossoms come to pass, upon that earthly-looking unliving creature? Scarlet blossoms! How wonderful they were! What were they, then, how could one lay hold on their being? Her mind turned to him. Him, too, how could one lay hold on him, to have him? Where was he, what was he? She seemed to grasp at the air.

He was dipping his face in the cold water—the slight shock was good for him. He felt as if someone had stolen away his being in the night, he was moving about a light, quick shell, with all his meaning absent. His body was quick and active, but all his deep understanding, his soul was gone. He tried to rub it back into his face. He was quite dim, as if his spirit had left his body.

"Come and kiss me," sounded the voice from the bed. He went over to her automatically. She put her arms around him and looked into his face with her clear brilliant, grey-green eyes, as if she too were looking for his soul.

"How are you?" came her meaningless words.

"All right."

"Kiss me."

He bent down and kissed her.

And still her clear, rather frightening eyes seemed to be searching for him inside himself. He was like a bird transfixed by her pellucid, grey-green, wonderful eyes. She put her hands into his soft, thick, fine hair, and gripped her hands full of his hair. He wondered with fear at her sudden painful clutching.

"I shall be late," he said.

"Yes," she answered. And she let him go.

As he fastened his tunic he glanced out of the window. It was still night: a night that must have lasted since eternity. There was a moon in the sky. In the streets below the yellow street-lamps burned small at intervals. This was the night of eternity.

There came a knock at the door, and the orderly's voice.

"Coffee, Sir."

"Leave it there."

They heard the faint jingle of the tray as it was set down outside.

Friedeburg sat down to put on his boots. Then, with a man's solid tread, he went and took in the tray. He felt properly heavy and secure now in his accoutrement. But he was always aware of her two wonderful, clear, unfolded eyes, looking on his heart, out of her uncanny silence.

There was a strong smell of coffee in the room.

"Have some coffee?" His eyes could not meet hers.

"No, thank you."

"Just a drop?"

"No, thank you."

Her voice sounded quite gay. She watched him dipping his bread in the coffee and eating quickly, absently. He did not know what he was doing, and yet the dipped bread and hot coffee gave him pleasure. He gulped down the remainder of his drink, and rose to his feet.

"I must go," he said.

There was a curious, poignant smile in her eyes. Her eyes drew him to her. How beautiful she was, and dazzling, and frightening, with this look of brilliant tenderness seeming to glitter from her face. She drew his head down to her bosom, and held it fast prisoner there, murmuring with tender, triumphant delight: "Dear! Dear!"

At last she let him lift his head, and he looked into her eyes, that seemed to concentrate in a dancing, golden point of vision in which he felt himself perish.

"Dear!" she murmured. "You love me, don't you?"

"Yes," he said mechanically.

The golden point of vision seemed to leap to him from her eyes, demanding something. He sat slackly, as if spellbound. Her hand pushed him a little.

"Mustn't you go?" she said.

He rose. She watched him fastening the belt round his body, that seemed soft under the fine clothes. He pulled on his great-coat, and put on his peaked cap. He was again a young officer.

But he had forgotten his watch. It lay on the table near the bed. She watched him slinging it on his chain. He looked down at her. How beautiful she was, with her luminous face and her fine, stray hair! But he felt far away.

"Anything I can do for you?" he asked.

"No, thank you—I'll sleep," she replied, smiling. And the strange golden spark danced on her eyes again, again he felt as if his heart were gone, destroyed out of him. There was a fine pathos too in her vivid, dangerous face.

He kissed her for the last time, saying:

"I'll blow the candles out, then?"

"Yes, my love—and I'll sleep."

"Yes—sleep as long as you like."

The golden spark of her eyes seemed to dance on him like a destruction, she was beautiful, and pathetic. He touched her tenderly with his finger-tips, then suddenly blew out the candles, and walked across in the faint moonlight to the door.

He was gone. She heard his boots click on the stone stairs—she heard the far below tread of his feet on the pavement. Then he was gone. She lay quite still, in a swoon of deathly peace. She never wanted to move any more. It was finished. She lay quite still, utterly, utterly abandoned.

But again she was disturbed. There was a little tap at the door, then Teresa's voice saying, with a shuddering sound because of the cold:

"Ugh!—I'm coming to you, Marta my dear. I can't stand being left alone."

"I'll make a light," said Marta, sitting up and reaching for the candle. "Lock the door, will you, Resie, and then nobody can bother us."

She saw Teresa, loosely wrapped in her cloak, two thick ropes of hair hanging untidily. Teresa looked voluptuously sleepy and easy, like a cat running home to the warmth.

"Ugh!" she said, "it's cold!"

And she ran to the stove. Marta heard the chink of the little shovel, a stirring of coals, then a clink of the iron door. Then Teresa came running to the bed, with a shuddering little run, she puffed out the light and slid in beside her friend.

"So cold!" she said, with a delicious shudder at the warmth. Marta made place for her, and they settled down.

"Aren't you glad you're not them?" said Resie, with a little shudder at the thought. "Ugh!—poor devils!"

"I am," said Marta.

"Ah, sleep—sleep, how lovely!" said Teresa, with deep content. "Ah, it's so good!"

"Yes," said Marta.

"Good morning, good night, my dear," said Teresa, already sleepily.

"Good night," responded Marta.

Her mind flickered a little. Then she sank unconsciously to sleep. The room was silent.

Outside, the setting moon made peaked shadows of the high-roofed houses; from twin towers that stood like two dark, companion giants in the sky, the hour trembled out over the sleeping town. But the footsteps of hastening officers and cowering soldiers rang on the frozen pavements. Then a lantern appeared in the distance, accompanied by the rattle of a bullock wagon. By the light of the lantern on the wagon-pole could be seen the delicately moving feet and the pale, swinging dewlaps of the oxen. They drew slowly on, with a rattle of heavy wheels, the banded heads of the slow beasts swung rhythmically.

Ah, this was life! How sweet, sweet each tiny incident was! How sweet to Friedeburg, to give his orders ringingly on the frosty air, to see his men like bears shambling and shuffling into their places, with little dancing movements of uncouth playfulness and resentment, because of the pure cold.

Sweet, sweet it was to be marching beside his men, sweet to hear the great thresh-thresh of their heavy boots in the unblemished silence, sweet to feel the immense mass of living bodies co-ordinated into oneness near him, to catch the hot waft of their closeness, their breathing. Friedeburg was like a man condemned to die, catching at every impression as at an inestimable treasure.

Sweet it was to pass through the gates of the town, the scanty, loose suburb, into the open darkness and space of the country. This was almost best of all. It was like emerging in the open plains of eternal freedom.

They saw a dark figure hobbling along under the dark side of a shed. As they passed, through the open door of the shed, in the golden light were seen the low rafters, the pale, silken sides of the cows, evanescent. And a woman with a red kerchief bound round her head lifted her face from the flank of the beast she was milking, to look at the soldiers threshing like multitudes of heavy ghosts down the darkness. Some of the men called to her, cheerfully, impudently. Ah, the miraculous beauty and sweetness of the merest trifles like these!

They tramped on down a frozen, rutty road, under lines of bare trees. Beautiful trees! Beautiful frozen ruts in the road! Ah, even, in one of the ruts there was a silver of ice and of moon-glimpse. He heard ice tinkle as a passing soldier purposely put his toe in it. What a sweet noise!

But there was a vague uneasiness. He heard the men arguing as to whether dawn were coming. There was the silver moon, still riding on the high seas of the sky. A lovely thing she was, a jewel! But was there any blemish of day? He shrank a little from the rawness of the day to come. This night of morning was so rare and free.

Yes, he was sure. He saw a colourless paleness on the horizon. The earth began to look hard, like a great, concrete shadow. He shrank into himself. Glancing at the ranks of his men, he could see them like a company of rhythmic ghosts. The pallor was actually reflected on their livid faces. This was the coming day. It frightened him.

The dawn came. He saw the rosiness of it hang trembling with light, above the east. Then a strange glamour of scarlet passed over the land. At his feet, glints of ice flashed scarlet, even the hands of the men were red as they swung, sinister, heavy, reddened.

The sun surged up, her rim appeared, swimming with fire, hesitating, surging up. Suddenly there were shadows from trees and ruts, and grass was hoar and ice was gold against the ebony shadow. The faces of the men were alight, kindled with life. Ah, it was magical, it was all too marvellous! If only it were always like this!

When they stopped at the inn for breakfast, at nine o'clock, the smell of the inn went raw and ugly to his heart: beer and yesterday's tobacco!

He went to the door to look at the men biting huge bites from their hunks of grey bread, or cutting off pieces with their clasp-knives. This made him still happy. Women were going to the fountain for water, the soldiers were chaffing them coarsely. He liked all this.

But the magic was going, inevitably, the crystal delight was thawing to desolation in his heart, his heart was cold, cold mud. Ah, it was awful. His face contracted, he almost wept with cold, stark despair.

Still he had the work, the day's hard activity with the men. Whilst this lasted, he could live. But when this was over, and he had to face the horror of his own cold-thawing mud of despair: ah, it was not to be thought of. Still, he was happy at work with the men: the wild desolate place, the hard activity of mock warfare. Would to God it were real: war, with the prize of death!

By afternoon the sky had gone one dead, livid level of grey. It seemed low down, and oppressive. He was tired, the men were tired, and this let the heavy cold soak in to them like despair. Life could not keep it out.

And now, when his heart was so heavy it could sink no more, he must glance at his own situation again. He must remember what a fool he was, his new debts like half thawed mud in his heart. He knew, with the cold misery of hopelessness, that he would be turned out of the army. What then?—what then but death? After all, death was the solution for him. Let it be so.

They marched on and on, stumbling with fatigue under a great leaden sky, over a frozen dead country. The men were silent with weariness, the heavy motion of their marching was like an oppression. Friedeburg was tired too, and deadened, as his face was deadened by the cold air. He did not think any more; the misery of his soul was like a frost inside him.

He heard someone say it was going to snow. But the words had no meaning for him. He marched as a clock ticks, with the same monotony, everything numb and cold-soddened.

They were drawing near to the town. In the gloom of the afternoon he felt it ahead, as unbearable oppression on him. Ah the hideous suburb! What was his life, how did it come to pass that life was lived in a formless, hideous grey structure of hell! What did it all mean? Pale, sulphur-yellow lights spotted the livid air, and people, like soddened shadows, passed in front of the shops that were lit up ghastly in the early twilight. Out of the colourless space, crumbs of snow came and bounced animatedly off the breast of his coat.

At length he turned away home, to his room, to change and get warm and renewed, for he felt as cold-soddened as the grey, cold, heavy bread which felt hostile in the mouths of the soldiers. His life was to him like this dead, cold bread in his mouth.

As he neared his own house, the snow was peppering thinly down. He became aware of some unusual stir about the house-door. He looked—a strange, closed-in wagon, people, police. The sword of Damocles that had hung over his heart, fell. O God, a new shame, some new shame, some new torture! His body moved on. So it would move on through misery upon misery, as is our fate. There was no emergence, only this progress through misery unto misery, till the end. Strange, that human life was so tenacious! Strange, that men had made of life a long, slow process of torture to the soul. Strange, that it was no other than this! Strange, that but for man, this misery would not exist. For it was not God's misery, but the misery of the world of man.

He saw two officials push something white and heavy into the cart, shut the doors behind with a bang, turn the silver handle, and run round to the front of the wagon. It moved off. But still most of the people lingered. Friedeburg drifted near in that inevitable motion which carries us through all our shame and torture. He knew the people talked about him. He went up the steps and into the square hall.

There stood a police-officer, with a note-book in his hand, talking to Herr Kapell, the housemaster. As Friedeburg entered through the swing door, the housemaster, whose brow was wrinkled in anxiety and perturbation, made a gesture with his hand, as if to point out a criminal.

"Ah!—the Herr Baron von Friedeburg!" he said, in self-exculpation.

The police officer turned, saluted politely, and said, with the polite, intolerable *suffisance* of officialdom:

"Good evening! Trouble here!"

"Yes?" said Friedeburg.

He was so frightened, his sensitive constitution was so lacerated, that something broke in him, he was a subservient, murmuring ruin.

"Two young ladies found dead in your room," said the police-official, making an official statement. But under his cold impartiality of officialdom, what obscene unction! Ah, what obscene exposures now!

"Dead!" ejaculated Friedeburg, with the wide eyes of a child. He became quite child-like, the official had him completely in his power. He could torture him as much as he liked.

"Yes." He referred to his note-book. "Asphyxiated by fumes from the stove."

Friedeburg could only stand wide-eyed and meaningless.

"Please—will you go upstairs?"

The police-official marshalled Friedeburg in front of himself. The youth slowly mounted the stairs, feeling as if transfixed through the base of the spine, as if he would lose the use of his legs. The official followed close on his heels.

They reached the bedroom. The policeman unlocked the door. The housekeeper followed with a lamp. Then the official examination began.

"A young lady slept here last night?"

"Yes."

"Name, please?"

"Marta Hohenest."

"H-o-h-e-n-e-s-t," spelled the official. "—And address?"

Friedeburg continued to answer. This was the end of him. The quick of him was pierced and killed. The living dead answered the living dead in obscene antiphony. Question and answer continued, the note-book worked as the hand of the old dead wrote in it the replies of the young who was dead.

The room was unchanged from the night before. There was her heap of clothing, the lustrous, pure-red dress lying soft where she had carelessly dropped it. Even, on the edge of the chair-back, her crimson silk garters hung looped.

But do not look, do not see. It is the business of the dead to bury their dead. Let the young dead bury their own dead, as the old dead have buried theirs. How can the dead remember, they being dead? Only the living can remember, and are at peace with their living who have passed away.

THE END

CPSIA information can be obtained at www.ICGtesting.com
Printed in the USA
LVOW080838050112

262488LV00002BA/87/P

9 781420 933406